"Theresa Scott's historical romances are tender, exciting, enjoyable, and satisfying!"
—*Romantic Times*

HUNTERS OF THE ICE AGE

PASSION AT THE DAWN OF TIME
YESTERDAY'S DAWN

"Now you will come with me." It was an order.

For answer, Terah tried bucking him off by heaving her hips and torso, but he would not budge. "Get off!" she cried.

Her body felt soft under him, and her struggles excited him. He dipped his head and mashed his lips against hers.

Terah's eyes widened in disbelief and shock and then she struggled harder.

He broke off the kiss and looked down into those furious green eyes. "You are a fierce saber-tooth tigress," he said. "Did you know that?" His voice was caressing and his obsidian eyes were amused. "What a fighter," he murmured. He lowered his head and kissed her again; this time his lips were gentle.

Other Books by Theresa Scott:
APACHE CONQUEST
FORBIDDEN PASSION
BRIDE OF DESIRE
SAVAGE REVENGE
SAVAGE BETRAYAL

THERESA SCOTT

YESTERDAY'S DAWN

HUNTERS OF THE ICE AGE

LOVE SPELL **NEW YORK CITY**

This story is for every human being who feels, or has ever felt, angry at God.

LOVE SPELL®

January 1994

Published by

Dorchester Publishing Co., Inc.
276 Fifth Avenue
New York, NY 10001

If you purchased this book without a cover you should be aware that this book is stolen property. It was reported as "unsold and destroyed" to the publisher and neither the author nor the publisher has received any payment for this "stripped book."

Copyright © 1994 by Theresa Scott

Cover Art by John Ennis

All rights reserved. No part of this book may be reproduced or transmitted in any form or by any electronic or mechanical means, including photocopying, recording or by any information storage and retrieval system, without the written permission of the Publisher, except where permitted by law.

The name "Love Spell" and its logo are trademarks of Dorchester Publishing Co., Inc.

Printed in the United States of America.

With my deep appreciation and special thanks for technical assistance to the following people:

Andy Appleby, fisheries biologist, Olympia, WA, for information on animal behavior;

Patty Bergman, Olympia Library;

Mr. Dan Bigger, Department of Natural Resources, Olympia, WA;

Dr. Rob Bonnichsen, anthropologist, Oregon State University, Portland, for information on the hunting of elephants;

Dr. Richard Michael Gramly, archaeologist, Great Lakes Repository, Buffalo, NY, for information on the excavation of the Wenatchee site in Washington State;

Christopher S. Johnson, PA/SA, for medical consulting on wounds and afflictions;

Don Meatte, archaeologist;

Eunice Santiago;

Dr. Keith Williams and his wife, Deanna, for their generous hospitality and information about the Wenatchee area;

and Jan Pierson, who wields a lethal red pencil.

*indicates Wenatchee Clovis archaeology site where tools were found that are believed to be 11,000 years old.

Map shows present-day place names.

Chapter 1

11,200 years before present

The half-grown boy carried his hunting spear with pride. It was a man's hunting spear, and his father had helped him work the stone blade. Together they had traveled a day's journey along the river, searching for the strongest, stoutest tree to make the spear haft. Together they had fashioned the blade, hitting the rock core with deer antler, knocking clean flakes of chert off until a thumb, run carelessly along the fine edge of the blade, bled easily. Together they had wound thin, strong deer sinew around the base of the spear point, fixing the stone blade firmly into the slit of the stick.

And this day was the first time that the boy had received an assent from his father when he

11

had asked the question: "Today, Father? Today may I bring it?" His father's gruff nod had set the boy's heart to pounding and he had taken up the man's weapon and followed his father out of the hide-covered dwelling.

The boy's heart beat with strong pride as together, he and his father, Kran, walked through windswept draws between rolling hills. Tufts of grass blew before them like wavelets upon a gray sea. Here the wind always blew. The wind kept away the mosquitoes and other flies, but it was cool too. He was thankful for the bison-fur robe he had tied about his strong young frame.

They walked parallel to the river and above it. Between the hillsides where they walked there grew moss and lichens and tough grasses. Were he to climb one of the hills, the boy would be able to look down and see green and yellow willows and lush thickets of plants that grew near the water. Between the hills and the river grew a sparse forest of stunted lodgepole pine.

Kran and his son came to a break between hills and they stopped. As always, their eyes turned to the Giver of Life River. The surface of the water flickered white from tiny waves the wind rustled up.

If he was to follow the river south, thought the boy, he would come again to the lands where he was born, where he had spent most of his life. It was only once every two or three years that his band, the Mammoth People, traveled to these barren rolling hills and basalt cliffs. His people came in the fall, in the Season of the Geese

Flying, to hunt the huge bison. Grass-fatted bison meat made a tasty change from a constant diet of river salmon.

This day I become a man, exulted the boy as he trotted alongside his father. *This is the day!* He knew it.

His happy thoughts went back to the vision quest he had undertaken but one moon ago. He had walked alone into the hills. All day he had climbed the high hillside until he reached the long ridge that overlooked the river. There he rested upon a small shelf. And it was on that ridge that he had buried the precious black obsidian spear tip his father had helped him make. It was an offering to the Great Spirit.

And then the boy had fasted for four days without eating a single piece of meat, a single root, and with nothing to drink but Giver of Life's water, which he had carried in a bison bladder. The boy had rolled in the earth's dust, he had sprinkled drops of water in the eight sacred directions, and he had purified himself with prayer.

He had prayed silently; he had prayed aloud. He had prayed sitting down, and he had prayed standing up, but it was his prayer of standing with his arms held up to the eternal blue sky and calling the Great Spirit's name aloud that had finally brought him his vision.

Then the boy sank to his knees, in utter amazement and wonder, as a huge mammoth appeared in front of him. The mammoth was a vision, he could tell that, but it was real too. The boy could see the mammoth's black hairy hide, see the wrinkles around its eyes, almost smell the beast's fetid breath. For a terrible moment the mammoth spoke to him, lifting its huge snout and mouthing strange sounds.

But the boy could not understand the words. He rose to his feet and took a step toward the mammoth, then froze in mid-step, waiting in an agony of indecision and wonder as his mouth opened and closed in a frantic prayer for understanding. The boy strained toward the mammoth, reaching, striving to hold the vision, to keep it from slipping away. But he could not hold it. His hands dropped to his sides, powerless, as the vision vanished. *The Great Spirit does not do what man wants,* he remembered the shaman saying. *The Great Spirit does the unexpected.* And now the boy saw for himself that it was true. . . .

In speechless awe, the boy stared into the wind, willing the mammoth to return. But it was gone. He swallowed, and his body trembled. He had just seen a vision of the mightiest animal on earth. He had been hugely blessed. The mammoth was *his* Name Animal now. Henceforth he must respect the mammoth, give it gifts, and always thank the Great Spirit for the presence of the great beasts upon the earth. In return, the mammoth would respect him and would fall to his spear whenever the boy had need of its meat. Hunting the huge animal would come easier to the boy now than to other men, now that he had had such a strong vision. It was a bargain of sorts between him and the mammoth, a bargain sealed by the vision, and the boy knew he would honor the mammoth until his dying day.

He had been happy after the vision, assured that his full initiation into manhood was very close upon him. He need only kill an animal with his new spear. Then he too would take his full and rightful place amongst the Mammoth People—with the other men, with his father, with his cousin. Yes, it was a good world he lived in, he reflected as he walked along beside his silent father.

"Behold." Kran's grunted word brought the boy out of his reverie. The father pointed with his chin at a lumbering mammoth that had suddenly emerged from around the bend of the river. It would be extremely disrespectful were he to point his spear at the beast now that it was his son's Name Animal. While of course the boy did not tell his father the whole of his vision, he was able to tell his father that it was the mammoth that had become his Name Animal. Kran's Name Animal was the bison, and everyone in the band agreed that he had remarkable success slaying the large, horned beasts.

They stood downwind of the mammoth, but he had not seen them yet. The boy thought that mammoths probably could not see great distances, though they could smell well and their hearing was acute. The mammoth was drinking from a small pool alongside the river, where water was warmer. The boy and his father watched in amusement as the great beast sucked up the water and sprayed it over his back.

"Let us go closer," urged the boy. Now that the

mammoth was his Name Animal, he felt more confident around such a behemoth. Heretofore, he had been very careful to keep his distance. Mammoths hated man and were difficult to hunt. That was why the boy's vision was so important, not just to him, but to the Mammoth People. The vision gave assurances of successful mammoth hunting, and all members of the band would profit thereby.

The boy smiled to himself, watching the great beast. "Closer," he urged.

His father looked reluctant, then shrugged. "It is your Name Animal, my son. I understand your interest." They moved slowly down the draw toward the water, trying to dislodge as few rocks as possible. They did not want to alert the animal.

The boy saw that it was a bull mammoth. Usually the females stayed in family groups, and the males wandered about alone except at mating season, when they joined the female herds. But mating season was past, so this bull was not as dangerous; still, it was wise to keep several man's lengths away from it. Mammoth could charge unexpectedly.

The mammoth seemed not to notice them. It was too intent with digging with its trunk on the other side of its body. The boy could not see what the elephant was scratching at, but he was curious. He walked closer still.

"My son," cautioned Kran. "Beware. Do not anger the animal. They are very strong, very powerful. We are but two men."

The boy paused in mid-step. The blood pounded thickly in his chest at his father's words including him as a man.

Just then the mammoth swung its great head toward them. It must have heard Kran's words also. The animal swung fully around, and the boy saw a great gaping red gash in the animal's side. He had been wounded.

The fine hairs on the back of the boy's neck stood up in alarm. Wounded mammoths were extremely dangerous.

Suddenly the beast waved his trunk in the air, catching the human scent. Its small ears flapping, it started toward them at a run. The mammoth was charging them!

"Flee!" yelled Kran.

For several paralyzing heartbeats, the boy just stood there.

"Flee!" yelled his father again.

The boy started running.

The mammoth gained on them, waving its trunk and blasting forth with a terrible trumpeting. Kran and the boy raced in front of the thundering beast, the boy's young legs taking the lead over the rough terrain.

Kran stumbled, then regained his footing. He whirled with his spear out, desperate to defend himself. He lunged, barely able to get an accurate thrust in his allotted heartbeat of time. The spear pierced the thick skin over the mammoth's lungs, one of the animal's most vulnerable spots. For a moment the beast faltered, and Kran jerked away just as his spear snapped in two. He ran. The behemoth steadied and came on, taking heavy plodding steps as he gained on the fleeing man.

The boy kept running.

Suddenly Kran's loud screams raked the boy's ears. Shivers coursed down his back. He, too, stumbled, then glanced over his shoulder at the marauding giant.

"Help!" cried Kran. "Help meeeeeeeeeee!" His hands were outstretched in a desperate plea to his son. Then he fell under the trampling front feet of the enraged beast.

In that moment, the image of his father's tortured face and inert body burned into the boy's memory forever.

The boy dropped his spear and ran—away from his father. Young legs pounded the uneven ground, pumping up and down, up and down.

Furious snorts whistled through the maddened beast's trunk and urged the boy onward. The ground shook from elephantine steps thundering behind him.

He heard his father's helpless cry, "Help meeeeeeee!" And yet still the boy ran, terror infusing his blood and lacing his body with the desperate strength he needed to escape.

How long he ran, he would never know. It was his whole lifetime. It was a single heartbeat.

When the boy could no longer hear the raging snorts of the bull, when he could no longer feel the earth shake from the pounding feet, even then he did not stop running. He thought perhaps he would die running.

Finally, far behind him, he heard a weary snort.

He whirled in time to see the bull sink to its front knees, its trunk weaving, head drooping. The boy stood, chest heaving with burning breaths, watching in disbelief as the huge hairy black mammoth knelt. He watched it struggle to rise, kicking with its back legs, striving for a foothold, but then it collapsed again. Death had reached the bull mammoth, and with a last wild trumpet, the great beast succumbed.

The watching boy suddenly realized that the beast before him was the one he had seen in his vision.

Taking a great sobbing breath, the boy started running back. He must rescue his father, he thought, his bloody feet pounding over the rough terrain. *Father, Father,* went the chant in his head. He ran on, the wind whistling in his own lungs now as it had in the mammoth's.

And when he came to his father's still figure, the boy's very breath felt sucked out of him. Kran lay still. Too still. With a sick, guilty horror, the boy slowly bent to kneel beside the prone figure. His cold lips trembled, hovered over his father's ear. "Father?"

His whisper drifted away on the wind.

"Father?" His hands like claws, the boy took hold of his father's head. "Father, hearken to me!" He lifted his father's head, searching Kran's eyes with desperate intensity. "Father! You must understand—" The boy broke off when he saw that his father's eyes stared back at him lifelessly.

He dropped Kran's head and ran his hands

feverishly over his father's body, over his chest, trying to find some sign of life. Chest lifting, breathing, heartbeat, some sign, anything. He saw then his father's legs, one twisted at an odd angle, the other broken and white bone protruding. The mammoth had broken his legs and trampled his body. No one could survive such a great weight upon him.

The terrible finality struck the boy. His beloved father was dead.

"No!" howled the boy. "No!" Kran could not be dead! They had just started to hunt. The boy was just beginning to be a man! His father could not be dead! He needed his father!

"Do not go! Do not leave me!" the boy screamed. No answer. Not a twitch, not a gasp, to say that his father was alive. Nothing.

"Father?" His voice faltered. "I love you, Father. . . ."

"It is difficult to lose a father," said the shaman. Miserable, the boy stared straight ahead, shrugging off the compassion in the soft voice. He stood rooted to the ground beside Kran's body. Around the boy stood his people—cousins, aunts, uncles, neighbors he had known since childhood. They gave him consoling glances; one or two tentatively patted his arm. The boy turned away from every one of them.

"Come, we will bury him," urged the shaman.

The boy knew the shaman did not want the saber-toothed cats and wolves and other scavengers to get at Kran's body. The boy did not want the remains defiled either, but somehow, he felt immobile, lifeless, as though he had no will or energy to move. He could not help his father in death either.

"Come," the shaman prodded.

The boy glanced once at the old man. Huge bison horns sat atop the shaman's head to make him look powerful, but the old wrinkled face contrasted strangely with the horns. The boy's aunt came up to him and took him firmly by the arm, pulling him away from the magical power of the shaman. She was his mother's sister, and he knew she was trying to be kind, but at this time he needed the company of men, not women. He shrugged her off, and she walked away, but not before he saw the hurt look on her face. Her son, a cousin one summer younger, regarded him with reproach, but said nothing.

The boy's thoughts were whirling like a dust storm. *What do I do now? Father's dead. I am alone. I killed him.* The chaotic messages whirled around in his brain. He faced the shaman, wanting to speak. He could not carry this secret. He must tell him, tell someone. But the shaman's eyes were closed, his hands lifted to the sun, and he was gently chanting. When he opened his eyes there was a dazed look to them and the boy thought perhaps he should wait to tell what had happened.

Then shame rushed through him. How could he tell this old man, a man whom he had grown up respecting? How could he tell him that he had run from his father's killer? That his father had cried out and instead of helping his father, the boy had chosen to save himself. How could he say the words? The contempt on that old face, on the faces of his neighbors, his aunt, his cousin— no, it would be too difficult to look upon.

He had lost his mother when barely weaned. Now his father was slain. Who else did he have? Only the Mammoth People. Were he to tell them what had happened, they would drive him away. Who wanted a coward in the tribe? The People needed brave men, men not afraid to risk their lives, not afraid of fighting, of dying. And he, the boy, was such a one. He had been afraid— very, very afraid. He had not wanted to die like his father. Everything in his body and brain and blood had screamed out to him to run, to save himself.

No, he was not the kind of man they wanted in the tribe. Yet the thought of leaving them, of going off into the tundra to be by himself, was too horrible to behold. He looked at his aunt's back, at his cousin, at the old shaman. He had known these people all his fourteen summers, his whole life. They were his world.

He could not make himself turn and walk away. He could not leave them, though it was best for them. *Again, the coward,* he reproached himself. *Only in these two things,* he vowed. *Only in running from Father-Killer and only in not wanting to leave my people. I will stay,* he thought. *I will stay and be brave; I will show them day by day that they did right to keep me. Never again will I flee.* His lips tightened as he made the silent vow.

He did not see a certain pair of dark eyes watching him, a silent sneer upon the face of another, watchful young boy. He saw only his own weakness, his own cowardice.

When Kran's body was buried and the chanting done, the Mammoth People started across the shallow plain to where the mammoth carcass sat, still on its knees. The boy straggled behind; he was the last one, the whipping wind wiping the tears from his cheeks. Some part of him hoped for punishment. Perhaps a saber-toothed cat would jump on him. But nothing happened, and he arrived at the place where Father-Killer sat. The boy looked at the huge beast, at the flies gathering to gorge on the black blood. Two dire wolves slunk away. They would come back and eat what the Mammoth People could not carry.

The boy sat dully in a fog of grief while the butchering went on. He did not offer to help and no one asked him to. The low murmur of their voices came to him—not the words, only the sound of their voices—and he took the sound into him greedily. He was still with them, still with the Mammoth People. As long as he did not tell them the truth, he could stay with them. He poked with a stick at the ground, lost in thought.

The shaman came over. "Big tusks," he observed. The boy looked at Father-Killer's tusks. Yes, they were big, the longest tusks he had ever seen. The shaman glanced at the boy, then riveted his thoughtful gaze on the mammoth. He walked over to the great beast and began sawing at the

23

tip of one tusk. When his task was completed, he walked back to the boy. "Here," he said, holding out the sawed-off tip of the tusk. "Take it."

The boy wanted to scream that he would take nothing from the body of Father-Killer. The beast had taken everything he loved—his father. No, he wanted nothing, no reminder of such a terrible animal.

He turned away.

The shaman nudged him, pushing the rounded piece of yellowed ivory into his hand. The boy closed his fingers over the tusk. Then he opened his hand and let it drop to the ground. He shook his head.

The shaman frowned. He picked up the ivory and squinted at it. "It is very valuable," he said.

"Not to me," snarled the boy.

The shaman eyed the youth consideringly. He glanced at the mammoth once more, then his gaze drifted off to the small pile of rocks where Kran lay buried.

"This," he held up the piece of ivory and shook it in front of the boy's eyes, "is very powerful."

"I do not want it."

"It is a powerful token from the mammoth. It goes with your adult name."

"What name?" The boy was guarded now. He had not expected to get an adult name. That was supposed to come after his first kill with the spear he and his father made. But there would be no such kill now, he thought sadly. Kran was dead. Anguish tormented his soul and twisted his features.

Then a perverse thought entered his head. Punishment. That is what the ivory would be. Punishment for the death of his father. He would take it and wear it, as a bead around his neck. It would be a constant reminder to himself that he was a coward, that he had run when the person whom he loved most had needed him. Yes, it was fitting. He reached slowly for the ivory piece.

Solemnly the shaman handed it to him, an expectant look upon his face. The boy said nothing, only closed his fist around the yellowed chunk and clutched it to his heart.

The shaman nodded and grunted, then he muttered, "Your adulthood comes upon you in a terrible way, my son. The agonizing death of your father marks your entry into manhood." The boy's fist tightened on the ivory, but he said nothing. The shaman called the Mammoth People over. Standing before them, the shaman spoke of the mammoth, he spoke of Kran's burial, and then he put his hand on the boy's head. "I will now give him his adult name," the shaman announced.

The Mammoth People waited in respectful silence.

"His name is Mamut."

Low murmurs greeted this announcement, and the boy saw several nods. They thought it was fitting that he be named after Father-Killer, did they? Well, so would he. He would wear the ivory piece and the name in constant memory of his own cowardice.

He stood, straight and tall, accepting the name.

The Mammoth People watching saw the sun glint off his shiny black hair. They stared at the handsome youth, and every one of them was pleased at the shaman's wisdom. He had named the new man well.

Chapter 2

Ten years later

Terah lifted her hand and shaded her eyes as she stared toward the mountains. The two-year-old on her hip shifted, whimpered, then fell silent.

Little Kell, who had seen four summers, tugged at Terah's leather tunic, but she ignored him. *It is so far!* she thought. Kell tugged again. "Thirsty," he muttered.

Terah laid a hand on his head. She, too, suffered from thirst. They all did, the baby most of all.

"It is not far," Terah said, trying to sound encouraging. *If only the two little ones were not so small,* she thought as her gaze fell upon taller, silent, blond Tika. Tika had seen eight summers, and sometimes she ran ahead of Terah. *Then we could walk more swiftly toward the mountain.*

All three children were the offspring of her older sister, Chee. Terah had no child, and she assuredly had no milk for the baby, the two-year-old.

Terah frowned. She was growing concerned about Tika because the girl had said little this day as the four of them had climbed through the passes between rounded, sparsely grassed, thickly graveled hills. Usually Tika's chatter kept the children entertained for a long time, but not today. *She knows*, thought Terah to herself. *She knows.*

"Why is it taking so long to find Grandfather and Grandmother's camp?" whined Tika. "It never has before. Mother finds it easily."

Terah tightened her lips. Tears welled in her eyes, but she said nothing. Now was not the time to speak. If she did, she might say too much, might tell them what had happened to their mother. No, she would not tell them. Not now. Striving to keep her voice light, she said, "Your mother told me"—she caught herself—"tells me what a strong girl you are." Terah swallowed her grief. "She—she would be proud of how far you have walked this day."

Tika stuck out her chin pugnaciously. "I can walk farther than Kell."

Kell, his big brown eyes reflecting his hurt, pushed at his sister. Terah's hand went between the two. "We will find water soon," she said. "Let us continue." The baby dozed on her hip.

Terah's eyes focused on the tip of the snow-covered mountain. She must find her parents' encampment soon. Tomorrow, she hoped. She and the children had already traveled for more than a day. They were weary from scrambling over the dry, rough terrain. They were out of water. They had one small piece of dried meat left.

Terah assessed the sky. No rain clouds, only the constant wind. How she preferred the quieter lands of the south, near Giver of Life River, to this lonely wilderness where the wind blew constantly. But the bison liked it; they wandered here and every year they called her people to them.

"We will find Grandfather and Grandmother soon, fear not," she assured the children.

"I want my dada," said Kell.

"Your father could not come with us," explained Terah patiently. "He had to find the special stone he uses for making strong spear tips."

"I want my dada." Kell's dark eyes sparkled stubbornly, and Terah felt a wave of despair. She doubted that he would see his father, Dagger, for a long time. Dagger did not know of Chee's death. He would be inconsolable. Terah hoped that when he found Chee's body, he would return to the Grandparents' encampment, as she was doing with the children. And that could take many days.

"Come," she coaxed. "As we walk, I will tell you the story of how El tricked the White Bird Maiden and made her his wife." Terah was using

29

all her wits to keep the children walking. To tell the story was almost more than she could bear because what she wanted to do was cry and cry for her sister, for the mother they would never see again. But she could not; she dared not. Once she started crying, she would never stop. So, instead, she gave a wavering smile to Tika, held out her hand to Kell, hiked the baby farther up on her hip and started forward once more.

"What think you?" asked the hunter, watching the distant, small figures walking across a small dry valley on the graveled tundra. "They do not know we are here. We could take them with ease."

"Yes," agreed his companion. His obsidian eyes narrowed as he watched the child-burdened woman. He glanced around, quietly surveying the grass-tufted hills. "But where is her man?" he asked. "What hunter lets his family walk across the hills without protection?"

"He is probably dead," said Spearpoint.

His companion nodded. Death came often in this land. It stalked men on the hunt, women in childbirth, and children at any time. "Must have been recent," Mamut observed. "That baby riding her hip looks small."

"It is good that she can have babies," observed Spearpoint. "Our people have need of children."

The shuttered expression in his cousin's eyes almost kept him from saying more. Though

Mamut's son and wife had died two winters past, their deaths were sharp and painful to him, the pain still raw. He never spoke of them.

"We need women," agreed Mamut. "That is why we came to this northern land—to hunt the bison and use the warm furs and horns to trade as gifts for wives."

Spearpoint snorted. "Gifts, hah! Even with all the gifts we have given, we could only pry one woman away from those stingy Frog Eater People. And she is older than my grandmother!" Disgust laced Spearpoint's voice.

He and Mamut had agreed that one of the other men of the Mammoth People could claim the woman. Spearpoint wanted an attractive mate, and if she could not be attractive, he wanted one at least young enough to bear him several children. He did not know what kind of woman Mamut wanted.

"We could capture this woman," Spearpoint suggested. "That way we can save the bride price. Then at the Meet-meet we can get other women, beautiful young women, with the bride price instead."

Mamut considered. He was one of the Mammoth men who hoped to get a wife this time when gifts were given at the Meet-meet. But there was wisdom in Spearpoint's words. If they could capture this woman and her children, he or Spearpoint would save on the bride price. At the next Meet-meet

31

perhaps Mamut could obtain a beautiful bride. Furthermore, if he traded the captive woman and her children, he could get a very beautiful, industrious bride. Cala had been very beautiful. A pang of grief assaulted Mamut's heart. He turned to his cousin. "We do need more women," he acknowledged.

Spearpoint's eyes lit up. "It will be easy," he assured Mamut.

"Perhaps it is better to give gifts for them," said Mamut, thinking suddenly of the disadvantages of what they were about to do. He indicated the woman in the distance, her back slowly receding from them. "Her people will not like it that we steal her. And if he is not dead, her mate will come after us. We may start a fight."

Spearpoint shrugged and stared at the distant figures. "I am not afraid."

He did not see Mamut flinch.

"As you said yourself," continued Spearpoint, "what man lets his woman and children walk out here alone? There are mammoths, there are wolves. There are saber-toothed cats." He stiffened suddenly and then slowly swung to regard his companion. "Lo! There is one over there." He pointed with his chin. Some distance from the woman, a tawny shape moved.

Eyes narrowed, Mamut now could see the yellow-and-black spotted form of a saber-toothed cat. The colors blended in well with the graveled hillsides. Dread filled Mamut's heart as he realized the big tiger was stalking the woman and children.

They had little choice now. If Mamut and Spearpoint did not take the woman, the tiger would.

Chapter 3

Mamut decided to scare away the saber-toothed cat—if it would go. Fighting saber-toothed tigers was very risky. Not only were the huge cats fierce fighters, but a single scratch from one sharp talon made a man's skin swell with poison. Often after a vicious fight with a tiger, a man went into a delirious hot trance and died from the affliction.

The single yellowed ivory bead strung on a leather strip around Mamut's neck bounced as he ran. If he had to, he would kill the tiger, Mamut thought grimly, no matter the risk. He had not backed away from a fight with an animal—or a man—since that fateful day ten summers before. Nor would he, ever again.

Mamut and Spearpoint started yelling and waving their spears when they were some

35

distance from the tiger. The sooner the tiger
knew they were after him, the better. But their
cries had another effect—the woman turned,
saw them, grabbed the younger child's hand
and began running away toward the hills across
the shallow valley. On the other side of the hills
lay Giver of Life River.

"She will have to run faster than that if she
is to get away from us," boasted Spearpoint
slyly, not at all alarmed by the head start the
woman had. Even were she to hide in the draws
between the hills, they would find her. And he
liked chasing tigers. After the tiger was gone,
he could chase the woman and children. It was
proving to be an exciting day!

The great cat roared and swung to face
them. Mamut could see its dagger-shaped
canine teeth and grimacing red maw. Mamut
raised his spear, still running. He felt strength
surge through his muscles and took careful
aim. From his youth, he had spent countless
days aiming at targets. He was accurate—the
most accurate of any man of the Mammoth
People.

At his side, he could hear Spearpoint's heavy
breathing. It was good to go into battle with
Spearpoint at his side. Mamut knew of no
braver hunter than Spearpoint.

The saber-tooth, a male in his full prime,
was not going to flee, Mamut saw. He was
going to stand his ground and fight. Beside
him, Spearpoint gave a happy *yip!* and Mamut
smiled grimly. Spearpoint *would* prefer the fight.

36

Teeth bared in snarls like the tiger, the two men circled the beast.

The great cat pawed the air, talons extended. Mamut jumped back just in time from one swipe of a big paw. Mamut watched the tiger lower into a crouch, about to spring. He yelled a warning to Spearpoint. Together the men threw their spears, Mamut at the heart, Spearpoint at the neck.

The tiger went down on his side, snarling and spitting. Mamut could smell its meat-soured breath, and he glanced away, nauseated. The glance was his undoing, for the tiger staggered up and launched himself at Mamut. Blood poured from the cat's wounds.

"Beware!"

Mamut heard Spearpoint's shouted warning and whipped out a heavy knife from his belt. The tiger sank down on him, his big teeth lunging at Mamut's head. The weight of the beast sank upon the knife. With a quick upward thrust, Mamut jabbed through tough fur and skin and into soft guts. He sliced the tiger's belly open, and hot intestines spilled over his arm.

The tiger, dead before it hit the ground, clawed reflexively, and its teeth snapped the air. Mamut heaved the animal off himself and backed away. Dismayed, he saw that he had three slashes from the tiger's sharp talons on his arm. He wondered when the hot sickness would come. He felt his head, where the tiger's teeth had grazed him. No injury there, just sticky tiger saliva in his hair.

Spearpoint was jumping up and down, yelling and exulting. He did a little dance around the carcass. He sang a song to the Great Spirit, thanking Him for delivering the beast's life into their hands. Mamut watched, also saying a silent thank-you. But somehow he was not ready to dance yet. Not until he knew no hot sickness would come from the tiger's three slashes on his skin.

Swiftly they stripped the hide from the saber-tooth, and Spearpoint rolled the bloody skin up in a ball. "I hope that woman knows how to tan hides," he joked with Mamut, then glanced back at her small frame disappearing into the distance.

Mamut laughed shortly. Ever since the Mammoth People had lost six women and eight children during the Winter of Death, the surviving ten men of the Mammoth People had been doing women's work. Spearpoint could now tan a hide as well as Mamut could. Verily, on occasion a tuft of fur blew away from a garment, leaving their clothing ragged-looking, but that bothered them little. Previously, neither had known what to do with a hide, but they had learned. Swiftly. Now they could dry meat in strips for winter, smoke and dry salmon for winter, and tell which plants were edible. Only two of their own women had survived the Winter of Death, but they and the Frog Eater woman had taught the survivors of the Mammoth People all they knew about preserving foods and animal hides. And the men did the jobs willingly. Most of the time. Even Lame Leg, the remaining child, helped, though not without complaint.

Spearpoint cut out the heart of the saber-tooth and began eating it. Blood dripped down his chin as he chewed a huge mouthful. Mamut cut off a slice of the tiger's liver and took a bite of the steaming meat. They did not eat too much, knowing they had to chase down the woman and children, but they needed the strength the meat would give them.

With a grunt, Spearpoint rose and wiped his mouth, staring out across the hills where the still fleeing figures of the woman and children were just disappearing. "She is going to get very tired, running like that," he joked.

Mamut grunted and wiped the last of the bloody liver from his mouth. He felt better, feeling the strength of the meat course through his body. "Alas, the wolves will get the carcass. It is unfortunate," he murmured. He did not like meat to go to waste, but this past Fall much meat had gone to waste. He and his men had killed plenty of animals, but they could not preserve them as well or as fast as the women could. Yes, it would be a good thing to capture this woman. She was fully grown, able to have children. She would know how to tan hides, weave baskets. Yes, she would be a welcome addition to the Mammoth People. And, best of all, she would cost them no gifts.

He surveyed the bare basalt hills critically. Still no male protector had appeared. She was alone.

"Let us go," he said to Spearpoint. The fight with the saber-tooth had restored his confidence and he was ready. Spearpoint balanced the rolled-up saber-tooth hide on one shoulder and carried his spear in the other hand.

Excitement coursed through Mamut's veins as he thought of stalking the woman. With a grin to Spearpoint, the two hunters set off at a jog.

Chapter 4

Terah knew she was running too fast for the children. If she kept to this pace, they would fall behind. Already Tika, the strongest of the three, panted heavily. Kell kept turning around to watch for the hunters and was now several paces behind Terah. The baby, Flori, had wakened from Terah's jostling run and was whimpering. She dared not put Flori on the ground to run because the toddler would soon be left behind.

With a worried frown, Terah forced herself to take slower steps. She glanced over her shoulder. The two men were trotting toward them, still far away. They did not look to be in any hurry.

While running across the valley, Terah had glanced backward several times and watched as the two strangers smote the saber-toothed tiger. Memories of Bron flickered across her mind, but she pushed them away. Now was not the time to think of her dead brother and his fatal fight with a saber-tooth. Terah hated and feared the great cats—as did every one of her people. Never had Terah thought she would be happy to see one of the dangerous tigers, but this time she was. The fierce beast had warned her of the hunters. She did not know if the hunters had been stalking the tiger or her and the children, but she would not tarry to find out. But now the animal was no longer an impediment if they wished to pursue her.

It worried Terah, too, how quickly the two hunters had slain the animal. Either the cat was old and sickly, which was unlikely, or those two hunters were deadly.

Terah felt sweat run off her brow. Even the wind could not dry her fear. Kell cried out once, and she reached for his hand. Flori clutched the front of Terah's deerskin tunic, and Terah was relieved that the baby knew to hang on. Children had to be strong and wise to endure in this land.

She led the children into a rocky draw. The hills were covered in loose gravel, and she and the children would only slide backwards if they attempted the hills. To make haste, they must traverse the rocky trenches between the hills.

If only she knew where her parents' encampment was. Then she would have help. The men of the Bison People would easily drive away the two intruders. If only she did not have the children. She could run faster and surely escape. If only, if only . . . But, she thought bitterly, she did not know the precise location of her parents and the Bison People. They were supposed to be at the foot of the mountain with the jagged tip. But she was still too far away from them; her people would never know of her danger, never come to her rescue.

Furthermore, she could not desert the children to save herself. Other than her old parents, they were the last remaining members of her family now that Chee—*Do not think about Chee*, she warned herself. *Think about saving the children.* . . .

She glanced back over her shoulder. The strangers were running after her. "Swiftly!" she urged the children. Within heartbeats they were swallowed up in the hills.

As she scrambled up the clattering rock, her mother's warnings echoed through her mind. Strangers were to be avoided; let the men talk with strangers, trade with them. Do not let yourself be seen.

"Why?" Terah had asked. She had noticed that even at Meet-meets, those rare times when nine or ten different bands gathered together, a happy time of excitement and socializing and feasting, the Bison People always kept to themselves. Bison men could visit the men and women of other bands, but they did not let their women visit.

"Why is it that Bison men can visit others but

43

Bison women must stay hidden?" she had asked her mother.

"That is how it is," her mother had shrugged. "That is how we do things." But Terah would not be put off with childish explanations. She wanted the truth. Her mother sighed and said, "Because sometimes men steal women."

A shiver went through Terah at those words.

"On occasion it happens that a man visits a Meet-meet, or he may even be out hunting, and lo, and he sees a woman he likes. He does not know her or know her family, but he wants her. Then sometimes that man will steal the woman away—away from her people, away from her lands—and keep her as his wife. He will not give gifts to her family. He will not tell the woman in a proper way that he wants to marry her. Such an unfortunate woman would never see her family again. We do not want such a woeful thing to happen to a Bison woman."

After her mother told her this, Terah wondered what it would be like to be stolen.

She glanced behind. She had an awful feeling she would soon find out. To be taken away from her family . . . Never to see her mother again, her father . . . "Faster," she urged Tika. The poor child scrambled up faster and Terah felt guilty. But those men would steal Tika and Kell and Flori, too. This must not happen. She must get away and save the children.

Terah peeked around a boulder. The men were closer now; she could see their long dark hair blowing as they ran. Yes, they were strangers.

She did not know them. Had they been to any Meet-meets? It mattered not. Here there were none of the Bison men to protect her and the children. It was best to flee.

Alas, the children were so very tired. Kell stumbled. They were all stumbling. Tika took Kell's hand to help him up, a scared look upon her face. Terah's heart sank. How long could the children keep climbing and running before they exhausted themselves?

She glanced over her shoulder once more. The men came on at a steady trot.

If the two men meant no harm, reasoned Terah, they would have turned away by now. They would have let her and the children continue on their way, unharmed. They would not be following her. No, these hunters were trouble.

Then a truly frightening thought came to Terah. What if these hunters wanted to *kill* her and the children? Perhaps they did not live by the rules of the Meet-meet and only stole women. Perhaps they killed them.

Terror surged through her, giving her new strength. They were perched at the neck of a trench between the hills. Before them lay more hills and more trenches to run through. "We must run!" she cried to Tika. Something in Terah's voice must have communicated her new fear because Tika nodded and used both hands to pull Kell along. For a short while, they were able to keep the driving pace, then Tika faltered. Again Terah's heart sank. She patted her white chert knife, tied at her waist, for reassurance.

Ahead, at the bottom of the passage they were scrambling down, she spotted a cluster of large boulders. There was a small space in the middle with boulders on three sides. "Only a little farther," she assured the children, through frantic breaths. "Just a little farther . . ."

"I want my dada," gasped Kell.

"We all do," assured Terah. Oh, how she wished Dagger were here. He was strong. He would defend his children and his wife's sister with his life. He had done so before. But alas, Dagger was in the hills somewhere searching out the secret source of the heavy white chert that he used to make fine speartips.

They reached the boulders and Terah dropped Flori to the ground. "Take her, Tika," she urged. "Hide her under the boulders. You too, Kell!"

She watched in relief as Tika guided Flori into a small space under one of the boulders. Kell was able to crowd into a tiny space between two of the boulders. He was well hidden. But the space where Tika hid was too shallow. The girl's arms and legs stuck out. Frantically Terah helped her dig out a bigger space.

When Tika was hidden as well as could be done, Terah spoke in what she hoped was a calm voice. "Bide here until I tell you to come out." She paused, fingering her knife. What if she died in the upcoming fight? What would the children do then? Sick with fear, she could only repeat, "Bide here!"

Terah turned to face the two intruders. She

watched them approach in their unhurried manner, easily descending the passage that she and the children had scrambled down so frantically.

Slowly she withdrew the knife at her waist and fingered the blade. It was made of the white chert that her brother-in-law prized so highly. Dagger had ground the edge fine and sharp. He had presented it as a gift to Terah so that she could easily slice through bison meat during the Fall Hunt. She knew the knife was of exceptional value. Chee's eyes had narrowed to mere slits when she beheld the gift. Terah knew that sometimes Bison men took more than one wife and often preferred to marry sisters because they worked well together and loved one another. A man hoped for peace in the household that way. But Chee would not like such an arrangement. Though she greatly loved Terah and Terah adored her older sister, still Terah knew that Chee would never share her man.

Terah had wanted to tell Chee that she had no wish to marry Dagger, for at that time she still thought she loved Bear, but she had not found the words. Instead, she had hidden the knife away under her bison robe, hoping never to use it for she had no wish to arouse her older sister's jealousy.

But now, Chee or no, Terah was glad of the gift. It was a fine, well-made weapon, especially shaped for her grip alone. Dagger's work would not be in vain. She would use this weapon to defend his children.

Terah took several deep breaths and tried to

calm the thrumming of her heart. The wait was long. She stood, long legs splayed, knife out, biding her time, waiting . . . waiting . . . and still the hunters came leisurely on.

When they were a short distance from her, they stopped. They said nothing to her, speaking only to each other. Unease stirred in Terah. They were too close. She sniffed the air, striving to catch their scent. She raised her white knife a little so that they would be sure to see it.

Finally one of them, the bigger one, walked toward her. He stopped a spear's length away.

She stared at him. He was big. The muscles on his arms and shoulders were massive. He wore a robe of ratty bison fur. The woman who had tanned the hides for his clothing did not know what she was doing, Terah thought in contempt. His hair, long and black, quivered in the wind. He looked fierce. She swallowed.

His eyes were as black as obsidian, his nose straight. His strong jaw clenched as he watched her. She noticed three long scratches on his right forearm, the blood recently dried. From the saber-tooth, she realized. She wondered if he knew the danger of such scratches.

She was younger than he had thought, mused Mamut. An amused grin twisted his firm lips. So young to have so many children. He stared at her. Her light brown hair blew to one side, giving him a full view of her face. He took a step closer.

Lo! Green eyes. I have never seen green eyes before. She had a flat, straight nose, high cheekbones, and a stern mouth. He searched her eyes, entranced. When she glared at him, he smiled to himself. He suddenly found that he could not drag his eyes away from her. His nostrils flared; his heart pounded. He knew he wanted her. Badly.

He decided he would try to capture her and the children without a fight, if he could. It would not do to hurt such a wild and lovely woman. And he and Spearpoint did not want to have to drag an injured woman or child back across the hills to his camp.

Terah, seeing the grin, raised her knife higher.

Alas, his weaponry was impressive. He wore several knives at his waist and carried a leather sling on his back above which poked several sharp spear tips. He had a pouch tied to one side of his waist and she wondered if it contained water. She licked dry lips.

His companion was similarly armed. How was she going to hold off two well-armed, grown men? She ruthlessly squashed her doubts. She had the children to think of, to defend.

"Drop the knife," said the man. He held out both hands, palms to her. No weapon. He still wore the amused grin.

For a moment, the wind blew Terah's light brown hair back across her face and she could not see him. Swiftly she pushed it back and behind her. So he thought to take her knife from her so easily and kill her without a squeak, did he?

"No," she said and raised the white knife. It struck her suddenly that she could understand

Theresa Scott

his words. He spoke the Bison People's language though he pronounced the words with a longer drawl.

"I do not want to hurt you," he said.

She stared at him, trying to decide if he was telling the truth or if he actually wanted to kill her.

"What do you want?" she asked at last.

He smiled, a wolfish smile.

"What do you want?" she repeated.

"I want you to come with us."

"No!"

He took a step closer. He pointed with his chin at his companion. Terah's eyes merely flickered to the other man before she brought them back again to the lethal male threat in front of her.

"We are two men," he pointed out reasonably. "You are one lone woman. With children." Terah's stomach clenched at mention of the children. He must have sensed her distress, for he added quickly, "Come with us. We will not hurt you—or your children."

He thought the children hers. Terah decided she would not tell him any different. She shook her head. "No," she said firmly. "You go away and leave us alone. I do not want to come with you. We have people nearby," she lied.

He laughed.

Terah's heart sank, and she raised the knife higher. Still amused, he glanced at it. "Give me the little knife," he ordered. He met her eyes and stepped toward her.

She stared at him, willing him to go away.

He closed the distance between them. She could smell him now. Smoke smell, leather, man musk. Her nostrils flared.

She stared up into those dark, deep-set eyes. He was so large, up close. His nose was straight, his cheekbones high. He had a strong chin with a cleft in it. She swallowed. His neck was strong and thick, his shoulders wide. He could easily kill her.

He seemed relaxed, uncaring of the threat her knife presented. She remembered how he and his companion had killed the saber-toothed tiger and she swallowed. "Beware! Do not come any closer," she warned. "I will kill you!"

Suddenly he reached for the knife and she lunged toward him, teeth bared. She brought the knife down and felt it scrape him with a jarring motion. He jumped back, a red scratch on his previously unscathed forearm. He was not amused now.

"Need some help?" teased his friend.

The intruder did not answer, but his black eyes had gone cold and assessing.

Mamut raged. Now he had a knife scratch to worry about. He was getting careless. A knife scratch was less likely to get infected than the saber-tooth's marks, but still it was not good. He reached for the woman, but she moved with him, her sharp white knife matching his movements.

With a fierce yell, he grabbed for her knife wrist. He squeezed tightly and the knife trembled in her grasp. Her eyes widened and he plucked the knife out of her numb grip. He tossed it behind him. "Now will you come with me?" Surely she could see it was useless to fight him. He was so much bigger and stronger than she.

"Never!" she cried. Terah's eyes filled with tears of frustration. She could not give herself and the children up without a fight. Desperation gave her new strength. She seized a handful of his thick black hair and gave a ferocious yank. Then she kicked at his crotch. Her foot missed and slipped and hit his muscular thigh. The force of the kick pushed him away.

Mamut grunted in pain from the kick. Still bent over, he heard Spearpoint chuckling. Salvaging his pride, his very manhood, suddenly became important to Mamut. He would subdue this green-eyed woman!

He straightened and lunged at her. His arms encircled her waist.

Terah felt as though she were in the suffocating hug of a cave bear.

Mamut kicked her legs out from beneath her and brought her down to the ground, himself on top. She gouged at his eyes with her thumbs. His eyes aching, he grabbed both her wrists and pulled them back over her head. She lay there panting. He stared down into her furious green eyes. "Now you will come with me." It was an order.

For answer, Terah tried bucking him off by heaving her hips and torso, but he would not budge. "Get off!" she cried.

He glared down at her. She ground her teeth, desperate to get free. Never to see her family again . . . She wanted to scream in frustration, but instead she opened her jaws and lunged for his nose. She missed when he jerked his head back, but she caught his cheek in her teeth. She bit down, hard.

He yelped. He tried to push her away, but she hung on, squeezing her jaws tight. He pushed her head back and slipped one hand between his aching cheek and her jaws. Her teeth promptly clamped onto his hand. With a frustrated cry, he pried her mouth off his hand.

Her body felt soft under him, and her struggles excited him. He dipped his head and mashed his lips against hers.

Terah's eyes widened in disbelief and shock and then she struggled harder.

He broke off the kiss and looked down into those furious green eyes. "You are a fierce saber-toothed tigress," he said. "Did you know that?" His voice was caressing and his obsidian eyes were amused. "Such a fighter," he murmured. He lowered his head and kissed her again; this time his lips were gentle.

When he raised his head, he saw that her lips still trembled from his kiss. He sighed. It had been a long time since he'd had a woman. Cala had died two winters ago.

"Come with me," he said softly. Spearpoint's idea to save the bride price faded. Now Mamut knew he wanted the woman for herself. He bent to kiss her once more.

Frantically, she turned her head to the side so that he could not touch her lips. He chuckled.

Flori, the baby, whimpered. That one lament gave Terah newfound courage. She writhed under the big male's grip and was able to free one wrist. She groped about on the ground and scrabbled up a handful of dust and gravel. She tossed it into his eyes.

With a yelp, he dropped her other wrist and rubbed at his eyes.

She tried to pull herself from under him, but he was too heavy and he firmly anchored her lower torso. Breathing heavily, she pushed at him, hoping that while he was blinded, she could get away. Alas, she still could not free herself. With both hands she seized the longest knife he wore at his waist and yanked it up. Her hands shaking, she held the knife point to the taut skin under his firm chin. "Do not move," she said in a low voice.

Mamut froze, inwardly scolding himself for letting his guard down with this she-tiger.

Terah ordered, "Get off me."

Slowly, with a little prick of the knife to remind him, Mamut moved to one side. In one swift move, Terah moved the blade to his throat and knelt behind him.

Mamut wanted to shake his head. This woman, so young, was a brave fighter. He felt a flare of grudging admiration. Just then, the blade of his knife touched the skin at his throat and he promptly forgot the admiration.

Terah smiled to herself now that she had the big hunter by the throat. "Get up," she said, savoring the power of having this stranger, this great, hulking man, do her bidding. "Move slowly, and I will not have to hurt you."

She watched him get slowly to his feet, his back to her. The massive muscles of his upper arms and shoulders tensed. She must be careful, she warned herself. The only thing saving her was one thin knife. . . . "Do not make any swift movements," she warned again.

Mamut ground his teeth and clenched his jaw. The only swift movements he wanted to make were to get this woman under him again. His body throbbed.

Suddenly the knife was torn past his throat, just missing his skin. The woman was thrown to the ground. Spearpoint had decided to join the fight and had come up behind the woman, throwing the stiffly drying saber-tooth hide over her head and grabbing her from behind.

Mamut whirled and launched himself on top of the woman. With one hand, he pushed her head into the saber-tooth hide and the ground. Spearpoint grinned at Mamut and tossed him a length of deer sinew. "Do you wish to bind her?"

With a dark look, Mamut grabbed the long piece of sinew and set about tying the woman's hands and feet behind her. It was with some satisfaction that he tested the last knot and found it well-tied.

Terah stared at the blackness inside the saber-tooth hide and the smell of the dead beast made her feel nauseated. Self-disgust flooded over her. Now she was caught, well and truly snared. She could not help the children. She could not even help herself. She kicked weakly when the hunter tied her feet, but her kicks had little effect against the knots he tied.

Sharp rock bit into her as she lay sprawled on her stomach, face down, listening to the muffled sounds around her.

She could hear one of the hunters—she thought it was the one who had sneaked up on her—talking to the children in a gentle voice, trying to coax them out from under the boulders. Then she heard coughing and choking sounds. Terah smiled grimly inside the saber-tooth skin. Next she heard a grunt and a sharp exclamation. The children were not giving in without a fight, either, she thought proudly. The baby whimpered.

"Friendly family," Spearpoint observed to Mamut. "The woman bites you and stabs you, and her children throw dirt in my face. Are you certain you want them?"

"We need women," answered Mamut shortly. His arm hurt, his cheek throbbed, and his pride smarted. "You were the one who said we should steal them. No gifts to pay, I believe you said." He grimaced at the vicious little saber-tooth cubs huddled under the rocks. "It would be easy, you said." He grimaced. The little animals looked well dug in. It would take the better part of the day to drag them out.

He stared at the woman, the lure in all this trouble. He walked over and tore the saber-tooth hide off her head and stood over her, frowning.

Terah blinked and rolled over. She glared up at the hunter whose knife she had stolen. "Let me go," she demanded.

She saw that her red bite mark graced his cheek and triumph surged through her.

The man caught her glance. He rubbed his cheek and glared back at her.

She stirred in the dirt. Her hands were securely tied and her feet just as securely.

"Tell those children to come out," he ordered. Terah stared at him, weighing her choices. If the two were going to kill her, they would have done so by now. These hunters were the kind of men who stole women, she was certain. They wanted the children too. She snapped her mouth shut mutinously, refusing to say a word.

Mamut stared at the woman in frustration, then back at the children, half-hidden under the boulders. He met Spearpoint's eyes and saw his own frustration mirrored therein.

Then inspiration struck Mamut. "We do not need these children," he said slowly. "They are too much trouble. Let us just take the woman."

Spearpoint opened his mouth to object, then caught Mamut's eye. "But what about the dire wolves?" He leaned over one boulder, making certain the children could hear him. "What about the saber-toothed tigers? They are very fierce. Many of them live near here. And how they like to eat tasty child meat!" Spearpoint looked smug.

The baby whimpered.

"I want my dada," growled Kell.

"Be quiet," snapped Tika.

Terah could hear the tension in her niece's voice. If the hunters took Terah away, then Tika would have to find her grandparents' encampment alone. Even Terah did not know where it was, for certain, because her parents moved camp every few days on their quest for food.

Despair gripped Terah. What should she do? If the hunters took only her and left the children, the little ones would wander among the hills, lost, prey to any animal or human that found them. Yet if Terah ordered the children to come with her, they would never see their family again. And these two hunters did not sound as if they cared about children. Oh, what should she do?

"I am going to have a drink of water," Spearpoint said innocently. Spearpoint made a big show of taking out his water sack and drinking from it. "This water is cool. It tastes good," he said.

The baby whimpered. Terah swallowed, reminded of how she had had no drink that day. She knew the children were thirsty, too.

She rose to her elbows, half-expecting to be hit back down, but nothing happened. She rose to her knees.

Mamut watched her struggle to her feet. He offered her no aid; he was still angry about the bite on his cheek.

"The children are thirsty," she said. She would not plead for herself.

Mamut shrugged as he leaned against one of

the boulders. "If they want water, they can come out and drink." Watching her idly, he took a swallow from his own bison waterskin, his black eyes assessing her as he drank.

Saliva coursed through Terah's mouth. She swallowed. "Do not leave them for the wolves," she blurted out at last.

The hunter merely shrugged again. His eyes played over her, then swung to the boulders where the children hid. "They are safe enough," he said. "As long as they stay hidden, the saber-tooths and wolves probably will not find them." He took another drink of water. "Although, if this wind dies down, the wolves will smell them." He shrugged as if to say it did not matter to him.

Terah turned away, looking at the boulders where the children hid.

She saw that the second hunter was regarding her closely. His lips were straight and tight, as if he were holding back his anger.

What should she do? If she ordered the children to come out, she was delivering them up to an unknown life with these hunters. If she ordered the children to stay under the boulders, she was certainly consigning them to death. She took a breath.

Before she could say anything, Mamut straightened and put away the bison waterskin. "Let us go," he said to the second hunter. The other nodded and picked up the stinking saber-tooth hide.

With a grimace, Terah said, "Bide a moment." The men kept moving. "Please."

The bigger one, whose knife she had taken, paused. Terah took heart. "Please," she asked with as much dignity as she could muster, "give the children a drink of water."

"Tell them to come out," he said, his dark eyes watching her gravely. Mamut could see that it cost the woman much pride to ask him, but by now he was certain she would ask for the children's sake, not for herself.

"Tika, Kell, Flori!" she called. She glanced at the hunter once more. His face was implacable. "Come out," she called softly.

After several heartbeats, Tika, all arms and legs, crawled out. She helped the baby out. Kell scrambled out, then stood, shaking the dust off himself. "I want my dada."

Terah wanted to weep. Kell would never see his dada again. Not unless she could escape with the children and return to the Bison People before they went south. It would be a daunting undertaking, escaping from these hunters and struggling across the hills, hoping to find the Bison People in time. She wondered if she should even attempt it, the risk of death wandering in the hills was so great. Yet how could she not?

The children were given water. Mamut untied Terah's feet and offered her the bison waterskin, but she turned her face away.

"Let us go," said Mamut gruffly. Let her be stubborn, he thought, that unwilling admiration rising in him again. She would not be able to travel much farther without water. He would leave her her pride for the nonce. It was little enough. And she had put up a good fight. She was brave.

Slowly the little band of captives and captors started back the way they had so recently run, but now at a much slower pace.

Chapter 5

Terah trudged along, Flori the baby riding on her hip. Now and then, Terah lifted her head to stare balefully at the broad back of the man walking ahead of her. Her captor, she thought scornfully. Well, he would not be for long. She and the children would escape as soon as she was able to make a plan.

Through eyes narrowed against the wind-blown sand, she observed for the tenth time that he was a tall man, taller even than Bear, the largest man of the Bison People. And his shoulders were wider, too. The wind in the hills whipped his long thick black hair back over his shoulders.

She gritted her teeth. She would have to be clever to escape this man. She could not outrun him, nor could she outfight him. That meant she would have to outwit him. That, she thought confidently, she could do.

Kell sat upon his broad shoulders. Terah had not wanted to relinquish her nephew to the giant of a man, but she had had no choice. Little by little, Kell had become tired and begun to lag behind. Frightened for him, remembering that their captors had once before been ready to leave the children behind, Terah had carried both him and the baby. She had kept on until almost exhausted. When the man had finally lifted the boy and put him on his shoulders Terah had felt a stirring of gratitude for his help. She quickly suppressed it.

Terah glanced behind her at Tika. The girl followed close upon her heels. And behind her walked their other captor, also tall and dark-haired. Now and then he would turn and search the hills behind them, on a constant look-out for saber-toothed tigers and big dire wolves.

Secretly Terah felt relieved that the two hunters were so vigilant. She had no wish to meet a saber-tooth. She smiled encouragingly at Tika, relieved that the girl was old enough to keep up with her. She was a stout-hearted Bison girl, Terah knew, and though she had not complained once since their capture, Terah thought that the girl must be near the end of her reserves of strength.

As Terah trudged along, she noted that the sun was setting. They would have to camp for the night soon. She wondered how many days of travel it would take to get to wherever her captors were taking them.

At last they found a small stream, the water ice-cold from a glacier far behind the ridge. Terah put the baby down and dipped her hands in the cool water. She splashed some of the freezing liquid on her face. It felt so refreshing that she splashed some on Flori too, and the little one gasped. Soon the baby and the two other children were playing in the stream while Terah searched for twigs and grass and lichens to burn for a campfire.

It did not take long for the men to make a fire. Kell squatted down beside the fire and stared at the men with expectant eyes. He pointed to his mouth, his meaning obvious.

Terah wished he had not done that. She did not want to ask these fearsome captors for anything. She glanced around, wondering what she could offer the children to eat. They had already consumed the last of the dried meat she had brought with her.

One of the men, the one she was most wary of, the one with the scratches on his forearm—the one, she thought smugly, that she had pricked with her knife—pulled out a chunk of dried meat from the leather sack at his waist. All four captives watched, mouths watering, as he cut it into pieces with a sharp obsidian knife.

Then he held out a piece of meat to the boy.

For a moment Terah hoped Kell would refuse it. She sighed when she saw the child take the meat with both hands and stuff it into his mouth. He was hungry, she thought guiltily. She had not carried enough meat to feed the children since they had been forced to leave Chee, and she wondered what she would have done if the hunters had not come along. She would have snared something, she assured herself stoutly—a pika or a squirrel or perhaps even a hare, but something.

She watched as the hunter next held out his open hand to Tika, palm up, with a piece of dried meat on it. He watched as Tika took a step toward him. Then the girl hesitated and glanced from the meat to Terah. Terah met her eyes, seeing the question therein. With a droop of her shoulders, Terah nodded. She could not ask her niece to starve. Tika snatched the meat off his hand and backed away several steps. She gobbled up the meat.

Flori toddled over and reached out a tiny hand. Terah held her breath as she watched the hunter carefully place a small chunk of meat on the child's palm. He smiled as Flori closed her hand on the meat and brought it to her lips. She pushed it into her mouth and began chewing.

Terah felt betrayed.

The hunter looked up suddenly and met Terah's eyes in challenge. "Can you provide better?" he seemed to be asking with those black, black eyes.

Terah looked away and gritted her teeth. Unaccountably, she felt abandoned by the children in their quest for food. And she felt humiliated that her family was so easily won over by a few hunks of dried meat. Yet what could she do? They needed to eat. She could understand that. Her own stomach was growling. It was not the children's fault that she had no food to offer them.

Terah stood up, intent on getting away from those dark eyes that seemed to be laughing at her. He rose, too, and moved to stand in front of her, blocking her way. He stared down at her, legs splayed, an arrogant look on his handsome face. He was not handsome, she corrected herself.

"Would you like some meat?" he asked.

She raised an eyebrow. She would show no fear to this man. "No."

"You are going to get very hungry," he warned.

She tightened her lips, the message plain that she did not want to eat of his food. Just then her stomach growled. He heard it, she knew, because his long eyelashes flickered. By no other sign, however, did he indicate that he heard the traitorous sound. He held out his hand, palm open, meat upon it, just as he had for the children. She turned away. She could not be bought so easily.

"We have much territory to cover on the morrow," he said. "You will not be able to keep up with us if you are faint with hunger and thirst."

"Then leave me behind," she said defiantly.

"Would you want that?" he asked, appearing to take her words seriously. "Would you wish to be left behind?"

"If you would leave me, that would be fine with me," she said stubbornly. But she could not let the children go on without her.

He studied her, trying to determine the extent of her rebellion. "No," he said at last. "We will not leave you."

"But we will get very sore carrying a big woman like you across the plains," observed his friend.

Since Terah was neither tall nor heavy, she knew him to be joking. She did not appreciate his levity, however, when her freedom was at stake. Anger flushed her face red. "I did not ask to be stolen," she pointed out stiffly.

"True," the first hunter acknowledged. "But you are with us now. It is best if you accept your lot."

"And what will that be?" she challenged. Perhaps now she could find out what they planned to do with her and the children.

"We are taking you to our people," Mamut answered. "You will live with us. One of our men will marry you and give you more children. You will be well treated."

Terah flushed. She thought that the way this man was looking at her meant that he had himself in mind as her husband. "And if I do not?"

He shrugged. "You have no choice."

Terah ground her teeth. "Do I have a choice

of husband?" she dared.

"No."

"What?" she screeched in outrage.

He smiled. "It is you who are the captive," he pointed out. "You have no say in whom you will marry."

"And you do!" she raged.

"Of course," they chorused together. Both men looked suddenly askance at each other, realizing that their thoughts had been running in the same direction. Who would be her mate?

Terah clenched her fists and gnashed her teeth. How unfortunate that her mother had neglected to mention the arrogance of women-kidnappers when she had warned her daughter. Terah stomped off in disgust and stopped at the edge of the flickering campfire. She was not so unmindful of her surroundings that she would go marching off alone into saber-toothed tiger territory.

"Aunt Terah?" asked Tika in a small voice. She felt guilty for eating the men's food, but she had been so hungry. And Aunt Terah looked so unhappy. . . .

"Aunt?" echoed both men, again looking at each other.

Spearpoint turned to the girl. "Is this woman not your mother?" He stared fixedly at the child.

Something in his voice warned Tika of the importance of her answer. Her eyes flicked to her aunt and back to the man.

"Tell us the truth, girl," said Mamut softly.

Tika looked down at the ground. "She is my aunt," she murmured. She glanced at Terah, then back to the men interrogating her. "She is my mother's sister."

Mamut nodded. He pointed to Kell and Flori with his chin. "And these children? Is the woman their aunt also?"

Tika's eyes flickered. She hesitated, looked at Terah. Terah kept her back to them all, but her outrage was evident from her stiff posture.

"The truth," prompted Mamut again.

Tika nodded. "They are my brother and my sister."

"Where is your mother?"

"Back at the campsite," answered Tika. She squirmed, uncomfortable with all the questions. Her eyes shot to her aunt once more.

Their mother is dead! Terah wanted to scream, but she did not. The children did not know that Chee was dead. When they had left, Chee had been lying there, paralyzed. She had pleaded with Terah not to let the children watch her die. And Terah had agreed to take the children and leave. But Terah would not tell the hunters that, nor the children. She planned to tell the children, later, in her own way, in a gentle way, of their mother's death.

Sorrow mixed with her anger as she turned to gaze at the little ones. The thought came to her that she was all they had now. They would never see their father or grandparents again. *Stop it!* cried an inner voice. *You will escape! They will see their family again.* Of course, she corrected herself. Of course. She would escape. She had but forgotten for a moment. . . .

Mamut regarded the young woman thoughtfully. Why had she been walking across the land with her sister's children? Where were their parents? Where were their people? Where was her husband?

He found himself asking the last question aloud. Tika looked at him and blurted, "She has no husband. Bear would not—"

"Silence!" shrieked Terah. She would not have her humiliation bruited about in front of these men. She may have nothing else, but at least she had the tattered remnants of her dignity. "Silence," she ordered Tika.

The girl gave her a hard glance and turned away. Terah started. Had the gift of a small piece of meat bought her niece's loyalty so completely? Terah's eyes narrowed.

Tika's chin came up. "I was only telling him that Bear did not—"

"Enough," hissed Terah.

"—want you."

Terah gasped and glared at Tika, totally betrayed.

"And-Bear-is-not-a-good-man-so-what-does-it-matter." Tika got out all in one breath.

Terah stared, amazed. What ever had gotten into her niece to make her tell such things? Did she not understand that these men were the enemy, that the less they knew about Terah and the children the easier it would be to escape?

71

She marched over and placed her hands on Tika's shoulders. Her hands were yanked off the child's thin frame by a pair of strong, dark hands. She glared at those hands and forearms—one of which bore her mark and the other three clawed welts from the saber-tooth.

Terah stared at the welts. They looked red and were beginning to puff. She lifted defiant green eyes and met those of the tall hunter. "Your arm is infected," she sneered. She hoped he would forget what Tika had just said about Bear not wanting her and concentrate instead on this new danger. "If it is not cleansed, you will get very ill." She could not keep the satisfaction out of her voice. How she resented being captured!

"I know," he said calmly. Mamut was certain his voice did not show his concern. He had known for some time that his arm was infected. It was one of the reasons he had pushed the children and woman at a faster pace than he wanted to this day. He must get back to his people and get help from the shaman or he would get the hot sickness.

He stared at the young woman before him. Her eyes were a vivid green, and he could see she was furious. And afraid. Did she really think it mattered to him whether some ignorant "Bear" wanted her or not? The man was obviously a fool to not want such a brave woman. Mamut had little use for fools.

He dropped her hands and took a step back, wanting to reassure her that he was not a threat to her. She was upset enough. "Come," he said his voice deep, reassuring. "Come and sit down and rest. You have traveled a long way this day. You need to rest. Come," he coaxed. "I will give you some water."

Terah stared at him, his soft voice lulling her. She was so weary. She allowed herself to be led back to the fire. She sat down, cross-legged, and Kell crawled over to her. His firm young body as he climbed onto her lap felt solid and reassuring. She held him tightly and bowed her light brown head until it touched his dark one.

Mamut could not keep his eyes off the woman. He continued to watch her as he handed her the bison bladder of water. She hesitated, her eyes flashing at him. He gave a nod, afraid that if he said anything, she would rebel and not drink. He and Spearpoint did not need a thirsty, hungry woman dragging for another day across the hills with them.

He gave a silent sigh of relief when he saw her take a sip. She lowered the bladder and he thought she was going to say something. She tightened her lips, however, and lifted the bison bladder once more. She took several good draughts of the water before she lowered the bladder once again. Glistening drops of water clung to her full lips.

Mamut licked his own dry lips.

Terah ran a slim brown forearm across her mouth to wipe away the water. Mamut's eyes followed her every move. He swallowed. He wanted this woman, he knew it now. She would be *his*.

He took out the leather pouch that held the

dried meat. He cut off another chunk with his obsidian knife and laid the meat carefully on a rock. He gestured to the children that they could help themselves to more meat. His gesture included the woman, should she want some. "Spearpoint," he said. "Come, I wish to speak with you."

Mamut's cousin yawned and looked up from where he had settled by the fire. "I was just about to fall asleep," he complained.

Mamut glared at him. Muttering, Spearpoint rose and followed Mamut a little way off from the fire. When he was certain he could not be overheard, Mamut said, "I want that woman."

Spearpoint stared at him in surprise. "You mean you are not going to let her choose one of us?"

Mamut frowned. "You heard me tell her she had no choice."

"Yes, but I thought you were trying to scare her. I thought we would take her back to our people and you or I or one of the other men would claim her. There are ten men," he pointed out, "and seven of them need wives."

Mamut's frown deepened. "You and I have first claim on her, as I see it," he said. "We are the ones who stole her."

Spearpoint shrugged. "I am new to this woman-stealing business." He regarded his cousin thoughtfully. "How are you going to keep the others from wanting her?"

"They can *want* her," said Mamut tersely. "They just cannot have her. She is mine."

"And what if I want her?" demanded Spearpoint belligerently. "I helped capture her. I saved you," he accused. "You were having a very difficult time of it, if you remember."

"I remember," remarked Mamut. He started to take off the belt at his waist, from which dangled his knives. Spearpoint saw the gesture and said, "Now, now, Mamut, it is not necessary to fight me for her favors. Let us share her."

Mamut glared at him. "That is not the way of the Mammoth People. I want her for myself. If you want her, tell me and we will settle this here and now." He continued to undo the string at his waist.

Spearpoint thought about it. His cousin outweighed him by the weight of a five-year-old child. He was also about a hand's breadth taller than Spearpoint. Still, Spearpoint could hold his own in any fight. But the thought of fighting this cousin, whom he loved and greatly admired, for the favors of a woman, however lovely, did not sit well with him.

"Would you like a gift for her instead?" Spearpoint suggested, not wanting to give her up entirely. She was beautiful and young and would give him many children. She would brighten his home and add love to his life, for he saw how kind she was to the children.

"No," said Mamut grimly.

"You have not heard what I was going to offer."

"Not interested," said Mamut.

"What about the last big chunk of obsidian that

75

Theresa Scott

I have been saving? It is the best obsidian there is," Spearpoint boasted. "You can make many fine knives and spear blades from it."

Mamut looked at him.

"It is as big as my foot," assured Spearpoint. "It is very valuable."

And it was a generous offer. "Not interested," said Mamut again. He was growing impatient with his cousin.

Spearpoint thought that perhaps he had not offered enough. "I will add my father's saber-tooth necklace. It is very precious to me, and brings great power to anyone who wears it. My father killed every single one of the tigers whose teeth are on it."

Mamut touched the yellowed ivory bead at his own neck. "I already have a necklace, thank you," he said. Spearpoint missed the note of irony in his cousin's voice.

"Very well, Cousin," said Spearpoint and Mamut was amused to hear irritation prevail in the younger man's voice. "I will give you the obsidian core, the saber-tooth necklace and"—he paused, trying to read Mamut's impassive face—"and a fistful of high-grade red ochre from the river bank. That," he said triumphantly, "is my best offer!"

And it was a magnificent offer. Mamut was impressed. "You will be certain to get a wife at the Meet-meet if you offer such fine gifts," said Mamut.

Spearpoint grinned confidently.

"Alas," said Mamut, "no."

76

"Mamut!" cried Spearpoint in disappointment. "What do you *want*?"

"The woman," said Mamut in an even voice.

Discouraged, Spearpoint muttered, "Very well, she is yours." He glared at his cousin. "But I do not think she is worth more than that," he said, petulant at being thwarted.

"We will see," said Mamut. The woman was brave. She would give brave children. It was enough for him. That she was beautiful and had an unusual color of hair and eyes was an added gift. He smiled at his cousin, magnanimous in his triumph. "You can still fight me for her," he offered generously.

Spearpoint shook his head. "No," he said. "I will let you have her, since you want her so badly." He took a step back to the fire, then turned to face Mamut once more. "Would you like to think about it? To get that red ochre takes much work. It is extremely valuable. And the saber-tooth necklace . . . a great many tigers . . . and the obsidian, only I know where to find it . . ."

"No, thank you," said Mamut firmly. "I will take the woman."

Spearpoint shrugged. "Very well," he said in defeat and started back towards the fire. Mamut watched him go. He had surprised himself at just how badly he wanted the woman. Spearpoint had indeed offered very generous gifts, and Mamut was bemused with himself for turning down the offer. Yet it also indicated that Spearpoint recognized the worth and value of the woman, too, else he would not have offered so much.

Mamut glanced around the area, alert for wolves and saber-tooths and lions, too, while he thought about the woman. He had lost Cala, his wife, two winters ago, and had been alone since then. It had been such a lonely time, and now, seeing the woman and the children, he realized anew just how lonely he was for a wife. And a son . . .

A ragged breath tore from his throat. When he and the other hunters had returned to find their women and children dead, they had at first thought that an enemy band had attacked and killed them all, leaving the bodies in such twisted, hideous positions. But there had been no enemies, no footprints—only Death. It had been something unseen, perhaps ghosts, perhaps something in the food or water, and so Mamut and the survivors had touched nothing. Even the wild rabbits that the children had tamed and played with were dead in their pens.

So Mamut and his people left everything and fled that woeful place, never to return. They had not taken a single piece of hide, a single dried root or chunk of meat, not a single knife with them. Nothing. They had not even buried the bodies, and to this day the memory of his little son, clutched in Cala's dead arms, brought terrible sadness to Mamut. His son . . .

He sighed and glanced back at the flickering fire. Perhaps the Great Spirit would grant him another son. From the womb of his new captive.

Chapter 6

When Mamut returned to the fire, he saw that the meat he had put on the rock had disappeared. He glanced at the woman. She swallowed and looked away. He smiled to himself. She was taking sustenance, but she did not want him to know.

The children had settled in close to her. The baby and the older girl slept; the little boy's head nodded and his eyelids fluttered.

"Get some sleep," Mamut suggested.

The woman turned her back to him.

"Spearpoint, I will guard them for the first part of the night. Wake me when you have rested."

"Very well, Mamut." Mamut caught Spearpoint's sullen glance; he was still angry about losing the woman. But he rolled over and soon was snoring.

Mamut could tell from her rhythmic breaths when the woman fell asleep.

He glanced up at the sky. Night watch was pleasant duty. Dire wolves howled in the distance. He heard a frustrated snarl from a nearby saber-toothed cat.

Mamut glanced at his forearm. The gashes looked dark and swollen. Urgency swelled in him, too. He needed to reach the main Mammoth People's camp in time for the shaman's help. He did not want to succumb to the hot sickness on the journey.

Spearpoint relieved him later, and it was Mamut's turn to sleep. He rested on his side and watched the woman breathe. Moonlight caught her hair and gilded it a glittering gold, like pretty rocks he had seen. Her long lashes made dark crescents on her cheeks. Possessiveness washed over him, and he was suddenly very glad he had told Spearpoint that he wanted her.

He fell asleep thinking of her. When he awoke, it was morning. He and Spearpoint fed dried meat to the children. Again the woman would not eat, and again Mamut placed pieces of meat on the rock. He and Spearpoint examined a likely chunk of basalt for making sharp knife blades, and Mamut pretended not to notice the woman pick up the meat and eat it.

The meat was all gone when they returned to the fire. *She is a stubborn woman,* thought Mamut to himself. *Brave, beautiful, and stubborn.*

They were on their way shortly after that. They walked all that day, halting only three times to rest. Mamut pushed them hard because of his injured arm, but he could see by midday that the children were not able to keep up with the pace he set, and so he was forced to go much more slowly than he wanted to.

It was not until much later that day that Mamut's arm began to pain him. He and Spearpoint found a shallow cave to camp in for the night. They and the woman gathered enough wood for a fire to scare away predators. Mamut moved his injured arm carefully. As he worked, he wondered what chants the shaman would sing to heal his arm.

Suddenly a man appeared on the other side of the fire. Mamut blinked. Was the hot sickness already upon him and causing him to see strange things?

From behind the man peeked a short woman and three small boys. Where had they come from? Did Spearpoint see them?

Spearpoint was staring intently at the newcomers.

Relief surged through Mamut; it was not the hot sickness causing him to see people that did not exist—there were strangers really standing there. "What do you want?" he demanded.

The man shuffled closer. Mamut held his breath. The squat, well-muscled man smelled as if he had been dragged through a freshly

Theresa Scott

gutted deer. His clothes and those of the woman were poorly sewn, and Mamut guessed that she too had much to learn about preparing hides.

"Where do you come from? Tell me!" Mamut tried to ignore the smell. His arm throbbed.

The man sidled up to him, waving his small sons closer to him. When the eldest boy did not move swiftly enough, the father snarled at him, "Antelope offal! Get over here!"

The boy started to whimper. His mother shuffled over and yelled, "Silence!"

The boy crept over to his father and cowered behind him. "You slinking sloth!" scorned the father. To Mamut, he said, "We are alone. We come from there." He jerked a stick in the direction of a tall rock. "I see you have three children. We do too."

He stared at Mamut's recently captured baby girl and little boy. But it was on the older girl, Tika, that the man's gaze lingered the longest.

Terah's fists and stomach clenched. Who was this dirty man with the long brown toe-nails that curled over his toes? His dirty beard seemed to move because there were so many bugs in it. And the smell! She herded the children downwind.

The stranger's little black eyes followed Tika's every move. Terah stepped in front of the girl to shield her from the man's intent gaze.

The short, powerful man gave a grunt and motioned his woman to come closer. But she did not move swiftly enough and he sneered at her, "Stinking dung, get over here!"

The woman quickened her pace. She, too,

was short and squat, her face lined from many seasons in the sun. Her belly was huge, swollen with a fourth child. The man fumbled at the large pack she carried on her back. He hauled out a rock. "Look at this!"

Terah recognized it as obsidian. The shiny black rock could be flaked into sharp blades that sliced meat or hide or wood. Obsidian was very valuable to her Bison people.

The man with the filthy beard marched up to Mamut. First the man pointed at the obsidian chunk and then at Tika.

Terah stared in growing alarm. He wanted to trade for Tika!

"I will give you this rock for the child. It is very valuable."

Terah clutched her niece to her. "No! No!" She shook her head frantically at Mamut.

Her captor's gaze swung between the child and the stranger. She saw him eye the obsidian. Surely he would not be tempted to trade her precious niece for a piece of rock!

Desperate, Terah forced herself to touch his arm. She avoided the arm with the deep scratches, knowing it must be painful. His skin felt warm under her trembling palm.

"Please," she whispered. "Do not do this." Her voice was hoarse with fear. "Do not trade her."

His obsidian gaze seared her. Terah flinched, but she refused to look away. "Do not trade for her," she faltered. "Mamut, please, she is all I have—"

He held up a hand to stop her plea. Would he

not even hear her out? Unknowingly, she gripped his arm tighter.

He did not want to see her beg. *She knows my name*, thought Mamut. Though somewhere in his mind that thought registered pleasurably, it was her eyes that held his full attention. They were the color of dark green leaves, he marveled. Or the green of the Giver of Life River, when it pooled, cool and deep. So green. So beautiful . . .

In that moment Mamut saw her—truly saw her—saw the passion in her, saw the love she had for the child she pleaded for. He felt as though a gossamer spider's web bound them, reaching from her to him.

Around them everything stilled, yet between them there pulsed life. The wind stopped blowing, the people surrounding them fell silent. Only *she* existed for him.

Terah stared up at Mamut and felt suddenly as though they were wrapped in a soft cocoon of awareness. As she looked into his obsidian eyes, she felt a strange stirring in the depths of her heart. There was a life force in this man, a life force that called to her, that promised wonderful things. Only he existed for her.

Then she shook her head, puzzled. The capture, the long walk, the hunger, it all must have affected her brain in some unaccountable way. She was badly mistaken. This man was not important to her.

Mamut frowned, trying to throw off the strange thoughts. *It must be the hot sickness*, he told himself. *The hot sickness is coming upon me and*

I am thinking that this woman is unique.

"I want the girl," insisted the stranger, crashing in upon their newfound awareness of each other. "Give her to me."

The harsh words jarred both Mamut and Terah. Terah's hand fell away from Mamut's arm. He took a deep breath and turned to the ill-smelling stranger. "No. No trade."

Terah heard the words, saw her captor shake his head, but it took several heartbeats before she understood his words. Tika was safe!

The burly man grunted and dug again in the pack on his wife's back. He pulled out a second chunk of obsidian, this one of reddish-brown.

Terah gasped. Among her people, the swirled red-colored stone was even more valuable than the black obsidian.

"I will give this to you, too. For the little girl." Saliva dribbled at a corner of his hairy mouth.

"No."

The squat man growled to himself. He turned and stared consideringly at his raggedly dressed family. The eldest son whimpered. The father grabbed the child by one ear and dragged him over to Mamut. "Here! Take him, too. Give me the girl."

Mamut regarded the trembling, crying young boy.

"Silence, you mouse turd!" snarled the father. The boy subsided into gulping sobs.

Mamut's lips tightened and he could barely trust himself to speak. "No trade. Go away."

An ugly frown creased the stranger's face. He stalked over to Tika and pointed rudely at her. "I want that one. I want her for my wife!"

Terah recoiled. Tika held on to her so tightly that Terah's stomach hurt. Kell and Flori started to cry.

"This girl will make a good wife!" He jabbed a finger at his own cowering woman. "I got this old woman when she was but ten summers old. Look at her now!" He spat in disgust.

Terah and Mamut and Spearpoint all turned to gape at the hapless woman, who tried to shrink into herself.

"Now she is all used up. All she gives me are three puny sons. Stupid woman! She births many babies, but they all die! Useless turd!"

The woman started crying softly.

"Silence, you sniveling maggot!"

The woman's sobs turned to chokes.

Terah's hands clenched and she clutched Tika tightly.

"I can give many babies!" crowed the stranger. He patted his crotch fondly. "Very good. I can make many babies!"

Terah gawked in horror at the man, then at his sobbing wife. Her lined, beaten countenance made her look years older than he did!

Tika moaned and buried her face in her aunt's waist.

"This little girl is just the right age. I will give her many babies! But first, since she is so little, we can have much fun! I will teach her!" His dirty face beamed at the prospect, and his beard jiggled up and down as he danced in little hops of joy.

Terah stared transfixed as two bugs crawled across his cheek. Her stomach quivered. He wanted to marry a seven-year-old child! It would be several years before Tika's first menstruation and then a year longer before she could birth any children. And this stranger's anticipated "fun" did not bear thinking upon.

Mamut swiftly read Terah's horror and fear for Tika. He snapped at the man, "Leave us. Now! No trade!"

The man halted his hopping dance and stalked over to Mamut.

The two men glared at each other. Then the squat stranger turned abruptly and picked up the obsidian chunks. He tossed them into his wife's pack. "We will leave. I do not like you. You are a stinking sloth!"

With vast relief, Terah watched the bedraggled family march away. Three times, the man gave longing backward glances at Tika. The fourth time, Mamut shook his spear at him and gave an ear-deafening roar.

The man started to run and left his family to straggle along behind him. His wife, weighted down by her pack and dragging the youngest son along by one arm, staggered last.

Terah turned to thank Mamut. He had helped her when she needed him. He had seen and responded to the danger to Tika.

But just as Terah was about to tell him of her gratitude for keeping Tika safe, another thought

Theresa Scott

intruded. How swiftly she had forgotten that he and his friend had stolen her and the children!

Terah's lips tightened. She would not thank her captor! She would not!

She turned and walked away from those questioning obsidian eyes. The words of gratitude died a strangled death in her throat.

88

Chapter 7

After the evening meal, Terah lay down, exhausted. The children had fretted at her all day as their captors had marched them along. Then to have a filthy, violent man want to trade for Tika seemed almost more than Terah could endure.

The children had devoured two fat rabbits, then promptly fell asleep. Terah no longer kept up a pretense; she willingly consumed every morsel of rabbit that the men offered.

Now she lay on the cave floor beside the children. Soon she drifted off to sleep.

It was much later in the night that a small sound woke her. She opened her eyes wide, her mind frantically trying to identify the tiny noise.

Spearpoint slept by the fire. Mamut was

nowhere to be seen. A finger of light in the east told her dawn would soon arrive.

Perhaps a bird made the noise, she mused, her eyes roving the darkened, boulder-strewn landscape. But a cautious sense warned her not to sit up just yet, not until she knew where the noise came from.

Suddenly she caught a glimpse of movement beside a large rock. There, just a short distance from the fire. She peered into the darkness. Had she been mistaken? No, there it was again. A movement. Something large.

Spearpoint slept on. Where was Mamut?

Kell and Flori slept on either side of her, but Tika had rolled away to a little distance and was positioned between the cave and the rock where Terah had glimpsed movement. Terah opened her mouth to scream as her blood pounded a sickening refrain: *Tika's in danger, Tika's in danger!*

Before she could even gasp, her straining eyes saw, creeping around the rock, the same squat stranger who had wanted to exchange the obsidian for Tika. Terah's stomach tightened in alarm.

Removing her little white knife from its place at her waist, she slowly extricated herself from between Kell and Flori.

Terah crouched, then sprang with a howl at the intruder. He halted; she could see his shadowed form, and she could smell him. He whirled to run, and Terah raced after him. She jumped on his back and her weight toppled him to the ground.

Grabbing a handful of his filthy hair, she yanked his head back and exposed his throat to the sharp blade of her little white knife.

"Make one move and you die," she hissed. She felt his muscles bunch under her, and she pushed the knife until it bit deeper into his skin. He ceased any movement. She jerked his head back further. He bellowed, "Get off me, you wolf vomit!"

Spearpoint awoke to that cry and sat up, looking around bleary-eyed.

From out of nowhere, Mamut appeared. He reached down and hauled the squat man up by the front of his greasy tunic. Terah tumbled off the stranger's back and landed hard on her bottom.

Mamut glared at the bearded stranger. "What are you doing here? I told you to go away."

The smelly man refused to answer.

"You came for the girl," snarled Mamut.

"He cannot have her," gritted Terah, getting to her feet. "I will kill him first!"

Mamut glared at her. She would do it, the little she-tiger, he thought. He saw the white knife in her hand and smiled grimly to himself. She was protective of those children—he could still remember the feel of his own blade held to his own throat by that delicate-looking hand.

He eyed the man. "You are to leave here and never come back. Do not follow us!" He gave the man a rough shake. "I will give you no more warnings. If we catch you again, I will let this woman have you! And she will cut you into little tiny pieces with her sharp white knife."

"I will do more than that," drawled Terah, dusting herself off. "I will cut off the male root of him! Then he no longer need look for child-wives!"

The man's eyes widened and he jerked, frightened, in Mamut's grasp. Mamut threw him to the ground where he landed in a sprawled heap.

"Leave us!" snarled Mamut. "And do not come back!"

The man scurried away into the darkness. Mamut jogged after him until he was satisfied that the man had truly left.

When he returned, Terah glared at him. "He was mine! There was no need to stop me!"

"You were going to kill him?"

"Yes! He was after Tika!"

Mamut shrugged. "I thought that if he died, so would his wife and children."

"They would be glad! His wife and children would be better off without him!" But Terah felt suddenly subdued. She had not thought about anything except her own overriding fear and anger at the man. She realized now that if she had killed the squat stranger, then his wife and children would likely have starved. A family needed a hunter and protector to survive in this barren land. And if the family did not starve, there was always the danger of a stalking saber-toothed tiger or dire wolf.

She turned away from Mamut's concerned look. "I would not have spared him," she said sullenly.

Mamut watched her walk away and shook his head. This woman was very strong, very brave. But he guessed that she did not know what it was like to have a man die by one's own hand. But Mamut knew, yes, he knew very well. And responsibility for another's death was not something he wanted to incur again.

The woman returned to the children and lay down. He was tempted to join her, but he had no wish to tangle with her and her little white knife.

Mamut went back to his bed. Dawn was lighting the sky, and soon they must rise and continue their journey. He lay still, willing elusive sleep to come, but the fight with the squat stranger had alerted his body.

Mamut sighed and rolled over. And came face-to-face with the grinning, bearded stranger. Clamped between his broken yellow teeth was a sharp obsidian knife blade.

Knowing that his surprise advantage was lost, the stranger sprang upon Mamut. The two rolled over and over on the ground, each seeking a death hold on the other's throat.

Though shorter than Mamut, the other had a powerful grip and finally succeeded in rolling on top of Mamut. He yanked the knife out of his teeth. One thick hand twisted Mamut's leather necklace to choke him at the throat, the other hand raised the knife, about to plunge it into Mamut's heart.

With a desperate heave, Mamut raised himself and pushed the man off balance. The stranger sprawled face down into the dirt.

Mamut grabbed the stranger's arm and forced it high behind his back. He plucked up the obsidian knife and held it to the man's jugular.

"Get up," Mamut ordered. "Get to your feet!"

The stranger growled and sullenly complied.

"Walk!" ordered Mamut. His opponent shuffled in the direction Mamut pushed him.

"Where is your family?" demanded Mamut.

The man pointed with his chin at a large rock. Mamut squinted. Yes, there was the round woman and her three little boys watching Mamut in stolid silence.

"I will spare you," growled Mamut, "for the sake of your woman and your sons." Mamut marched him a goodly distance away from the cave where Terah and the children slept. Finally he halted. "I will let you go. But I warn you, do not come after the girl child again."

Mamut glared at the man, willing him to understand. "If I kill you, there will be no one to feed your children."

"You cannot kill me, you maggot-eater!"

Mamut sighed. He had done what he could. He had no wish to make life more difficult for the woman and her children by killing her man.

Mamut backed away from the man, careful to keep out of knife range.

The stranger watched him, still grinning.

After a safe distance, Mamut swung around and began jogging back to his camp.

"Beware!" The sudden warning screech came too late.

Mamut was thrown to the ground, the burly arms of the stranger wrapped tightly around his ankles. The stranger jumped heavily onto his back and pressed his knifeblade to the base of Mamut's skull.

Mamut cursed himself for his foolishness.

"You stinking camel dung! I will take the little girl for my wife! And I will take your woman, too. They will all be mine!" He gave a hoot of laughter.

Suddenly the stranger coughed, and his heavy weight lurched to one side of Mamut's back as his wife gave him a shove.

That was all Mamut needed. He rolled over, teeth bared, and launched himself at his opponent. He grabbed the man by the throat with one hand and whipped out his own knife.

The fight ended swiftly. The bearded man's bleeding body lay face down on the gravel where he died.

The squat, pregnant woman walked over to the body and kicked it. One of the boys started to cry. "Be quiet!" she snarled.

Mamut turned to her. "If you speak to your sons like that, they will answer you in kind. You will then have become just like *him*." He pointed with his chin to the body.

The woman gazed at Mamut out of weary, reddened eyes, then at her crying son. Her shoulders slumped, and she held out her arms to the sobbing child. He ran to her. She gave him an awkward pat. Slowly, the other two boys drew closer to their bedraggled mother and brother until they stood in a little group, two of the boys crying, the eldest looking tense and angry. "I am glad he is dead!"

The woman nodded. "I am, too."

"You may come with us," offered Mamut. "We will keep you safe."

The woman shook her head. "No men. I do not want any man. No more."

Capturing one unwilling woman and her children was enough. He would not add to his troubles. "Where will you go?"

She waved Mamut away. "We visited my cousin's grandmother's camp but two days past. We will go to them. They will feed us."

"It is dangerous to travel alone," warned Mamut. "There are saber-tooths, dire wolves . . ."

The woman laughed harshly. "Nothing can be worse than what I endured with him." She pointed at the body with her chin. "No, you go back to your people. I will go to mine."

Mamut did not try to persuade the woman any further. She and her sons left, taking their few possessions with them, without another glance at the body.

When they were out of sight, Mamut scraped a shallow grave and put the body in it. He covered it with dirt, then hefted two boulders and placed them on the grave to keep predators from digging up the body. Now a second man lay dead at his hand.

With bleak steps, Mamut headed back to the cave.

Chapter 8

Terah stared at the men. Eight pairs of assessing, narrowed eyes stared back at her. Every man had black hair and dark eyes, as did her two captors. The men of this band were taller and bigger than Bison men. Three of them carried spears, and every one of them carried a knife.

Wearily, Terah gave a ragged sigh and let the baby slide off her hip. She did not want these strangers staring at her. It frightened her and added to her fatigue. Alas, she could not just will them away. This was their encampment.

Terah looked around at the place she and the children had been brought to. A small blue lake, fed by a tumbling glacier stream, lay glimmering a short distance away. A green border of bull rushes and willows circled the lake. Brown dried grasses framed the green. A huge rock formed a natural wall protecting one side of the encampment. It was a fine setting for a camp, she thought grudgingly.

Eight hide tents were staked in the shelter of the huge rock. The tents were set every which way. A look of disdain crossed Terah's face and she muttered, "These people are ignorant. They do not have the good sense to set their doors to face the east." Everyone knew that a dwelling should always be placed so that the doorway captured the first rays of the rising sun. And some of these tents were different from the Bison People's tents, which were made of tanned bison hide. Several tents of her captors were rounded and made of animal hides thrown over mammoth tusks. Terah frowned. Bison People did not hunt mammoths; the animals were considered too dangerous and unpredictable.

Terah felt Tika take her hand and clutch it until her nails dug into Terah's palm. The girl was afraid and trying not to show it. Terah shivered. She was afraid too. She squeezed Tika's hand, hoping to reassure her. Kell wrapped himself around one of Terah's legs and looked about him, his brown eyes huge.

After three long days of travel, Terah and the children had arrived at this encampment. They knew their captor's names— Mamut and Spearpoint. Of the two, she preferred Spearpoint. He joked. The other, Mamut, unnerved her. She sometimes caught his black eyes upon her, hot and assessing. Like now.

Mamut reached for Flori. On the long trek, Terah had occasionally let him carry the baby, but now she pulled Flori back. She would not let Mamut hold Flori, not now. He was the enemy.

She picked the baby up, glaring at Mamut the while, her green eyes defiant, daring him to take the baby.

Mamut stared at her for several heartbeats, then decided that she was feeling protective of the baby while surrounded by his people. He took a step back, but his eyes remained locked on hers.

Terah wanted to sag in relief. This close to him, she felt the clear threat of him. What that threat was, she could not say; she only knew he was far more dangerous to her than Spearpoint was. More dangerous than any of the other men staring at her.

"Where did you find her?"

"Whose children are these?"

"Where are their people?"

Terah tried to step back from the men pressing forward. Eager hands reached out to touch her hair and that of the children. One of the men had the audacity to walk up and pry Tika's mouth open. He began counting her teeth. Terah shrieked in outrage, "Leave her alone!" and threw herself between the poor child and the inquisitive male.

Theresa Scott

The man laughed. Mamut and Spearpoint
called for calm to prevail. Terah pulled Kell and
Tika away from the eager men. Flori reached
out to Mamut, and Terah swung her away.
She felt distinctly uneasy being the object of
so much curiosity.

"Where did you find them?" asked a man. He
had a tattooed spider on his right cheek.

Mamut gestured back in the direction they
had come. "Wandering about," he said.

The others laughed; several of them beamed.
They certainly seemed happy to see her and the
children, Terah had to admit.

"Whose woman is this?"

"What gifts did you give for her?"

"Where are her people?"

"Are there more women? This one is very
beautiful."

"Her children look healthy!"

The questions kept coming.

Mamut shook his head and held up a hand,
waiting for silence. At last the excited men
calmed down, and he was able to be heard.

"Spearpoint and I captured this woman and
these children," explained Mamut. A hush grew
over his listeners. Mamut saw frowns. One
man fingered his knife. They were thinking that there would be fighting, thought
Mamut. "A saber-toothed cat was stalking her
and the children," he explained. "Spearpoint
and I slew it." Spearpoint held up the dried
spotted skin. Nods and exclamations greeted
this sight.

102

"She has no man," continued Mamut, swinging to look at Terah. "These children are her sister's."

"Where is her sister?" demanded one, the man with the tattoo on his cheek.

Mamut shrugged. "I know not."

Terah clenched her lips tightly. She would not tell them of Chee.

"Where is the children's father?" asked another. "Surely he would want to protect such fine children."

Terah flushed at his words, vaguely pleased.

"My father is hunting for chert to make strong blades for his spears," volunteered Tika.

"Ssh," cautioned Terah. She did not want these people to know anything about her or the children.

Mamut stared consideringly at Tika.

"The children's father will come looking for them," warned a man. "He may bring men. He will want to fight."

Mamut frowned. "We were careful to hide our tracks. I do not think he will find us." Several black heads nodded slowly.

"Where are their people?" asked an aged man. He wore a headdress of wide horns and leaned on a stout stick.

Mamut shrugged. Spearpoint looked at the dirt and moved some with his toe. Neither answered.

The old man turned to Terah. "Where are your people?"

Terah tightened her lips. She would tell these

people as little as possible.

"How can you give gifts for her if you do not know where her people are?" demanded the old man.

"No gifts," said Mamut. "We stole her."

The aged man snorted and muttered, "Her people will not like that!" He stared at Terah and the children. "Young men," he said in disgust. "Hot blood."

He looked around at the gathered men. None of them seemed to share his concern. "Who will hunt meat for this woman? These children? Who will defend them against wolves and saber-toothed tigers?" His dark eyes sparked in challenge.

"I will," said Mamut, stepping forward.

Terah's eyes shot to him, and her mouth opened. Something in the region of her stomach clenched. Sweat beaded on her forehead. She stared at Mamut. His eyes locked with hers, and his nostrils flared. A possessive light burned in his narrowed dark eyes. A frisson of fear tingled down Terah's spine. He and Spearpoint had already decided who was to have her. And it was *him*.

Several of the men grumbled. The man with the spider tattoo marched up and grabbed a lock of Terah's hair. "I do not agree," he snapped. "She should choose one of us. I wish to court her."

Terah yanked the piece of hair out of his grasp, but he ignored her. He swung to face Mamut. "Why should you have her?"

"Because I captured her, Lern," said Mamut evenly. Terah's eyes fell to where Mamut toyed with an obsidian knife at his side. She glanced back at the man who dared challenge him.

"You were not there to help us, Lern," spoke up Spearpoint. "Had you been there, then surely you could have decided who gets her."

Terah glared at the men as they discussed what was to happen to her. They ignored her.

Lern was not mollified. "Why should Mamut get a young, healthy wife?" he sneered.

Spearpoint shrugged. "No one forced you to take the old woman." Lern's wife, Rana, several years older than Lern, was the Frog Eater woman whom the Mammoth People had given gifts for. Rana had not yet borne Lern a child, and the young husband was angry about this.

"If you do not want your wife," spoke up the old man who had questioned Terah, "then move her things outside your tent. We have ten men in this camp and only three women—four now with this captured woman."

Lern's brows rose, and his black eyes snapped. He managed to control himself, however, and address the older man with courtesy. Terah guessed from the way Lern was restraining himself that the old man was the band's shaman. "My wife shall stay with me."

"Why should you have another wife then?" asked one of the men. "You want to keep Rana. And you want this woman. You have no need of two wives! Not when other men have no wife at all!"

105

There was muttering amongst the men. Lern glared at the others.

"Lern, can you provide enough meat for two wives and three children?" asked the old shaman.

Lern glared at Terah. His black eyes were piercing and angry. He spun on his heel and stomped away.

Terah watched him go. She felt uneasy.

When she turned back to the rest, the men were teasing Mamut about his knife wound. "This woman is brave," acknowledged Mamut.

Terah flushed at his words, a curious warmth growing in her heart. She caught several admiring looks before she turned away. She refused to like these people, especially Mamut. She was a captive. She must flee with the children. Her face was stony.

The old man tried again. "Who are your people?" he asked, and Terah thought she detected kindness in his voice.

Terah glanced at Mamut.

He was watching her, could not take his eyes off her. *Mine*, he thought. *Mine*.

The aged man with the wrinkled face awaited an answer. Terah looked at him, her mouth set. She would not tell him anything.

Just then Kell clutched Terah's leg tighter, and she was momentarily distracted. She winced and looked down at him.

A child of her captor's people had drawn close to Kell, causing him to press up against Terah. She stared at the child, unable to tell if it was a girl or a boy. The child's clothing looked as thought it would fall off at any moment, so large and clumsy were the stitches piecing the rough hides together. The child's skin was encrusted in dirt. Piercing brown eyes glared out through shaggy black matted hair. The creature moved awkwardly toward Kell. A breeze carried its scent. This child had not bathed in some time.

Kell shrank into Terah's leg, pushing her off balance. Still the strange child came on, making odd walking movements. One of its legs was afflicted, Terah observed. The child dragged itself in front of Kell. Brown lips drew back, showing white teeth. Then the child spat, straight at Kell.

Kell jumped in surprise.

Tika spat back.

Terah pulled Tika away. Men guffawed.

Kell threw himself on the strange child and knocked it down. Flori jumped on the two now sprawled in the dirt and began pummeling.

"Arise," hissed Terah, mortified that they were fighting. She pulled the baby off the two in the dirt, thrust Flori into Tika's arms, then ran back to drag Kell off his opponent.

The men stood around and made comments.

"Weak fighter," observed one.

"Not so," contradicted another. "See how he grabs hair. Shows he will fight. He must do well when he fights saber-tooths."

"What he needs is a weapon," said another, and he bent to pick up a stick. Terah was certain he was going to hand it to Kell to strike the dirty child with.

107

With a cry of anger, Terah intercepted the stick and thrust it away. She yanked Kell off the child.

The onlookers laughed. Terah noticed that no one rushed over to pick up the dirty child. It was a girl, Terah saw, when the child rolled over and her ratty robe came up, exposing skinny buttocks and legs.

Terah managed to get Kell away from the girl. The girl child scrambled in the dirt, trying to get to her feet and falling back. She could not rise.

Terah yanked Tika and Flori away from the ragged child. When she turned back, she saw that no one had yet aided the girl child. Where was her mother? Did these people not help their children? Terah stomped over and extended her hand to aid the child to her feet.

The girl promptly bit her on the fingers. Terah winced. Several men hooted. "Lame Leg does not like people," one of them explained. "She would rather play with the dogs."

Terah frowned. Lame Leg regarded her with hostile dark brown eyes. Terah did not offer her hand again.

Just then Mamut lifted the dirty girl to her feet. She shrugged his touch away and stared at Terah. Her dark eyes dropped to Terah's bitten fingers, and a tiny smile crossed the child's face. Then she turned and shuffled away, limping. She left behind an acrid, unwashed smell.

Terah watched her shuffle over and sit down next to one of the tents. It was one of the smallest; the hide was poorly tanned, and it had a long tear on one side. Suddenly a gray shadow emerged from behind the tent and stalked over to the child. Terah's eyes widened. The shadow looked to be a huge wolf. She peered closer. It was a dog. Lame Leg threw her arms around the animal and buried her face in the strong neck. The beast licked the child's dirty hair.

So, Terah thought, *someone cares about that child.* She frowned thoughtfully, then turned back to find Mamut watching her. "Where is her mother?" she asked.

Mamut shrugged. "Dead." His dark eyes were suddenly shuttered and cold.

Terah wanted to inquire further, but the look in her captor's eye stopped her. She glanced at Lame Leg once again.

"Come with me," Mamut said gruffly. His dark eyes brooked no argument.

With a mutinous thrust of her chin, but deciding not to challenge him at this time, Terah reached for Tika's hand and led all three children along behind him. They walked past the old man, past the curious eyes of the other gathered men. Terah walked stiffly, looking straight ahead, seemingly unaware of the hungry eyes staring at her.

She watched Mamut's easy gait. She focused on his broad back and powerful upper arms. She swallowed and wondered suddenly why no woman had stepped forward to greet him. Surely such an attractive man would not lack for a mate. Terah reddened suddenly at the direction her thoughts were taking. The man was not attractive! He was rude. He captured women and children and did not know to set his tent in the proper direction.

But he had protected her and the children on the three-night journey, when she had heard the howl of dire wolves and the snarls of saber-toothed cats. She had even heard the growl of that dreaded beast, the short-faced bear, a fierce animal that could outrun a human being. Twice in the night while they rested, Terah had awakened and by the fire's flicker had seen Mamut, alert, his strong profile firm, his spear at the ready. Watching. Protecting. *He guards us well*, Terah thought, just before falling back to sleep.

This man, Mamut, had brought her safely to his people. Terah shrugged away the sudden rush of gratitude she felt. Any man could do that. Protect. Why, Dagger protected his family—actually, she amended, sometimes Dagger protected his family. He had not protected his family when he was off searching for the chert quarry. And they had sorely needed his protection. Terah tightened her lips. Any man could protect. It was what men did. It was expected. This Mamut had done nothing worthy.

And now that she thought of it, she looked around uneasily—where were the women? She remembered the old man saying that there were three other women here, but she had yet to see one.

As if conjured up by her thoughts, a woman of middle age suddenly emerged from a dwelling as they passed by. She was short and thin and slightly bent. She smiled. Terah felt suddenly grateful for this friendly face and wondered if the woman was Rana, Lern's wife.

Mamut led her and the children over to one of the larger tents, a rounded one. Although the tent looked large, the hide that covered it was surprisingly poorly tanned. Terah stared at it. The hides that Terah and the Bison People tanned looked much better than this one that had clots of fur still on the outside. She frowned.

"This is where you will dwell," Mamut told her. Terah wanted to dismiss the tent with contempt, but found she could not. A large roomy dwelling would keep her and the children safe from night predators. She bent and glanced inside the door. It was surprisingly neat. Furs were laid out for beds. She flushed.

Outside the dwelling lay a small pit circled with fire-cracked rocks. Racks for drying meat stood nearby. The racks were full of meat. She glanced around with a frown, studying her new surroundings. Why had these people so few women? They had plenty of meat. Did they make a practice of stealing women and then the women escaped? Were the men cruel?

Four of the men she had passed earlier came over to stare at her and the children. Two gray dogs walked up and sniffed at Kell and Tika. The children pressed away from the animals carefully, but seemed to pass the dogs' inspection. The animals loped away.

Terah wanted to take the children and hide

111

in the tent, away from Mamut and the others' curious eyes. Keeping her back straight, she forced herself to stand rooted to the ground. "Where are your women?" she demanded of Mamut. "Did they all run away?"

The tone of her voice indicated to Mamut that she thought such was the case. She looked past Mamut and saw a pregnant woman walk by. Ah, now she had seen two women. And one child.

Mamut reached out and took her chin and turned her back to face him. He stared down into those strange green eyes he found so beautiful. He wanted her. Desire soared through his body as he stared at her. She was here, she was his, recognized as such by all his people. He wanted her badly. He had captured her. No one had stopped him. She was his. His hand shook, and he dropped it so she would not know.

"Our women are dead," he said, letting nothing of his pain creep into his voice. "We have only four women. We have many hunters—ten. And few wives."

Terah wanted to tear her eyes away from the black gaze locked on hers, but she could not. She had seen a flicker of pain there, and it disturbed her. This man, hurting? This strong hunter, able to slay fierce saber-toothed tigers, hurting?

When he dropped his hand from her chin, she turned away and made a pretense of calling the children. She wanted to get away from him suddenly. She did not want to see the pain in those dark eyes, did not want to know that this man had feelings. . . .

Mamut watched her walk away, stifling the urge to follow her, for he knew that she needed time to adjust to her new surroundings. She needed time to become his woman.

Chapter 9

Terah lounged outside the tent as Kell and Tika played quietly. The baby was sleeping inside the tent. Terah felt almost peaceful. The children were safe, the sun was warm, and she could rest. For a moment the traitorous thought grew that she could enjoy living with the Mammoth People. Terah quashed the thought. She would not like these people, nor accept living with them. She would not.

She had expected Mamut to come to her in the past night, but he had not. Of course, she had not *wanted* him to come to her, only expected it. Since he had claimed her in front of all his people, then he would be dwelling with her, would he not? But he had not arrived at her new home at any time of the night, and she had awakened this morning with a vague feeling of dissatisfaction. Not disappointment, assuredly, merely dissatisfaction. She wished he would tell her of his plans.

She glanced around the quiet camp, searching for his tall, well-muscled frame, but she did not see him. Again, it was not disappointment she felt, she told herself. It was . . . relief, yes, that was it. Relief that he was not nearby.

Hunters had left camp this morning, Kell had told her. The little boy was an early riser and had peeked out of the tent and counted them as they were leaving. He had awakened Terah to tell her the exciting news and was most pleased with himself that he could hold up all the fingers on one hand and tell her that that was how many hunters had left the camp. Groggily, Terah had nodded and fallen back to sleep. She was tired because Flori had been crying in the night, and every time she wept Terah had awakened to console her. Terah knew the little one missed Chee and her milk. Water and dried meat could not replace Chee's breast milk.

Terah closed her eyes and let the warm sun heat her skin. How good it felt to be away from the wind.

She opened her eyes when a shadow blotted the sun from her eyelids. The thin, bent woman she had seen the day before stood in front of her now, holding a large wooden bowl. A delicious aroma wafted from the bowl, and Terah felt her mouth grow wet. It had been some time since she and the children had broken their morning fast, and then it had been to eat dried meat. With a start, Terah realized how hungry she was.

"Greetings. Would you like to eat some jackrabbit stew?" asked the woman. Kell and Tika stopped their playing and flew over, drawn by the meat smell.

"I am called Rana," the woman said. She pointed with her chin to one of the tents. "I live there with my husband, Lern."

Terah stirred herself and rose to her feet. The woman's round face was kind, her brown eyes gentle. The children plopped down, their bright eyes following the bowl as Rana lowered it and placed it on the ground in front of them. Though the smell of the stew assuredly drew them, yet they waited politely. Terah introduced herself and each of the children, then thanked the older woman for bringing the stew.

The two adult women sat down. The children dipped eager little fingers into the bowl, scooping up chunks of warm meat and broth and herbs. Terah strived to eat slowly, not wanting the woman to think she was as hungry as she truly was. Her teeth sank into the savory flesh. Oh, how good the meat tasted!

Rana ate a few pieces of meat, then sat back to watch the small family devour the remains. Terah, to her embarrassment, realized suddenly that she and the children had eaten as though they had starved for days. As she was wiping the juice from her chin, Terah glanced up to see Rana's gaze upon her. The dark brown eyes were strangely sympathetic, and Terah felt herself drawn to the woman.

"Where is the children's mother?" Rana asked. Terah shook her head, not wanting to talk about Chee and again she caught a sympathetic look in that brown gaze. The children stood up, licking their fingers, and then raced back out to play.

Terah studied the woman in front of her. An air about her invited confidences, and Terah was puzzled as to why that should be so. The woman looked very ordinary, yet there was something about her . . .

"I am from the Great Frog People," said Rana.

Terah was puzzled. "I thought your people were the Frog Eaters."

Rana frowned. "Pah, that is an insulting name. My people do not eat frogs. We *revere* them." She studied Terah. "I see that you are not trying to insult me. But you did not know this. Only outsiders call us Frog Eaters. My people take our name from the magnificent animal the Great Spirit created to warn our people. The frog gives many warnings. When any dangerous animal walks the ground, looking for our camp, the frog warns us. He goes silent. Then we know a saber-tooth or a bear is looking for us."

"But does that not get confusing?" asked Terah. "Howbeit, if a hare hops by, the frogs go silent, too. Your people will be in great fear because they will think a saber-tooth stalks them."

Rana laughed. "Oh no, that is not a problem. We have hunters who watch, too."

Terah smiled. Evidently the Great Frog People were practical and did not rely completely on frogs for warnings of danger.

"We have many stories about frogs," continued Rana, "and about how frogs help people."

Terah shook her head. She had never thought about frogs helping people before. What an unusual idea it was.

Rana laughed at her bewilderment. "Every animal helps people," she said. "That is why the Great Spirit made them."

Terah stared. "Only to help people?" she echoed. "Perhaps the Great Spirit made animals for their own enjoyment, not to help people at all."

Rana chuckled. "Perhaps," she shrugged.

"And how can flies possibly help people?" argued Terah. "Or mosquitoes?" Terah did not like flies or mosquitoes, the little scourges.

"Ah," said Rana wisely, "flies and mosquitoes are food for the frogs. And the frogs help people."

"Ah, so it is," agreed Terah, awed by Rana's logic.

"The Frog is the Great Spirit's favorite animal."

"I differ with you," said Terah politely. "The bison is the Great Spirit's favorite animal. My people, the Bison People, know this."

Rana looked at her in astonishment. "How do your people survive without killing bison?"

"What do you mean?" asked Terah. "Assuredly my people kill bison. We eat the meat, we tan the hides for soft clothes, and we carve the strong bones for tools. We *need* the bison."

Rana frowned. "We Great Frog People respect

the frog. We use its name. We do not kill it. How is it that your people call yourselves Bison People, yet you hunt and kill the very animal you are named after? That is very odd."

Terah answered, "Our hunters are adept at slaying the great beasts. It is because our hunters are so skilled that we can take the name Bison People."

Rana regarded her askance. She shrugged. "It seems our ways are very different," she observed.

"Yes," agreed Terah. Terah felt uncomfortable with this realization. She was just beginning to like Rana and now they had discovered that they were different. Terah sighed. She supposed she would not be able to like Rana anymore. Perhaps Rana would not like her now, either, because they were so different.

Terah looked around, anxious for something to say, something to take away the uncomfortable feeling. "That is a fine drawing of a frog you have on your tent," she observed politely. Rana's skin tent was brown with a stylized frog painted in black. The frog had big red eyes. "It must have taken you a long time to grind the red ochre for the frog's eyes."

"Thank you, it did," said Rana, equally politely. "I drew it to remind me of my people." She sounded sad. "But my husband abhors it."

"Oh," said Terah. She had already seen Lern's anger about his wife. She thought that Rana had a burdened life married to the young hunter. "How is it that you came to live with the Mammoth

People?" asked Terah delicately.

Rana smiled. "The Mammoth men came to my people. They brought many gifts. They wanted women. We Great Frog People had only two unmarried women at the time, myself and another. The Mammoth men promised to treat us kindly, to give us children, to let us visit our people. My people asked for so many gifts that the Mammoth men could only afford one woman—me."

Rana sounded very sad. "I did not wish to come with the Mammoth men even though they gave such expensive gifts. They gave mammoth ivory and red ochre," she said with a note of pride.

Terah stared blankly. While her people valued red ochre highly, they did not use mammoth ivory. Terah guessed from the pride in the other's voice that mammoth ivory was also very valuable and so she nodded when she caught Rana's questioning gaze upon her.

"Why did you not wish to come?" prodded Terah.

Rana looked down at the brown dirt in front of her. "My husband had recently died," she said. "I had been married to him since I was but a girl like you. I was grief-stricken at losing him." She looked up at Terah and there was a sheen of tears in her eyes. "I had raised two children with him. I am an old woman. I do not think I can have children any longer. I rarely go to the menstruation tent any more. I told my people this. They told me to keep silent. They wanted the gifts."

"They forced you to go to the Mammoth men!" cried Terah indignantly.

Rana looked at her with a sad smile. "I am not young and fiery like you," she said. "My children were grown. Both dwelled with husbands in other bands. I was of little consequence to my people. They told me to go, because they wanted the mammoth ivory more. It was very valuable." The old woman's chin came up. "So I went. I would not stay where I was not wanted."

Terah privately agreed and nodded.

"I came with the Mammoth men. When we arrived here, I was chosen by Lern." Rana's voice went flat as she said this last.

"Are you—are you happy with Lern?" Terah wanted to know.

Rana turned away. Terah gasped. There was a yellow bruise on Rana's cheek. Rana heard the gasp and turned back to face Terah. "I had years of happiness with my first husband," she answered. "With this one"—she shook her head— "with this one, I have sadness."

That did not answer Terah's question, so she waited.

"This one is impatient. He is angry much of the time, and he is secretive. I do not understand him," said Rana. She looked at Terah assessingly.

Terah stared at Rana's cheek.

"Sometimes he strikes me," murmured Rana.

Terah's jaw tightened. "That has happened among my Bison People," she said slowly. "It is not right for a man to smite a woman. Not all men do so," she added hastily. "Dagger, Chee's husband, did not do such a thing, but some men do." Bear would probably strike his wife, she thought suddenly.

A heavy silence hung between the two women. Terah was afraid to say any more. She did not know what to do to help Rana. Her own predicament was difficult enough. What could she do to help another?

Rana slowly got to her feet. She picked up the empty wooden bowl and looked at it. "I am glad you like my cooking," she said.

Terah chuckled, relieved at the simple joke. Perhaps they could pretend that all was well, that there was no danger to either of them. "Come and visit me again," she offered cheerily.

Rana looked at her, eyes sympathetic, as if she understood Terah's discomfort. "He does not strike me every day," she said. "Only sometimes."

Terah's false smile faded. Very well, the problem was not going to go away. She too stood up and met Rana's gaze squarely. "Once is too many times," she said.

Rana nodded. "It is." She turned to go.

"Rana?"

The thin woman turned to face her, a questioning look upon her face.

Terah held out a hand. "I—I—" What could she say? *Come to me and I will help you?* Terah had three children she had to help escape, besides herself. *Do not let him smite you?* And how could Rana stop him? Lern was strong.

Terah's hand dropped. "I thank you for the food," she said in a weak voice. She sighed.

Rana nodded. "We will eat together another time," she said.

Terah smiled. She liked Rana. She waved a hand. "Yes, we will."

Chapter 10

Terah was pensive after Rana left. She wondered if Mamut was the kind of man to strike his wife. She wondered if all the Mammoth men did such things. She tightened her lips, more determined than ever to escape. She would not stay where she could be struck or beaten at a man's whim.

Her thoughts drifted to Bear. When Rana had been telling about Lern, Terah had wondered if Bear might be the kind of husband to clout his wife. The more she thought about it, the more convinced she was that he would do such a thing. And oh, how she had once wanted to marry Bear.

Not that he had wanted to marry her, Terah remembered bitterly. Bear had merely wanted to take her into a cave and do secret things with her, things that were done between a husband and wife.

But Terah had wanted to marry him.

She had already told her father to reject an excellent marriage offer from Dagger's brother, One Shoe. One Shoe had earned his name because he had once returned from a hunting expedition wearing only one of his high moccasins. The other he had yanked off his foot and thrown at the short-faced bear that was pursuing him. The smell of the leather moccasin had distracted the hungry bear long enough for One Shoe to escape. Everafter among the Bison People, he was known as One Shoe. Strong and comely as One Shoe was, Terah was waiting for Bear to ask her to marry him.

Terah's father had promised that he would give an expensive dowry gift to the man who married her. He had fashioned two spears, with sharp tips made from the white chert that Dagger so prized. The shafts of those spears were made of a strong, straight wood and then painted with red ochre. Those two beautiful spears were to be Terah's dowry. She knew they would look fine in Bear's lodge. And so she had waited.

Terah had admired and yes, loved, Bear since her fourteenth summer. He was the best Bison hunter. When other Bison men brought home a brace of hares, Bear brought home an antelope. He could outrun every Bison man. He could swim across the widest part of Giver of Life

River three times when other men flagged after one crossing. Bear could wrestle any Bison hunter to the ground to take a prize. At the Meet-meets, it was always Bear who won the wrestling matches against the men of other bands.

And Bear was handsome. Terah frowned. Not as handsome as Mamut, now that she thought of it. With resolution, Terah pushed aside thoughts of her captor.

Bear was very convincing with words, too; that had been part of her downfall. Her thoughts drifted back to that terrible day.

"Come with me for a walk," Bear had suggested. His light brown eyes had met hers, and he had smiled that friendly smile of his. Terah had been ecstatic that he had asked her. Earlier, she had seen him talking with Gita, one of the prettiest Bison maidens. Terah had seen Gita shake her long dark hair and stride off. A dark, glowering look had crossed Bear's handsome face then, but when he caught Terah watching him, he had shaken himself and put on that friendly smile of his and sauntered over to her. Terah wondered briefly while she looked into those light brown eyes if Gita had refused to walk with Bear. More fool, she. Terah would not refuse such a handsome, admirable man.

They walked along, getting closer to the caves that tunneled back into a hillside. Terah paused, suddenly nervous. "My father told me not to go up to the caves," she said.

"Your father meant, do not go up to the caves

unless you have someone to protect you." Bear's voice was pleasantly deep. He leaned closer and Terah's heart beat faster. "I will protect you, little Terah." The way he drew out her name made her heart soar to the clouds.

She glanced up at the caves, then back at the encampment where the Bison People were camped. No one had noticed her or Bear.

"Very well," she conceded. Her heart beat rapidly. She should not be going with him up to the caves. There were saber-tooths; there were wolves.

"It is a chance for us to be alone, to get to know one another," murmured Bear as if he could read her thoughts.

Terah smiled weakly and gave him her hand to help her over a steep part of the hillside.

Bear smiled at her and led her on.

When they got to the caves, Terah stopped and listened. She did not hear any growls or scurrying. Perhaps the caves were not occupied by animals, she thought hopefully.

"I have come here many times," said Bear. "It is safe." Indeed, he could probably go wherever he wanted, he was so strong, thought Terah.

"Come, I want to show you something," he added. If only she had turned back at that point, Terah regretted later. But she looked into those light brown eyes, so clear and sparkling. That smile, so friendly. She had known this man all her life, was sure she loved him and wanted to marry him. She put her trembling hand in his and let him lead her into the nearest, biggest, darkest cave.

"Sit down," he invited. He lowered his spear and took off his knife belt and set it aside. Terah did not want to sit. She hesitated, then drew back a step toward the opening.

"See," said Bear in that same reassuring voice, as he took several steps with her. He walked her slowly back out into the bright sunlight. "You can see our encampment."

They stood at the mouth of the cave, and he pointed with his chin to where the tents stood. She could see the tiny cookfires, see the smoke blow away. "There is your parents' cooking place," added Bear helpfully.

Terah looked to where he indicated. Yes, she could see it. Her mother and Chee looked so tiny. The children looked like little dots. Terah had not realized that she and Bear had climbed as high as they had. She raised her hand to wave to her mother and opened her mouth to cry out a greeting.

Bear swiftly grabbed her fingers and clamped his own strong hand over her mouth. Seeing Terah's eyes widen, he smiled and whispered, "Let us not tell them we are here. This will be our secret place to come."

Terah's wide eyes stared, then she relaxed. Bear looked so playful, and she had known him so long—what was the harm? They would exchange kisses, and he would ask her to marry him. Why should she not stay quiet? She had longed to marry this man since her fourteenth summer. A man like this one would feed her and their children well, would protect her and keep them all safe from the animals that roamed. He was strong. She nodded her head, and he took away the hand covering her mouth. The hand clutching her arm slid lightly down until he was once again holding her hand. His grip felt firm. She gave a little pull to slide her hand out of his grasp, but he tightened his fingers. And smiled.

She smiled back. It was on the tip of her tongue to ask him to marry her, so lost was she in those golden eyes. But before she could say anything, he gave a little tug and led her back into the cave.

"Come," he invited once more. He sat down and leaned against a rock. He looked comfortable and at ease. His manner was friendly, reassuring.

Terah smiled at him. She was the woman with him, not Gita, came the victorious thought. Terah's smile grew wider.

She sank down on her knees beside him. He patted the sand, indicating she should sit right next to him. After a tiny hesitation, she moved closer and sat down.

"Why not take this off?" he asked, gently taking the hem of her deer tunic. He tugged at it and she came toward him. He lowered his lips to her and kissed her. She felt clumsy and pulled back. "More," he murmured, and pulled her toward him. They kissed and then his hands moved over her. "Let us get you out of these cumbersome clothes," he said.

Terah's head came up and she looked at him, askance. Taking off her clothes was more than she expected to do.

Bear's eyes grew suddenly hard. "Do not think to change your mind, little Terah," he said. "You know why I brought you here."

She heard the heavy note in his voice, and alarm grew in her mind for the first time. She pulled back, but he lunged for her. He grabbed her and pushed her to the cold sandy floor of the cave. She could feel the grit digging into her naked back, for he had half-ripped her deer tunic off her. In fear and desperation, she clutched the garment to hide the lower part of herself and cried out, "No, Bear! No!"

He was pulling at her hands now, trying to get her to drop her hold on the robe. "Let me," he panted.

"No!" she cried again. This was not what she wanted, not how she had imagined he would ask to marry her!

"Come here," he grunted, yanking her to him by both her elbows. Her head jerked back from the jolt, and she felt a sharp pain streak up the back of her head. For a second, blackness swirled in front of her. She was going to die, she knew it.

Then she erupted, kicking, fighting, biting, every part of her moving. She screamed too. Terah was fighting for her life now.

"Let me go!" she screamed. She yanked his hair and kneed at his groin. He grimaced but hung on, trying to climb on top of her. She struck out at him. Then she remembered his knives. With one arm she batted at his eyes, with the other hand, she scrabbled frantically on the cave's sandy floor for one of his knives or the spear. Whatever weapon she could find she would use on him. She had to get away! But her hand found only sand.

Bear pushed her down and threw himself on top of her. His hand groped under the tunic and he was fumbling and touching her where he had no right to touch. She bucked and tried to throw him off. She screamed as loud as she could. She felt something stiff and hard press against her leg, and she struggled frantically. Another heartbeat and he would be inside her!

In the next breath, he was suddenly torn off her and thrown against the far wall of the cave. Dagger and his brother, One Shoe, stood there. Dagger glared at Bear, panting. His brother stared at Terah's naked body.

"She does not want you!" Dagger yelled at Bear. "We could hear her protests from far off where we were hunting!"

One Shoe finally tore his gaze from Terah's nakedness. He bent and picked up her tunic, not meeting her eyes while he shoved the torn garment at her. But it was too late; she had already seen contempt on his face.

Dagger snarled at Bear, "Be more careful who you take with you to your cave! At least make certain she wants you!"

132

Terah, at first relieved by her brother-in-law's timely intervention, winced at the disgust she now heard in his voice. So Bear had taken other women to this cave, women who knew that he expected to mate with them. She flushed in humiliation that both her kinsmen had known that Bear did this and had seen her thusly.

One Shoe swung to face her. His eyes blazed in contempt. "I do not want you for my wife," he spat. "Anyone who goes with Bear does not deserve to be my wife!" He stormed out of the cave, leaving Terah clutching the tunic tightly to her.

Humiliation ate at Terah, and she wanted to yell after him that she had not known that Bear was going to do this. But only a croak issued from her throat. What good would it do to tell One Shoe? He did not want her now, would not want to offer marriage for her again, and he certainly blamed her even though it was Bear who had tried to force her.

While Terah dressed, Dagger pinned Bear face-first against the cave wall. When Terah's clothes were arighted, they left the cave. Bear's insult followed them down the hill, "You are wrong, Dagger! She wanted it! She was begging for it! Begging!" Then slyly, "Perhaps you will do better with her!"

Bear's words added to Terah's anger. She flicked a glance at Dagger, but he would not look at her. *He believes Bear,* she thought. *And he thinks that I am a woman who mates with any man.* She opened her mouth to say something

133

in her own defense. Then she closed it. She *had* wanted Bear's kisses, she *had* followed him into the cave, but it was not the way it sounded when he yelled after Dagger. Bear made it sound so . . . so dirty!

Bear had turned her innocent desire into something humiliating and horrible. Desire was something beautiful, not shameful as these men made it out to be. In her heart she knew this.

When they reached the camp, Dagger let her find her own way to her parents' hearth. Terah scurried into the tent and told no one what had happened. After that day, she was careful never to be alone with Bear again.

Terah's lips twisted in an ironic smile. After the ordeal with Bear, there were no more marriage offers. She wondered what lies Bear had spread about her. One Shoe ignored her. Bear's face was cold, and his golden eyes were merciless whenever he looked at her.

Terah's father had made six spears with white chert points and red ochre hafts. Still no marriage offers. He increased her dowry to eight spears, an amount unheard of among the Bison People, but the results were still the same: no husband for Terah.

But Terah did not want a man. Not anymore. A man could humiliate a woman too easily. They fanned her desire and then used it against her. She wanted nothing to do with any of them.

Thus had matters stood until Dagger gave her the little white knife. He did not say anything, but Terah had wondered if he wanted her to protect herself the next time a man attacked her. But when Chee frowned at the knife, another thought entered Terah's mind. Perhaps Dagger wanted her as a second wife. Chee seemed to think so. And Terah's father might give her to him, over her objections, over Chee's.

Chee!

She had forgotten about Chee. Terah glanced at the children. They were pretending to hunt birds, playing happily with tiny spears and a dead bird that they had found.

Terah peered inside the tent. Flori slept on, the sound of her soft little breaths reassuring.

Terah crept back outside the tent. How was she going to tell the children that their beloved mother was dead?

Chapter 11

Mamut felt sheepish, but not sheepish enough to turn his steps back to hunting. No, he was loping alone across the desolate hills, drawn back to the Mammoth People's encampment, with one thought only—to see Terah. When he had departed from camp earlier that morn with the other hunters, he had hoped that they would swiftly find an antelope or a camel or, if nothing else, one or two jackrabbits. Then they could return to the main camp by nightfall. But the hunters were not finding game. Mamut realized that the Mammoth People would have to move their encampment in the next few days because game was becoming so scarce.

And his people had yet to find the valuable bison herds.

It was difficult biding time until the bison

came. But then, the hunters of the Mammoth People were well known for their patience.

This Fall season, the Mammoth People had taken a gamble. The Moon of the Geese Flying was the time when the salmon swarmed in the creeks. Most years at this season, the Mammoth People could be found much farther to the south, fishing on the banks of Giver of Life River for the salmon that kept the people fed through the winter.

This year the Mammoth People had decided to leave the Giver of Life River basin and travel north along the river into the dry, sparsely treed wasteland of the tundra because there was something the Mammoth People needed and wanted—women. If they killed enough bison, they could bring back the warm furs and bladders and horns as valuable trade items to exchange at the Meet-meet for women.

The Mammoth People hoped, too, that they could kill enough of the huge bison to put away much dried meat for winter. Bison meat in the Moon of the Geese Flying was rich and full of fat and warmed a man to his very bones when he ate it.

But the Mammoth People were taking a risk. If they did not find the bison herds by the end of the Moon of Geese Flying, they would have to return to the south and catch the last of the salmon harvest. If they were vigorous in their fishing, they might still get enough salmon meat to preserve for the long winter ahead. But then they would have to wait until the following year to get enough valuable trading goods for the women they needed.

After the salmon run, there would be a big Meet-meet on the banks of Giver of Life. Many small, scattered bands of people wandered in to trade at the Meet-meet, and some of those bands would be looking to make alliances with the Mammoth People, alliances strengthened through marriage.

Yes, it was a good plan, thought Mamut in satisfaction. In fact, he had been the one to suggest it. None of the Mammoth men had questioned why he had wanted to hunt bison and not mammoth, though they all knew that the ivory from one long tusk of a mammoth would pay the bride price for six or seven women with ease. But it had been several years since the Mammoth men had hunted the great woolly mammoths. Their mammoth-hunting skills were waning. They would do better to hunt the huge bison.

As for Mamut, he had no wish to pursue one of the great woolly mammoths. Ever. And now that he had found a woman for himself, Mamut was not so eager to hunt this day, either. Instead, he wanted to see her.

When he entered the camp, he was relieved that no barking dogs heralded his arrival. Mamut wanted to sneak up and watch his captive woman without her seeing him. Perhaps he would learn more about her that way.

Lame Leg's dog, Wolf Boy, came up and sniffed at Mamut. When Mamut reached out to pat him, Wolf Boy growled low in his throat, but then Wolf Boy growled at everyone—except Lame Leg. Mamut glanced around, looking for the girl child, but he did not see her. Probably resting in her tent from the heat of the day, he thought. When she was not staying to herself, the girl would limp after one of the women, usually the Frog Eater woman, Rana, and follow her about as she worked on camp chores. The foreign woman seemed to tolerate Lame Leg better than the two adult Mammoth females did.

Lame Leg's mother and father had died in the Winter of Death, and the girl had not been taken into the home of either of the two surviving Mammoth women, Benaleese or Kutchka. Mamut guessed it was because Lame Leg's mother had never wanted her. The other Mammoth women knew this and did not seem to care for the child either. When the Frog Eater woman married into the band, she had tried to treat the girl kindly. But Lame Leg was fearful and a little cruel and unpredictable. Most times she preferred to stay by herself.

The other members of the Mammoth People ignored her. Only Mamut and the old shaman stopped to give the girl a haunch of meat after a successful hunt. And when they did, she snatched the meat away and growled at them just like her dog.

He had observed that Lern's wife would attempt to teach the girl about cooking and drying meat and tanning hides, but it seemed that Lame Leg did not particularly want to learn any of those skills. She preferred to stay with Wolf Boy, her dog. Mamut did not know if or how the child would ever grow to be a woman. And the Mammoth People needed women so badly.

Mamut's moccasined feet made no sound as he padded up to one side of his tent. It was turned in a different direction from the day before and he shook his head, wondering to himself at his captive's strange ways. Then he shrugged. If she wanted to move the tent around, he would not object.

He had let Terah and the children sleep there, alone, last night, while he slept under the stars, wrapped in a musk-ox hide he had tanned himself. Most of the fur had come off the hide. The night had been cool and the robe was of indifferent warmth. Mamut thought that the sooner he persuaded his new captive to let him into his tent, the warmer he would be.

He sank down on his haunches to watch Terah and the children. She was sitting near a large willow frame, using a sharp stone to scrape dried meat off the hide of the saber-toothed cat that he and Spearpoint had killed. It was good to see that his captive woman was industrious.

Terah wiped her forehead with the back of one hand. Scraping the large hide was taxing work, but it had to be done. She flipped the hide over and began scraping off the hair. When the hide was scraped clean, she rested.

141

"Children," she called softly. She could not put off her next, most onerous task for another day. She must tell the children about Chee.

Flori, Kell and Tika all looked up. There was something in their aunt's voice and a look on her face that spoke to them of seriousness. Terah beckoned them over.

"I must tell you something," she said, when three pairs of bright eyes had settled upon her. How to tell them? she thought wildly. How to tell them that the mother they loved was dead?

She paused, taking a deep breath. "Children," she began hesitantly. "I love you very much, and there is something I must tell you."

Solemn big eyes stared at her.

Terah swallowed. "Your mother—" She stopped. Tika's green eyes were wide, and Terah watched a shadow come over them. The girl stopped breathing. *She knows*, thought Terah. "Your mother is dead," Terah blurted out, wishing she could say it some other way. "Your mother was dying when we left her."

Kell's head dipped to one side, watching her in curiosity.

"She—she loved you very much, and she did not want you to have to watch her die."

"Mmmmphut," said Flori, pointing at her mouth.

Terah smiled weakly. The child could not be expected to understand what Terah was telling her.

"Will we see her again?" asked Kell.

"No," answered his sister shortly.

Terah's heart contracted at the pain in the girl's voice. She reached for Tika's hand and gave the little dirty palm a squeeze. "Your mother has gone to a happy land," she said. "She cannot come back."

Tika began to cry, and Terah's own sorrow deepened. It had been so difficult leaving Chee alone, to die. . . .

"Please," Chee had pleaded. "Do not let them see me die. It will be too horrible for them." Her big green eyes stared at Terah as Chee had lain upon the ground, unable to move, unable to get up. Both Terah and Chee recognized that Chee was dying.

"I think it was the mushrooms," Chee had gasped then. "Did you eat any?" she asked, concern for her children making her voice sharp. If Terah got sick and died too, who would look after the children?

They had picked the mushrooms that last evening, and the children had not wanted any. Terah had been too tired to eat more than the fat bird they had cooked. Only Chee had eaten the small grayish-white, round mushrooms that she had found growing in a circle.

Terah had shaken her head as she sat beside her sister. The leaf poultice Terah had put on her sister's heated body slid off unnoticed. She wiped the sweat off Chee's glistening face. *So much sweat,* thought Terah. *Who would have thought Chee could have so much water in her?* "No," Terah reassured her sister. "I did not eat."

Chee closed her eyes in relief. Then her eyes opened, and Terah thought Chee was going to vomit again, but she did not. "Bron died," Chee whispered hoarsely. "He died a terrible death. We watched. Do you remember?"

Terah nodded. Their older brother, Bron, had died a slow, agonizing death, disemboweled by a saber-tooth. It had taken him two days to die, and his moans and screams still echoed in Terah's nightmares. "I remember."

Terah saw Chee's hand move, a palsied shake, and knew her sister was trying to touch her. Terah took the paralyzed hand, which grew cold even as she held it.

"Do not let them see me—" gasped Chee. "Do not let Tika—she will understand more than the others—do not let her see me die. . . ." Chee's face crumpled and so did Terah's. Terah sat, sobbing, beside her sister.

After a while, Chee's voice came weaker. "Take the children. Go back to our parents. . . ."

"No," said Terah stubbornly. "I will not let you die alone."

"Take them," said Chee, her voice a little stronger, desperate. "I beg you, Sister. Do this for me." Her green eyes were bulging a little, and Terah wanted to cry some more. "I am dying. . . ."

"No!" cried Terah.

"Yes. Take the children and go! Dagger will find me. He will bury me. It will be right with the Great Spirit."

Terah knew that Dagger would not find Chee's body before the dire wolves or saber-tooths or

144

other scavengers got to her. Chee's dead body would be torn apart by predators and be bare bones by the time her husband found her. Terah's face crumpled again.

"I love you," Terah cried.

"And I love you," Chee whispered. Then her voice came a little stronger and harder. She met Terah's eyes. "If you love me, take my children back. Do not let them see me like this, dying—"

Terah had cried some more then. When she had exhausted her tears, she had nodded, still miserable. She bent over Chee. Her lips touched the hot, wet forehead in a gentle kiss. "I will go, my dear, dear sister," she whispered. "I will take your children."

Chee closed her eyes, and a shudder went through her body. Her face seemed to relax. Terah's eyes filled once more as she looked at that beloved face. As she watched Chee's slow breaths, she thought of the years with Chee, of Chee holding out a flower to her, Chee talking with her, Chee laughing and singing with her, Chee who loved her children. . . . And now it was all over. Beautiful Chee was dying. There would never be anyone else in her life like Chee.

Terah stroked her sister's thick dark hair one last time. Then, blinded by tears, she rose and walked with dragging steps to the little tent the children slept in.

"Come," she told Tika, Kell, and Flori, shaking each of them gently. "Wake up." Terah's voice was low and sad. "We must leave. Now."

And the sleepy children had risen, placed their

trusting hands in their Aunt Terah's, and walked away, leaving behind their dying mother.

Terah blinked back new tears as the memories flooded over her.

Kell said, "I want my dada."

Terah wondered if Dagger would look for them. By the time he found their tracks, *if* he found their tracks, many days would have passed. She did not think that Dagger would be able to follow the old trail and find them. She shook her head at Kell, unable to speak. At last she took a deep breath. "Your father loves you. Your mother loved you," she said, and then her voice broke. Both parents were dead to these children, one through actual death, the other because his children had been taken from him. Fresh tears poured down Terah's cheeks.

Tika lifted her head from her quiet crying. She saw that Terah was still crying. Tika crept closer to Terah, and her long thin arms wrapped around Terah's waist. Terah hugged the girl to her, the strong young body of her niece reassuring. She patted Tika's hair and made soothing sounds, but she could not take the child's grief away, nor her own.

Kell got up and walked away. Flori poked at an ant in the dust as it walked a little crooked path. She stood up and started to follow it.

A warm, firm hand suddenly gripped Terah's shoulder. She looked up. Wet, green eyes met dark, piercing black eyes. It was Mamut, she realized, wondering vaguely where he had come from.

Mamut squatted down beside her. He handed her a leaf to wipe away her tears. The compassion on his face was so unexpected that Terah felt new tears rise in her. "Thank you," she murmured, dipping her face in the leaf.

She raised her eyes slowly and looked at his face. It was kind of him to be there, to share her sorrow. Then her eyes dropped to his forearm. The three gashes from the saber-toothed cat were red and angry-looking. Around the wounds, small white feathers were stuck here and there by tiny dabs of pitch. The shaman's cure.

Slowly she raised her eyes to his face again. Mamut was watching her; the sorrow on his own face reflected the sadness she felt.

"I heard," Mamut said softly. "I heard you tell the children. . . ."

Terah shook her head. "I did not want you to hear," she murmured. "I did not want you to know anything about us." She shook her head slowly.

"I want to know about them. About you. You are all part of my family now."

"I do not want to be!"

He shrugged and his handsome face hardened. She did not have a choice. He reached out and touched Terah's hair.

Tika suddenly looked up from where she had her head snuggled against Terah's chest. Tika wiped her eyes, then got up and walked over to where Kell was stalking a tiny bird.

Terah felt deserted.

Once more her eyes dropped to Mamut's puffy

red forearm. She raised her eyes and locked upon his. Her grief receded for the moment as she gazed into those deep, obsidian eyes.

This man is in danger of dying. Does he know that? she wondered, searching his arrogant, strong face.

Chapter 12

Mamut followed his captive woman's gaze to his forearm. The shaman had sung and prayed over his wounds, and the old man had assured Mamut that the feathers would drive the evil out of his arm. Mamut did not want the hot sickness to come, but he felt worse now than when he had set out that morning.

Tears still streaked the woman's face, and Mamut dragged his thoughts away from his own concerns. When he and Spearpoint had decided to steal this woman and the children with her, he had not thought of all the problems that would come from that one simple decision. Now as he saw the grief on her face, he felt great sorrow for her. The two youngest children did not recognize the loss that she spoke of, but Mamut thought that the older girl, Tika, understood very well what her aunt had told her.

Mamut sighed and fingered the yellowed ivory bead on his chest. He thought of his own father and his own terrible loss when Kran died. Unlike himself, Terah did not have to carry a basketful of guilt with her sorrow at her sister's death. Did she?

"That is why we found only you and the children walking in the hills," he said.

Terah reluctantly nodded. "My sister was dying. She had eaten a poisonous mushroom. She did not want her children to have to watch her die. My brother—"

Terah stopped, wondering if she should say any more. Mamut was the enemy. Then she decided that he would gain no knowledge of where she and the children would flee to when they escaped even if she did speak of Chee's death. And it did feel better to share her sadness with someone. "My brother, Bron, died a terrible death when I was a little girl. My sister and I watched his agony, held his hand. Chee did not want her children to go through that, to hear her screaming in pain—"

Mamut nodded. He felt a grudging respect for the dead woman for having thought to spare her children the misery of her death. A brave woman. Terah came from a family of brave people, thought Mamut in envy.

"Where is their father?" He had wondered this for some time.

Terah looked at him, trying to read the

striking, impassive face before her. She gave up and said, "He left us at a small camp and went on ahead to get white chert for his speartips." That was not telling him very much, she assured herself.

"White chert," mused Mamut. He knew of a white chert quarry. It was a two-day walk from where he had found Terah and the children.

"It is a secret place," said Terah. "He did not want us to know where it was."

Not so secret, thought Mamut. *All Mammoth men know of the chert quarry.* He glanced at her, his eyes narrowed. "He did not take his son?"

"Kell is too little," observed Terah. "He is only four summers."

"I would take my son with me to a quarry," said Mamut. "It is important for men to know where good stone for spears can be found. My son would remember; I would show him landmarks on the way. Four summers is old enough to learn this."

Terah did not like the implied criticism of Dagger. "Well, you do not have a son, do you?" she snapped. "How can you say what you would do or not do?"

Mamut looked at her and for a moment she saw rage in those black eyes. "I had a son," he snarled when he could get his voice under control. "My son is dead." Then he rose and walked away, shaking with anger.

Terah watched him go. She suddenly felt much sorrow for what she had said. The man had listened to her pain, and she had done naught but rouse his. She wished she could take the words back.

There was pain all around, it seemed. She thought of the children, of the grievous news she had given them. That afternoon, as she watched the children and scraped at the saber-tooth hide with a stone scraper, she was as kind and patient as she could be with them. They played close to her, looking up often, now and then running over for a hug to reassure themselves that she, too, was not going to go away and leave them.

At last, most of the dried flesh and fat was scraped off the saber-tooth hide. The children were playing quietly, settled.

Perhaps she could yet give Mamut some kindness, Terah mused. He had assuredly given her kindness in her grief.

She told Tika to watch Kell and Flori and headed off to the river with a tightly woven basket. She needed water to mix with fatty deer brains to make a paste for tanning the hide.

She walked along the little trail to the river. Deep in thought, she passed a gray lizard sunning itself, then a deer carcass. It was four days old, and Rana had kindly advised Terah that she could use the brains from that carcass for her tanning. Flies buzzed over the carcass, and Terah barely glanced at it, so caught up was she in thinking about Mamut.

As Terah was dipping the basket into the lake and catching the clear, cool liquid, it came to her suddenly how she could help Mamut. He needed to wash his wound. Feathers and sap were fine for his shaman to stick on his arm, but those gashes were infected. If they were not cleaned, they would become more pus-filled and putrid. Why, he might even lose an arm—or worse, die.

Die? Why should she care if he died? she wondered. But she found that she did care, a tiny bit. She remembered the kind look on his face as he handed her the leaf to dry her tears. Selfish interest merged with her new, confused feelings. If Mamut died, she reasoned suddenly, she might be taken as a mate by another man, a less kind man, a man perhaps like Lern, who would strike her. That would never do. No, perhaps it was best to save Mamut. At least he was kind—when he was not kidnapping women and children.

She found him making knife blades. She watched his strong hands knick off the sharp blades of black rock with a deer antler. Her eyes widened when she recognized the stone as obsidian. She could use a good obsidian knife, with a keen, sharp blade. Such a knife made slicing meat a pleasure.

Mamut looked up, and she smiled at him. Warily, he narrowed his eyes. "What do you want?" he asked after some time. He flaked off another blade, appearing completely uninterested that Terah stood there, but his heart pumped strongly and his pulse quickened. She intrigued him, this captive woman of his, with her long, floating, golden brown hair and her tilted green eyes.

"Come with me," she said, struggling to keep her smile in place. She thought he did not want her there, but she was determined to help him and help him she would. "Walk with me to the pool by the river."

"What is the name of your people?" he surprised her by asking.

Taken aback at first, she answered, "The Bison People."

"Are all Bison women so bold?"

She flushed. Then she realized that he was still angry at her for what she had said about his not having a son. That knowledge tempered her answer. "I am sad for you that your son is dead."

"I did not mention my son." The words were cold and clipped, but the look he shot her was uncertain. He set aside the obsidian and stared at her. She met his eyes and would not look away. With a sigh, he got to his feet.

Terah smiled inwardly. He must be a little bit curious, she thought.

"Why the pool?" he asked, following her. He liked the dress she wore. It was different from the dresses the Mammoth women and Frog Eater women wore. Terah's dress, of tawny deer hide, came down to a point at the back and in the front below her knees. Slits up each side showed a generous amount of tanned, graceful leg. He thought perhaps she got cold in the winter in such an outfit, but he liked to see her in it. The garment was decorated across the front and shoulders and hem with long fringe and tiny white beads. Her people must have traded for the beads because he had never seen their like before.

"Why the pool?" he asked again. She was walking ahead of him and he liked the way the leather of her dress rolled smoothly at her hips with each step.

"You will see," she answered. They reached the water. "Kneel," she commanded. She pointed with her chin at the water.

"Are all Bison women as bossy as you?"

"No," she answered. "The other Bison women are much bossier. I am considered gentle and sweet."

Mamut thought he detected a hint of a laugh in her voice, but he could not be certain. After all, he did not know his captive woman all that well. Nevertheless, he thought he liked her.

Slowly, watching her, he sank to his knees. The water was cold and refreshing. He felt foolish, though, kneeling in the water, while his tanned, green-eyed captive watched him.

"Stretch out your arms," she ordered.

He did so, not knowing what to make of this new, playful side to her.

Terah lowered his arms, still stiff, to the water. She began splashing water on his forearms.

"Stop that," he ordered. "You will get the feathers wet."

"I will do more than that," she promised. "I will take those feathers and that pine pitch right off!" She slapped more water onto his arms and then started scrubbing with her fingers.

"Ouch!" he yowled.

Terah stopped and looked at him. "I am not trying to hurt you," she assured him.

155

"Let me know when you *do* try," he said dryly, gritting his teeth against the pain.

When she had taken all the feathers off and most of the pine pitch, she looked at her handiwork. "Yes," she muttered.

Mamut was feeling very wary by now. "The shaman put those feathers on there," he said. He trusted the shaman. "That pine pitch and those feathers were supposed to keep the evil from hurting my arm."

Terah looked at him. "Yes," she agreed, "it did that. But now it is time to try something else.

"We Bison People," she explained, as she led him along the little path back to the encampment, "are well known for our knowledge of plants and medicines."

"We Mammoth People," said Mamut, "are well-known for our revenge."

His message was not lost on Terah. She glanced over her shoulder at the discomfited man. "Now, now," she soothed. "It will feel better soon."

Mamut wondered about that. The skin on his arm throbbed with pain, and he was very worried that the water had destroyed the power of the feathers and pitch. He did not like putting this much trust in his captive. What if this was her way of avenging her capture? The Mammoth People were not the only people who sought revenge, he thought uneasily.

They reached the deer carcass that Terah had spotted earlier. She bent and plunged her hands into the entrails of the dead deer. She rummaged around inside the carcass. When she brought up her hands, she was holding several white, squirming maggots.

"Come here," she said enticingly.

The anguish in Mamut's eyes was sweet to behold. Let him know what it felt like to have another person doing something to him. What she was doing was not like the torment he had meted out to her when he had captured her, but still it was something. The Mammoth People were not the only ones who liked a little revenge.

"Hold out your arms," she commanded. "Straight."

She saw the dread in those dark eyes and reveled in it.

Yet he held out his arms. Mamut wanted to see exactly how far this woman of his would go to kill him. For that was surely what she was trying to do.

One by one she plopped the plump white worms on Mamut's injured forearm.

He winced.

She smiled. "Here's another one," she said encouragingly, as though she were giving him a fat juicy berry. She placed the last maggot carefully on a piece of dead skin.

"Now," she said in satisfaction, "we will leave those little ones to eat."

Mamut gritted his teeth, his strong jaw clenching and unclenching. "And how long will that be?" he asked with remarkable restraint.

"Two days," she smiled. Terah was enjoying herself. It was most pleasant to wreak destruction

157

on one's captor, she decided. And to save his life while doing so.

Mamut gnashed his teeth. "Two days?"

"Two days."

Mamut felt foolish and vulnerable standing there with maggots eating his arm. "Do Bison men do this?" he asked.

"Only the wounded ones." Terah sobered. "If maggots would have saved my brother, I would have put them on him, too. But my brother's intestines were too shredded by the saber-tooth," she explained. "Nothing could save him."

Mamut had been thinking that the woman was trying to kill him in a new and dangerous way. But now, seeing the sadness on her face as she spoke of her brother made him reconsider. "You truly think this will help?" he asked doubtfully.

She nodded. "It will."

"Two days?"

She nodded again.

Mamut drew himself up to his full height. "Thank you," he said as sincerely as he could muster. Then he walked away. He could not take it if she were to laugh at him. He felt foolish.

Lern did not help matters when he inquired as to why Mamut was holding his arm so stiffly. Lern started laughing when Mamut told him about the maggots. Mamut wished he had told Lern to go away instead.

Mamut walked past Tika and the other two children. They had skinned the back off the dead bird and were throwing dirt on the wet skin. "We are tanning hides," Tika called to Mamut as he walked by.

He nodded stiffly, half-surprised that the child had addressed him. Tika ran up to him and looked at his bleeding arm. "Ah," she said. "You have an infected arm. We, too, put maggots on poisoned cuts."

She obviously thought Mamut had placed the maggots there himself. "You have seen such a thing before?" Mamut asked.

Tika nodded. "It is one way to clean a deep wound." Mamut stared at the child. Perhaps the Bison People *did* know more about healing and medicines. Mamut did not think he had known such things when he was the age of this girl. He had not even known such a thing as an adult!

With a blinding flash of smile, Tika ran off to "tan" hides.

Mamut walked thoughtfully through the camp.

Two days later, Mamut's arm was healing well and he was able to pluck off the maggots. He placed them carefully back on the deer carcass. "Thank you," he told the maggots humbly.

Terah watched from a short distance away. Something in the region of her heart quivered when she heard him say those words. She frowned to herself. She did not want to like this man who had taken her from her people.

She had waited for three nights for him to come to her tent. Waited and worried about what she would do, how she would fight him

Theresa Scott

off. He had not come. He had not even ranted about the maggots, instead going about his daily work as though he wore maggots upon his arm every day. She had thought he would be more upset by the plump white worms than that. But a little part of her was pleased that he had trusted her.

She turned away. If she kept thinking about Mamut like this, she would not want to escape. Or, if she did escape, she would convince herself to come back with her father to offer Mamut the eight dowry spears. Perhaps Mamut would like that.

Terah shook her head. She must stop thinking about the man.

Chapter 13

Mamut stiffened. He lifted his nose to the wind, and his nostrils flared. Something smelled—badly. He darted behind a boulder, careful to keep the glittering, smooth-flowing Giver of Life River in his sight. The bad smell wafted from that direction.

Then he saw them. A herd of mammoths had come to drink. Mamut's jaw clenched as he watched the giant black, brown, and sand-colored behemoths. Memories of his father's death swept over him. His blood pounded furiously in his chest; sweat beaded his forehead. He wanted to run!

With grim resolve Mamut forced himself to stay where he was. The mammoths were far away, he reassured himself. He was hidden. He was upwind from them, so they could not smell him. They had poor eyesight, so they could not see him. They did not know he was there. He was safe.

Gradually Mamut's racing heartbeat slowed to a normal pulse.

He stared at the large herd pensively. He had not seen mammoths in this area for several years. Well, what matter? he asked himself. He and his people were searching for bison, not mammoth. None of his people wanted to hunt mammoths. *He* certainly did not. His people wanted bison. It was bison robes that they could trade for wives, fat bison meat that they could dry for the approaching winter.

He should continue his hunt for bison. But something held him fixed to the boulder he had sought refuge behind. It had to be a sick fascination, he mused, that held him rooted to the spot, staring at the great beasts as they lumbered around in the water. One large female yanked at the lush water plants that grew near the river's edge. He watched as she pulled the dripping greens into her mouth; her great jaws chewed as green leaves plopped back into the water. A calf frisked at her side. Another of the beasts, a brown yearling, moved slowly out of the water and began to browse on a clump of dry grass.

How long he stayed watching the great woolly animals Mamut did not know. It was only as the sun was setting that he realized he had let the whole day go by without pursuing a single antelope or camel or horse, or any game his people could eat. He shook himself. What terrible spell did the mammoths weave around him?

He remembered his vision quest, before he became a man. The Great Spirit had gifted him with the eerie sight of a mammoth. And upon the heels of that vision had come his father's death by Father-Killer.

No, mammoths meant naught but danger to Mamut. Nothing good could come from his sick fascination with the beasts. Nothing good at all.

The Great Spirit smiled upon him, and Mamut found a young she-camel wandering in a canyon near the camp. He killed her with a single spear stroke and quickly skinned her. Now that dusk had descended, he must be careful of scavengers.

Even as he thought thus, a movement to the left caught his eye. Two dire wolves, their large gray-and-black bodies blending in with the encroaching night, growled. One of them sat down, her yellow eyes gleaming, her big tongue lolling out of great jaws. Dire wolves had jaws that could snap a bison bone in two. The other dire wolf padded on a tiny trail, back and forth nervously, clearly waiting for Mamut to leave so that he could approach the fresh, bleeding camel carcass.

With clean, sure movements, Mamut sliced off the back haunches of the camel. He wrapped them in the hide. With swift, economical motions, he butchered several more choice pieces of the carcass. Then he stood slowly.

Theresa Scott

The two dire wolves growled, and the pacing male stepped back.

"So, you do not want a fight," muttered Mamut. He glared at the yellow, gleaming eyes. "You want that meat, but you want to take it easily this night." He chuckled to himself. He was willing to share the camel, now that he had the best pieces for his family. Family. How strange that felt, to think of his captive woman and the children as his family. He shrugged.

Settling the large, tightly wrapped bundle of meat on one shoulder, he backed away from the camel remains and continued to watch the wolves warily. The female rose from her haunches, her tongue still lolling, obviously anxious for him to disappear completely. She gave a sharp, short bark.

With one last chuckle, Mamut backed several more steps. The dire wolves slunk over to the camel. Mamut heard the crunch and snapping of bones, the gobbling of meat chunks. He turned and strode away, knowing the wolves were content with their easily won meal this night.

He strolled into camp and dropped the bundle of meat outside his tent. He could hear the children inside, and the low melodious murmur of his captive woman's voice. A crackling fire burned in the small fire pit and cast its light on the tent opening. Mamut ducked and stealthily looked into the tent.

The children and Terah were playing a little

game with laced fingers and two white pebbles. Evidently Flori had just won, for the others hooted and laughed at her antics. Mamut felt a satisfaction creep over him as he watched them. It was a good thing to have a woman to return to, he reflected, thinking of the many times since Cala's death that he had returned to a dark, empty tent. It was time to let his grief go, time to live again, time to love. . . .

No, he did not have to do that, he told himself. It was enough to enjoy his captive woman. He did not have to love her. After all, if she did not suit him, he could proceed as he had first planned and trade her at the Meet-meet for a beautiful wife. But now, watching Terah, Mamut had sudden doubts that he would ever find another woman as beautiful as this one at any Meet-meet.

Her light brown hair swayed as she moved her head, now putting her hands behind her back, hiding the pebbles. Her small breasts jutted with the movement and Mamut's eyes fastened on them. He swallowed. He had given her three nights to grow used to his camp, his tent. How much longer could he wait before tasting the fruits that were rightfully his?

Kell clapped his hands in glee and dived for one of Terah's hands. She laughed as he burrowed behind her.

Mamut wanted to be part of this. His dead son, his dead wife, had been with him so long he had forgotten what it was like to laugh and play.

165

They had not seen him, so he backed away from the tent. He stood and gave a little call. All activity inside the tent ceased, and he heard Terah caution the children. Something in his heart twisted at the realization that she was warning them about him. An inexplicable longing washed over him, but for what, he did not know. Was it to be accepted by her? Accepted by the children? He wished he knew.

Cautiously, Terah poked her head out of the tent. She thought she had recognized Mamut's voice. Yes, it was he. She crept out of the tent and looked up at him.

He stood before her, an amused twist to his well-formed lips. He poked at a bundle with his toe. "Meat," he said. "Camel."

With a little cry, Terah scooped up the bundle. She loved the taste of sweet, pink camel meat; it was considered a rare treat among the Bison people. "Oh, thank you!" she exclaimed.

Then she caught herself and fiddled with the bundle nervously. Of course he would feed them—that was his responsibility, was it not? He had captured them; he had claimed them in front of his Mammoth People. Of course he would provide meat; it was expected.

And with taking the meat went a sense of obligation to him that Terah could not shake off. She did not want it, that obligation, but she felt it nonetheless. Perhaps she should give the meat back. Tell him that she would provide for the children, that she could pick enough plants, find enough roots to feed them. But when she opened her mouth, the words did not come. For she wanted the meat. With it, the children would grow strong. She herself would stay strong. Hunger was a constant enemy in this land and in her life. Anything that vanquished hunger was good.

She opened up the bundle, instantly seduced by the fresh red slabs of flesh that lay therein. She raised her eyes to his watchful, handsome face. "Thank you," she said again, with as much dignity as she could summon. Unconsciously, she hugged the bundle closer to her chest.

Mamut read the struggle on her face. She wanted the meat, but she did not want it. A strange notion of compassion swept over him as he considered her dilemma. She was proud; she was brave. He knew that. And she did not want to take anything from him. He watched those vivid green eyes drop to the fresh meat. But he knew she wanted that meat. He would have to remember that she favored camel meat so strongly.

He smiled at her, understanding her dilemma, but wanting it solved his way. After all, she was his captive. What he wanted was more important that what she wanted. He put his hand over the meat. "I killed that camel. I brought this meat to you. I give it to you." He wanted it clear to her that she was receiving food from his hand. "You cook it—for yourself, for your sister's children. And for me." He watched her out of amused obsidian eyes.

Anger flared in her. She wanted to throw the

meat in his face, but something—some cunning, some primitive desperation—held her at the last moment and she did not. "I do not like this," she said at last. "I do not like receiving meat from you."

He shrugged. "You ate of the dried meat I gave you. You have lived on the meat my people killed and dried since you came to live with us. How is this any different?"

But it was different. He knew it; she knew it. This meat would forge a bond between them. He giving her the meat, she eating it. If she accepted this meat, she would be accepting him, Mamut, and recognizing a place for him in her life. Terah felt this at a basic, elemental level. She looked down at the meat once more. The smell of it came to her, enticed her.

Inside the tent, Flori whimpered. Tika hushed her.

The children. Terah had forgotten the children. This man's presence was so strong and overwhelming that she frequently forgot everything around her except him.

"The children are hungry," he pointed out softly. Mamut had no qualms about using the children against her. He inhaled her unique fragrance, so close was she. He closed his eyes for a moment as he imagined her coming to him, naked. . . . He opened his eyes and waited. He did not want to upset the delicate moment. The moment when she took a step toward him of her own accord. . . .

Terah glanced from him to the meat once

more. So much rests on this, she thought.

Flori whimpered again. With a deep breath, Terah nodded her head. Once.

Mamut let his breath out. So, she had succumbed. Now it was only a matter of time before he would have her. He straightened.

Something had changed between them. Terah felt it; Mamut felt it. Some kind of bargain had been made. He had agreed to provide meat, she to eat it. Terah felt suddenly uncomfortable and vulnerable and trapped. This was not what she had expected when she had come as a captive to these people. She had expected to stay to herself and escape with the children at the earliest opportunity. But now, something had changed.

And what, she mused, would he want in exchange for the meat?

Chapter 14

He had gone hunting. Again. Terah's full lips
tightened as she placed the long white root on
a flat stone, then pounded it with a rounded
stone. She picked up the squashed white fiber,
turned it over, and threw it down on the flat
stone. Then she pounded it again. Hard.

She continued to pound the white root until
it was naught but a flopping, flat, unappetizing
mess. She should be glad he was so conscientious, she scolded herself. Happy that he cared
about hunting and providing plenty of meat
for herself and the children. And what did she
want meat for anyway? Taking his food made
her feel vulnerable. And she certainly would
not admit to missing him!

She slapped the flattened white tuber on the
flat stone and pounded some more.

Tika came over to watch. The girl frowned. "Mother says to pound the bullrush tuber gently."

"Your mother is dead," said Terah. Then she began to cry. How had it happened? she stormed. Here she was with three children to look after, captive of a man who made her senses rage in confusion, and her sister was dead! It was all too difficult to cope with.

She lifted tear-filled eyes to Tika and saw that the child's face had crumpled in misery. *Oh, what have I done? The poor child.*

She reached for Tika and held her. Both of them cried. Terah wiped Tika's tear-streaked face and rubbed her back. "Your mother was correct," Terah acknowledged when she could speak. "The root of the bullrush plant should be pounded gently. The flavor is much better that way."

Wiping her tears, Tika took the stone from her aunt and picked up a second long root. She placed it carefully on the flat stone and began pounding it with the smooth pounding stone. Terah watched the rhythmic motions, and at last a tiny smile curved her lips. Tika had learned well from Chee. . . .

Chee. Why had the Great Spirit taken Chee? Terah asked herself in despair. Why could her sister not have lived? The children needed their mother so badly. Why did the Great Spirit have to take her sister, her beloved only sister?

There was no answer but the gently pounding stone. Terah turned away so that Tika would not see her tears again.

"There," said Tika, satisfied that the root had been pounded enough. "That is how you do it, Aunt."

"Thank you," said Terah, hiding a sad smile. She placed a consoling hand on Tika's shoulder for a moment. The child patted her hand absently and ran off to play with Kell.

Terah watched her go, sorrow in her heart. How was she going to take care of Tika, see that the child grew to be a woman? How was she going to take care of Kell and Flori? Despair etched itself on her mind. She needed help to raise these children, she thought. The help of her Bison People would be best. And the children needed their father, Dagger. Oh, what could she do? Terah sighed. How had this ever happened to her?

She should be planning their escape, that was what she should be doing. The little pieces of dried meat she had been hiding away were going to feed them on their flight back to the Bison People.

But time was against her. She had waited this long because there was always someone guarding the Mammoth camp. But the longer she waited, the more difficult it was going to be to find the Bison People. The Bison People were wanderers; the Mammoth People were also wanderers, and the Mammoth People's wanderings were taking her and the children farther away from her Bison People. And if she *was* going to flee, Terah had to get back to her people before the end of the Moon of Geese Flying, because then her people would be wandering south once again, following the Giver of Life River, and she would never, ever see them again. . . .

Oh, what a woeful mess I am in, Terah lamented, as she pounded another of the long roots. She caught herself just as she was going to mash the root to a fibrous pulp. She lowered the pounding stone gently onto the tuber.

Presently Terah rose and walked over to the meat racks. Flori ambled over. Terah lifted the already dried strips of camel meat and put them in a half-filled basket nearby. She stoked up the embers under the meat and laid a chunk of wood on the fire. Flori handed her a second piece of gnarled wood, her little face solemn. Terah thanked her and added the wood to the embers. When the fire was smoking, Terah placed new strips of the pink meat along the sticks above the smoke. A combination of smoke and sun would effectively dry and preserve the meat.

At least she and the children would have something delicious to take with them when they left, Terah thought with a tiny glimmer of hope as she surveyed the dried camel meat in the basket. She would use the meat she had accepted from Mamut to flee to freedom.

She heard a tiny grunt behind her and whirled suddenly. She lunged for Flori, just in time to pull the child out of the flames. A heartbeat later, and the child would have been badly burned. Terah's heart pounded as she recognized how close the child had been to the fire. Shaking, she clutched Flori to her and staggered away from the smoking fire.

After thoroughly soaking Flori in the lake water, Terah carried her over to examine the saber-toothed tiger hide that she had left to soak in a large, tightly woven basket that held a gray ooze of deer brains and water. She put the child down and lifted the skin out of the water and started to wring it out. Her arm muscles bunched and she panted heavily, trying to wring the heavy hide. Flori watched, hazel eyes huge, her little blond head cocked to one side.

Rana approached and set down her basket. "Would you like some help?"

"Yes," answered Terah gratefully. Together the two women wrung and knotted the hide. As she worked, Terah noticed a dark bruise on Rana's left cheekbone. Terah's lips tightened, but she said nothing.

A splash behind her made Terah whirl around just in time to see Flori dipping her hands and splashing in the thick gray ooze. Muttering to herself, Terah grabbed Flori up just as the little one was about to lick the acrid-smelling fluid from one of her wet hands. Terah groaned. The ooze would have tasted terrible and would have made Flori sick.

Terah shook her head and met Rana's eyes. The older woman's dark eyes twinkled. "It has been some time since my own children were small. I had forgotten how swiftly they can move."

Theresa Scott

Terah chuckled. She put Flori firmly on the ground and warned the little girl to stay away from the ooze. Terah carried the still dripping saber-tooth hide over to the willow frame. Flori followed; so did Rana, chatting quietly.

Terah used a sharp deer bone awl to make little holes along the sides of the hide. Then she laced a strand of leather through each hole and lashed the hide to the upright willow frame. She pulled the hide tightly, stretching it as much as she could.

Rana grunted. "You do a fine job of stretching the hide," she said admiringly.

"Thank you," said Terah without thinking. "My mother and Chee taught me well." Chee again, she thought and a pang of sorrow clenched her heart. She looked at little Flori; the child's eyes were the same shape as Chee's. Terah sighed, her grief a terrible weight upon her slim shoulders.

Face downcast, Terah reached for the camel hide and her sharp scraper and began the repetitive task of scraping the dried meat and fat from this hide.

Rana watched her for a moment, then squatted down beside her, picked up another tool and began scraping. Flori, watching them, picked up a little rock and began sawing at the hide, too. She used both hands on the pebble and put all her efforts into the task. Terah smiled, unable to keep back her amusement at the child's work. The three worked in silence for some time.

Rana sat back when the camel hide looked

clean of meat. "Let us walk down to the pool," she said.

Terah rose to follow her and reached out a hand to Flori. The three walked down the path to the water. They had almost reached it when Rana halted. "Behold."

Terah stared. "What?"

"Soon it will be very dry. No rain."

Terah looked at her and frowned. "How do you know this?"

"Frogs," answered the older woman.

"The frogs told you?"

The older woman nodded. "Verily, it is the frog's elder brother, the toad, that tells me." She pointed with her chin.

As Terah watched, a toad dug itself into the mud, its great back feet working at the earth like paddles.

"There is another," said Rana.

Terah spotted the third toad on her own. "Perhaps they ready themselves for winter early," commented Terah. Even though she was not one of the Great Frog People, she knew that toads hibernated in winter.

Rana shook her head. "No, too early. These toads prepare for drought."

Terah digested this in silence.

"If there is no rain," continued Rana, "then the bison will be forced to search out the Giver of Life River for water. Perhaps it will make our men's work easier, if the bison come to us."

Terah nodded. Bison. That was where Mamut was. Waiting for the bison herds to come.

"Why are they called the Mammoth People if they hunt bison? Why do they not hunt mammoth?" Terah asked idly as they reached the edge of the shallow pool.

Rana shrugged. "I do not know. My husband will not hunt mammoths, I know that." She halted and turned to look at Terah. "I think he is afraid." In a normal tone of voice, she went on, "Yet I notice that these Mammoth People have many implements made from mammoth bone and tusk. I think they must have hunted them at one time. And Benaleese, my sister-in-law, takes every opportunity to brag about the valuable mammoth ivory necklace she always wears."

Terah smiled. "You do not like Benaleese?" So Benaleese was Lern's sister. They bore a sly, handsome resemblance.

Rana shrugged. "Benaleese does not respect frogs."

"Oh." Assuredly a serious flaw in Rana's judgment, thought Terah.

Rana asked, "Have you met her?"

"She has walked by my tent once or twice, but she has not stopped to visit."

"Hunnh, and she will not stop, if I know Benaleese."

Terah waited for Rana to fill her basket, then they started back up the trail to the camp. Flori ran after a mouse. They reached the camp, and Terah looked up to see Lame Leg limp over to where Kell and Tika were building a small pretend fire. It was the first time that Terah had seen the Mammoth child offer to play.

Tika had gathered eight long sticks and was trying to make a meat-drying rack, but the sticks kept falling down and she was becoming frustrated. When she saw Lame Leg, she bared her teeth in an unwelcoming grimace.

Terah eyed the children. Neither Kell nor his sister welcomed the Mammoth girl, but they did not attack her either. Tika went on with her work of building the miniature drying rack. After standing by herself for some time, Lame Leg glanced at Terah, saw her watching, and limped away.

Terah's mouth twisted at seeing the discouraged look on the dirty little face. One side of the skinny child's body could be seen behind the loose stitches on her tunic. Such a garment was suitable for summer, thought Terah, but winter was coming soon and the child would freeze wearing such poorly sewn clothing.

"Who sews for Lame Leg now that her mother is dead?" asked Terah, settling herself at the camel hide once more. She flipped it over and began scraping the hair off.

Rana reached for a scraper. As she watched the girl limp away, Terah caught a wistful expression on the older woman's countenance. "Nobody sews for her."

"How did she get that tunic then?"

"She sewed it herself."

Terah sat up straighter. The sewing was not so bad if one considered that a child of ten summers had done it.

"How did Lame Leg's mother die?" she asked

179

Rana, remembering Mamut's shuttered face when she had asked about the child.

Rana shrugged. "The same way they all died— in the Winter of Death."

"Ah, yes, the Winter of Death." When Mamut's son and wife had died also. Terah scraped the hide thoughtfully. Flori, bored with scraping, got up and waddled over to where Kell and Tika played. She began drawing in the dust.

Terah kept an eye on the children as she continued to scrape. "What happened in the Winter of Death?" she asked.

Rana shrugged again. "I do not know the whole of it. My husband does not see fit to tell me everything." There was a curious flat note in the older woman's voice whenever she spoke of Lern. Terah waited, scraping.

"The hunters came back and the women were dead. The children were dead."

"Starvation?"

Rana shook her head. "There was still food. They had an antelope carcass nearby. No, it was not starvation. Several of the men thought it was ghosts. Some thought it was poisonous food."

Terah nodded. "My sister, Chee, died from eating a poisonous mushroom."

Rana's expressive eyes were sad upon hearing this. She reached out a hand and touched Terah's shoulder. Terah went still. "You loved your sister very much," Rana observed softly.

Terah nodded, biting back tears. "I did."

"And now she's gone."

Terah nodded again. Tears dripped from her

eyes. Rana patted her shoulder, saying nothing more, but Terah took comfort from the old woman's presence. She reached up and touched the worn hand. Rana gave her hand a little squeeze. Terah wiped at the tears with the back of her other hand. "I—I do have the children," she said softly.

"Yes, Chee lives on through them." The calmness in the old woman's voice soothed Terah.

They both went back to scraping. "You were telling me about the Winter of Death," prodded Terah after a little.

"Hunnh," Rana murmured softly. "As I said, some thought it was ghosts that killed them, some thought it was bad food." She paused and looked around. Satisfied that no one would overhear them, she leaned forward and said, "But I think it was the rabbits."

"The rabbits?" Rana was a curious woman at times, thought Terah. She stopped scraping and eyed Rana. "Rabbits? How can rabbits kill people?"

Rana stopped scraping too and met Terah's eyes in full measure. "Because," she said in a stern voice, "rabbits can carry a bad disease, a rabbit fever. It sweeps through like a plague. My Great Frog People know about this. And there were rabbits that winter. Rabbits that some of the children had caught and tamed. Some of the families even took the rabbits into their winter caves when it was cold, so dear had the rabbits become to the children." Rana shook her head. "Living that close to wild rabbits is not good. Not

181

good." The old woman shook her head once more and went back to scraping.

Terah began to scrape once again also, pondering the old one's words. "Does Mamut know you think this?" she asked after a while. It might console him in his loss to know how his wife and son's deaths had happened, Terah thought.

But Rana shook her head. "I do not speak of it," she answered. "If I did, I think the Mammoth men would just laugh at me. That is what Lern did, when I made the mistake of telling him what I thought."

Terah's eyes flew to the dark bruise on Rana's face. "He has been striking you again." It was not a question.

"Hunnnh, yes." Rana did not meet her eyes.

"Rana," Terah laid a hand gently on the older woman's shoulder, remembering the kindness and understanding that the old woman had given her just moments before. "You do not have to stay with Lern. You can leave him. Put your things outside your tent," she urged Rana. "That is what the old shaman said," she reminded her.

The old woman heaved a great sigh. "Then I would have no husband. Who would hunt for me? I have no son, no son-in-law. And these Mammoth People are not merciful. You see how they treat Lame Leg. And," she demanded, "where would I live?"

"You could make a tent for yourself," answered Terah stoutly. "You know how to tan hides. You would make a better dwelling than these tents," she made a careless gesture with her hand, dismissing the ragged tents surrounding them.

Rana smiled grimly. "And once I had made my tent, child. What then?" She shook her head. "What man will court an old woman? And I do not know how to hunt. I would have to eat a diet of lichen and moss and little tundra flowers for the rest of my life—which would be short. Hunnh, no, thank you. I will stay with my husband."

Terah felt exasperated with the woman. "And so you will stay, and get hit," she exclaimed.

Rana shrugged as if to say, if it must be so.

Terah turned away. Sometimes she did not understand her new friend. They were very different. Perhaps Frog Eaters—no, she corrected herself, perhaps Great Frog People thought differently from Bison People. No Bison woman she knew of would stay with a man who beat her. At least Terah did not *think* a Bison woman would.

Terah regarded her new friend uneasily as she continued to scrape the camel hide. How could *she* tell Rana what to do? She, Terah, was not an older woman who faced certain abandonment should she move her things outside her tent. She was young and fair enough to find another mate if Mamut struck her.

Terah gasped inwardly. How could she even be thinking of Mamut as her mate? She flushed and scraped harder.

"Careful," warned Rana. "You will put a hole in this camel hide if you scrape it in so determined a fashion."

183

Chapter 15

Terah watched Mamut stride into camp with a young, long-necked, buck antelope slung around his shoulders. She watched as he surveyed the camp, looking for something. Her breath caught in her throat when he met her eyes and she realized he had been looking for her.

She swallowed, staring her fill at him as he strode toward her. His black hair blew back from his high cheekbones, and she could see the strength in those broad shoulders. Her eyes dropped to his flat, muscled torso and followed the clean line from slim waist down long, leather-clad legs. Unbidden, her eyes lingered on the tan pair of leather leggings he was wearing. They looked about to split at the leg seams, and the knee-high moccasins he wore looked about to separate from the soles.

Terah frowned. In the rocky tundra lands, a hunter needed well-made leggings and footwear for the rough terrain. Her eyes lifted to his face once again, and her heart beat faster. He was smiling at her, the curve of his mouth devastating her. She wanted to melt into the ground.

Mamut swung the antelope down and dropped it on the ground at her feet. Terah went to reach for one of the half-grown buck's horns, but a movement from Mamut stopped her. Negligently, he placed one foot in its scuffed, torn moccasin on the neck of the dead antelope.

He was signaling her that he was the owner of the antelope, she realized. She drew her hand back. He met her eyes, and she saw the amused twinkle in those obsidian depths. She met his gaze unwaveringly.

"For you," he said. Then he took his foot off the neck.

Terah reached for the antelope's horn once more, and this time Mamut did not stop her. She had started to drag the beast over to the fire area for butchering when she caught his eyes still upon her. What did he want? she wondered.

"Lame Leg has no one to hunt for her but her dog, Wolf Boy," Mamut observed.

He was watching her carefully, and Terah suddenly wondered if he was testing her in some way. What did he want? An acknowledgment from her that he had killed the antelope?

She straightened, her mind whirling. "Your spear ran red with blood," she said politely. "Thank you for the antelope. It is a fine animal."

"I will share," he answered just as formally. Yet still he waited. What was it? She was unable to guess what he wanted. Better to ask him outright, she decided. "What is it you want from me?" she asked, tilting her chin in the air a fraction.

He took a step toward her, then two, and she was staring at his broad chest. She swallowed and lifted her eyes to his. He reached out and pushed a strand of her hair gently behind one of her ears.

Terah trembled at his touch.

"I want," he said, and his voice drifted away as he gazed at her. Mamut forgot what he wanted. She stood before him, half-defiant, half-afraid, and thoroughly desirable. He wanted *her*. That much his body was telling him. Instinctively, Mamut lowered his head and kissed her. The touch of her lips sent a shock through him, and he reached for her, pulling her to him.

Terah's eyes widened when she felt his lips meet hers. Then, before she could protest, he was pulling her into his arms and holding her. His lips were warm. He was so solid and strong, she wanted to go limp and let him hold her and never let her go. For a moment she gave into the wonderful feelings. Then he raised his head and gazed down at her. "I will come to your tent.

Tonight." His husky voice held a deep note that licked at her like the flames of a brush fire.

Dazed, she raised one hand to her mouth, touching her so recently bereft lips. "I—I think not," she murmured. Her first objection was that the children were in the tent. They would hear . . . everything. With an inward gasp, she scolded herself. She should not be entertaining any notions about him at all! Except to escape him.

She tore herself away, grasped the antelope by both horns this time, and began dragging it. But now she was conscious that he could hold the meat as ransom for her behavior. She shifted her hold on the antelope, pretending it was heavier than it was, while she read him through downcast eyelashes. Disappointment flickered over his face and then was gone. She would have expected anger on his handsome visage—but disappointment? Well, she was disappointed too, but not for the same reasons, she told herself. He was disappointed that he could not come to her tonight. And she was disappointed because . . . because he could not come to her!

She gave a furious tug on the antelope horn, and the neck twisted.

Mamut said nothing as he watched his captive woman struggle with the dead beast. Then, with a sigh, he walked over, took one of the long curved horns, and helped her drag it to the fire.

Kell and Flori and Tika came running over to see the animal.

"Ooooooh." Tika sighed admiringly. Terah shot her a look, then smiled to herself. The animal

188

was an impressive size and would yield plenty of meat.

"Tika," said Terah, as she pulled her little white chert knife from her belt. Just then she saw Mamut glance at the weapon. Terah met his eyes defiantly. This was the knife she had fought him with. She expected anger in his gaze, but met only amusement twinkling in those dark eyes. She bent down and began skinning the antelope. "Tika," she said again, trying to ignore Mamut's presence, which was like trying to ignore a saber-toothed cat, "would you please take this haunch of meat to Lame Leg?"

Terah saw by the look on Tika's face that the child did not wish to do any such thing. "Never mind, then," said Terah. "I will invite her to sup with us. She may not know how to cook antelope."

"She knows," said Mamut, and a smile played about his mouth. His captive woman was kind; he liked that. He had meant to suggest that she give meat to Lame Leg, but he had forgotten about the crippled child and her dog once he had stepped close to this enticing woman.

Terah was watching him in curiosity. "How do you know she can cook?"

He shrugged. "I bring her meat at times, as does the shaman. We do not want to see her starve. Our people need females."

With a snort, Terah turned away. She did not need to be reminded about how his people needed females. Why else was she here? Her movements were precise and skilled as she sliced off a chunk of meat.

"She will not eat with you," said Mamut after a while.

"Who?" Terah focused intently on butchering the antelope. That way she did not have to acknowledge the forbidden attraction of the man watching her.

"Lame Leg."

"Oh." She kept butchering and setting the pieces aside. Some of the meat she would dry, to take with her and the children. She smiled a secret smile. He thought to keep her, did he? Well, he might be able to kill saber-tooths and antelopes and camels, but she had a few skills of her own.

Mamut saw the tiny smile and leaned forward, intrigued. The children drifted away to play again. This time they were digging holes in the dirt, pretending to dig for roots. Kell objected to this game, saying he wanted to hunt, but Tika was adamant. With a sigh, Kell began pawing at the earth.

"Why do you not want me to come to the tent tonight?"

The audacity of the man! "Because we are not married. Because you captured me. Because you did not come to my father and ask for me. And—and I do not like you." *A lie,* she said to herself. She felt wary. Her desire for a man—Bear—had let her into trouble once before.

Mamut went very still. He regarded her closely. "If I went to your father and asked for you, would you consent to marry me?"

"No!" she snapped, but a little voice in her mind cried, "*Yes!*" She silenced it.

Mamut relaxed and shrugged his massive shoulders. "Then it is well I did not ask for you, is it not?" he said in a hard voice. He did not like being rejected by this woman. Her kiss had not rejected him, he remembered.

He walked up to her, uncaring that the children were there, that any passing member of the band could see him. He stared down at her. She glared back at him.

"You had better understand one thing," he said, his voice a low growl. "I captured you and I am keeping you. You are my captive!" He tapped his massive chest with his thumb for emphasis. Her wide eyes followed his gesture.

"No," she said, stepping forward to meet him. Her heart pounded and she thought sweat beaded her forehead, but she refused to back down. She was shaking in anger. "*You* understand something!"

Mamut waited, his frown ferocious.

"I am not going to stay here and be your captive! You may have the strength, but you do not have the right!"

"The right?" he laughed. "You stubborn woman! I have the right that my strength gives me. And that is to keep you here."

He glanced at the children. "Besides, where would you go? You have three children to care for. To feed. To provide meat for," he said pointedly.

"I can hunt for them," she said.

"Antelope?"

"If I have to."

He laughed.

"Rabbits," she said, stung by his mockery.

"Rabbits," he sneered. "Oh, very good. The children will grow very big and strong on rabbits."

She thought it sounded feeble herself. She stuck her chin out, not willing to give up. "I will not let you come to my tent." She wished now that she had not told him she was planning to escape. The words had slipped out in her haste and anger. Perhaps he had not noticed. She would not mention it again.

She did not have to. Mamut was already angry enough that she was refusing him. He leaned closer. His big hand closed upon her arm. She tensed and he felt the strength of her in surprise. But then, he had seen her drag the antelope, and he had certainly felt her strength that day when they had first struggled. *She is strong*, he thought. And that made him want her all the more. "You cannot win against me," he growled, his gaze searing her. "I can take you whenever I want to."

True, she conceded. "I will fight you with everything I have in me. I have already been attacked—"

Her hand flew to her mouth. She had said too much.

Mamut's eyes narrowed. This sounded interesting. "You have been captured before? If so, you should know you have no choices."

She wanted to shriek. "Captured? Is that all you

have on your mind? No, I have not been captured before! Once is enough!"

"Once is never enough."

"What are you talking about?" she glared.

"Who attacked you?" he barked, anger rising at the man who had hurt this woman.

"I do not wish to speak of it."

His grip tightened. "Tell me."

"Why? You cannot do anything worse than has already been done to me."

His eyes widened in disbelief, and he dropped his hand. "Beaten? Raped? What was it?" he snarled.

"Those are things that you would do to me, so what does it matter?"

She sounded dispirited all of a sudden. He did not like to see his Bison captive like that. "I will not beat you nor rape you," he growled. "I do not need to resort to such tactics."

She glared at him. He was so handsome no woman would ever refuse him, she thought resentfully. He was sure of himself, too, the fool.

She turned her back to him.

He swung her around to face him.

"There are Mammoth men in this very camp who beat their women," she spat.

He frowned. "You speak of Lern."

"If you know that he beats Rana, why have you not done something to stop it?"

"What can I do?"

"Tell him to stop! It is not right that he beats her. He will kill her." Inspiration seized her. "And you know how you Mammoth men need women."

"I do not choose to tell Lern how to live his life."

"Then you think it is fine for a man to beat his wife." Her voice was dead as she said the words.

He lifted her chin. "I did not say that. I said I did not wish to interfere in Lern's life. I do not beat women. I never, ever struck my first wife, Cala. I loved her—" He stopped at the sudden look upon Terah's face.

A spasm of pain crossed Terah's face, and Mamut was surprised at the reaction. "What is the matter?"

She turned her face from him. He loved his first wife. What chance did she, Terah, have for his love? Until now, she had not realized she had even been hoping for it. "I must get on with the meat preparation," she said in a dull voice.

"What did I say?" he asked in genuine amazement.

"Nothing." She shook her head. "I was just . . . coming to my senses."

"I think not," he snapped, irritated.

"Think what you want," she returned, but with little bravado. She had to get away from this man—she had to! If she stayed around him for much longer, she would get so confused she would be begging him to come to her tent, children or no.

"I need some water," she said to him. She had to get him to leave so that she could think clearly.

"Carrying water is women's work."

"Oh, well, just go away then." What was the

danger? She would never beg this man to come to her tent, ever!

Exasperated, he stomped off.

"Mamut," she called softly.

He halted, his back to her.

"Among Bison men, carrying water is not women's work."

Was that an apology in her voice? He swung around to face her. She was watching him, her green eyes gleaming.

He watched her, sensing that she was testing him in some way. He walked back to where she stood beside the dead antelope. What did she want? He tried to read her face, but he saw only those green eyes. He leaned forward, about to get lost in them once again. Then he caught himself. "I do not beat or rape women," he said at last. "I will not hurt you. But I expect you to behave like a wife."

"I am not a wife!" she snapped. "We are not married. You have not asked my father for me. My father has not given you the spears."

"What are you talking about? What spears?"

She sighed impatiently. "The gifts! My father has not given you the dowry gifts that go with me."

Mamut stared at her, then frowned. "The Mammoth People," he stated carefully, "give gifts *to* the woman's family. We do not take gifts *from* the woman's family." The very idea bothered him. "And who gets the children?" he demanded.

She looked at him askance. "Why, the woman's family, of course. That is why we give the gifts.

When the man accepts the spears, then he knows that any children of the marriage belong to her family, not his. That is the agreement."

"No," he said evenly, "it is not." His obsidian eyes flashed. "Not with the Mammoth People. We men give the gifts to the woman's family so that the children belong to us, the men!"

"Why, that is foolish!" Terah had never heard of such a thing. Suddenly a horrified look crossed her face. "You cannot have the children!" she shrieked.

"What children?" he asked, bewildered.

Her eyes wide in shock, she stared at him. "Our children," she croaked in a tiny voice.

He went off humming.

Chapter 16

The children would not go to sleep. Terah ran a weary hand across her brow. Would they ever fall asleep this night? Dusk was descending outside the tent, and she thought the pale light was keeping them awake.

Kell and Tika had just accused each other of taking up all the space under the bison robe. Now they were engaged in a full-fledged pushing and wrestling match under the covers.

"Stop!" ordered Terah, to no avail. The pushing and shoving became even more frantic. Bison robes went flying across the tent. Terah crawled over and placed a hand on each of the combatants. "You must stop this," she said sternly. "It is time to sleep."

By the time the children had finally finished arguing their respective cases for why they

should each have three-fourths of the bed,
Terah was exhausted and had lost her concen-
tration. Unable to remember what Chee would
have done in such a situation, she drew a line
down the middle of the bed. "This side," she said
firmly, "is Kell's. This side"—equally firm— "is
Tika's."

"No!" cried Kell and Tika together.

Terah tried to encourage herself that the children had at least agreed on something.

"This is mine," said Tika, drawing the line
across the bed. She was sitting on the upper
half of the bed.

"Mine!" yelled Kell, leaping onto the second
half of the bed.

Terah agreed swiftly. Anything to get the
children to go to sleep! Finally the children
settled down, lying at right angles to how they
normally slept in the bed, but Terah was too
tired to care. "Just go to sleep," she moaned.

Soon she heard tiny little snores coming from
Tika and slow, even breathing coming from
Kell. They were asleep! Terah said a prayer of
gratitude to the Great Spirit.

But now Flori started to whimper. Terah
rose to peer at the little one, only to find
that the child had wet the bed robes. Flori,
at two summers of age, had been doing very
well at relieving herself outside the tent. But
sometimes she slipped up.

Terah padded over to find a small rumpled
hare hide. She stuffed it with moss that she
kept in a basket in the tent for just such

occasions. She tied the diaper around Flori's chubby little bottom. Rubbing the child's back, Terah crooned a lullaby. As she sang the words, she watched Flori's little eyes close, the lashes long upon her cheek. She could tell the moment Flori passed into sleep. Her rosebud mouth was pursed, and she looked unutterably sweet to Terah.

A pang of sadness that Chee was not here to see her daughter shot through Terah, followed swiftly by a great relief. They were asleep at last! Now *she* could rest.

Terah lay in the tent, listening to the wind, staring into the blackness. She was too restless to sleep this night. She began to wonder if Mamut was going to come to her as he had said he would. She wondered if her refusal meant anything to him. She wondered if all the noise from the children had scared him off.

It was sometime later that she awoke to a sound just outside her dwelling. She sat up, blinking in the dark. Someone was entering the tent!

The nerve of Mamut! she thought in irritation. She fumbled for her white chert knife. Perhaps she could brandish it and convince him that she meant what she said. But before she could pick up the knife, two hard hands seized her. One hand clamped cruelly over her mouth, the other anchored her waist. She was dragged over and pulled up against a hard male body.

Her nostrils flared. A sour, unwashed smell greeted her nose. This was not Mamut! she thought in alarm. She widened her eyes in the dark, trying desperately to glimpse her attacker. She caught a flicker of a tattooed spider. A harsh chuckle in her ear gave her another clue. It was Lern.

"If you scream, the little ones will walk the Death Trail this very night."

Terah shuddered. Lern began planting wet sloppy kisses on the back of her neck. Her skin crawled. She struggled against his tight grip. He chuckled low in his throat, obviously amused at her struggles.

She was not amused. She was frantic. It was happening again, she thought wildly. First Bear, now Lern. What was it about her that made men think they could attack her?

Furious now and uncaring of the danger, she let loose an angry yell. Lern jerked and stared at her. Obviously he had thought his threat to kill the children would be enough to silence her.

Well, it was not, she thought and kicked out at him. She snatched up her knife and, with teeth bared, snarled at him, "Get out!"

He grabbed the hilt of the knife and they struggled. Terah held on to the knife, but he dragged her across the tent floor. She was reaching with her other hand to yank on his hair when he raised his fist. Another second and his fist would come crashing into her face.

Suddenly the tent flap opened, and a large arm encircled Lern's throat and yanked him out of the tent.

On her knees, panting, Terah scrambled after

him. No one was going to deprive her of her victory!

From outside the tent came a series of grunts and thuds. She blinked, trying to see what was going on. Rana's fire lit part of the camp, and she saw that Mamut was on top of Lern. Lern had stopped struggling. Terah heard the hate in his voice as he growled, "Let me go!"

Mamut, in a rage and panting, wanted to kill Lern. That Lern should dare to attack Mamut's captive, *his* woman, was beyond understanding. Mamut's fingers were at his enemy's throat and squeezing. Suddenly a restraining hand touched his shoulder.

"Let him go," said the shaman in a calm voice. "Do not kill him."

"He deserves death," snarled Mamut.

"Perhaps," said the shaman mildly. "But that is not for you to decide. Let him go."

Mamut's nostrils flared as he stared down at Lern's fearful, upturned face. *So easy*, he thought. *It would be so easy to kill him.* Lern deserved it, after what he had tried to do. Mamut knew that Lern was in the tent for one reason—to rape Terah. Anger went through him and his fingers tightened reflexively.

Lern's eyes bulged and he gasped.

Terah watched Mamut. She wanted him to kill Lern. At this moment, she loathed Lern with such intensity that she could barely breathe. "Kill him!" she cried.

Her exclamation caused Mamut to glance at her. Chest heaving, eyes wild, she looked furious.

"Kill him," she said again. But Terah was not seeing Lern laying there, with Mamut's fingers around his throat. She was seeing Bear. All her fury and rage at Bear was added to her fury and rage at Lern. She was an inferno of fear and rage. "Kill him!"

Lern reached up and touched one of Mamut's hands. Gently. In supplication. Lern's brown eyes pleaded.

Mamut glared down at him. He had known Lern all his life. Lern was part of his band of Mammoth People. Mamut shook his head, trying to clear it. If he killed Lern as his heated fury told him and as his captive woman demanded, Mamut would be murdering a man of his own people. Did he want to do that? Death was forever. His father's death had taught him that. His father and another were dead by his hand, and he had to live with that knowledge every single day of his life.

If Lern was killed by Mamut's hand, could Mamut ever feel right about that? He looked down into Lern's black, frightened eyes, and all of a sudden Mamut knew that this day he would spare Lern.

Slowly he removed his hands from Lern's throat. Lern took a great gasp of air. Mamut swung off Lern's chest. "Get up," he growled.

Lern felt his throat with cautious hands, then carefully sat up. When he saw that Mamut did not attack him, he gingerly rose out of the dirt.

Around them had gathered the Mammoth People. They were all there—Spearpoint, the shaman, Rana, Kutchka, Benaleese with her older husband, Spark, the six other Mammoth men, and finally, Lame Leg, holding on to Wolf Boy. All of them had crawled out of their tents and come running to see what had happened. Now they stared at Mamut and Lern and Terah.

Terah, seeing Mamut move off Lern, wanted to leap upon the downed man herself. Then she caught a glimpse of Rana's face. The older woman looked drawn and pale, and her eyes were focused intently on her young husband.

Rana did not want Lern to die, Terah suddenly realized. But he deserved to die, she thought grimly. Why, he had raised his fist to strike Terah just as he had raised his fist to strike Rana so many times before. He deserved to die!

Mamut watched Lern. "Stay away from my tent," he snarled. "Next time I will not spare you." Whether he would or would not spare Lern, Mamut did not honestly know. He only knew that this one time he would not carry the burden of Lern's death. "Do not attack my woman again!"

Lern stared at Mamut. Then he looked at the shaman. "You must not do this again," said the shaman soothingly. "It is wrong to attack women. It is wrong, too," said the shaman in a loud voice, "to strike a woman." Several pairs of eyes shifted to Rana and back to Lern.

So, thought Terah, others in this camp know that Lern smote his wife. Why did they not stop it, then?

eresa Scott

Murmurs swirled around them. "It is cowardly," said one man in a stern voice. Lern jerked as though he had been struck. He found something fascinating to stare at on the ground.

"You are stronger than a woman. You should not clout one."

"We need our women, our children," rang out Spearpoint's voice. Terah could hear bitterness in it. "Did you learn nothing from the Winter of Death? How many times must we lose women and children before you value them? Your beatings could kill Rana."

"And you could have killed Terah," snarled Mamut. His eyes were hard. "Do not come near her, or the children, again. If you do, I will demand that the Mammoth People banish you."

Several loud murmurs went up from the gathered people at this statement. Evidently the Mammoth People would assent to Lern's banishment, if asked.

A gasp rose from Rana. She covered her face with both hands. Banishment was a terrible penalty to a man or woman. It meant being driven off from the Mammoth People and wandering alone, for the rest of a miserable, solitary, probably short life. The banished person was treated as though he was dead. No one spoke his name. His family held a burial ceremony. As far as the Mammoth People were concerned, after a man was banished, he did not exist.

Lern lifted a trembling hand to Rana. He pried one of her hands away from her tear-stained face.

oter
204

Terah expected Rana to snatch her hand away. After all, the man had beaten Rana several times. Why should she help him?

Rana stared at her husband, then slowly her fingers intertwined with his.

Terah felt angry and bewildered. Was he going to take Rana to their tent and beat her in his frustration?

Head down, leading his wife, Lern walked through the surrounding people. Men and women stepped aside. In silence, Lern went to his tent. He ducked and entered. Rana turned to look at the gathered people. Then she too ducked and entered the tent.

The Mammoth People began to stir themselves and return to their tents.

Mamut turned to Terah. "I will stay in the tent with you," he announced.

Terah nodded, albeit reluctantly. "It is safest," she whispered. Then her anger returned. "I wanted you to kill him," she hissed.

Mamut regarded his Bison captive woman. He shook his head. "I stopped him. That was enough. To take a man's life is a serious thing. It is the worst kind of stealing. You steal all the things that man will ever do or think or love. You steal all the good things he would have done as well as the bad."

Terah frowned. She did not understand this Mamut at all.

Mamut sighed. "He will not come after you again."

"If he does, I will kill him," said Terah tersely.

Mamut shrugged. "Then you will live with him in your head," he said.

"What do you mean?"

Mamut fingered the ivory bead at his throat. "I mean," he said softly, "that if you kill a man, it is something you will always remember. Whether you do it intentionally or accidentally, it is something you will live with every day of your life." He saw the disbelief on her face. "Oh, sometimes you will forget. For a short time. You will see a beautiful sunset, and then a tiny reminder will come to you that the person you killed will never see such beauty ever again. Or you will feel love for a child, and a tiny reminder will come to you that the person you killed will never, *ever*, again feel love like you are feeling."

Mamut reached for a strand of her hair and gazed into her eyes. His own were as black as night. "Killing is something done when there is no other choice. I prefer not to do it."

"Some people deserve to die," gritted Terah.

Mamut nodded. "Yes, they do. But to take the responsibility to kill them is a serious thing. For you. That is what I am trying to say. It hurts you, too. Do you understand what I am saying?"

"No."

Mamut regarded his woman thoughtfully. She had no doubts about killing, he thought. Probably she had never killed anyone, only wanted to. Well, he hoped that she would never find out what it was like to be responsible for a man's death. "Come," he said, holding back the tent flap. "It is time to sleep."

Terah glanced at him, but she could detect nothing in his expression or voice that said he was going to take up where Lern had left off. Reluctantly, she followed him into the tent. His tent.

Chapter 17

Terah sank slowly onto the bed robes where she usually slept. She could not take her eyes off Mamut, though he was only a deeper shadow in the darkness of the tent. She could hear Tika's tiny snores, Kell's slow rhythmic breaths, and Flori's faster ones. Part of her mind registered that the children had slept through Lern's attack. But then her thoughts flew back to Mamut. What was he going to do? What did she *want* him to do?

Mamut glanced around, his eyes adjusting to the dim light. He saw the sleeping children, the wide eyes of his captive woman, and the small space of the tent. There did not look to be enough bed robes for him. "I will get my musk-ox robe," he said gruffly and left.

Terah let out her breath when he left, feeling

a twinge of reprieve and something else. Disappointment? But she did not have long to dwell on her feelings before he was back, outside the tent.

She stared straight ahead—at his long legs, then up past the blanket, past the wide shoulders until she met his eyes. There was a bemused expression on his face, as if he wondered what to do next. That could not possibly be, she thought. He had all the power. He could do whatever he wanted. The thought sent a tiny thrill of excitement down her spine.

He glanced to where she lay. He shook the musk-ox robe, and little pieces of fur drifted down. He must have tanned the hide himself, she thought irrelevantly.

He crawled into the tent and set the hide down beside the robe where Terah sat. She inched away, but he noticed the telltale movement. *She is afraid,* he thought, and anger at Lern for attacking her flared up once more inside him. Yet if Lern had not attacked her, then Mamut would not be here, inside the tent, planning on how he could have this woman. His heart beat faster as he sat down. He thought she gave a little start, and he wondered if she would run out of the tent. He thought not; the children were here, and she would not leave them. The children. What, he thought, tapping his chin with a long forefinger, was he going to do about the children? He did not think he wanted to claim Terah for the first time with little breathing bodies all around him—little breathing bodies that could awaken at any moment.

He glanced at the tent opening. Perhaps he could entice her to walk with him down by the water. He did not think anyone would come into the tent tonight. Not after his fight against Lern. And Lern assuredly would not attempt another attack. He had looked too humiliated after the Mammoth People had raised the possibility of banishment.

Mamut surveyed the sleeping children. Yes, the children would be safe if he left them for a little while.

He glanced at Terah. She had not yet lain down; she was watching him, her eyes huge. He felt another flare of anger at Lern for his attack. Now she probably thought he would attack her as Lern had done. And he could not deny the pulsing in his body. He could feel the aftermath in his body of the alertness, the exertion, the excitement of the fight. It would be a welcome change to channel that excitement into lovemaking.

He stretched, every one of his senses taut and alive. He was thoroughly aware of the desirable woman next to him. "I cannot sleep," he muttered. "That fight with Lern is keeping me awake." He glanced at her, and he saw her shrink back a tiny bit. "You, too?"

Terah nodded. But it was not Lern's attack that was keeping her from her rest. It was Mamut. His closeness, his warmth, his strength, his immense desirability . . . She tried to shake the spell of him away. She could not. She took a deep breath. She wanted him, had for some time. How could she pretend otherwise? She had been straightforward

211

in her desire for Bear, and that was a feeble desire compared to how she wanted this man. She shifted restlessly. What was she going to do?

"Would you like to go for a walk?" he broke in on her thoughts. The question sounded casual to her, as though he did not care one way or the other about her answer.

Terah glanced at the sleeping children. "Do you think they will be safe?"

He shrugged. "Lern will not leave his tent for the rest of this night." Terah heard the confidence in his voice and believed him. "He has been shamed in front of the Mammoth People. He will want to hide for a time."

"You sound as if you know Lern well," she could not help but observe.

"I do. I have known him all my life."

"Do you like him?" Curiosity pried at her. She did not like Lern, but she wondered if Mamut did. After all, he had chosen not to kill the man.

Mamut sighed and shrugged. "I care little for him." He shrugged. "But I do not wish to carry his death on my mind."

Mamut met her eyes, and she strained to see him in the dim light. "Do you want to walk?" he asked again.

"Yes."

He let out his breath. He had not realized her answer meant so much to him. If he could get her down by the water, away from the others . . . He tried to slow his racing heart, a futile gesture.

He rose, keeping the musk-ox robe in front of him. He did not want her to see the hard evidence of his desire for her. He walked to the tent flap and turned. She had not moved, was still watching him. "Come," he said softly.

As though in a trance, Terah rose. She ducked out of the tent behind him. They passed by the other tents, quiet now. Fires had burned down to embers. There was the occasional snore as they passed a tent, but calmness reigned.

Wolf Boy padded up to them, and Mamut put out his hand. The dog laid his cold, wet nose in the man's palm and wagged his tail slowly. Then he padded away. Mamut said, "Wolf Boy is guarding the camp. He will alert me with his barks if there is any trouble."

Terah felt relieved. They would not be leaving the children alone. And not for long.

She followed Mamut down the rocky, narrow trail that led to the pool by the river. They came close to the still, quiet body of water. Mamut halted. Two deer, one obviously the mother, the other her half-grown fawn, bounded away at their approach. Some of the animals, like deer, chose to drink water at night, but most preferred to drink in the day, when they could watch for predators sneaking up on them.

Terah glanced around. Bullrushes grew at the edge of the lake. Stars winked overhead in the indigo sky. Here was quiet, peace, all very welcome to her after Lern's earlier attack. She let herself relax.

Mamut glanced around, looking for any sign of saber-tooths or dire wolves. He saw nothing and sensed nothing. He thought they would not come so close to the camp in any event because the Mammoth People had been camped near the pool for some time. For too long, assuredly; there was little game left in the area. And still the bison herds had not come. Resolutely, he pushed aside thoughts of survival.

Tonight he would concentrate on the beautiful woman at his side. He turned to her and took her hand. She hesitated, then reached out and placed one hand in his. He closed his hand upon her slender fingers and smiled to himself.

He led her to a grassy spot near a willow tree. He glanced around, again looking for saber-tooths. Nothing. He dropped the robe and sank down upon it. The soft grass cushioned the musk-ox robe. He gave a little tug, and Terah followed him. They sat together, looking out at the water. The moon was rising, peeping from behind a hill, and its silvery light gave a cool glow. Mamut relaxed. He could watch for dire wolves easily by its light.

The moon also lit the soft brown hair of the woman beside him. Unbidden, his fingers reached out and touched the soft texture. She gave a tiny start. He said soothingly, "Your hair is very beautiful."

She bowed her head for a moment, not knowing what to say. He put a finger under her chin and lifted her face, forcing her to meet his eyes. "You are very beautiful."

Terah tried to close her eyes against the soothing words, to shut out the caress in his voice. But she leaned forward, infinitesimally. He noted the reaction. So, she liked words in lovemaking. He would give her words.

It had been a long time since he had had a woman, and his body was reminding him of that fact. Cala had died two, almost three winters ago, and he had been without a woman all that time. He had missed Cala so much. He looked at Terah, wondering if this woman was going to mean as much to him as Cala had. He pushed the thought away. It did not matter. She was his; she could not leave. He owned her. What matter if she meant anything to him or not?

He leaned forward and touched her lips with his. They were soft and pliable. She was willing, he thought, and his heart leapt. He reached for her and drew her closer to him, groaning in his need. It had been too long.

Terah closed her eyes and let him kiss her. At first, she felt only the warmth and gentleness of his kiss; then, as he pulled her closer, his desire lit hers. She reached up and put her arms around his neck. He needed no further encouragement. They clung to each other, his lips moving on hers. Terah thought she would scream from wanting him so much. Instead she groaned.

His hands roamed her body now, and she did nothing to stop him. He was touching her skin under her robe, and he began pulling at the deerskin tunic she wore. She gave a little giggle at his haste. "Let me," she said, and pulled it off over her head.

He gasped when he saw her breasts in the moonlight. He touched them, gently, reverently.

He did not think he could wait much longer for her.

The touch of his hand on her breasts roused Terah and she leaned forward into the firmness of his hands. He was kissing her again, hot, hard kisses. He groaned and had to stop while he peeled off his leather leggings. In an agony of desire, she waited. He kicked the garment away and pulled off his moccasins. Both were now naked on the robe.

He looked at her perfect body in the silvery light. "Lo! You are so beautiful," he breathed. He wanted nothing more than to have her under him.

He pushed her gently down on the robe, and she went willingly. Terah gazed up at him hovering over her, the white ivory bead of his necklace catching the moonlight and gleaming dully. She smiled at him, welcoming him openly. He was so strong, so handsome to her. And she wanted him.

He positioned himself over her and pushed steadily into her. She gave a gasp, and her face convulsed.

She has not been with a man before, he thought. And he felt a humble gratitude that he should be the first man for her. Something savage and primitive in him snarled that he wanted to be the *only* man for her.

He drew back a tiny bit. "I will be as gentle as I can," he told her. She pushed at his shoulders, as though trying to push him off her.

"No," he murmured, kissing her. "We have gone too far for that."

She stopped pushing as his kisses warmed her again. She pulled at his shoulders and he went with her, breaking through the tiny skin barrier that would keep him out. He felt her tense, and with inhuman will, he halted, not wanting to hurt her. He felt her relax again, and then he plunged forward. He could not stop himself. "Too long without a woman," he muttered. Then an overwhelming, sweet explosion filled his head and body.

Terah watched him, feeling him fill her. She felt him stiffen, then collapse on top of her. She frowned. What was this all about? Was this all there was to making love?

Mamut bent his forehead down to hers and closed his eyes. He had seen the disappointment on her face and he wanted to chuckle, but he was too exhausted. He had satisfied Cala too often and seen too many hungry glances from other women to worry about Terah's disappointment. He knew he could satisfy her.

He slipped out of her and began to kiss her again. He caressed her, running his hands over her smooth body. Soon she was panting once more, her soft gasping breaths a delight to his ears.

And he was more than ready for her. He surged into her, his hand between them, moving her delicate bud in slow circles.

A feeling grew in Terah, a deliciousness that grew and spread outward from the center of her body. The sweetness built until she wanted to scream. Then she exploded, and it was as if her

217

brain convulsed completely. She turned inside out and back again. She clutched him to her, wanting him to hold her forever.

When she went limp, Mamut smiled to himself in masculine satisfaction. It had been good for her.

Terah came out of the massive explosion in a daze. This was what it was like to make love, she thought. This was what it was like!

She wrapped her arms around him, the beautiful haze she was in so relaxing that she felt limp. She felt beautiful, too, and desirable. And all because of this man. She hugged him to her, wanting to stay with him forever.

Chapter 18

Terah sat outside the tent, her mind working as swiftly as her busy hands that stretched the camel hide. Her intimate parts were sore this morning.

Tika and Kell played "bison hunt" nearby and Flori napped in the tent.

Terah pulled on the hide. Last night had been a joyous entry into womanhood for her. Mamut's tenderness and skill came back to her, and she shivered in remembrance. Self-consciously, she glanced around, but no one noticed the red flush on her high cheekbones.

So this was what being a woman was about, she thought happily. This knowledge of a man, the joining together of bodies—and yes, of hearts. And those kisses. It was all so sublime. She felt joyous too, that her desire for a man,

Theresa Scott

that immense feeling of attraction that had been so cruelly deadened by Bear, was now brought to life again with Mamut. And *this* time, desire had led her well. To be a fulfilled, physically pleasured woman was a marvelous thing.

After their lovemaking, she and Mamut had returned to the tent. Terah had gone willingly to him then, proud and naked. They had slipped under the bedrobes, and she had cuddled up beside him. When she fell asleep, it was with one brawny arm wrapped around her waist. She thought to herself at the time that he was holding her as though he would never let her go, that he shared her desire.

But in the morning, when she had awakened, soft and shy, Mamut was gone. She had tried to stave off the feeling of loneliness that washed over her. She tried to concentrate upon her happiness in being a woman, but still the loneliness crept in, like an unwanted dire wolf skulking at the edges of a feast. She missed Mamut terribly and wanted him with her. She wanted, too, to reassure herself that last night had truly happened. That they had made beautiful love.

Then Terah halted in mid-pull on the camel hide. Why had Mamut been so eager to leave her? Did he, could he. . . . She swallowed. Perhaps Mamut did not find her attractive.

Shaken at the thought, she looked sideways at her light brown hair. It fell to below her shoulders. She stroked it. Soft. Her hair was pretty; her mother had always told her so.

She reached up and stroked her face, feeling

the cheekbones and slanted eyebrows, her nose—
a tiny bit too flat perhaps—and her wide mouth.
Her face was beautiful; her eyes, too. Chee had
told her that.

But, she mused, perhaps Mammoth men were
only attracted to women who had brown eyes
and black hair, like Benaleese. Even pregnant,
Benaleese was lovely. And Rana's dark eyes and
graying hair were attractive remnants of her
younger beauty. Terah frowned. Perhaps that
was it. Mamut did not find her attractive.

Terah tapped the stretched hide with one finger
as she pondered. She no longer lied to herself
about her attraction to Mamut. He was wonderful to look upon with his rugged face, his black
eyes, his massive shoulders and long legs. She
sighed. Everything about him attracted her. He
was far better looking than One Shoe or Bear.
Remembering Bear, she frowned. Why had she
been attracted to Bear? Oh, yes, it was because
of his skills in running, wrestling, and hunting.
Well, Mamut did all those things and did them
very well. Far better than Bear, she thought in
satisfaction.

Terah stretched another section of camel hide,
tugging at the tawny skin. A dreamy look crossed
her face as she thought of Mamut.

Presently, she looked up from her hide-
stretching and saw Benaleese walk by. Terah
gave a polite nod, but Benaleese either did not
see her or pretended not to. Terah shrugged. It
did not matter to her what Benaleese did.

She watched the pregnant woman walk past.

221

Benaleese would deliver her babe in another month or so, judging by the size of her torso, thought Terah. Benaleese walked past Lame Leg's ratty tent. She gave the dozing girl a sharp kick and continued on her way. She reached Rana's tent and called out a greeting. Receiving a reply, she ducked and entered.

Terah stared. The casualness of Benaleese's brutality appalled Terah. She walked over to Lame Leg. The child took one look at her and crawled into her tent. Terah frowned and went back to the hide she'd been stretching. The fear she had seen on Lame Leg's face told much. The child was not used to kind treatment, expecting only cruelty.

Uneasily, resolving to treat the child with dignity, Terah went back to stretching the hide. After a while her thoughts meandered back to Mamut. She wondered if Mamut would go to her father now and ask for her. The idea held great appeal. And if Mamut wanted her for a wife, he must understand that it was her father who should be the one to give the spears. That was how marriages were arranged among the Bison People. That was how marriages should be arranged with all people.

Though now that she thought on it, gifts had been given to the Great Frog People for her friend, Rana. And Rana had deemed it right and proper for the Mammoth people to give gifts for her when she had married Lern.

Terah frowned. There was also the matter of children. She wanted the children, any children between her and Mamut, to be *hers*. She was certain of that. Her father giving the spears promised that. Perhaps if Mamut gave his gifts to her father, and her father gave the spears to Mamut . . . no, no, it would not work. That was not the Bison People's way. And the Bison People's way was the correct way. Mamut must receive the spears from her father. That was the correct thing to do.

Having settled that matter in her mind, Terah glanced at the children. Tika was rolling around in the dirt, bellowing. Obviously she was the wounded bison. And Kell was the mighty hunter. Terah smiled to herself. All the talk in camp had been about the bison hunt. Her smile faded. Except that the bison had not yet appeared. She hoped that they came soon so that the Mammoth People would be able to dry much meat for winter. The mornings were cooler now, and winter was not far away.

She glanced at the clouded sky, and a sudden thought jolted her. The longer she stayed with the Mammoth People, helping them get ready for winter, the less chance she had to escape and find her Bison People. But now she did not need to escape, she soothed herself. Now Mamut would ask her father for her.

And to be honest with herself, there were many days when she did not feel like planning an escape at all. Tika and Kell and Flori were settled in with the Mammoth People. They had plenty of food to eat. They lived in a big tent, with strong men to guard them from predatory animals. She noticed

Theresa Scott

that the children asked less and less often about their parents.

If Mamut were to ask her father for her in marriage, she would be very happy to stay with the Mammoth People. As long as Lern kept away from her, at any rate.

She looked down at the skin she was preparing. This skin would make fine warm leggings for Mamut for the winter. Terah smiled to herself. She could surprise him with the leggings. And she had almost finished making a beautiful set of thick-soled moccasins from the spotted saber-tooth skin. The moccasins reached midway to the knee, in the Bison People's style of footwear. Terah had hidden them away in a corner of the tent. All she needed were some beads to decorate them with. Yes, they would also make a fine gift for Mamut.

Terah wondered if she should just ask Mamut outright if he would ask her father for her. But if he said no, she could not stand the thought of his rejection. If he did not want her, she thought perhaps she would die. She had thought she wanted Bear, at first, but that wanting was as nothing compared to how she wanted Mamut now. Yet what if he turned out to be like Bear? She had thought Bear was kind. How mistaken she had been! What if she made the same mistake with Mamut?

She thought back about him—his defense of her against Lern, his kindness to her and the children, his gentleness when making love. No, she decided judiciously, he was not like Bear.

224

Mamut did not act like a sweet and friendly man and then change into a raging animal.

Would Mamut ask her father for her?

Her thoughts were interrupted by Spearpoint's sudden appearance in the camp. Terah glanced over and saw Spearpoint waving his arms and doing a little dance. She rose to her feet.

"We found the bison!" he cried in jubilation. He held up all the fingers on both hands. "A large herd of them!"

So that was where Mamut had gone, Terah thought. Bison hunting. She sighed. A little part of her wished he had stayed to linger with her this morning, instead of being so conscientious and going off to hunt for his people. Still, he was an admirable man. He knew his people had to find the bison before harsh winter arrived, and so he had done all he could to help them. She felt torn between chagrin and pride in him.

The Mammoth People were dancing around and giving happy cries in their excitement at finding the bison.

Spearpoint held up one finger. "We killed one of them!" There were more happy cries at this news.

Then the camp erupted into purposeful activity as the four adult women ran to take down their tents and collect all their belongings in preparation for the move to the butchering grounds. Skinning knives were swiftly sharpened, tent hides rolled up, and dried meat pulled off the meat racks and stuffed into baskets. Tika and Kell ran to the water to fill the bison bladders.

When they returned, the two children put their hands to their heads in imitation of bison horns and swung at each other, bellowing excitedly.

When they had finally packed up everything, Terah sent Tika over to help Rana. Then Terah caught a glimpse of Lame Leg, awkwardly taking down her tent. Terah marched over with Flori, set the baby down and swiftly rolled up the tattered hide that had housed Lame Leg. Wolf Boy ran in excited little circles.

It was a happy group that followed Spearpoint to where the hunters had found the bison. Terah was surprised at how far back into the hills they had to walk. They came to a glacier creek as wide as two men; its icy waters churned a path between the hills. Spearpoint led them up the creek toward the source for some distance. Then he disappeared through a draw. Terah and the children struggled along, single-file, carrying the bundles and baskets and belongings. Each footstep had to be placed with care because of the sharp rocks.

Terah had not seen Lame Leg for some time. With Flori riding on her hip, Terah retraced her steps back along the treacherous path. She caught sight of Lame Leg, straggling far behind the rest of the Mammoth People. The ragged child was the last one through the draw. Terah worried that wolves might attack the child. Without saying a word, certain that Lame Leg would refuse were Terah to ask, Terah took a big basket from the child's grasp and set it on her other hip. Thus lightened, the limping child was able to catch up to the others. When at last they passed through the draw to the other side, Terah handed the basket back to its owner.

"Thank you," murmured Lame Leg. Dark brown eyes gazed unblinking at Terah through the long, matted hair that covered part of the child's face. Terah nodded acknowledgment and walked over to where Tika and Kell were sitting after their climb through the draw.

Now that they had made it through to the other side, Terah glanced around. She surveyed a flat plateau that stretched for a great distance. Yellow, waving grass rippled gently across the plateau toward her. The north edge of the plateau dropped away sharply.

Terah stared. For so long she had seen only brown hills and green, tree-lined river that she had thought the world could not look any different.

She watched the bison herd. There were about twenty of the huge animals. The bison were at a distance and looked small, but Terah was not fooled. A bison was a huge animal with a spread between its two sharp horns that was greater than the length of a tall man.

Several of the beasts dozed in the wallows they so loved. These wallows were dusty shallows that each animal scooped out for itself. Terah watched as one of the big animals rolled in the dust, its back legs kicking the air as it sought to cover its thin flanks with a coating of dust to keep off the biting flies.

A few of the bison stood nosing at the grass.

Usually bison preferred to eat early in the morning and at dusk. It was midday now, and most of these animals lay in their wallows and chewed their cud. The few nosing the grass were not particularly hungry, she thought.

As Terah watched, one of them lifted its great shaggy head with its huge standing mane. He sniffed the air. Terah knew that bison had an excellent sense of smell but very poor eyesight. That was why they grazed facing into the wind, so that they could smell any approaching danger. Terah relaxed because their strong bison scent was being blown toward her by the wind. The bison did not yet know that the Mammoth People were watching them.

The lead animal, a bull, looked around for a time, shaking its great shaggy head uneasily, then resumed nosing at the grass once more.

Terah spotted the carcass of the one dead bison that Spearpoint had reported earlier. It looked huge. To another bison, it probably looked as if it were asleep in its wallow. She hoped the dead animal was a cow. The hide of a bull bison, although warm and woolly, would be wasted. A bull's hide, thick as Terah's two thumbs placed side by side, was just too thick to be tanned properly.

Terah watched as the hunters stalked the great beasts. She narrowed her eyes, searching for Mamut, but she could not pick him out at this distance.

The men walked slowly, carrying their spears and atlatls—notched sticks that spears fit into.

Atlatls gave added penetration power to a spear thrust.

The men moved slowly to the north, toward the drop-off. She guessed their strategy at once. This was how the Bison People hunted too.

The hunters, careful not to do anything to scare the bison, kept walking in a steady line toward the north. The bull bison who had sniffed the air began moving toward the north also. It was a natural reaction—bison instinctively avoided being outflanked. Several of the other bison got up from their wallows and began following the lead bull.

The hunters herded the unwary bison toward the drop-off. Which man was Mamut? She peered into the distance at the line of dark human shapes outlined against the pale grass.

The bison moved docilely in the direction the men wanted them to take. The lead bull began trotting.

Terah smiled to herself. Hunters had to know how a bison thought in order to kill it. Her Bison People had made a study of bison habits. She knew that bison were gregarious and liked to stay together in family groups, the cows more so than the bulls. This herd boasted seven calves born the past spring. They were now half-grown. Bison birthed calves every year. Sometimes a cow would be followed by a calf, a yearling, and a two-year old. Terah preferred the meat of cows under three years old. The older the animal, the tougher the meat. Bull meat was toughest.

Bison were also erratic and unpredictable, she

knew. Sometimes wolves could walk unmolested through a herd of bison. At other times a bison would charge a wolf.

It appeared that, for this herd, everything was going well with the hunt. The unsuspecting animals were approaching the drop-off.

Now Spearpoint moved forward, urging the women and children to start walking, too, and begin waving their arms. It was time to stampede the animals.

Terah strode forward, careful to keep an eye on little Flori. Kell and Tika ran ahead, waving their arms, delighted at being part of the hunt. Terah realized that this was their first hunt, and she glowed inside at their enthusiasm.

The cries and flapping arms of the humans sufficed to feed each animal's fear until their restive trottings became a full-fledged stampede.

At last Terah was able to pick out Mamut, taller than the rest of the hunters. She smiled to herself at seeing him move toward the herd. He was brave, she thought, brave and strong. She watched with pride as he shook his spear and called to the animals to keep moving.

Suddenly the lead bull did a sharp about-face, using his front hooves to pivot. One moment he was careening forward toward the cliff, the next moment he had whirled and was racing back the way he had come, head down and charging.

She gasped. Mamut stood directly in his path.

Mamut watched in disbelief as the bull charged him. His mind flashed the knowledge that the huge animal would surely impale him on those sharp horns.

No! he thought, forcing himself to stand his ground. He began waving his arms and kept walking toward the charging bison. *I will not run. Not this time!* Unbidden, the memory of his fright as a youth, his terrible flight from Father-Killer the mammoth, entered his mind even at this crucial moment—the moment of his death. And it tainted this moment even as it had tainted—no, rotted—every waking moment of his life.

I can never get away from it, from the fear, he thought as he watched the bison hurtle onward, great head down.

Mamut halted, fear filling him, willing himself to wait until the last possible moment before fleeing. Bison were known to charge and, sometimes, to turn and run. He stood ready to risk his life that this bull would run from him.

The fear washed over him, the fear that had stalked him since he was a boy. He gave in to it. He felt shaken through his whole body. And when he looked at the hand that had raised the spear—without conscious message from his brain—he saw that it too shook.

But he could not, would not, run any longer. He had run all his life, he realized. Run from the knowledge that he was a coward, the knowledge that he lived with his people under a terrible pretence. Now he would face this charging animal and die. But he would die not as he had lived, a coward, but would die free—free from the fear, free from the terrible rot of cowardice.

These thoughts swirled through his brain in a pulsebeat before calm overtook him. He gripped the spear, hoping for one good thrust before he went down under the great pounding hooves. He raised his spear arm, man against giant beast. He drew his arm back, readying for a powerful thrust, the thrust that would either kill the beast or kill him, and with eyes squinting for better sight, judging, calculating, he marked the best place to strike the oncoming animal, a thundering mass of heavy, angry bull.

Mamut threw the spear with all his might.

It bounced off the stone-hard forehead of the charging bison.

Mamut stood weaponless. He looked into the snorting, drooling, brown, hairy, horned face of Death and began his death chant.

Chapter 19

Mamut waited to feel the agony of sliced flesh and the ripping torment of goring horn. He sang the words of his death chant with extreme solemnity, knowing that now he would go to meet the Great Spirit. He was ready.

Suddenly the charging bison slid to a halt, flipped about as neatly as he had done when first starting the charge and dashed off—toward the cliff again.

Mamut blinked and shook his head, the words of his chant dying on his lips. He looked around him, feeling a relief that made him want to sag to the grass at his feet. A trembling coursed through his body. And then he started to laugh.

He saw the old shaman watching him, a thoughtful look upon the wrinkled face, but

Mamut shook his head, too overcome with joy and relief and freedom to be able to say any words. He thought he caught the ghost of a smile from the old one, but it vanished as the shaman ran after the stampeding herd.

Mamut wiped his face with a hand, still shaking, and pressed forward, shouting at the bison. He watched as they ran over the drop-off. It was a drop the height of four tall men and some of the animals would die instantly.

Exultant, Mamut retrieved his spear and inspected the sharp stone point for damage. Satisfied that there was none, he shook his spear at the retreating bull. "I have won!" he cried. "I am free!"

But even as he shouted the words, he wondered if he was truly free. The knowledge that he was a coward, that he had run from Father-Killer when Kran had needed him the most—that fear had dogged him his whole life. Could one bison bull charge wipe clean that cowardice? Deep in his heart, Mamut thought not.

The bull bison obligingly leaped from the cliff.

Later, the Mammoth men ran to the cliff's edge and climbed down the rocky shale slope to where several bellowing, maimed animals lay among the dead. The maimed bison were swiftly dispatched by a spear thrust through the heart or liver.

When all the bison were dead, the women and children clattered down the sliding shale goat trail that led to the bottom of the cliff.

The stench of dead animals made Terah want to hold her breath at first, but she gradually got used to the smell.

Mamut glanced around for Terah. He saw her working on a fat cow with Tika. Kell and Flori clambered over the carcass. Lern's wife, the Frog Eater woman, squatted nearby and gleefully butchered a half-grown calf.

Mamut's eyes narrowed as he watched Terah split open the bison along the spine to get at the hump meat. Then she chopped and pulled until the forelegs came off. Next, she scooped out the innards.

She handed choice morsels out to the children. Kell chewed happily on the liver, sprinkled with drops of bile. Blood ran down his chin and his little mouth pouched out. His brown eyes twinkled.

Terah caught Mamut's eye and smiled at him as she handed a dripping piece of liver to Tika. Mamut wondered if Terah was remembering how it had been for them last night. Or was she smiling because of the successful hunt?

He watched as she deftly cut into the meat, slicing chunks that she would cook immediately over the fire and setting aside other pieces of meat for the smoking racks.

He remembered those same hands running over his body last night, sending shivers down him. It had been very good between them. He stared at her a long while, unable to take his eyes off her. He wanted her even now. She was a good woman, this captive. She knew how to butcher a cow, how to dry meat, how to take care of children. She would make an excellent wife. At that thought, Mamut turned away. Such a strong woman would not want him for a husband. Not if she knew the truth—that he was a coward. The bull's challenge had only resurrected the memory of Father-Killer.

Lost in his thoughts, he walked over and began butchering a large cow. Terah watched him go out of the corner of her eye. For a moment, she had thought she read interest, desire, and . . . more? Then his face had gone cold, impassive, and he had turned away.

She touched her hair for reassurance. Was she not attractive? Did he not want her? She frowned as she watched him, his broad back and powerful muscles holding her green gaze for long moments as she watched him butcher the cow.

Then Flori cried out and pointed to her mouth. With a dispirited little sigh, Terah cut off another piece of liver and handed it to the child. Around Flori's little pink mouth were streaks of bison blood. Terah smiled. The children were happy. They had more meat to eat than their little stomachs could hold. It had been a very successful hunt. The meat from these animals would feed the Mammoth People for much of the winter.

After the innards were cleaned, Terah tackled the meat around the pelvic girdle and lastly, the hind legs. She would not take the meat from the neck and skull. That took too much work for too little meat.

After a time, Terah glanced around and wiped her sweating forehead. Everywhere she looked there was activity. Rana butchered a cow next to her, Benaleese was busy hauling on the front hoof of a calf. The shaman was wiping a sharp knife on his leather-clad leg. Wolf Boy and Lame Leg worked together on a bison bull. Terah could hear the crack of bones between Wolf Boy's sharp teeth. She saw Lame Leg try to cut into the tough bull hide.

Benaleese watched Lame Leg too. Benaleese caught Terah's eye and pointed at the girl with her chin. Benaleese's lips contorted in a mocking laugh.

Terah shook her head. She rose and walked over to Lame Leg. Lame Leg was trying to split the bull down the spine as she had obviously watched the adult women do. Her knife could not pierce the thick skin of the bull.

Terah squatted down beside the girl and touched her shoulder.

Lame Leg started. She shrank away from Terah's touch.

Terah hastily withdrew her hand. "It is best," she observed in a quiet voice, "if you butcher a cow or a calf. Bulls are too tough—the meat is stringy, and the hide is too thick to tan."

Lame Leg glared sullenly at Terah through black, tangled hair. Then she glanced at Wolf Boy chewing on one of the bull's hind legs.

"Bulls make good meat for dogs," said Terah,

"but not for people. Come," she added, "I will show you how to butcher a cow."

Lame Leg said nothing, only turned away and tried again to cut through the bull's matted hair. Terah waited, but Lame Leg showed no inclination to follow her, so she went back to the carcass she had been working on.

She is compassionate too, thought Mamut, and a shaft of pain arrowed into the region of his heart. *She is kind to Lame Leg.* Why had he found this woman just when he was so acutely aware of his own failure?

He turned away, his knife slipping a little on the blood-wetted meat in his inattention. It would not matter when he had found her, he told himself. He still would have to face his cowardice. That she would find him abhorrent when she knew the truth, was all too plain to him. *A strong, brave woman would not want a coward for a mate,* he told himself bitterly.

His heart felt as bitter as the bile juice he squeezed onto a piece of warm bison liver. Yet he had no stomach for the treat. He walked over and handed it to Lame Leg.

The child snatched the meat from his hand and gobbled it up, blood smearing half her face as she stuffed as much into her mouth as she could. When she was done, she held out her hand for more.

Mamut shrugged to himself. The child had never asked him for anything of her own accord.

He went back and sliced off another chunk

of liver, sprinkling more bile juice over it. He walked back and handed it to her. Again she gobbled it down. This time she did not ask for more. She went back to slicing at the bull hide. As Mamut walked past Wolf Boy, the dog growled over the bloody bull haunch. Mamut returned to the cow he had been butchering. When next he glanced at the bull carcass, Lame Leg was gone.

Terah noticed when the child joined her; one moment she was talking to Rana, the next she noticed the faint whiff of unwashed child smell that told her Lame Leg was nearby.

Terah continued to slice through the rump of bison, making thin strips to dry over the smoky fire. Tika and Kell were on the cliff above them, tossing down dry bison chips for fuel for the fires. Spearpoint worked with the children. He guarded them against any wandering saber-tooth or dire wolf lured by the enticing scent of rich bison meat.

Terah explained what she was doing and watched as Lame Leg tried to copy the thin slicing action. Terah ignored the frown that Benaleese turned in her direction. Terah sighed when she saw that the slices Lame Leg made were thick and chunky. The child did not seem able to slice meat properly. Even so, Terah said nothing, only continued to slice and explain as patiently as she could.

Terah glanced around for Flori. The little one was bending over one of the smoky fires. She reached out to touch the flames. With a yelp, Terah leaped to her feet and dragged the child away just as Flori was about to pick up one of the hot orange embers. "Pretty," said Flori.

Terah groaned as she gripped the little hand and inspected it for burns. Fortunately, there were none. A mere heartbeat later, and Flori would have been badly burned.

Terah dragged the child back with her to the cow carcass and thrust a small rock in her hand.

"Slice," she commanded the child. Flori willingly tried to cut the meat with the dull stone. It would take her a long time, thought Terah, satisfied that she had found a way to keep the child from wandering off. When she glanced over at Lame Leg to see how the girl was doing, she caught a tiny, knowing grin on the girl's face.

Then Lame Leg leaned over Flori and made encouraging sounds. She glanced at Terah, still with that tiny grin—now of complicity—and met Terah's eyes through the thick mat of her hair. Terah smiled back.

And the tall, well-muscled man who watched her felt more lost than ever.

Chapter 20

The bison were butchered, several of the hides tanned, and most of the meat dried. The men and women hurried to dry the last remnants of the meat because the cool weather had arrived. Soon the Mammoth People would move through the hills again to follow Giver of Life River's wide banks south to the wintering grounds. The Mammoth People were jubilant. They now had a goodly supply of dried meat and the precious bison robes they needed for trade at the Meet-meet.

It had been a successful time, thought Mamut. He should be feeling happy. Instead, there was a dragging at his heart. He stayed with Terah every night now, in their tent. He made love to her often, whenever they could slip away from the children, but still he felt a sadness. He noticed that she had not asked him to ask her father for the spears. He thought perhaps she felt a fondness for him, but not enough to want to marry him.

Since the bison charge, Mamut had been almost contemplative. He recognized that something in him had changed, but what it was he could not discover. Some part of him still felt the old fear about his cowardice, but there was something new that the bison bull had given him. Something about standing and facing his fear.

He went to talk to the old shaman, who was squatted beside the creek. The old man listened patiently as Mamut spoke. He nodded as Mamut recounted the bison charge. The shaman had been there that day and had watched the bull charge Mamut. He also had been there the day that Kran died, and the similarity of the two events had not escaped his agile mind.

There was a long silence between the two men after Mamut had spoken. "You say you have confusion in your mind. In your life. What do you wish to do?" the old shaman asked at last.

Mamut shrugged. Dare he say what he truly thought?

But the shaman just watched him out of wise old eyes, and Mamut found himself suggesting what he had heretofore barely considered. "I want to seek another vision," he said.

The old man nodded. Mamut, as a youth, had confided the details of his first vision to the old man. When Mamut had spoken then of the big black mammoth of his vision, the old man had been reluctant to say much. Mamut later wondered if something in the vision had been a warning, a warning that only the old shaman understood. But it mattered little now. The warning, if there had been such, was about the death of Kran. No, he corrected himself, it was more. It was a warning about Mamut's cowardice. Since the time of his father's death, Mamut had felt distant from the Great Spirit, almost banished from the Great Spirit's presence because of his own craven actions.

But the bison bull charging him had given Mamut a tiny glimmer of hope. Perhaps he could change, he thought as he watched the old man. Perhaps as an adult, he could go on a second vision quest and right his life.

When the old man said nothing, merely nodded again to indicate that he was listening, Mamut continued. "I think that perhaps the first vision was a warning."

The old man raised one eyebrow at this and nodded again.

Taking heart, Mamut plunged on. "If so, the time of that warning is long past. I need something to guide me for my adult life—for this time and beyond to when I am old."

The old shaman frowned thoughtfully. He stared into the churning waters of the creek. Mamut waited.

"The Great Spirit," said the old man slowly, "is Unknowable."

Mamut nodded.

"It defies our human hearts and minds to know or understand the Great Spirit or how the Great Spirit works." The old shaman smiled at Mamut. "Having said that, I must tell you that I have spent my life studying the ways of the Great Spirit."

"Of course," answered Mamut. "That is what a shaman must do."

The old shaman raised one brow. His eyes twinkled, but he did not answer the confidence in Mamut's voice. "It is very likely," he said thoughtfully, "that there is more that the Great Spirit wishes you to know." He eyed Mamut. "This restlessness I sense in you, this testing yourself against the bison bull . . ." He stopped as Mamut's eyes narrowed. "What would you call it?"

Mamut shrugged. "Preparing for death." His calmness, his death chant, and his acceptance that this time he would not run as the bison charged him, all came back to him.

The old man waited. When Mamut said nothing else, the shaman continued, "I think it is wise for you to seek a vision at this time."

Mamut waited a while, but the old man said no more, only stared at the white bubbling water of the creek.

Mamut was reluctant to leave. He felt that he did not know enough to seek a vision. Oh, he knew what rituals to do—the fasting, the praying, burying a sacred object as a gift to the Great Spirit. But he did not know what to ask for, how the Great Spirit worked. He wanted more from the old man.

He cleared his throat. "You say that you have spent a lifetime studying the Great Spirit."

"The *ways* of the Great Spirit," corrected the old shaman mildly.

"The ways, then," said Mamut a little impatiently. "Could you tell me something of what you have learned?"

The old man looked at him. "You ask me to give you what I have worked a lifetime to learn?"

The enormity of what he was asking for appalled Mamut for a moment. Then he nodded his head doggedly. "Of what use is it if only one person knows?"

The old man stared at the creek for some time, then he looked at Mamut. "Very well," he answered. "I will tell you some of the things I have learned, but I do not know if they will help you. They may even hinder you."

Mamut shrugged. He doubted his relationship with the Great Spirit could become any more hindered.

"The first thing that I noticed," said the old man, "is that there are no rules as to how the Great Spirit works."

It was Mamut's turn to raise an eyebrow.

Undaunted, the old shaman continued, "I want to tell you that it seems the Great Spirit likes to do the unexpected. And then when He does the unexpected, the unexpected He does is always better than what I expected."

He smiled at Mamut's confusion. Perhaps he saw it as a challenge. "Then," he went on, "the Great Spirit often acts through the ordinary. You do not know that it is the Great Spirit acting until much later and after much thoughtful reflection. And then you understand how amazing the ordinary event that happened assuredly is."

"Like what?" Mamut demanded.

"You wish to know where the Great Spirit has acted in your life?" the old man wanted to know.

"I know He gave me the vision, saved my life from the charging bull . . ."

"Those are special moments, not ordinary ones," nodded the shaman. "The Great Spirit acts that way also. And those times are easier to see." He did not, however, offer to help Mamut find the ordinary moments in his life that were amazing, that came from the Great Spirit.

"He sent me Terah. . . ." persevered Mamut.

"Perhaps," said the old man.

"What do you mean, perhaps? If it happened, the Great Spirit willed it."

The old man sighed. "People are free to act," he answered. After a while he offered, "The Great Spirit can bring good out of terrible pain."

"If this is another of your rules about how the Great Spirit works, I do not understand," said Mamut. He wondered if the old man thought that it was a painful thing that Mamut had made Terah his captive. Perhaps that she was a captive was painful to *her*. . . . He quashed the thought.

"Sometimes the Great Spirit works at a slower pace than we would like."

What does that mean? thought Mamut in exasperation. He thought about it. He had struggled with the terrible pain of his cowardice throughout his adult life. It seemed a long time. Was the Great Spirit able to bring some good out of his pain? Was He going to bring the good *now?* "Is the Great Spirit bringing good out of something painful in my life?" he asked cautiously.

"Of course," answered the old man. "The Great Spirit is amazingly merciful. That is a part of the unexpected."

Mamut thought it was time to stop asking about the ways of the Great Spirit. It was too confusing. It was a good thing though, he thought, that the shaman was able to figure out some of the ways of the Great Spirit.

With as much dignity as he could, Mamut thanked the old man and rose. The shaman continued to squat and watch the foaming creek. He gave an absent wave to Mamut as the younger man strode off, his mind whirling.

Chapter 21

He would, decided Mamut, assuredly go on the vision quest. He glanced around at the people in camp. There were still a few smoky fires with meat racks, but not many. At Terah's fire pit there was no meat drying on the racks. She had completed the drying procedure. He looked around for her and saw her walking down the dusty trail to the creek. She was swinging her hips and an empty bison bladder.

Mamut dragged his thoughts away from her. He had only a few days for his vision quest. Could the Great Spirit be hurried? He should have asked the shaman. Well, there was no hope for it now. He must go on his quest and then he would have the answers to his fear, his cowardice, and how it all tangled up his life.

He walked past Spearpoint and Lern. They

were talking as they worked at repairing tools. Spearpoint was sharpening an obsidian knife that had been dulled in the bison butchery. Lern was polishing a wooden spear shaft.

Spearpoint called Mamut over. Mamut would have preferred to avoid Lern, but he decided to stop and visit with Spearpoint. And Lern had acquitted himself well enough in the bison hunt. He had killed two cows, enough meat to keep his Frog wife very busy slicing and drying the meat and tanning the hides.

Mamut sat down. Spearpoint and Lern had been discussing the wives that the Mammoth men were going to trade for at the Meet-meet. The shaman had not said if he was going to obtain a wife, but the five other unmarried hunters all wanted wives. Lern wanted a second wife, but when he mentioned it, Spearpoint caught Mamut's eye and shook his head. Obviously Spearpoint thought that Lern did not need, or perhaps he did not deserve, another wife.

Spearpoint himself spoke volubly about how he expected to find a wife once they reached the Meet-meet. He had a long list of the qualities he expected in a woman.

" . . . and she should know how to tan hides," Spearpoint said, glancing down at the poorly tanned antelope hide tunic he wore. "And she should be able to sew—little, delicate stitches that keep out the cold and rain . . ." Again he looked down at himself.

Spearpoint's large stitches left gaping holes

in the seams of the antelope hide. Mamut smothered a smile and glanced down at his own leather leggings that Terah had made. The hide was smoothly tanned, the stitches tiny.

" . . . and she will not nag at me to go out and hunt when I want to stay by the warm fire . . ."

Terah always welcomed him to the fire, thought Mamut. Her green eyes lit up when she saw him. And her voice carried a happy lilt.

" . . . and she will be pretty. Not too fat, not too thin . . ."

Like Terah, added Mamut to himself.

" . . . and she will have warm feet at night. I hate cold feet in bed . . ."

Terah had warm feet, very warm feet.

Mamut only half-listened to his friend. Terah had other, more important qualities, too, that Mamut liked in a woman. She was kind to the children, worked hard, spoke knowledgeably of medicines and gathering plants. She cooked well; everything she made was tasty. She got along well with the other women. She was generous to Lame Leg. She was beautiful. . . .

Why then did he not tell her that he wanted to ask her father for her? Because—he shifted restlessly—if he married her, she would become a Mammoth woman, and then she would find out that he, Mamut, could not kill mammoths. After that she would leave him—he pictured his strong, brave Terah with a contemptuous sneer on her beautiful face. Aimed at him. He squirmed where he sat.

251

But as long as she remained his captive, he assured himself, he had the upper hand. He did not have to tell her the truth about himself, he did not have to trust her. . . .

Spearpoint's voice cut into Mamut's tormented thoughts. "What about you, Mamut?" he asked. "Are you going to trade for a wife at the Meet-meet?"

Mamut's head came up. "I already have a—" He was about to say wife, then thought better of it. "Perhaps," he said instead. His voice gave no hint of his feelings or of what he had been thinking.

"Perhaps I might," he said, unaware that at this moment Terah was passing behind him on the trail back from the creek.

She paused when she saw the men. Mamut's back was to her. The water-filled bison bladder was heavy. It would be good to rest for a moment, she thought. She lowered the bison bladder to the ground and rubbed her lower back as she waited, not listening to what the men were saying.

Spearpoint saw her. So did Lern.

Spearpoint guessed that Mamut loved Terah. Who would not? She was lovely. But Mamut's answer had surprised him. Thinking he must be mistaken, Spearpoint pressed further. "You would have two wives?" He frowned, inadvertently. Mamut was beginning to sound like Lern. He was getting greedy for women.

Terah heard the word 'wives'. She started to listen to what the men were saying.

"Two wives? Why not?" said Mamut carelessly, playing with the idea. Truly, he had not thought about obtaining another wife since he had come to Terah's bed. He remembered that before he had captured her, he had entertained half-formed plans of obtaining a wife at the Meet-meet, but those ideas had faded once he had met Terah.

"You are a good hunter," goaded Lern. He was smiling a sly grin that Mamut did not trust. "You can easily provide enough meat and hides to feed and clothe *another* woman and her children." His voice was unnecessarily loud.

Mamut saw through Lern's plan with ease. Lern thought that if Mamut took a second wife, the other men would agree that Lern could take a second wife too.

But Terah would not like a co-wife, thought Mamut. She was too strong, too confident of herself to let another woman share her life. That was fine with Mamut; he did not actually want another wife. He just wanted to play with the idea.

"There is some truth in what you say," admitted Mamut.

Lern smiled triumphantly.

Ah, you do not win—yet, thought Mamut. "But I am satisfied to wait."

He saw Lern's smile fade.

Toying with Lern amused Mamut. The other hunter had made too many sly digs and innuendos about Mamut in the past. It was almost as if he knew Mamut's secret; but no, he could not know. Mamut gave in to the dislike he felt toward Lern. A second woman would increase his status among the Mammoth men, too. "When I take a wife," he began.

"You mean a *second* wife," enunciated Lern clearly.

Mamut shook his head. "The woman I have now is a captive. She is not a wife," he corrected. "Therefore the wife I take at the Meet-meet will be my *first* wife."

He did not hear Terah's smothered gasp. But Spearpoint did. Spearpoint frantically tried to catch Mamut's eye, but Mamut ignored him. He was watching Lern.

Lern's smile was malicious. "You will make your captive woman, *Terah*, a *slave* to your first wife?" he asked impudently.

Mamut gave a short bark of laughter, though not denying Lern's assumption. The thought of Terah as a meek slave to another woman amused Mamut. He smiled tolerantly. Why, Terah would probably take out her sharp little white chert knife and chop off the hapless woman's hair! Lern had no idea whatsoever what Terah was like.

Terah did not wait around to hear his answer.

"I think that I will not—" Mamut stopped. It was obvious he had lost his audience. They were staring at someone or something behind him. He swung his head around in time to see Terah stomping off toward the tent.

He swung back to the men, a stricken look upon his face. Had she heard? Spearpoint's slow nod and grimace told him the answer. So did Lern's sly grin.

Mamut rose at once. He turned on his heel and strode after Terah.

Spearpoint frowned at Lern. He had long ago stopped sharpening the obsidian. "That was cruel."

Lern's eyes narrowed in anger. "He deserved it. He has come between my woman and me."

"Your beatings have come between your woman and you," responded Spearpoint.

"A man has a right to correct his own wife," snarled Lern.

"That may be," responded Spearpoint. "But not with his fist. And a *man* does not have a right to smite his wife until she is blue with bruises."

Lern flushed. "Rana has food, she has shelter," he muttered defensively.

Spearpoint snorted.

"I do not strike her," said Lern. "I have never struck her. She lies."

Spearpoint looked disgusted. "I have heard her screams. The whole camp has heard her screams. I have seen her bruises. Like the one she wears on her cheek this day."

Lern flushed again. "She walked into a tree."

Shaking his head, Spearpoint got to his feet. "I am going to get sick," he announced in disgust.

"Do not puke on me," answered Lern, scrambling to get out of the way.

Spearpoint rolled his eyes and stomped off in the direction Mamut had taken. Perhaps he could help his friend. Lern followed, once he was certain that Spearpoint was not going to vomit on him.

"Get packed," Terah ordered Tika as she rushed past the girl and headed straight for the tent.

"But we do not leave for five more days," protested Tika, holding up her hand with five fingers displayed. "You told me that this morning! And I want to play!"

She and Kell and Flori were chopping up a hare carcass as if it were a bison. The animal had been neatly split down the backbone and thin, stringy strips of dirt-covered pink meat hung on a miniature drying rack. It was Flori's chore to chase the flies and dire wolves away.

"We must pack. Now," hissed Terah. She slammed into the tent and threw the bison bladder she was carrying into a basket. Water splashed over the bedding, but she cared not. She plopped down on the robes and put her head in her hands and sobbed.

"That is why he does not ask my father for me," she whispered to herself. "He plans to take another wife, a *first* wife!" The word sounded obscene as she hissed it. She kicked her heels into the robes and flung her arms around in her agitation.

"Terah!" It was Mamut's voice, outside the tent.
She froze.

"Terah! Come out here."

"No!" she cried. "I refuse!"

Mamut frowned. What to do now? Lern had known all along that Terah was there, listening.

And he, Mamut, had been played for a fool. The fact that the condemning words had issued from his own mouth only increased his wrath. "Come out!"

"Never!"

He ground his teeth. "If you do not come out, I will come in there."

"Try it!"

Just then, his poorly tanned musk-ox hide, the one he always slept in, came flying out the door of the tent. Bits of fur fell off it. He leaned down to peer into the tent and was hit by a moccasin full in the face. He jerked back. She was angry!

Spearpoint and Lern arrived at the tent. Spearpoint said, "Let her calm down."

Mamut glowered at his friend. "And how many wives do you have to give me such advice?" he demanded crossly.

"Yes," said Lern smoothly. "Do show us how to treat a woman, Mamut. You know so much."

Mamut swung around to face the man he wanted to throttle. "Leave," he snarled.

Lern, with a smirk, sauntered away.

Spearpoint frowned. "You said you wanted another wife," he pointed out reasonably.

Another moccasin, followed by a second bison robe, came flying out of the tent. "Now I can see why," observed Spearpoint. "I did not know she was like this. . . ."

"Leave," snarled Mamut. His fists clenched. He was not a man to fight his best friend, but if it came to that . . .

Spearpoint took in the red face of his friend,

the clenched jaw, the obsidian-hard eyes. A basket, full of dried meat, whooshed out the door and spilled over the ground. "I am leaving," Spearpoint said with considerable dignity. He walked away.

"Terah!" growled Mamut.

"Go away!"

"I cannot go away," said Mamut striving for patience. "I live here."

"No longer."

"Terah!" His voice held just the proper amount of masculine threat. He congratulated himself.

Silence.

Now what? he wondered. All was quiet. No sobs coming from the tent. No sounds.

Cautiously, he bent to peer inside. "Terah?"

He ducked back just as another full basket came sailing toward him. He felt grateful for his hunter's reflexes.

"Terah," he said in a stern tone. "We need to talk about this."

He heard what sounded like a growl in answer. Was she looking for her little white chert knife? He should have remembered she kept it hidden in the tent. Now she was armed.

What was he going to do? He turned his head to look for a stick or something to poke in the tent, to jiggle, to see if she attacked it, when he noticed that he had an audience.

Rana with her bruised cheek was standing, arms crossed, frowning ferociously. "Do not strike her," she warned.

Lern stood peering from behind the Frog tent

where he lived. He was smiling. "Afraid?" he taunted.

The shaman had come up and was watching Mamut with something akin to pity on his face.

Lame Leg half-stood, half-leaned on Wolf Boy. The big dog sat, tongue out, ears pricked forward in interest.

Benaleese waddled up, her hands holding her bulging stomach as she hurried.

Mamut struggled to regain some kind of composure. It would not do to let his people see him beg and plead with his captive. He waved his hands at the others. "Go away," he said. "It is all a mistake. Everything will be fine."

Lern laughed.

Mamut ground his teeth. "Please leave," he said through gritted teeth. How could he speak to his captive woman with all these people watching?

Tika and Kell were holding hands and watching him. Flori was eating some dirt.

Lame Leg limped over. She stopped when she was in front of Mamut.

He spared her a glance. "What is it?"

"Do you hit her? Do you kick her?"

Mamut stared at the child. Hitting and kicking was something Lame Leg knew well. She had been hit and kicked many times in her short life. Some of the anger seeped out of him. "No," he said slowly. "No, I do not hit her. Nor kick her."

There was silence around them.

"Good," said the child. Then she limped over to her dog. "Come, Wolf Boy. We play." And they went off.

Mamut watched them go. It was the first time he had heard Lame Leg speak so many words. Then he eyed his audience. "Leave," he demanded.

Benaleese, still holding her burgeoning bulge, reluctantly waddled back to her fire pit.

Rana, with a last disapproving stare, swung on her heel and returned to her Frog tent. She frowned at her husband, and Lern watched her, a guarded expression upon his slyly handsome face.

Spearpoint and the shaman left.

There was only Tika and Kell and Flori left watching him.

In irritation, Mamut said, "Stop eating that dirt, Flori."

There was a cry from the tent, and Terah barreled out the door. "Flori!" she cried. "Do not eat dirt!"

Mamut was relieved to see Terah was not armed. He did not feel up to disarming a knife-wielding woman, not this day. He blocked the tent door so she could not re-enter the dwelling.

"We need to talk," he said.

"Then talk."

Her voice was so cold that for a moment Mamut wondered if he had imagined the warm woman he thought he knew.

"What you overheard . . . It is not like it sounded."

She waited. Her face was impassive, and Mamut searched the green depths of her eyes. He saw that she was keeping him out.

"It was—just plans, that is all," he said. "We were making plans for when we reach the south."

"And your plan is to acquire a wife."

"No—well, yes—I mean no. It had been. Before I captured you, that is."

"It means nothing to me," said Terah, her green eyes as frozen as permafrost when they met Mamut's. "Whether you gain a wife or not is no concern of mine." *Because I will not be here,* she added silently. *I am taking the children and escaping at the first opportunity.*

"You are very understanding," he acknowledged grimly, wondering if she cared if he took another wife or not. She did not seem to care for him. Perhaps he should take another wife. But then why was she throwing things at him? He stared at her. This woman did not seem to love him. There it was, love again. He wanted love. He searched her eyes. There was no love there, only coldness. He tried again. "I—I did not intend to take a wife. I have you, after all."

"A captive," she sneered disparagingly.

"It is true that you are a captive." Why was this going so badly? "But you do all the things a wife does. You cook, you tan hides—very well, too. You know how to sew. . . ."

Her eyes dropped to the leggings she had made for him. *A gift,* she thought bitterly. What a fool she was!

His guilty glance followed hers. "Did I thank you for the leggings?"

"Yes."

He stared at her, his obsidian eyes bemused.

Theresa Scott

What could he say to her that would take away her anger? She was right to be angry, he thought with a twinge of guilt, if she had expected to be his wife. He wondered if her anger hid her hurt.

It was not as though it was a terrible thing for her to be a captive, he mused. She received food, shelter, protection from wild animals. If he and Spearpoint had not killed that saber-tooth and captured her and the children—why, she would be white bones glistening in the sun at this very moment.

But the real reason, and he knew he did not want to face it, was this—if he married her, he would feel completely committed to their union. And then he would feel obliged to tell her about Kran's death and his own cowardice. The secret was getting too heavy to live with.

He wondered for a moment why he had never felt obliged to tell Cala, his first wife, about Kran's death. Cala had been from the Bird Feasting People. She had been several years younger than Mamut. She had seemed tiny and fragile, and he had felt very protective toward her. At the time, he had not thought she needed to know about his lack of courage. The secret had not seemed so heavy then.

But with Terah it was different. She was strong and as brave as a saber-toothed tigress. No, it was too much. He could not tell her. He did not want to see her contempt, her hate for him. Better that she dislike him for keeping her a captive, or even for taking a second woman, than that she learn of his cowardice.

"I did not actually *plan* to take a wife," he said.

He saw the contempt in her eyes. She thought he was lying. And in a way he was. He had planned to—before meeting her. But now, if he was going to take a wife, it would be her. "I am not interested in the women at the Meet-meet," he said at last. His face was sullen, uncaring. He had to protect himself. He would not take a woman at the Meet-meet. It had been a foolish idea to pursue, he thought now.

Terah saw the uncaring; it was directed at her. She could think of nothing to say to add to the lies he had told her. Strange, she had thought more of him than this. He has always seemed honest with her before. Now she could not get past the shuttered look in those black eyes.

She turned away. "I will make the evening meal," she said, her voice conveying her indifference to him.

"Very well," he answered. But he did not feel hungry.

Tomorrow he would set out on his vision quest. Perhaps the purification rituals he must do to seek the vision would cleanse him of the lie he was now living with her. He knew she thought he did not want to marry her. He did; but he could not give her the honesty that would come with that commitment. Tomorrow. He sighed.

Chapter 22

Terah was miserable. Mamut had been absent from the evening meal. She had picked at her food and watched the children wolf down the tasty bison meat. Now Mamut lay beside her. He had entered their dwelling later, after the camp noises had died down.

He might as well be out hunting, she thought miserably, *or in another encampment, so far apart are we.* She lay stiffly to one side of the bedrobes, careful to let no part of her body touch his. And it seemed to her that he was just as careful not to touch her. She moved one stiffened leg. She could not sleep; her thoughts raced, yet she wanted Mamut to think she was asleep. Then he would not try to make love to her. Her lips tightened. Tomorrow she would escape.

"Terah?" Mamut could not sleep. He did not

like lying next to her, unable to touch her. He could feel her woodenness from where he lay, her back to him. He wondered what she was thinking, feeling. The very air of the tent felt close and heavy.

He reached over to touch her shoulder, but then he paused, his hand hovering in the air. He could feel her body warmth, yet there was a protectiveness, a stiffness to her that he could not penetrate. He drew his hand back.

He felt obliged to stay with her in the tent because Lern might attempt another attack. The man was sly enough to attempt it, in Mamut's judgment. Mamut would not leave Terah and the children defenseless again. He resolved to ask Spearpoint to guard his family when Mamut left for his vision quest on the morrow.

"Terah?"

No answer. Terah's eyes flicked wide open, and she stared into the darkness. She would take the children and leave. Let him take a wife, let him go to the Meet-meet, let him go to *ten* Meet-meets and choose any woman he wanted. It was nothing to her! *Then why,* came the little voice that so plagued her, *do you have this awful pain in your heart?* Hunger, she supposed. She had eaten little at dinner. *A different kind of hunger,* supplied the little voice helpfully. *A hunger for love. A hunger for a man.*

Terah gnashed her teeth. Silently. She would not speak to him. If she did, she feared she would erupt into a screaming, pleading mess. She had so wanted him to love her, wanted him to ask her father for her. And now the death of that wanting tasted bitter in her mouth.

"Terah?" He could not go on the vision quest without telling her. She might think he rejected her even more than she already did. "I go on a four-day journey. I leave in the morning."

Silence, though he thought he detected a shudder run through the stiff body next to him.

"I am going to seek a vision."

Terah's eyes remained wide open. Why was she so relieved that it was a vision quest that drew him away from her? A wife, a vision quest—what difference? Either one, he was not hers.

Her lips thinned in the dark. Bison men went on vision quests also. The acid thought came to her that Mamut would better profit from spending his time studying what went on right in his own dwelling, not seeking after the Great Spirit for something.

Then she sighed. Perhaps it was best. Perhaps the Great Spirit would tell Mamut how important she was in his life. She smiled, liking the idea.

Then her smile disappeared. The Great Spirit always *took*. He took her brother Bron. He took Chee. The Great Spirit had never, ever done anything to help Terah of the Bison People. She would not expect any help now.

Her heart felt like a lump in her chest. It mattered little what Mamut learned on his vision quest. When he returned, she and the children would have escaped, and it would be too late for her. Mamut would never find them again and there would be no hope for a marriage between

267

them. A small shudder shook her frame.

Mamut thought he heard a tiny groan. Perhaps she would miss him. . . . "I will ask Spearpoint to guard you while I am gone."

Alarm shot through Terah. Did Mamut suspect she would escape?

"Spearpoint will hunt for you and keep Lern away."

Ah. She relaxed. He suspected nothing, then.

"Spearpoint will sleep close by at night."

Still no answer. How, Mamut wondered, could they ever talk about what was wrong between them if she would not speak? He got up on one elbow and leaned over her, trying to see if she was awake, if she had even heard his words.

He thought her eyes looked squeezed shut, her breathing a little forced and uneven. She was not asleep. He sank back down again and stared at the dark fur of the dwelling. "Terah, I know you are awake."

No answer.

He sighed heavily. "When I return—" What? Things will be better? I will be different, a new, calmer, wiser man from what I learn on my vision quest? He frowned. What, indeed, could he say?

He would do well not to hold out false hope, he decided. "When I return, it will be time to move south."

There, that should please her. She would enjoy seeing the winter camp along the river. It was sheltered from the winter storms. And when the Mammoth People traveled to the Meet-meet, there would be many pretty things for her to see—

necklaces, bracelets, finely sewn clothes, needles and awls, baskets and bowls. Things that would enhance her beauty and things that would make her work easier.

The bison hunt had been successful; he was greatly enriched. He could trade a valuable set of wide, gently curved bison horns for a beautiful present for her. Yes, that is what he would do. He would get Terah an expensive present, perhaps a necklace. He smiled into the darkness. She would like that—a beautiful white bead necklace. He could not marry her, but he could treat her well and give her fine presents.

His quandary resolved, he rolled over and went to sleep.

Terah stared unblinking into the darkness. Tomorrow. She sighed.

Chapter 23

One day earlier, some distance to the east, a man named Dagger stood on a hilltop looking out over the vastness below him. And nowhere over the humps and bumps of the hills and the brown seams of the valleys did he see a single sign of those whom he sought so desperately.

He squatted down, his shoulders slumped in despair. He had hoped upon reaching the very highest hill, the Mountain of the Badger, that when he gazed out, he would see at least something of the people, some sign. . . . But it was not to be.

He hurled a brown leather sack to the ground, heedless of where it landed. "What good is the white chert if I cannot have my family?" he cried aloud. Only a hawk wheeling overhead heard him.

He stared out over the land, caught up in a terrible remorse. He had gone to the hidden quarry for the white chert, as was his wont whenever he had need of new stone to make the lethal spearpoints so necessary for survival in this ferocious land. He remembered coldly turning his back on his wife's pleas to take the children and herself with him, just this one time. Surely the chert quarry was not so secret, so important that he could not take his own children with him? she had begged.

But Dagger was adamant. It was his secret, *his* stone, and he would not share the knowledge of the quarry place with anyone. Well, he reproached himself now, head drooping, he had his chert. He had his precious white stone. But, alas, now he had no wife, no children.

He'd spent several days at the quarry, fashioning spearheads, and he had been triumphant when he had made the final, best one. Reaching into the now-despised leather sack, he pulled out the spearhead he sought. It truly was a beautiful piece of work, he marveled anew. It was hard to believe that *he* had made it, so cleanly chipped were the flakes.

He hefted it in his hand. The weight was balanced, the flutes perfectly placed in the middle. Yes, he thought, he had never made a better weapon.

Slowly he let the spearhead slide from his hand to rest upon the gravel. He had the spearhead he wanted, but no children, no wife.

When Dagger returned to the campsite where

he had left his wife, her sister, and the children, they were gone. This caused him no alarm. He had not even bothered to follow their tracks. He had assumed they had tired of waiting for him and headed back to the grandparents' encampment.

It took him three days to find the grandparents' encampment. They had moved. In their doorway, he deposited a freshly killed deer, killed with his new white chert spearhead.

His in-laws had ignored the meat and stared at him. Dagger had been stunned to learn that neither his wife nor his children nor his sister-in-law had yet returned. He had squirmed as he watched the anger and disgust on his in-laws' faces when they realized he had returned without his family. How did a man lose a family? his father-in-law had demanded harshly. Even Dagger's brother, One Shoe, normally the most loyal of men, looked disgusted.

Dagger had stayed only long enough to sup upon a strip of dried meat that his mother-in-law had pressed upon him. She, at least, seemed to have some understanding of his dazed state.

Dagger had lost track of time in his search for Chee and Tika and Kell and Flori. Chee, his lovely green-eyed wife. He could still see her pleading with him to take them to the quarry. And Tika, his firstborn. She was so playful, so concerned, so sweet. . . . He sighed. And Kell—was his son Kell dead and his body food for lions this very moment? And what of little Flori, so young yet that she could not speak whole words, but he still loved her. He loved them all. He wondered if his sister-in-law Terah was dead, too. At one time he had thought perhaps he would take her as a second wife, but not now. If he ever found his family again, he would be content—no, more than content. He would be a man who knew what he had and valued it every day of his life.

Tears welled in Dagger's eyes and rolled down his cheeks. He did not try to brush them away. Who did he have to act the man in front of here, on this hilltop? The hawk?

How long he cried he did not know. The sorrow of losing his family lay like a terrible dullness in his chest. *Too much time has passed now,* he thought, *for me to even hope that they are. alive.* All that remained was to search until he found their bodies. At least then he would not have to live with the not-knowing.

Slowly he gathered together his things, the food, the bison bladder, his spear, the leather sack with the large chunks of white chert inside. He would start his search once more. He squinted at the sun. Still half a day left in which to find them.

He had almost forgotten the white chert spearpoint that lay on the ground. As he reached for it, a thought seized him. He held up the perfect point and looked at it assessingly. Yes, it would do.

With trembling heart, Dagger got to his feet, his legs shaking from the enormity of his thought. What if—what if he gave the most precious thing he still had? Would the Great Spirit understand that he was asking for a trade? The white chert and the beautiful spearpoint in exchange for his family? Did the Great Spirit bargain with men?

The hope that entered his heart at that moment crushed Dagger's doubts. He would offer the chert spearpoint and yes, another great chunk of the stone, the biggest chunk he carried with him, if only the Great Spirit would let him find his family. *Alive*, he dared to add.

Fingers trembling, cutting himself accidentally on the sharp blade in his haste, Dagger pulled out the large chunk of chert he was going to offer. Would the Great Spirit want it?

Dagger hoped He would. If not, he had nothing else to offer.

Dagger placed the rock on the gravel and beside it, the graceful spearpoint. He wondered if he was a fool to leave such a valuable stone tool and chunk of white chert here on the mountain top. Then he quelled his doubts. He wanted his family, did he not? What other way was there, then?

With new confidence sprung from hope, Dagger walked away. He did glance back—just once—at the stones; he could not help himself.

No, he admonished himself. They belonged to the Great Spirit now. He had made a bargain, he and the Great Spirit. He would find his family, and the Great Spirit would have the precious stone.

A hopeful smile cracked Dagger's brown face as he took another step. He would find them. With the Great Spirit's aid, he would find them.

Just then, the hawk above him wheeled once more, gave a great scream and swung to the west.

Dagger was no fool. He turned his steps to the west. Already the Great Spirit was helping him.

Chapter 24

Dawn's pale gold fingers were just creeping over the hills when Mamut slid from the woman-warmed bedrobes. He dressed, pausing now and then to glance at Terah as she slept. Regret seized him, and he suddenly wanted to give up on his possibly fruitless vision quest and stay instead with this bewildering, slumbering woman.

He sighed and his sense returned. He would go on the quest. He *must* go on the quest else he would never resolve his fear and cowardice and he could never be a man, the kind of man that a woman like Terah seemed to instinctively demand and the kind of man that he wanted to be.

Mamut slipped out of the entry-way and into the cool, clear morning air. He passed with quiet tread the other dwellings where other Mammoth People slept.

When Mamut went to cross in front of Lame Leg's tent, Wolf Boy gave a low throaty growl. Mamut whispered to him, and the big dog caught the man's scent. The animal's large head sank back down on his forepaws and he closed his eyes, prepared to go back to sleep. Mamut patted the dog's head. "Guard the camp," he ordered. The dog thumped his tail once and then went still. Mamut skulked past Lame Leg's tent.

He stopped at Spearpoint's dwelling. The young hunter was just awakening. He yawned and nodded when Mamut told him of the planned quest and then asked him to guard Terah and the children. "See that you get back in time for the move south," warned Spearpoint. "I do not want to have to move your woman and those unruly children all by myself."

Mamut grinned to himself. It was Spearpoint's way of telling him to take care of himself. And he had every intention of doing so.

Mamut left the camp in a better frame of mind than he had been in the night before. He felt rested and ready for what he was about to do. One did not undertake a vision quest lightly.

He carried no food with him, only a bison bladder of water. He could refill it at a creek in the hills if need be. In his right hand, he carried his best spear, with its carefully prepared tip, for protection against any marauding saber-tooth or dire wolf or lion. In his left hand, Mamut carried a newly sharpened black obsidian blade. This he would bury on a hillside near his vision place as an offering to the Great Spirit, just as he had done on his first quest.

He jogged along, feeling himself grow lighter. It was good, he thought, to go on this quest. Terah was safe; Spearpoint would take good care of her and the children. Now was the time for Mamut to concentrate on the Great Spirit.

That night he camped on the top of a hill overlooking a creek. He had decided to stay away from the creek because of night predators. A cacophony of growls, grunts and hisses from unseen deer and wolves and lions failed to keep him awake, however, and the next day's sunrise found Mamut trotting onward on his journey.

After the second day of traveling, his protesting stomach had given up. An occasional sip of water from the bison bladder now sufficed for his needs. He felt stronger, sharper, clearer in his thinking.

The new dawn found him standing on the Mountain of the Badger, a hill that the shaman had once mentioned. Mamut drank in the quiet and breathed deeply of the cool air. The mountain's height gave him a view across the hills and sharp valleys. Farther away, a long, shadowed crevasse grew where the Gift of Life River flowed.

Mamut felt calm. He prayed to the Great Spirit. He buried his obsidian offering. And then he sat down to chant and wait for his vision.

It came when he had drifted into a strange state; he felt suspended between earth and sky. One moment he was chanting, and lo! the next moment a great, whitish, ghostly mammoth was walking up the hill toward him. The animal's feet did not appear to touch the earth. An eerie quiet surrounded Mamut and lay over the land. His heartbeat speeded up as the hoary, frosted giant approached. A white mammoth! he thought. What means this?

Without further thought, Mamut stumbled to his feet, prepared to run. Dread seized him, and still the behemoth came on.

It was happening all over again, some part of his mind screamed. He was running from a mammoth *again!* It was like that terrible day when Father-Killer had chased him.

When the great beast was so close to Mamut that he could see ragged clumps of shaggy hair on its snaking trunk, the vision-animal suddenly swung to one side. It glared at Mamut out of one fierce, red-rimmed eye.

Mamut wanted to scream his fear aloud, but his vocal chords were paralyzed. So were his legs. He could not move away from the beast. The only part of him that still lived, still moved, was the blood flooding through his veins, pumped by a frantic heart. This was not a vision—this was a nightmare!

The mammoth swung its big head back once again. It raised its great trunk in the air and appeared to be sniffing. The trunk waved back and forth, back and forth, seeking, seeking . . . until Mamut, watching, felt bewildered and dizzy from the motion. Then the trunk lashed out and wrapped itself around Mamut's waist.

He could not move.

His skin prickling, Mamut felt the rough scrape of shaggy hair slide against his skin. He breathed in the musky smell of mammoth and squirmed against the constriction of trunk muscles slowly squeezing the very breath out of his body.

Fear sliced through him, and he cried out to the Great Spirit. The mammoth shifted a little as though getting a better footing. Mamut gasped, desperate to draw air into his aching lungs.

Now he could move his arms, his hands. He placed both hands on the trunk and sought to push away from the behemoth. The tip of the animal's trunk curled round and touched Mamut, as though seeking out the threat of the man. Mamut grabbed the sensitive tip and twisted the skin as hard as he could. The great beast gave a terrible roar that hurt Mamut's ears. A hot blast of air erupted from the giant's lungs and hit Mamut in the legs.

Suddenly the beast let him go, and Mamut fell to the ground. He lifted himself, shaking his head to clear it. He had to get out of the way, had to! Or the beast would trample him as it had his father.

Then to Mamut's utter stupefaction, the mammoth swung round and started ambling down the hillside! In disbelief, he watched the great white rear of the beast slowly descend the sharp, gravely hill.

It came to him, then, in a voice that was somehow partly inside his head and somehow partly outside of him, that he would have another

281

chance to fight the mammoth—in one last, final
confrontation. Mamut *could* prevail in the fight—
if he was prepared and if he was strong enough.
If he was not, he would walk the Death Trail, just
as his father, Kran, had done.

Mamut sank to the ground, exhausted. The fear
had drained out of him somewhere in the vision
and all he felt himself to be was an empty husk.
How could he prepare himself to fight a mammoth? How could he strengthen himself enough
to kill a mammoth, he who had never hunted or
touched a mammoth in all his adult years? He did
not know the rituals, doubted even if the shaman
knew the rituals that would prevail against one
of the giants.

And yet he must learn them, or learn whatever
it was that would ensure that he prevailed against
the great beast. For if he did not, he would lose
everything that held any meaning to him—the
children, Terah, his life.

The vision had been clear. If he could not kill
the white mammoth, he would die like his father,
trampled to death by an enraged mammoth.

He rolled over onto his back and looked up at
the huge blue bowl of sky above him. He blinked.
How long had he wrestled with the mammoth?
Much time had passed. He sat up, disoriented
and dazed, and looked around him.

And then he saw it. A beautiful, perfect
spearpoint lay but a foot-length away from him.
The blade caught the sun's rays and glowed white.
Next to it lay a large chunk of white chert rock.
Neither the stone nor the spearpoint had been

there before his vision. Mamut was certain of it. He would have noticed.

With new hope, he hefted the spearpoint. The stone felt warm from the sun. An idea formed in his mind as he gazed at it. He held the blade up to the sun and watched as the stone took on an almost living cast. It was strong, thick, with no fractures.

Suddenly it came to him. The Great Spirit had given him this spearpoint as a gift. This deadly white chert blade was what he would use to kill the mammoth. And from the thick chunk of white stone he could make several more speartips.

When it came time to face the hoary mammoth, he would be ready, thought Mamut grimly, and he would use those spears to kill it.

Then and only then would he truly be free!

Chapter 25

Terah awakened to the sound of sobs. Swiftly she glanced at the children. All three were still asleep. Relief coursed through her. The crying was not from the children. The muffled sound seemed to be coming from outside the tent. Who, then?

As she swiftly dressed, she could still hear the sobs. She paused in the act of straightening her deerskin tunic. Silence. Had they stopped? She strained to listen.

No, they were quieter, as if whoever was crying was trying not to let anyone hear.

Terah crept from the tent, suddenly remembering that this was the day she had planned to flee from the Mammoth People. She followed the sounds, at first to Lame Leg's tent. When she peeked inside, she heard the child's deep, even breathing, saw the matted head. Lame Leg was not the one sobbing. Who then?

Wolf Boy opened his eyes and raised his head. When he saw Terah, he thumped the ground with his tail, but he did not growl. She was thankful for that. When it came time to leave, she did not want Wolf Boy giving the alarm. At the thought of leaving, she felt a tiny pang of despair. She had grown to know and like the Mammoth People. She took a breath and cautioned herself. She *must* leave—for her sake and for the sake of the children. She would not stay with a man who did not love her. . . . She caught herself. Love? How was love a part of her decision?

Exasperated with herself, she paused, listening for the sounds. They seemed to be coming from the Frog tent. Was it Rana? She crept closer and paused.

Now she was certain that the sounds were coming from Rana's tent. Terah sat back on her heels, wondering what to do. Perhaps Rana was crying because of something Lern had said—or, more likely, done. He had probably struck her again. And if Lern was in the tent, and in a rage, would he attack Terah also, if she came to inquire about the older woman's welfare?

She frowned; she had not heard a man's voice, only the sobs.

Terah sighed, wondering what she should do. She wished that Lern and Rana would get their domestic life in order. She did not want to see Rana's tear-stained face as the first sight of the morning. Yet, what could she do? The woman was crying . . . and she was, moreover, a friend.

Taking a deep breath, Terah called out at the entry-way. "Rana?"

No answer, but the sobs stopped. Terah heard some loud sniffing. "Rana?"

A quavery, "Y-yes?"

"Rana, it is Terah. I have come to visit you."

"It is very early for a visit, Terah," came the muffled answer.

Was Lern with her? Was she afraid? "Yes, it is early," agreed Terah. "If you would like me to come back another time, I will do so." There, she had made the offer. If Rana dismissed her, so be it. Terah almost hoped the older woman would tell her to go away.

There was a rustling inside the tent, then a trembling brown hand pulled back the animal skin at the doorway.

Terah gasped when she saw Rana's face. She had not meant to gasp, it was just that she was so unprepared for the bruises—and sadness and tears, too. "Rana!" she cried, sinking to her knees in front of the older woman. "What has he done to you?"

Rana buried her face in her hands and sobbed. "I cannot hide it any longer," she said brokenly. She looked up, and the right half her face was covered in black and yellow bruises. Red welts crossed the bruises. There were black bruises on her arms. Some of her hair was pulled out.

Terah felt sick. "You have got to—"

"What?" asked Rana. "I have got to what?"

Terah stared at her friend. She did not know what to say. She remembered the time she had recommended that Rana take her things out of the tent and leave the marriage, and Rana had said no. Rana had made it clear that she would not leave Lern. She did not want to have to "eat little tundra flowers." Terah gazed at Rana as her thoughts stumbled. "What," she asked at last, "do *you* want to do?"

The older woman shook her dark head. "I do not know any more," she sobbed at last. "Please tell me what to do." Her voice was pitiful. Her face was pitiful.

Terah did not know what to say. She cast around, trying to think of something. If she told Rana to leave Lern, then she, Terah, would be taking responsibility for Rana's life. If she told her to stay, it amounted to the same thing. No, it was Rana herself who must make a decision, not Terah.

Terah had Flori and Tika and Kell to think about. How could she advise another woman what to do?

Terah continued to squat by her sobbing friend. At last she said cautiously, "What choices do you have?"

Rana shook her head. "I know not."

Terah sighed. "Has this ever happened before? With any of the other Great Frog People, in your old village?" she ventured.

Rana nodded. "It did."

Terah brightened. "What did the woman decide?"

Rana sobbed harder. "Nothing."

Terah frowned. "Nothing? You mean she just let her husband keep beating her?"

Rana shook her head. "She died."

Terah grimaced. No help there.

"He killed her."

"Oh." Nausea welled in Terah's stomach, and she tried to concentrate on not getting sick. "Rana," she said finally, "that is what will happen to you if you continue to let Lern beat you. He will kill you. Every time he smites you, he smites you harder. You are more bruised. One day, you will be dead from his blows."

Rana sobbed harder. "I have nowhere to go, no one to help me. I do not know what to do."

Terah felt helpless. She patted Rana's arm, feeling the gesture was futile.

"What can I do?" Rana looked at her, eyes red from weeping.

Terah sighed. "What do you want to do?"

"Stay with Lern. He will apologize. He will be kind to me, again. Like he was before."

Terah was glad she had not suggested anything. "Stay with Lern then," she said in a stony voice. She felt as though she were consigning her friend to death, but she did not know what else to say. If Rana would not help herself, how could Terah?

"He loves me, I know he does."

Terah just stared at Rana. How could the woman believe Lern *loved* her? She opened her mouth to say something, but Rana said, "He told me he loves me."

Terah choked back a rude snort. Rana glanced

289

up at her. Terah's disbelief must have shown on her face.

"He told me," Rana said again. "After—the last time."

"You mean after he struck you the last time?"

Rana nodded. "I was going to leave—perhaps go to the shaman for help. Or perhaps come to you." She glanced sideways at Terah to see what Terah thought of that admission.

For a long moment, Terah kept her face impassive. What could *she* have done to help Rana? Kept her with her, she supposed. Made sure that Lern stayed away. But she would have needed Mamut's help in that. She sighed then. Mamut. He had chastised Lern for hitting his wife. Perhaps Mamut would have helped Rana. Perhaps not. It was too late to know, now. This was the day that Terah was taking the children and leaving and so she would never find out if Mamut would have done more to help the Frog woman.

"I told him I was going to leave."

Terah wanted to shriek her frustration. "Why did you tell Lern you were going to leave? That was just warning him!"

Rana grimaced. "It got some results," and her voice held a note of pride. "That was when he told me he loved me. He begged me not to leave, pleaded with me."

Terah had difficulty picturing Lern pleading with his wife.

"But I was determined." This time Terah had difficulty picturing the Great Frog woman as determined. Rana's unblinking gaze met Terah's.

Terah squirmed inside at the sight of the purple bruise that puffed out over Rana's right eye.

"I even reminded him that I cannot give him children—something that he beat me for in the past."

Terah winced, but at least it was getting easier for Rana to admit that Lern had hit her.

"I thought that if I reminded him, he would let me go. But he said—" The older woman lifted her chin proudly. "He said that he loved me even if I could not have children. Then he begged me not to leave. He told me that if I left him, the other men would laugh at him. All the people would laugh at him and mock him and say that he could not keep his wife."

True, thought Terah. But she doubted people would be laughing. They would be relieved.

"So, are you still going to leave him?" asked Terah. She held her breath, dreading the answer.

Rana slowly shook her head. "No, I have waited a long time for that man to say he loves me. And now that he has told me that he loves me, I am not going to leave him."

"You told me you could not hide it anymore that he beats you," said Terah. "That is what you said when I first came to your tent this morning." She was hoping that Rana would realize that if she stayed with Lern, she would continue to be beaten.

Rana shrugged. "My bruises hurt then. I was desperate."

"Do they not still hurt? And are you not still desperate?"

"No," said Rana stubbornly. "Lern loves me. And I love him."

Terah's green eyes flared with indignation, and she bit her lip to keep from screaming at Rana. *Leave the man!* she wanted to cry out. But mercifully, for Rana's sake, Terah remained silent. She could not, however, resist saying one thing. "Rana, I am afraid for you. Very afraid. I am afraid that if you stay with Lern, one day his beatings will kill you."

Rana shrugged. Her eyes watered a little, but she gave no other sign that what Terah said had affected her. "He did not break my jaw," she said finally. "It is not so bad." She took a deep breath. "If he had broken my jaw, then perhaps . . ." Her voice trailed off.

Terah's shoulders slumped. There was nothing else she could say or do. She turned away from the older woman. "I must go now," she said quietly.

Rana looked startled. "Go where?"

Terah glanced back at her friend and bit her lip, wondering if she should tell her plans to Rana. The older woman had enough to contend with. Then, deciding that Rana would not tell anyone of her escape, Terah answered, "I am leaving the Mammoth People. I am taking the children and going back to my people."

"Leaving? Going out into the hills by yourself?" Rana looked shocked, and Terah regretted the impulse to confide in her. "Do you even know where your people are?" demanded Rana.

Terah felt the flush rise in her cheeks.

"You do not know where your people are,"
Rana shrewdly answered her own question as she
watched Terah. Then she observed, "I thought
you liked Mamut."

Terah's cheeks flushed hotter.

"You do," again Rana answered herself. "And
he seems to like you. At least he does not beat
you." She caught herself, suddenly realizing what
she had said. "A man can care for a woman and
still beat her," she added tentatively. "Like Lern.
He—he cares for me."

Terah thought that Rana did not sound as certain as before. Then she sighed. Rana would have
to decide what to do with her own life. *She* had to
think of escaping, and of surviving the search for
her parents while guiding and feeding three little
children. *That* was what she had to think about.

"You will not tell—" Terah began.

Rana shushed her. "I will not tell anyone. Your
secret is safe with me."

Terah felt embarrassed that she had ever
doubted the older woman. She glanced down
at the ground. "Spearpoint is supposed to watch
out for me," she said tentatively. "I—I hope that
my escape does not cause bad feelings between
Mamut and Spearpoint."

Rana lifted her puffy right eyebrow. "You have
to escape first," she observed dryly.

"I will," said Terah in a voice like stone.

Rana gazed at her thoughtfully. "Before you go,
there is something I would do for you," she said
and rose. Her feet buckled and she almost collapsed. Terah reached out to steady the woman.

293

Rana groaned. "I—I felt dizzy for a moment," she explained sheepishly.

Lern's beatings, thought Terah angrily.

Rana leaned heavily upon Terah for a moment. Then she gave a feeble push, to stand on her own. "Come," she said and led the way slowly down to the creek. Terah followed, wondering what the Great Frog woman had in mind.

When they reached the creek, Rana pointed at the thin trickle of water in the wide, dry streambed. "Drought," she said, and Terah suddenly remembered that Rana had predicted drought earlier in the season. She nodded.

Rana picked up a stout stick that lay near the creek and began pounding the dirt with it. She kept pounding, and the rhythm was soothing to Terah's overwrought nerves.

Suddenly Terah jumped back as a huge, dark green toad crept out of the dried mud at her very feet. To Terah's surprise, more toads began to creep out of the ground. Soon, the two women were surrounded by grayish-green toads, all climbing out of the little shelters they had built to hide from the dryness. "They think that it is raining," explained Rana to Terah. "The pounding stick sounds like rain to them."

Rana had a rare smile of satisfaction upon her face. *She loves these toads*, thought Terah and she was glad there was something good in Rana's life.

Terah watched as Rana laid down the stick, careful not to injure any of the toads with it. Then the Great Frog woman raised her arms and began singing. She swayed as she sang.

Hear me, O toads! Hear me, O frogs!
Go where my friend goes! Guard her steps,
little scouts!
Hi yi yi yi! Hi yi yi yi!
Hear me, O frogs! Hear me, O toads!
Call out your warnings! Your great voices
will tell her when you see an enemy!
Hi yi yi yi! Hi yi yi yi!

A tear of gratitude spilled down Terah's cheek as she listened to the words. She felt humbled that Rana would do this for her—disturb the toads and ask their protection for her.

Terah turned to Rana and hugged her. "Thank you," she said. "Thank you for awakening your friends, the toads, and asking that they watch over me on my journey. I know that now I will get back to my people safely."

Rana smiled; the black and yellow bruises on her face looked hideous.

Terah hesitated, but she could not resist asking, "Why did you not ask the toads' protection for yourself?"

Rana shook her head and put her fingers to her lips. "The Frog Power only works when you ask for a gift for someone else, not for yourself." She smiled sadly.

Terah stared at her. "Then I will ask the frogs and toads to guard you," she said decisively.

She swung around and faced the grayish green creatures. Some of them were burrowing back into the earth, unable to feel the rainwater they had expected.

Terah stamped the ground to gain their attention, then she raised her arms as Rana had done and imitated the swaying movement, too.

> *Hear me O toads! Hear me O frogs!*
> *Stay with my friend, Rana! Keep her safe!*
> *Do not let her husband hit her!*
> *Hi yi yi yi! Hi yi yi yi!*

Rana watched with an approving gleam in her eye. When Terah had finished her song, Rana said simply, "I thank you, friend Terah."

Later, Terah was very quiet as she led the way back to the tents. Her friend, Rana of the Great Frog People, leaned on her occasionally as they traversed the path. When they reached the encampment, the Mammoth People were stirring. Smoldering fires were being lit anew with dried bison dung. Wolf Boy was stalking between tents. Another day was beginning.

Chapter 26

Lo! She was free, rejoiced Terah, as she and the children climbed into a narrow, rocky draw between two basalt-covered hills. They were leaving behind them the dirt-brown tents of the Mammoth People.

Spearpoint had come to her and told her he had decided to go hunting with Lern and the shaman. He expected to be back at camp by nightfall. Would Terah and the children feel safe until his return?

Terah had looked blandly into his dark brown eyes and flushed at the deceit she intended. He did not deserve to be so deceived, yet what else could she do? She *had* to escape. So she had nodded and murmured the correct words and waited until the hunters had walked away into the hills. Then she had taken the children and left.

No one had seen them leave the Mammoth People's camp. No one could tell Mamut until he returned from his vision quest.

Unfortunately, in her hurry to leave, Terah had snatched up the basket of meat only to find it half-full. She had taken it anyway. Now she glanced down at the basket worriedly. The dried meat would not last them longer than two or three days. They must find her people before then, or she and the children would starve.

"This basket was full of meat yester eve," she said to Tika. "I do not understand why it is only half-full now."

"Oh," answered Tika. "Kell and I were playing dire wolves with Lame Leg. Lame Leg was the baby wolf and I was the mother wolf. Kell was the father wolf. We had to feed the baby." She looked at Terah with large green eyes.

A sinking feeling invaded Terah's heart. "And so you gave your 'baby' dire wolf the meat," she concluded weakly.

"Yes," answered Tika. "All that she could eat. She was a very hungry baby."

Tika and Kell climbed the draw between the hills without complaint. Flori whimpered and Terah picked her up and tied her onto her hip with a long, wide length of leather, a baby carrier thong such as Terah had seen Benaleese make.

Terah could not stop herself from glancing back several times, but there was no pursuit. She hoped she and the children would not stumble across Mamut in their flight.

They made their way slowly through the draw

and came out the other side into a long, narrow wash. At least the Mammoth People would not be able to see her now because of the hills between her and the creek, Terah thought in satisfaction. She and the children could follow this wash until they were safely out of the Mammoth People's territory.

Mamut would never find them. The thought left her strangely downcast. She pushed him from her mind and slogged on.

But her hopes began to flag at the end of the third day of freedom. Dusk was falling. She managed to find a little sheltered area where the side of a hill guarded their backs. A large boulder protected one side. They would spend the night at the corner where hill and boulder met. She hoped dire wolves and saber-tooths would not catch their scent.

Nights were the worst. Danger abounded, and that was when she thought of Mamut. Of his strength, his protectiveness, his warmth, his lips . . .

She dragged her thoughts away from Mamut and peered into the basket. By the failing light she could see that there were three small pieces of dried meat left. She hefted the bison bladder. It was still one-quarter full of water. At least they had enough water for another day or so. But after that . . . it did not bear thinking, she decided. She would find her people. She had to.

For the first time, she thought of the Great Spirit. *Help me find my people*, she said in a slight, swift prayer. No more, though. For she was becoming very angry at the Great Spirit. She was beginning to realize that it was the Great Spirit's fault that she was in this mess. The Great Spirit had let Chee die; the Great Spirit had not prevented Terah's capture and that of the children. The Great Spirit, she went on as her anger grew, had let Bron, her dear, beloved brother, die in pain and agony from the saber-toothed tiger claws. And the Great Spirit, so powerful, so almighty, could easily lead her and the children to where her parents' encampment was now—but did He? No!

She handed out the last of the three chunks of meat to the children. She would not eat— had not, in fact, eaten all that day so that the children would have enough food. She took a tentative sip of water. She must calm herself. To rail at an uncaring Great Spirit was not going to help her, she reasoned with herself, but reason did not help. Her heart was incensed that things had come to this pass for them.

Kell, his brown eyes sleepy, took the meat from her. He chewed it slowly. Flori held out her plump little hand for her piece and Terah gave it to her. The child chewed with gusto. But Tika glanced sharply up at Terah as her aunt handed her the last chunk of meat from the basket. *She knows*, thought Terah, *she knows that we are in serious trouble*. A sense of failure washed over Terah that she had fled with the children when so ill-prepared.

Terah swallowed and lifted the water bladder

to her lips once more. She took a careful swallow of water. At least she had the water. When the children were finished eating—uncommonly quickly to Terah's way of thinking—she let them each have two swallows of water.

When she had them settled on a bison robe she had taken when they'd left the Mammoth camp, she sang them some songs and told a story. "Now, go to sleep," she said softly. This night, to Terah's great surprise and gratitude, they snuggled into the robes and went to sleep.

She slept too, but fitfully, haunted by a dream where she left tiny signs along the trail so that Mamut could find them. But in her dream he did not come after her. . . .

They slept that night and on into the next morning. Only the heat of the day awoke them. They each took two sips from the water bladder and then rose from the cramped little place they had slept in.

Terah stepped back from the boulder and glanced around. It was going to be a hot day. She looked back down the wash where they had come. No one was following them. She supposed that was good. "Come, children," she said, her voice as encouraging as she could make it, and they set out.

By the end of the day, all four were drooping. There was no food, except for a handful of tiny withered berries they had found. Those were swiftly consumed by the children, and the water in the bison bladder was now down to one-eighth.

Enough for one more day, thought Terah in despair. Oh, where were her people? Tomorrow, she thought in desperation, she would climb the ridge and look out over the hills toward where she thought the Giver of Life River should be. Trapped as she was down between hills, she could see nothing but the closest hills. But from the great height of the ridge, she would be able to look out over the vast rolling hills and spot her people. Surely she would see them!

The next morning, Terah set out with a determined look upon her face. The children trudged after her, but they were traveling at a slow pace, slower than Terah would have liked. She had to get to the ridge top. She gritted her teeth. That ridge was her only hope of finding her people in time.

By midday the children were fretful and crying. They stopped often to rest. Terah gritted her teeth. She had to push them to the ridge. She had to.

She glanced back the way they had come. No pursuers. She and the children had dragged themselves across the narrow wash, which was not so narrow when one was counting every step. Then they had climbed one of the smaller hills. The ridge lay behind two more hills, and then it was a steep climb up the gravel-covered slope. She took a breath and clenched her jaw. She could do it. She would do it. Nothing was going to stop her from reaching that ridge!

Night fell. They had not reached the ridge. They had not reached the hills in front of the ridge. Discouraged, Terah plunked herself down on the coarse dry gravel. Tika and Kell and Flori flopped down beside her. The only sound was their panting.

"I want water," said Kell.

Terah held up the water bladder. Fluid gurgles came from the bottom of it. The last of the water.

"Mmmmphhh," said Flori, pointing at her mouth.

Terah lifted exhausted eyes to the child's face. The child looked drawn and tired. Guilt prodded Terah's conscience. Because she had fled from the Mammoth People, the children were now thirsting and starving. Terah shook her head. "No food." Flori pointed to her mouth again. "I am sorry, little one. There is no food."

"Stop it!" said Tika irritably. She swatted at her sister's outstretched hand. "There is no food!"

They were all impatient and irritable with one another, Terah saw, as Kell joined in and started hitting at his older sister. Terah stopped the fight.

"Children," she said tiredly, "we must not fight. We are hungry, but we must still treat each other with kindness." Her own stomach felt hollow and empty and sore as she said the words. "Tomorrow, at first light, I am going to climb to the top of the ridge. From there, I will see Grandmother's people. Then we will know where they are, and we will climb down and find them." Terah hoped it sounded easy to do.

"Are you—are you leaving us?" asked Tika, her green eyes wide.

"No," said Terah firmly. "I will climb the ridge and then I will return to you."

She saw Tika's frown. "It is too far and too difficult a climb for small children," Terah explained.

"I am not small," said Tika.

"We want to come," said Kell.

Terah shook her head. "You cannot. We will all be too tired."

"But," objected Tika, "what if a dire wolf gets us?"

"I will see that you are safe before I leave," Terah answered. But she knew that she could not ensure the children's safety. If she were not so hungry, she could think better. Two days with no food was a very long time, she had discovered. And she was so tired.

She roused herself. "After a sound sleep, I will be strong." Some part of her mind jeered at her. If only she did not have to leave the children and climb . . . yet she could not continue to drag them with her. They were too exhausted. If only, she thought angrily, the Great Spirit would help them. But no, the Great Spirit had turned his back on her, as usual, and was of no help at all!

The children were still asleep when Terah awoke the next morning. Dawn lit the sky, and the air was fresh. She glanced down at the children. Tika lay on her back, with one arm thrown to the side. Kell had snuggled up to Flori. Flori slept half-burrowed into the robe, her rounded rump pointing skywards.

Terah glanced around; no saber-tooths, no dire

wolves were in sight. The sweet sound of a little bird pierced the air. Terah shook Tika gently. "Wake up," she whispered.

Tika sat up, abruptly. "You are still here."

Terah nodded. "I go now. There is water in the bison bladder. Enough for all of you, if you take tiny, tiny sips." Terah licked dry lips, reminded that she had not had any water because she had saved it for the children. "I will be back as soon as I can."

"What if you do not come back?" Tika looked older than her eight years, her small face drawn in the thin rosy light of sunrise.

Terah met her niece's gaze and squeezed the young one's shoulder. "I will come back." *How can you promise so?* came the jeering little voice. *A saber-tooth could get you, you could die of starvation . . .* Terah silenced the nagging voice of fear. "I go now." She took several steps, then turned around. She stared at her niece. "Know that I love you," she said softly. "I love you very much."

Tika nodded. "And I love you," she said, her little voice so formal, so adult.

"I will return," said Terah in what she hoped was a confident voice. "Wait here for me."

Tika nodded, her big green eyes solemn.

Terah turned and began walking toward the ridge. Her steps were light though her heart was heavy. So much depended upon her reaching that ridge. She would be able to see where her mother's people were; she would be able to see any green patches of trees and plants. Those would

305

indicate water. She must make it to the ridge, she must! She thought she heard a choking sound behind her, but when she glanced back, Tika was buried in the robe again. *I must have been mistaken,* Terah thought. She was hearing things. She wondered if that happened when a person went for two days with so little water and no food.

She concentrated on putting one foot in front of the other. Her body responded to the rhythm, and she was soon crossing the draws between the hills at a good pace. The children really had made walking much slower, Terah thought. She wondered how they were doing with Tika in charge. She quickened her pace. She must get back as soon as she could.

Terah finally reached the bottom of the ridge. Half the day had passed, half the day of trudging over the rough rocks. Half the day of leaving the children alone. By now, saber-tooths could have attacked them, or dire wolves, or perhaps just the slow heat of the sun was burning them. . . .

Tortured now, Terah wanted to run back to the children. But it was so far! She struggled against the fear. There was no choice but to push on. She was closer now to the ridge than she had ever been.

She started to climb up the gravel, taking ten steps and sliding back five. Several times she attempted to climb, but the big chunks of rock were slick and she kept sliding down. Despair drove her. *I must make it to the top. I cannot stop now!* She grabbed hold of a leathery tundra plant growing in a crack and hoisted herself up a little farther. "The children are depending upon me," she murmured to herself over and over again.

With painstaking effort, she finally dragged herself on hands and knees up the steep incline. Sliding back down bloodied her hands and knees, but she kept crawling. Finally, exhausted, panting, thirsting, she came to a little ledge of hard rock. She was half-way there. But she was tired. She would just rest a little. . . .

No, came an inner voice, *get up and keep climbing.* But oh, how good it felt to rest . . . she was so tired. . . .

Somehow she dragged herself onward. She left the little ledge. The rock was not so loose here, but she had to place her feet in cracks and crevices to keep a foothold. She dragged herself up the cliff until she reached the overhang of the ridge.

"Just a little farther," she encouraged herself. "Just a little farther . . ." The rock she had gripped broke away and she jerked, sliding down the slope a little. She managed to grab a piece of rock that held firm. She held on, panting. "Just a little farther . . ."

Then she closed her eyes. It was all too impossible. She was so close to the top, but she could not do it. She was too tired. She would slide to her death on this barren hillside, and the children would starve to death or be eaten by wolves. Bitterness swept over her. *Where is the Great Spirit?* she wondered. *I need help!*

But only the soft sighing of the wind met her

Theresa Scott

despair. "I cannot give up," she whispered. "I will not give up." She reached out and, foothold by foothold, climbed back up until she was at the overhang again. She stood there panting, her feet frozen into the crevices, her knuckles white from gripping the rock. She had to get above the overhang, and then she would be done!

Cautiously, she reached out, trying to feel the rock above the overhang. It was gravel, nothing to hold on to. She carefully replaced her hand and felt above with the other hand. Gravel there, too. Despair gripped her. What was she going to do? She was so *close*. . . .

She groped again; still only gravel. Nothing to hold on to. She glanced to either side. There, if she moved a little to the side, she could get some new handholds, closer to the top.

Slowly, cautiously, she inched her way across the rock. Her foot slipped. Gravel from the broken rock tumbled down and bounced off the rocks below. Terah swallowed. That could have been her body. *Do not think about it*, she told herself. *Keep going.*

This time when she reached up, she felt an outcrop of solid rock on the top of the overhang. She gripped it, and her hand curled around the rock. She tugged. It held solid. She put a little of her weight on it. Still solid. Carefully, she moved until both hands were on the rocky outcrop. Her feet were glued to the crevices. She put more of her weight on the outcrop. Then a foothold broke and one foot dangled. She gave a little cry of fright.

She hung on to the outcrop and realized suddenly that she would have to kick free her anchored foot and lift herself up. "I can do it," she repeated through gritted teeth. But her arms were getting tired. She dangled from the cliff, clutching the outcrop, her lower body swinging free of the cliff. "Great Spirit," she prayed. "I am angry with you, furious with you. You must know that. But I do not want to die. Please help me. There are three children waiting for me to save them. Please let me live." She gritted her teeth. How angry she was to be begging the Great Spirit for her life. The Great Spirit had never listened to her. Yet what else could she do? She was desperate.

There was no answer. No surge of strength, nothing. In fact, the strain on her arms was beginning to hurt.

"Great Spirit," she tried again. "I need your help. You took my brother Bron. You took my sister Chee. Please do not take me!"

No answer. She hung there, dangling above the rocks. The pain in her arms was intense. Her stomach was hungry. She knew the hunger had weakened her. How long could she hold on before she dropped and slid and bounced off the rocks below to her death? Not very long, she answered herself.

"Great Spirit," she moaned. "Help me."

A little wind pushed at her. She dangled, her feet hanging. She put her feet back to the rock. That took some of the weight off her arms. Carefully, she moved one foot closer, as if walking up the cliff. Then she moved the next foot. Taking

Theresa Scott

little steps, she was able to work her way up
until she could throw one leg out and over the
overhang. She half expected the overhang to fall
away, but it held. With her leg, she was able to
pull herself up. She inched her way up until her
torso lay on the overhang. Panting, she lay there,
half on the cliff, one leg still over.

She peeked down. The cliff fell away before
her, the brown rolling hills, and in the distance
she could see a green line of trees where the Giver
of Life River cut through the hills. With a tiny
sigh, she pulled her leg up and collapsed on the
ridge. She had made it! But she was weary, so
weary. . . . She would just close her eyes for but
a heartbeat. . . .

She awoke to a quiet stillness.

And perched on a black rock, watching her, sat
an old man.

310

Chapter 27

He wore a white bison robe, seamless. He
looked familiar to Terah, like someone she
had known, but she could not remember when
or where she had last seen him. His face was
wrinkled, homely, perhaps even a little ugly.
White hair fell to his shoulders. His dark eyes
sparkled.

Terah sat up and inched away from the cliff
toward him. Completely forgotten was the reason she had climbed the cliff in the first place.
"Who are you?" she asked at last.

"The Great Spirit," came the answer, but he
did not move his lips when he spoke. Terah
heard his answer in her head, yet the words
were clear.

"The Great Spirit," she repeated. A sense of
awe filled her, but not an overwhelming awe

as she might have expected. It was a comfortable awe. She was momentarily distracted and looked out across the land. She could see the distant green trees that lined the Giver of Life River valley. Toward her rolled the brown hills, then the darker basalt gravel and rock of the cliff she had climbed.

The old man pointed with his chin to a pillar of black rock in a bend of the Giver of Life River. The rock was far north of where Terah had been traveling. "Your parents are there," he said.

"Thank you," she answered. There was a peace, a calm in her heart, and a gratitude. She felt at ease with him, accepted. Even her anger at him was accepted. She could feel it. "May I—?" she reached out a hand and took a step toward him. "May I touch you?"

"If you wish. Though not all people wish to touch me."

It came to her that many people were busy with their lives, and distracted, and did not think it important to touch him. She detected no censure from him for that, it was just the way things were. A longing grew in her to touch him, even if it was a tiny, light touch. Slowly, carefully, she reached out and touched his hand. Suddenly she felt dizzy and heard singing.

She woke up. She saw that she was still on the clifftop. "I had a vision," she thought to herself, looking around for the Great Spirit. "I saw the Great Spirit!"

There was no one with her. She moved back from the cliff and fell asleep once more.

She woke again in the presence of the Great Spirit. This time, she was wearing a white bison robe too. She walked around on the ridge top looking down at the rolling hills below. There were several other people on the ridge top with her, none of whom she recognized. They all wore white bison robes. Terah heard women singing the most beautiful song she had ever heard.

The Great Spirit had a thoughtful look upon his face. Terah went over to him. "My brother—Bron," she said. "I would like to know how he fares."

Immediately she saw Bron, but not as he had been when she had last seen him. Then he had been dying, and his face was tortured by pain as he clutched the bloody remains of his stomach. Now he was a happy, youthful, bronzed young man, his torso flat and strong and healed. He raised his spear and ran after a young antelope. He threw his spear, and the antelope fell. In triumph, he glanced at Terah, beaming. It came to Terah that he was happy and whole and very content to be where he was. The terrible grief that had been with her ever since his death lifted. Bron was safe; he was happy. She did not need to carry the anger and bitterness of his loss with her anymore.

"Thank you," she said to the old man. He nodded.

She enjoyed the calm and peace on the ridge

top, but after a little while she began to wonder about Chee. "May I see Chee?" she asked the Great Spirit. "I loved her very much. I did not like it that she died." She looked into the Great Spirit's eyes. "Chee has three children, as you know. They needed her. I wanted her to live."

The old man looked at her, and it was a kind glance, but she did not see Chee, and he did not give her any words in her head in answer. She was puzzled, but accepting. If the Great Spirit thought she did not need to see Chee, she could accept that. She was very accepting of everything in this state. It came to her that she was loved and accepted right now, at this very moment, as she was, with her angers and fears and griefs and hopes. There was a rightness to it all. And the gift of the Great Spirit's presence was very precious to her. He was kind; she could make her own choices. And he liked it that she had wanted to touch his hand. She would always cherish this vision of him, she knew.

She awoke again, and she was no longer wearing the white bison robe, only her ordinary deerskin tunic. She sat up slowly and glanced around.

Chee, her sister, was there. Terah's heart gave a little leap. She sank back to the hard ground with a smile. She was dying; she realized it now. Seeing Chee told her that. No food, little water, the exhausting climb . . . it had all been too much for Terah. She hoped the children would be safe.

And how kind of the Great Spirit to send her sister's comforting spirit to her as she had requested. Terah felt a sweeping rush of gratitude at the mercy He had shown her. And now she sensed that all would go well with Tika and Kell and Flori. And Mamut . . . What of him? She realized drowsily that she wanted his life to go well too.

Terah lay quietly on the desolate ridge top. A sad smile cracked her dry lips, but there was a peaceful look on her exhausted, lovely face as she waited for her death. She closed her eyes and let out her breath.

Chapter 28

When Terah woke up, Chee was still there. She was building a small fire. Terah blinked, wondering why the afterlife place looked so much like the clifftop she had climbed to. She sat up.

Chee looked over at her. "Finally, you are awake," she said.

Terah was surprised that people could sound so impatient in the afterlife. She had thought it would be all peace and acceptance, as she had found earlier. She blinked. Chee was still there. "We are both dead, then?" she asked cheerfully.

Her sister stared at her. "I am not dead," she answered in amusement. "Perhaps you are."

Ah, so like Chee. Terah wanted to throw her arms around her sister. She looked to see if she had arms. Yes, she did, and they moved in the normal manner. "Where is the old man in white?" she asked.

"Who?" answered Chee.

"The old man."

Chee shrugged. "There is no old man here." She turned around in a full circle. "No, no old man," she assured Terah.

Terah was puzzled. "No more teasing," she admonished her older sister. "We really are dead, are we not?"

Chee walked over. She squatted down and stared into her sister's eyes. Green met green. "I am not dead," she said slowly. She reached out and pinched Terah's arm.

"Ouch!"

"There. You are not dead, either," said Chee. She got up and walked away, humming, and started to gather little tufts of grass for the fire.

Terah frowned. If Chee was not dead, and *she* was not dead, then what had happened? Her body felt light, but that could have been hunger— and thirst. She remembered the Great Spirit very clearly. He had been real. She watched Chee, realizing at last that her sister had put a hare on to cook over the flames. Soon the sizzle of the cooking meat and the tantalizing smell drifted over to Terah's nostrils. Her stomach growled. She licked dry lips. "Do you—do you have any water?"

Chee pointed with her chin to a bison bladder lying on the ground.

Terah rose and staggered over to it. She lifted the water bladder to her lips and drank. In her haste, the water bubbled over her lips and ran down her chin. The cool liquid soothed her throat, and she thought the wetness of the water the most beautiful feeling she had every experienced. The bladder was half-full, so she lifted it and poured some of the precious fluid over her face. The water ran into her hair and up her nose, and she gloried in it.

Chee came up behind her. Terah turned and met her sister face-to-face. They were of the same height and had the same green eyes. Chee's hair was black, while Terah's was a light brown. And Chee's build was fuller, Terah's frame slimmer. But there was no doubt that they were sisters.

They hugged and Terah clutched Chee tightly. "I am so glad you are alive," she whispered. Tears gleamed in both women's eyes. At last, Terah dashed the wetness away and the two pulled apart.

"And I am glad to have found you, dearest sister," said Chee. "Now that you feel better," she added, "I want you to tell me where my children are."

"The children," gasped Terah. "I forgot about the children."

Chee frowned at this admission. "If I did not think you had been without food and water, perhaps for days, I would take offense at that remark."

She turned away and walked back to the roasting hare. Terah guessed that Chee had already

319

taken offense. She hurried after her sister. "I have not been away from the children more than a day," she said, but even as she said it, guilt struck her. To leave the children alone for even one day in this terrible terrain could mean leaving them to their death. Terah knew it and Chee knew it.

Terah glanced at the roasting hare, then turned to see where the sun was. It lay low on the horizon—late afternoon. She turned back to the hare. "After we eat, I will be strong enough to show you the way back to the children," she said, hoping her voice sounded confident. Verily, Terah did not know if they could find the children before dark fell, but she had to try.

Chee nodded halfheartedly. She, too, had her doubts about finding the children before nightfall. They ate in silence, Terah's thoughts occupied with worry about the children. Suddenly she looked up and said, "How is it that you are not dead, sister? When I left you, we both were certain that you were dying. I would not have left you otherwise."

Chee was gnawing on one of the hare's hind legs. She looked up. "The sickness passed. I fell asleep, and when I awoke the hotness had gone, I could move my body once again. . . ." She shrugged. "I think it was the mushrooms I ate."

"I am glad you are alive," said Terah, and her voice echoed the fullness of her heart. "I cried so much for you and missed you . . ."

Chee nodded. "I thank you, little sister," she said, and Terah could hear the love in her voice. They finished eating, then Chee stood. "I will pack away this meat for the children."

Terah nodded, hoping that they would indeed find the children alive and well and able to eat. Then she remembered the vision she had of the Great Spirit. At the time, she had had the feeling that the children were well. She clung to that thought. "Let us go," she said.

They put out the fire and set out. Chee led her to a path that came up the back of the cliff. It was much easier terrain to travel than the cliff-face that Terah had climbed.

They plodded steadily onward, and Terah felt encouraged and hopeful because they seemed to be traveling at a goodly speed. Perhaps they *would* reach the children before night fell on the land.

As they walked, they talked, each telling by turns what had happened to them since Terah had last seen Chee. They also kept alert for saber-toothed tigers and dire wolves.

One time a wolf began to follow them. Terah expected a pack, because dire wolves liked to travel in family groups, but it seemed that this one had no brothers or sisters. She and Chee threw rocks at the wolf and watched in relief as he slunk away. Terah thought to herself, *The Great Spirit is watching over us. I just hope He has guarded the children as well.*

At last they reached the area near where Terah had left the children. Now she marveled that she had gone and left them on their own—but she had been desperate, she reminded herself, desperate to locate the grandparents' encampment.

Terah stopped on a small knoll. She raised one

hand to shade her eyes as she searched for the hill and boulder where she had left Tika and the others. Dusk was falling, and the boulders and terrain all appeared gray. It was difficult to pick out one particular boulder. Still, she gazed at the landscape.

"Do you see them?" asked Chee.

Terah did not wonder that her sister's voice shook. No mother could remain calm knowing that her children were all alone somewhere in the gathering darkness. Terah half-expected her sister to run screaming down the knoll, driven frantic in her fear. But Chee did not. She did, however, reach for Terah's hand.

Terah's hand ached from the rockhard grip of her sister. Gently she pried her fingers loose. "I see it," she said and heard Chee expel her breath. "Come," said Terah, knowing that each step she took was forced now. What if the children were not there? Or dead? She shook her head slowly, trying to drive such fears from her mind. "Come," she said again.

Chee needed no urging. They walked down the knoll and headed west toward the boulder that Terah had spotted.

Yes, it was the right one. Their pace increased until they were running over the rough gravel as they drew ever closer to the boulder.

Suddenly Terah jerked to a stop in mid-step. Her sister halted beside her. Both stared in disbelief into the gathering gloom.

A flickering light, as though from a fire, was coming from behind the boulder. Who was there?

Chapter 29

The two women stared at each other. "Who?" whispered Chee.

Terah's eyes widened. "I do not know," she answered. She knew the fear she saw in Chee's eyes was a reflection of her own.

The two held a whispered conference. Quietly, carefully, Terah took out her white chert knife and headed toward the boulder.

Chee scraped a shallow pit to hide the bison bladder and the meat so that predators would not be drawn to the food. Then she set out to creep behind the boulder on the lee side of the hill.

Terah's heart thumped heavily in her chest as she ran low over the ground. *Who is with the children?* she wondered frantically. *Had Tika managed to build a fire?*

Theresa Scott

Then Terah's fear grew because she suddenly realized that she had left no flints for Tika. No, this was not a fire built by Tika. Who, then? Had Mamut returned early to the Mammoth camp and followed their tracks out into the hills? Had he chanced upon the children?

The possibility that it was Mamut who had built the fire brought a sense of relief to Terah. Yes, it would be a good thing if it was Mamut with the children. They would be safe with him. She began to hope that it was indeed Mamut.

She was not prepared for the pang of disappointment that twisted her heart when she finally peeked around the boulder and saw who it was.

Then she smiled slowly to herself. It was Dagger—Tika and Kell and Flori's father. Chee must have recognized him at that same moment, for a blood-curdling scream pierced the night and then Chee was hurling herself at her husband. Dagger had half-risen, alerted by a stone dislodged by one of the women's steps. His wife's happy attack pushed him to the ground.

The children stared in disbelief. "Mama! Mama!" They were on their feet and dancing, pulling at the two adults, screaming and jumping about as though demented.

Terah, grinning, slipped around in front of the boulder and watched the happy scene. The children looked well. The remains of a young antelope lay near the fire, and a full water bladder was next to the meat. Dagger had done well for his family.

When the noise and jumping and happy cries

324

finally died down, young Tika glimpsed her aunt. "Aunt Terah!" she cried and flung herself into Terah's arms. Terah laughed and caught the child to her and hugged her. *If I ever have a child*, she thought, *I want one just like Tika.*

She held the child to her and Kell and Flori ran up, too, wanting a hug. Chee and Dagger stood by the fire, arms locked around one another. They held each other as though they would never, ever let one another go.

Terah saw the glisten of tears on her sister's cheeks. She noted that Dagger's eyes were suspiciously wet, too. She bent to hug Kell and Flori, to give her sister and brother-in-law time to compose themselves. Bison men and women were very proud.

At last the children plopped down by the fire once more. Terah stayed with the children while Chee and Dagger retrieved the cache of bison bladder and cooked hare meat that Chee had buried. The children kept asking why Mama and Dada were taking so long to come back, and Terah launched into a third story to keep them entertained. Finally, Chee and Dagger returned with happy, satisfied smiles on their faces.

Terah felt an inexplicable longing for someone to share her life with, someone who would bring a beaming smile to her face as Dagger had done for Chee. Her thoughts crept to Mamut. *He* had brought a smile to her face, she thought, and more than once.

But she did not have time to wonder for long about how Mamut would feel when he returned to the Mammoth camp and found her gone, because the children were talking and Dagger was talking and then Chee was talking, and Terah lost the thread of her thoughts.

It was late that night when the happy children finally fell asleep, Tika in her mother's arms, Kell and Flori on either side of Dagger.

Terah stared moodily at the fire and wondered what life held for her. When she returned to her parents' encampment, would she find a mate among the Bison men?

She wrinkled her nose. None of them could compare to Mamut. She would be a fool to hope otherwise. She had learned much during her stay with the Mammoth People, and one of the things she had learned was that she wanted a man that *she* desired. And who desired her. She wanted a man who cared about *her*, and not just about her body. And she definitely did not want a man like Bear, who was led by his loins from woman to woman.

At last, exhausted by all that had happened during the last four days and nights, Terah fell into a deep sleep.

She was awakened late the next morning by the children arguing loudly over who was going to be the dire wolf and who was going to be the antelope. Kell was screaming that he was tired of always being the animal who was killed. Flori was sniffling because she was being left out of the hunt. And Tika was fuming because she had played the antelope the last time. It was her turn to be the dire wolf, she insisted.

Terah smiled to herself and rolled over, content to let Chee handle the children. Dagger wisely decided to go off hunting. When he returned, this time with a young deer, the children were energetically digging for roots. They cooked and ate the deer and saved the meat for the return trip to the grandparents' encampment. Dagger assured Chee and Terah that it was only a two-day walk, a slow walk, to the camp.

They started out and soon found a creek. They filled the bison bladders with fresh water. Terah's steps lagged behind the others. She was going back to a group of people where there was no man for her.

She remembered that the Mammoth People attended Meet-meets and sought out wives. Perhaps she could talk her family into attending a Meet-meet. Perhaps she could meet a young man there.

The image of Mamut sprang into her mind. She shoved it away. Then she brought it back. If she saw him at a Meet-meet, picking out a wife, she would ignore him. She would saunter past him, dressed in her best tunic and beads, and just ignore him. Treat him as if he were not there. She would have smiles for the other young men, assuredly. But not for him. No.

The more she thought about it, the better the idea seemed. She would talk her parents into visiting the next Meet-meet.

Chapter 30

Mamut's eyes narrowed to glittering slits as he watched his prey, the little family band, walking across the tundra. Three children and three adults—and one of them was Terah. He recognized those swaying hips, that provocative stride. So she sought to escape him, did she? And she had almost succeeded.

Upon Mamut's return to the Mammoth People's camp after his vision quest, a visibly anguished Spearpoint had met him before he even reached the camp. Mamut thought he knew his cousin well, but he was unprepared for the contorted face, the wringing hands, that foretold grim news.

"I did not think she would escape," Spearpoint began, and Mamut's heart sank. Then the tidings worsened. Terah had taken the children and fled somewhere into the hills. Spearpoint had followed the tracks, then lost them when Terah had wandered through a creek, a trick Spearpoint recalled teaching her when they had traveled to the bison hunt.

Gone was the mood of relief and challenge and hope that Mamut had enjoyed since he'd had his white mammoth vision. In its place was loss—mixed with a terrible anger and a consuming, raging desire to find Terah and drag her back, in bonds if necessary.

He castigated himself that he had been so foolish as to trust her. *See what comes of trusting a woman,* he snarled savagely to himself. He experienced a twinge of fleeting gratitude that he had not told her about his fear of mammoths. It seemed she ran from him anyway, without even knowing of his secret cowardice.

What had gone wrong? he had wondered over and over as he pursued the tracks she had left. Spearpoint had pointed out her tracks and the creek where they had disappeared. Mamut had picked up her trail farther down the creek. It seemed that vengeance and grim patience brought more success in tracking a fleeing woman than apologies and hand-wringing. Mamut knew he was not being fair to Spearpoint, but he was angry. Spearpoint should have known better than to leave a captive woman unguarded. Especially a woman who had been so difficult to capture at first, and one who insisted upon carrying a dangerous little white chert knife!

Had one of the Mammoth People guessed his

secret cowardice and told her? Perhaps the shaman—he might have guessed, for the man was
an astute reader of people. Yet he also had an
integrity about him ... no, it would not be the
shaman who said anything.

Who then? Who did not like Mamut? Perhaps
Lern? Lern often made jokes about Mamut.
Mamut knew the man was jealous of him,
disliked him for some reason, but then Lern had
always been like that, since they were young men.
That was just Lern. Mamut was certain that Lern
knew nothing of that accursed day when Mamut
had run from the mammoth Father-Killer and left
Kran to die. No, it was not Lern who would have
told her.

Then what? Mamut now felt a perfect fool
for expecting that she would be there when he
returned. He had not anticipated that she would
flee him. He thought she had finally accepted her
place among the Mammoth People as his captive.
Also, she had three children to look after. What
woman fled when burdened with three small
children?

He had told her he would come back. He
was not deserting her. Surely she knew he
cared about her. There had been that one
little incident about obtaining a second wife
at the Meet-meet, he admitted to himself, but
surely she had become reconciled to being his
captive. What did she want?

Well, now he would find out, he thought, his
jaw clenched as he watched his prey trudging
ahead. Mamut was too far away to see if Terah

carried the little white chert knife at her side, but knowing her, she probably did. His eyes fastened on her buttocks, and he had to drag them away to study the terrain.

He felt impatient waiting for them to stop and camp for the night. From the unhurried pace the family traveled at, Mamut guessed that they must be in their own territory. The male, black-haired, tall and thin, did not appear unduly apprehensive. Now and then he searched the terrain for predators and Mamut was careful to keep still and low when he did, but the male did not exhibit the nervous demeanor he had shown the day before when Mamut had first sighted them. Then the male had been keeping a constant watch of the surrounding landscape. Well, if they were near their destination, Mamut would have to get closer to steal Terah.

The little family group came to a bush-sheltered spot on the bank of a creek, and the male looked around. When he nodded, the women set down the children and their few bundles.

Mamut watched them lazily, biding his time. The children played, and the women set about making a temporary camp. Kell started to wander off and the male—probably the father, Mamut had decided by now—fetched him back, the boy kicking and yelling. Mamut was close enough to hear Kell yelling something about hunting saber-toothed tigers, and he chuckled to himself. The boy was brave, no doubt about that. Later he saw the father leave, taking Kell with him. Mamut watched as the man patiently showed the child how to set a bird trap. Then when the bird was trapped, the man let Kell use a tiny spear to kill it.

He is teaching the boy well, Mamut thought approvingly. He would do as much for his own son. At the thought of a son, Mamut's eyes shifted back to the camp where Terah was. The women were talking as they worked.

Just then he froze. Flori was toddling into the newly built fire. Tiny flames and smoke licked at the wood. Grimly, he silently willed Terah to turn around and see the little one. Terah whirled and pulled the child out just before the fire burst into big flames. Mamut let out a sigh of relief. Flori was safe. Children, he reflected, could exhaust one.

Wearily, he took a sip of fresh water from the bison bladder. Then he chewed on a piece of dried meat while he waited for the sky to darken fully.

He must have been more tired than he thought. Mamut sat up in disgruntlement and rubbed his eyes in disbelief. He had slept the night away! Dawn was breaking as he leaped to his feet, peering out over the tundra to see what the family band was doing. If they were still asleep, he could sneak up and—

But they were not still asleep. Something had awakened them. It sounded like frogs croaking. Flori started crying, then Kell joined her. The frogs had awakened them and now he saw the black-haired woman sit up. The mother. At least, he was fairly certain she was the mother. The children seemed to rely on her and stay close to her, closer even than to Terah. He hoped she was the mother because when he took Terah, the children would be dependent on the male and the dark-haired female. In the time he had come to know them, Mamut had grown to love the children, and he did not want any harm to come to them.

He was fairly certain they were the parents, though he remembered Terah telling him that the children's mother was dead. Perhaps the woman was a second wife to the male, a step-mother to the children. Whoever she was, the children loved her. He could steal Terah away without hurting the children, Mamut thought, relieved.

Suddenly he stiffened. He smelled smoke, and the family had not yet lit a fire this morn. He scanned the horizon of hills. There, sloping in a gradual descent down to the river, was more smoke. The family had seen it too. The male was pointing out a blue plume of smoke blowing slowly across the green sward of trees near the river.

Mamut frowned. They were closer to her Bison people than he had realized last night. He had better proceed with his plan. Quickly he grabbed up his few implements, a knife, his spear, the water bladder, and a small sack of dried meat that he tied at his waist.

He started off toward the family band at a lope. Terah was the first to see him and give the alarm. Mamut saw the male glance his way, then say something to the children. The dark-haired female snatched up the two youngest—strong woman—and began running toward the smoke. The male gestured at Terah; she had pulled out her knife.

Mamut grinned to himself when he saw the familiar weapon. Brave Terah. It was obvious that she wanted to stay and fight.

It was just as obvious that the male wanted to make a run for it. With some arm-waving, he finally bullied Terah into running. When he saw that she had obeyed him, he started at a slow lope after her.

Once again Mamut was impressed. The male would buy time for his family to escape. Well, thought Mamut grimly, it was not the family he was after. It was Terah.

Mamut gained steadily on the fleeing family. The black-haired woman and children were still ahead, but the female was struggling. The male ran over to take Kell from her. With only Flori on one hip, she was able to run faster. Tika streaked far ahead of her family, and Mamut grinned to himself to see how well the child ran. He heard the father yell to Tika to bring help.

Terah was the last one, straggling. Mamut smiled to himself. He guessed that she wanted to fight and saw her chance now that the male was preoccupied with rescuing Kell. Mamut increased his strides until he rapidly gained on her.

The male looked back once and saw Mamut

gaining on Terah. He stopped, but the female must have said something to him because he began running again, still carrying Kell in a race toward the smoke. *Intelligent man*, thought Mamut. *He chooses to save his children, not his sister-in-law.*

She was Mamut's.

As Mamut approached Terah, he once again had to admire her courage. She stood, legs splayed, water bladders and bedrolls tossed carelessly to the ground behind her. Of course her little white chert knife blade filled one hand. It reminded him fondly of the first time he had seen her.

"Come with me," he said.

"No." Terah wanted to tell him to back away, but the words stuck in her throat. She hardly dared breathe as she stared into those smoldering black eyes. His strong jaw clenched, and she wanted to run her fingers over it to ease his tension. She wanted to touch that straight blade of a nose. . . . She felt faint as her eyes wandered over his broad shoulders, his naked chest, the leather pants that *she* had made for him. Her knees felt so weak that she thought she might collapse right where she stood. The knife blade in her hand shook from her trembling, and she had to clench her fingers lest the knife fall to the ground.

Her own jaw tensed. Her body might tremble with desire for him, but she would *not* give herself up to this man who wanted only her subjugation, her body, but not her love.

"I do not want to hurt you," he said.

"You will not dare." She raised the knife a little higher in threat. She tossed her head and her brown hair blew back from her lovely, sculpted face.

How he wanted her. His eyes burned into hers. "What is it you want?" *I will give you anything.*

"I want to be with my people." *A lie*, she thought. *I want to be with you. But you do not want me—except as a slave, and that I will not tolerate.*

"What would it take for you to come with me?"

She looked at him, wondering if he would ask her father for her. She bit her lip. Should she suggest it?

While she was eyeing him, he took a few steps closer, then looked past her. The other family members had disappeared. He could not afford to dally long. He glanced back at her.

"Well?"

"I—" she took a breath, "I want you to offer for me."

He frowned. "You mean in marriage?"

She nodded, her green eyes intent on his.

Mamut ground his teeth in frustration. Why did she have to ask for the one thing he could not, would not, do?

"No," he answered.

She tightened her lips. "Leave, then." She had been a fool to think that he would marry her. What arrogance the man had to think that she

337

would be willing to go back into captivity with him!

Suddenly, several warriors with raised spears appeared in the distance, the river and the smoke behind them. They were running up the long slope to where Mamut and Terah stood. So, the male of her family was bringing reinforcements.

"I ask you one last time," Mamut said evenly. "Come with me. I will treat you well. You will have plenty of food, shelter every night, people around you who care about you. I will give you a valuable necklace. I will even give you beautiful children." On this last, he smiled slightly. He could not come any closer to asking her to marry him. Could she not see that? He held his breath, awaiting her answer. And still the warriors, five of them, came on.

Terah stared at him, memorizing everything about him—his black-as-night hair blowing back from the hard planes of his face, his obsidian eyes, his lips. . . . When she was an old, lonely woman with no children and no husband, she would remember him thus, she thought. She could not, would not leave and go with him when he cared not a whit for what she wanted, yet she could never be satisfied with any other man—not after knowing Mamut. She was doomed to a lifetime of loneliness, she thought unhappily.

Mamut's eyes narrowed. Three more warriors had joined the first five. Eight against one. Not good odds. He could wait no longer.

He dropped his spear, came in under her, grabbed her knife hand, and squeezed until she dropped the weapon. Swiftly he threw her over his shoulders and picked up his spear. *Not like the last time,* he thought in triumph. This time she had no chance to use her knife or to fight him. He scooped up her knife and began jogging.

Pain shot through Terah's arm when Mamut grabbed her. She gasped when he threw her over his shoulders and the air was knocked out of her. When she finally gasped a huge breath, she found herself held tightly. And though she kicked and struggled, her efforts availed her nothing.

"You cannot do this!" she croaked in his ear.

"I can."

"My people will capture you! This time *you* will be the slave!"

It is possible, he thought, jogging faster. If he could make it to the next hill, the Bison warriors would not find them. "If I," he panted, "put you down, will you run?" If she would run next to him, they could make better time away from their pursuers.

"Yes," she said sweetly. *I will run back to my people!*

She is too accommodating, he thought, and he did not set her feet on the ground.

They were almost at the hill. He could hear harsh shouts and yells behind them. He darted around the base of the hill and glanced around. They were between two steep hills; sharp, sliding slate rock covered both hillsides. He looked around frantically, finally spying a crevice. He ran over and untangled Terah's hands. He dropped her to the ground.

"Slide in there," he ordered.

"No," she said and crossed her arms in defiance.

Mamut glared at her in frustration. If she did not hide, he would have to fight off eight men *and* hang on to her, too. What was he going to do?

"You could beat her," came a voice from the hill above.

Mamut looked up. There stood Lern. It was he who had given the advice. Beside him was Spearpoint and five other Mammoth warriors. Never in his life had Mamut been so glad to see his people.

"I do not beat women," Mamut answered. To Terah he said, "Climb up to them."

She did.

Once they were on the hilltop, the Mammoth warriors—eight men and one captive woman—stared down at the Bison warriors swarming into the narrow draw.

The pursuers searched the lower part of the hill, one of them checking the crevice where Mamut had sought to hide Terah.

Mamut smiled grimly to himself as he watched the frustrated men gather together, all talking at once about where their prey could have gone. One of them happened to glance up to the hill where the Mammoth warriors stood.

"Give us back our woman!" he shouted in rage and he shook his spear at the Mammoth men.

Mamut recognized him as the black-haired male who was Tika and Kell and Flori's father. Then another man, older, his long gray hair tied back in a wolf's tail, stepped forward, and Terah gave a little gasp. Mamut's eyes narrowed as he glanced from Terah to the old man. He gripped her arm and could feel a tremor go through her. *That is her father,* he thought.

Terah raised a trembling hand in a gesture of unconscious pleading to the gray-haired man who stood down in the draw. "Father!" she cried.

Mamut saw the old man clench his fists, and for a moment he felt pain such as the old man must be feeling, helplessly watching a loved and precious daughter being stolen from him. The insight left a bitter taste in Mamut's mouth for what he was doing, but he had little choice. He had need of a woman. And not just any woman. Terah.

"Give her back," shouted the old man, raising one spear. The white speartip caught the sun. Mamut remembered that Terah had said her father would give eight spears for her.

He did not answer. The Mammoth warriors waited in silence, desperate men in enemy territory.

The Bison warriors spoke amongst themselves. Then the younger man, Dagger, called out, "We will take the woman from you!" Great shouts arose from the Bison men beside him, and they shook their spears ferociously at the intruders. "We will fight!"

Mamut looked at the grim faces of his Mammoth men, again grateful for their help. He did not want to risk their lives, but he knew they would fight for him if he needed them to. Their presence attested to that.

Mamut's deep voice echoed in the hills as he shouted boldly, "If you dare to fight us, we will kill you! Then your families will have no fathers, no warriors to protect them! Think carefully, Bison men. Think how many of you will die for one mere woman."

The Bison men conferred amongst themselves. At last Dagger's voice could be heard once more. "We will fight. We do not let strangers steal our women!"

Terah felt a fierce pride in her people. They were not going to let her go! They were going to fight for her! She would see her family again! She whirled to see how Mamut would answer Bison bravery.

His obsidian glance was on her, implacable, assessing. He saw the proud smile on her face. "You like this, Terah?" he asked softly. "Do you like it that your brother-in-law must spill his blood for you? That the old man who loves you, your father, will die an agonizing death with a spear through his heart because he fights for you? How precious will your freedom be to you then, built on the blood of your menfolk?"

Nothing he could have said could have silenced and devastated her more than those words. A picture of Dagger dying, and of her father holding his bleeding chest, etched itself on her brain. Her hand went to her mouth in sick horror. The children would have no father, her mother would be left alone. . . . "No," she murmured, "oh, no!"

Mamut watched her face as the meaning of what a fatal fight would do to her family dawned on her. "Men will die this day, Terah. And some of the dead will be Bison men. There will be mourning in the tents of the Bison women."

Then he turned to face the waiting Bison men. "She will not come with you," he called out. "She chooses to stay with me."

The Bison men were shaking their fists at the usurpers. Terah closed her eyes against the sight, but she could hear Bear, of all men, shouting insults.

Dagger yelled out, "She does not choose you. She ran from you. She pulled her knife to fight you. That is not choice!"

The Bison men were roaring now, and her eyes flew open. She saw two of her people break out of the huddle and start to climb the hill, rage contorting their faces as they scrambled up the slope. "You cannot steal our women!" One of the warriors was Bear, the other was One Shoe.

Terah's heart slammed in her chest. The Bison men were brave, she had no doubt of that. They would come up and attack the Mammoth warriors and blood would be spilled—Bison blood.

"Stop!" she cried, the veins in her neck standing out with the force of her shout. "I go with him." She reached out and gripped Mamut's arm and felt the muscles contract under her touch.

"Terah!" It was her father's anguished voice. "We know you do not want to go with him. We will save you!"

She closed her eyes and took a breath, hoping

343

her people would not damn her forever for what she was about to say. When she opened her eyes, she felt a new calmness steal over her, an acceptance such as she had felt back on the mountaintop with the Great Spirit. "I carry his child!" she called down to her people.

"No!" The great shout went up from her father and the other Bison men. It was a shout of anguish and fury and despair.

Mamut glanced at her, his obsidian eyes widening in surprise. Then his attention flew back to the Bison warriors. He knew what that cry of despair meant—they had finally recognized Mamut's claim. Mamut turned to Terah once again, and her wide green eyes were upon him. He read the surrender therein. "They believe you. It is good that you said this; now there will be no fight."

Her eyes filled with tears. "There will be no fight," she agreed. And then defiance flared in her eyes and strengthened her voice, "But I will make your life a living nightmare."

He looked at her, his face impassive, his eyes revealing nothing. He thought of the constant torment of his cowardice. "It already is."

Chapter 31

It still looked the same, thought Terah as, surrounded by Mammoth warriors, she was marched into the camp where the familiar tents sat. She spotted her previous habitation, in the same place it had been when she fled.

Wolf Boy, growling low in his throat, strutted over to sniff the newcomers. Mamut patted the dog. Wolf Boy's growls dwindled away, and he let them walk through his camp.

Mamut led Terah to the tent they had shared. As they passed the Frog tent, Terah caught a glimpse of Rana, her face showing new bruises. Sorrow was etched in the dark circles under her friend's eyes. Terah wanted to look away, unable to bear her friend's pain. She forced herself to meet Rana's puffy eyes. "Your frogs gave warning," she said at last and watched as

Theresa Scott

a tremulous smile teetered on the old woman's mouth.

Benaleese glanced up from where she was resting by the fire, her hands propping up her heavy torso. When she saw Terah she frowned. Terah gave a little wave. Benaleese turned away. Terah frowned; Benaleese had not changed. She was still preoccupied with her own thoughts and feelings, and nobody could pull her out of that preoccupation. Terah wondered when Benaleese was going to be delivered of her baby. She shrugged. The baby would come when it was ready; babies did that.

Lame Leg shuffled over to stare from behind dirty matted hair at Terah. The girl leaned against Wolf Boy's back for additional support. Terah smiled at the girl and received an answering little twist of the lips. Terah accepted it as a smile.

The shaman walked over to the returning warriors, and while Mamut and Spearpoint and the others discussed her most recent capture, Terah slipped away to the tent.

Everything looked the same in the Mammoth camp, but it was all so different for her now. She was a captive once more, true, but this time without Tika and Kell and Flori. She missed their happy little games and longed for Flori's plump little body to hug whenever she wanted to. There was none of Tika's chatter on the return trip, and Terah wondered if she would ever again see Tika and Kell and Flori.

346

And this time there was nowhere to run. Terah could not go back to her Bison people. She remembered how the Bison men had watched in silence when she departed from the hilltop with the Mammoth warriors. Their silence had fallen immediately after their protests when Terah had told them she carried Mamut's child. Bear and One Shoe had hastily slid back down the slate hillside to join the other Bison men, leaving Terah feeling alone and bereft. The knowledge that she had saved some lives proved to be of little comfort when faced with her people's anger and despair and resignation.

Tears filled her eyes now at the memory of her father's last farewell gesture to her. He had looked so old, so gray, standing there with bent back, watching his youngest daughter being led away by strangers. He had looked so sad, she thought, leaning upon his spear. Her last glimpse of him had shown him with bowed head, staring at the ground while Dagger spoke solemnly to him.

Later, Mamut had asked her if she was indeed pregnant. Terah gave him a look that could have frozen a glacier. She refused to speak to him unless it was necessary. Telling him whether he was to be a father or not was, in her opinion, not necessary.

The next days at the camp passed slowly, and Terah felt distinctly uncomfortable whenever she was alone with Mamut. She had been alone with him so seldom, she realized now, when the children had been with her. Now there was no distraction of children, no rescuing Flori from the fire, no resolving differences between Tika and Kell. There was nothing— only Mamut.

And Mamut was in a torment of his own. He had forced Terah to return with him, but gone was the loving, kind woman he had known. In her place was a stranger, a woman who regarded him out of frozen green eyes, who kept away from him as much as possible, a woman who was obviously indifferent to him. At times he despaired that she would ever again want to be with him, to laugh with him, to share a sunset with him. Yet when he thought of returning her to her people, he would shake his head. He could not part with her. And so he kept her and continued to suffer.

Three days after Terah had returned to camp, the Mammoth People packed up their belongings and began the move south for the winter.

Mamut walked at the head of the slowly moving line of burdened Mammoth People as they wound their way through the hills. He was leading them to the Giver of Life River. They would follow that river south until they came to their winter fishing banks. Terah walked at the end of the line, by her own choice.

Lern came up to her. "You do not like me, do you?" he observed.

Terah glanced at him, but continued plodding along. She wondered if he would go away if she did not answer him.

When he saw that she refused to answer, he gave her a kick. "Answer me, woman."

She turned on him fiercely then, and her hand made a grab for the white chert knife at her hip. In the blink of an eye, the knife was in her hand, the point aimed at Lern. Through gritted teeth, she said, "No, I do not like you."

Lern glanced around. The others were following the curving hillside around the bend of the draw. No one was paying any attention to the rear of the line. He smiled. He had chosen his time and place wisely.

He seized the knife from her, ripping it out of her hand. The knife clattered to the ground.

She glared at him with loathing.

He stared back blandly. "When Mamut dies, I will take you for my captive."

She gasped. Whatever was he talking about? "Mamut is not going to die."

"Oh?" He cocked an eyebrow at her. "How can you be so certain?" He glanced away, looking at the sky, at the hills. "This is a dangerous land. Many bad things can happen to a man here."

That was true enough, she thought. Her mind was racing frantically. Why was he telling her this?

His brown eyes returned to her. "Something might happen to Mamut." His eyes bored into hers assessingly. "Would you like that?"

Terah gaped at him. Obviously her private troubles with Mamut were known to others in the camp.

349

"What—" she licked dry lips. His eyes followed the tip of her tongue. "What are you planning to do?"

He stared at her, then took a step back. "I? Why, Bison woman, I am not planning to do anything."

He is lying, she thought. *He is planning to hurt, even kill Mamut.* Numbly, she tried to think. Should she pretend to go along with him so that he would tell her of his plan? As angry as she was with Mamut, she did not want him hurt or killed. How could this man even think that was what she wanted?

She tried a tentative smile and saw his eyes darken. *He wants me*, she thought, and she struggled inwardly with how to use that knowledge. "You . . . uh . . ." she could barely get the words out. They finally came out in a seductive whisper, "You want me for your wife?"

He looked at her. "I will keep you as a slave," he said arrogantly. "If you are good to me, I might, in time, make you my wife."

"When Mamut is dead," she added quietly.

He nodded.

She looked out over the hills as if considering. "What—" she tried again. "How are you going to kill him?"

He answered cryptically, "I will not kill him. Others will."

"Others?"

"The ones he is so afraid of," said Lern enigmatically. "He fears them. Runs from them."

350

Terah felt a little bewildered. What was he talking about?

"You see, when Mamut was a boy, he killed his father."

Terah gasped.

Lern grinned. "You did not know? I was sure he would have told you." He laughed as though at a private joke.

Terah shook her head numbly. "He never . . ."

Lern lifted an eyebrow. "He never said anything about it? Strange." He pretended to consider this. Then he added, "When you are my captive, I will treat you better than Mamut does. I will give you presents."

And beat me, she wanted to add but bit her tongue. "What of—" she swallowed. "What of Rana? Does she know you plan to take a second wife—I mean, captive?" Seeing his frown, she added hastily, "I mean a captive in addition to your wife?"

His frown cleared. "Oh, Rana. She will not mind." But he did not sound quite so confident to Terah. She decided to pry more information out of him about his planned murder of Mamut. She forced herself to lean closer to him. "Do you want to kill Mamut so you can have me?" she purred sweetly.

He looked at her. "No, not just for you. I—" He hesitated.

She widened her eyes as she stared at him, willing him to give her more information. "I do not like him." She nodded encouragingly. "I hate him." His voice sounded bitter.

351

Now we are getting to the truth, she thought.

"I want to kill him because he deserves to die."

She raised an eyebrow but said nothing, fearing words would halt his confidences.

"Mamut ran." Lern was staring at her now but not seeing her. His body tensed. "Mamut ran when he should have stayed and fought for his father. Kran cried out to Mamut for help. And Mamut kept running . . . away. . . ." Lern's glassy eyes focused on her for a heartbeat, but he did not see her. He was watching something in his mind. Something painful. "Mamut is a coward!"

To Terah's great surprise, Lern gripped both her arms and held her immobile. "He is a coward," he hissed. "He deserves to die!"

She wanted to pull free, but his grip was too strong.

"I saw it," he cried. "I saw it all. Nobody knows that. But I saw what happened to Kran and—"

He released her then. Terah stared at him as his face crumpled. He turned away and presented his back to her for the space of several heartbeats. When he swung round to face her again, his face was impassive. A shadow of pain flitted through his eyes and was gone.

"Do not think you can use this against me," he warned. "No one will believe the word of a captive woman."

Terah could only shake her head. What was he talking about now? "I will not tell anyone. . . ." Who would she tell? *What* would she tell? She was not even certain she knew what information she could use against Lern.

He yanked her up close to him and glared down into her eyes. "If you tell anyone . . ." He shook her.

"Unhand me," she hissed.

When he let her go, he smiled and added, "But who would you tell? You are only a captive woman. No one will listen to you.

"Although Mamut might listen to you," he added consideringly. Then he laughed. "But that does not matter. Mamut is a coward. And Mamut will die soon." He grinned engagingly. "Then you will belong to me."

She shuddered inwardly.

"And it is a beautiful way for him to die," Lern mused. "He fears them so. What better way than to have to face them, knowing he is mad with fear all the while?" Lern laughed.

Terah wondered if the man was deranged.

"Lern!" It was the shaman. Terah jerked guiltily to see the shaman watching them through narrowed eyes. Lern took a slow step away from Terah.

"I am coming," called Lern.

He glanced back at Terah as the shaman walked toward them. "Not a word of this to anyone, my sweet bird. When Mamut is dead, there will be time enough for us to talk!"

Terah wanted to scream her disgust. Instead she bit her tongue and nodded shortly.

"Come," said the shaman. "We need you to help carry Benaleese."

Lern shrugged. "Where is her old husband, Spark? He should help her, not I, her brother."

Theresa Scott

The shaman snorted. "Her husband went hunting. Why now, when the baby is due, I do not know, but he did. She needs your help." To Terah he gave a brief nod. "Mamut awaits," he observed.

Lern's stern glance at her ordered Terah to say something.

"I go to him," she answered.

Lern smiled, pleased. Evidently she had given the correct answer, thought Terah. Her thoughts were in a turmoil. Now she was a conspirator to Mamut's murder. And if Lern succeeded in killing Mamut, she faced a miserable life as Lern's captive. Oh, what was she going to do?

Chapter 32

The Mammoth People reached Giver of Life River. Terah stared around her. The river was wide here, as wide as ten men lying head to toe. Several large rocks jutted out of the swirling blue depths. A great flock of ducks rose into the air, squawking in protest at their arrival.

Giver of Life River was the biggest body of water that Terah knew of, and she was relieved to be back at its riverbanks. She set down the rolled tent and water bladders she had been carrying, then sauntered down the rocky slope to the water and waded in. The cool water felt good as it lapped at her toes.

Rana set down her possessions and ambled over to the water. Terah watched as Lern helped Benaleese to the water. Lern's face was dark with anger at something his sister had said,

355

and he shoved her in his irritation. Despite her bulk, Benaleese elbowed him in the stomach, and Lern doubled over.

Other members of the Mammoth People were now setting down their bundles and wandering over to the river. Lame Leg shuffled to the bank, her hand gripping Wolf Boy's back for support. Wolf Boy slurped the water.

Willow trees lined the banks of the river, and green trees provided a screen several foot-lengths thick. Long grasses grew in quiet waters that pooled near the shallow banks. Terah watched as a crimson-headed salmon swept past her in its long journey upstream. Everywhere the river touched, its waters brought life to the land.

After a while, the shaman lit a small fire and laid the special, sacred plants in a smoldering pile on the tiny flames. He called out his thanks to the Great Spirit for guiding the Mammoth People safely once again to the source of all life, the Giver of Life River.

Terah said a silent thank-you also. It was good to be near the river once more. She knew that the rest of the journey would be easier as the Mammoth People walked south. Fish would be caught from the river's roiling depths, and game animals like antelope and camel and sloth would easily fall to the hunters' spears.

Even as she thought this, she glanced upstream to see a herd of mammoths move away. Evidently the presence of the Mammoth People disturbed them.

Lern followed her gaze. He stared at the mammoths and then turned back to Terah. He grinned, and she felt as if she had just been caught up in something evil. He nodded as if she had suggested something, then turned casually away. His tense body, however, betrayed his interest in what he had seen.

That night, the Mammoth People sat around the campfires, talking and telling stories. Stars twinkled overhead, and the night was quiet and beautiful. The fresh, damp smell of the river scented the air with its wealth of water.

Rana told a long tale about frogs, and Lern snorted in disgust at the end of the tale when the Great Frog hero saved his people. Terah did not miss the contempt that crossed Lern's face, nor the anger that crossed Rana's. Lame Leg sat leaning against her dog, of course, and Benaleese, still not delivered of the baby, lay asleep on a bedrobe.

Terah turned away from the others, waiting for Mamut to approach her. He had stayed away from her during the day, as he had every day since he had recaptured her, but he had slept next to her every night.

She felt restless this night, and she guessed it was because of what Lern had told her. She should say something to Mamut, she thought, warn him—but about what? Lern had been too vague in his plan for her to be able to say anything more definite than "Lern wants to murder you." When the others were settled in and snoring in their bedrolls—no one had bothered

357

to raise the tents as they would not be staying long—Mamut walked over to her. He sat down next to her, and she turned to look at him.

"Let us go for a walk," she suggested in a low voice. This was so contrary to her behavior of the past few days that she caught him by surprise.

Remembering what their "walks" had often led to when they had left the children in the tent, Mamut stared at her. Was she wanting to make love?

He rose swiftly and led her downstream. When Terah was certain they could not be overheard, she said, "Lern does not like you."

He shrugged. He had known that ever since he was a young man.

"He calls you a coward—"

No sooner were the words out of her mouth than Mamut seized her by both arms and swung her around to face him. His gaze was harsh, his teeth clenched as he forced terse words, "He told you that?"

Terah stared at him, her eyes wide in fright. She slowly nodded.

Mamut saw the fear, and his lips tightened. He dropped his hands.

Terah relaxed a little. "He—he says he wants to kill you." Then she turned and fled back to the camp. She did not know what effect her words would have on him, nor did she want to stay to find out.

Mamut watched her retreating figure. Lern! Why could the man not leave Mamut alone?

Lern was always there with his petty insults, his nasty jibes, his cruelty. And the net of people he tormented was widening. First Rana, then Terah, now Mamut.

Mamut's fists clenched. Something would have to be done about Lern. He would have to be told that he could not go on interfering in people's lives.

He thought back upon Terah's words. So, Lern wanted to kill him, did he? Mamut mused. There were a number of ways the man could do it. He could attack Mamut openly with knife and spear. But that was unlikely. Lern was not an open, straightforward man. He would choose a sneakier method. Perhaps a hunting accident or a knife in the back when Mamut was asleep. Or he could try drowning Mamut when the men went fishing, Mamut thought uneasily. Well, whatever method he chose, Mamut was not going to let Lern kill him.

And as for Lern telling Terah that Mamut was a coward, he would have to be very careful. He did not think that Lern knew anything; he could have said it as a way to create trouble between Terah and Mamut. As if there was not enough trouble between them already, thought Mamut with irony.

As Mamut wandered slowly back to camp, getting his temper under control, he mused upon how Lern planned to kill him.

Chapter 33

The next morning, Mamut found out precisely how Lern planned to kill him.

The Mammoth People went slowly about the tasks of catching and eating the morning meal of fish. After they had cleaned up and doused the fires, Lern asked all the men to meet with him at the Frog tent.

Terah was just dumping the breakfast fish-bones and putting out the fire. Today the Mammoth People would move farther south, following Giver of Life River. But when she saw the men gathering, she felt curious and, ostensibly collecting her possessions, she moved closer to listen.

"My sister, Benaleese," Lern began, "is going to have her babe very soon. Let us stay here and wait. It is a hardship for my sister to travel so late in her pregnancy."

Mamut stared at Lern. Benaleese's husband, Spark, stared at Lern. The shaman and Spearpoint stared at Lern. How unusual, thought Mamut, for Lern to be concerned about his sister's hardship.

Lern met the silent stares sheepishly. "My wife suggested it this morning. She says that Benaleese needs rest. Childbirth is hard work." He shrugged as if to say he did not know.

There were several wary nods from the men. "It is good," said the shaman at last. "We can wait here for your sister to give birth."

Lern smiled slightly. Mamut's suspicions heightened.

"My wife tells me also," continued Lern, "that firstborn babes take a long time to arrive. Sometimes two days, sometimes three." He held up three fingers and threw out his chest, preening in the listening men's attention. "If we are to wait here, we could do some hunting."

Several of the men nodded their heads in agreement. Mamut held his breath.

Lern pointed upstream with his chin. The mammoth herd they had seen the day before sported in the water.

Dread seized Mamut. Now he knew exactly how Lern planned to kill him.

"Let us go mammoth hunting," said Lern.

His black eyes swept over the Mammoth men, lingering a heartbeat longer as he met Mamut's narrowed eyes in challenge. Lern smiled in contempt.

Mamut gritted his teeth. The other men were speaking amongst themselves, discussing the proposed hunt.

"We have not hunted mammoth for a long time."

"Do you know the proper rituals, O Shaman?"

The shaman nodded affirmatively. Mamut's heart sank.

"I do not like mammoths. Too big."

"Lots of meat, though. And tusks!"

"Tusks are very valuable. We can get many women at the Meet-meet if we bring in mammoth ivory."

"Too much work. Let us hunt antelope."

This last was met with a snort of disgust.

Mamut roused himself from his grim thoughts. "We are not prepared to go after mammoths," he said, speaking with as much authority in his voice as he could. "It takes much training. Much planning. And you cannot kill just a single mammoth."

He pointed with his chin at the herd. "Think you that a mammoth mother will let you walk up and kill her babe? Or that the old grandmother who leads the herd will eat twigs as you are busy killing her daughters?"

The men stared at him, considering his words, and Mamut began to feel hopeful. "No, they do not stand by idly and let you kill. If you kill one mammoth, you must kill the whole tribe. Mammoths make it a family fight."

"What he says is true," Spearpoint murmured.

"Listen to me," Mamut said. "Hunting mammoths is a very serious thing. Not something you do because you do not feel like hunting antelope today." His gaze met the other men's squarely. "There is no such thing as killing one mammoth."

The shaman nodded, and Mamut knew that he meditated upon what he had just said. If the shaman was convinced of the danger, surely the others would be too. Mamut began to relax, sensing that he had narrowly averted a mammoth hunt.

Lern cleared his throat. "What you say is obvious," he began. "Mammoth men know better than to hunt one mammoth. We can kill the whole tribe if we work together."

Mamut glared at him. "If we hunt mammoths, it may mean that one or more of us is killed. We Mammoth People are few in number. We cannot afford to lose a single hunter."

Lern shrugged. He glanced around at the men. "I say it is worth the risk. We will have enough meat for winter, we will be rich in mammoth ivory, and therefore we will be rich in wives."

"We are Mammoth men," put in Benaleese's husband, Spark. "Mammoth men hunt mammoths. We have not hunted mammoths for many years. It is time."

Lern smiled at his brother-in-law, and Mamut wondered if Spark had been privy to Lern's plans, but the big man's face was impassive.

The men considered Spark's words.

Mamut shook his head. He felt shame deep inside himself that he spoke against the hunt. There were many advantages to his people if they hunted the mammoth. But there were terrible risks too. And he knew that Lern would make it even riskier for him, Mamut.

"You lost Kran to the mammoth," said the shaman softly. Mamut jerked. Had it been anyone else who said those words to remind him of his father's death, Mamut would have fought him. Yet it was the shaman, and Mamut respected him too much to smite him.

"Perhaps," continued the shaman, "it is the memory of Kran's death that discourages you."

Mamut met his gaze steadily. "I have not hunted mammoths since that day," he answered. He felt the blood rush to his face at this admission and wished he had kept silent.

The men were quiet now. Mamut added, "It is a reminder of the risks. Men get killed."

"You do not want to hunt mammoths," said the shaman. It was not a question.

Mamut shook his head. "No, I do not." Shame washed over him as a little voice in his head taunted over and over, *You are afraid, you are afraid. . . .*

Lern sneered. Mamut braced himself.

"I think," said Lern slowly, "that you are a coward."

A gasp went up from the listening men. The shaman cut his head sharply to Lern. Lern ignored the frown on the shaman's face. Spearpoint and the others were frowning too.

Dread tied Mamut's gut in knots.

"You are a coward," Lern repeated in a louder voice, drawing himself up to his full height. "The day your father was killed, you *ran* from the mammoth. Kran called to you for help, and you ran away! I saw you! You let the mammoth kill him! You killed your own father!"

Mamut would have accepted a spear in his chest rather than hear the words Lern was saying. And the Mammoth men—several of them stared at Mamut in shock.

The disgust in Spearpoint's eyes made Mamut turn away in despair. His gaze surprised Terah's; she had been listening. He thought he read contempt on her face. *Now she knows what I am*, he thought, *and she is disgusted too*.

Terah met his glance. She had heard Lern's words—indeed, the whole camp had heard Lern's words. She waited for Mamut to defend himself. When he did not say anything, she looked away.

The shame and anger upon Mamut's face was too painful for her to behold. She would not add to it. *Why is it that men do this to each other?* she mused bitterly. Bron, her own brother, had fought the saber-toothed tiger for mere sport, to prove his bravery. She would gladly have Bron back safe and considered a coward than have him test himself in that fatal fight. All the Bison men and women had thought Bron brave. And yes, he was brave. He was also dead. Her heart twisted in anguish for Mamut. Evidently he had made a different choice from Bron.

Mamut swung back to the men, forcing himself to meet their gazes. Spark glanced away. Spearpoint would not meet Mamut's eyes. The shaman frowned at him, then his glance slid away.

Desolation seized Mamut, and he could say nothing to defend himself. What was there to say? He was a coward. He had acted the coward, and his father had died because of it. In some small way, there was a tiny relief that his terrible secret was revealed at last. Now he would not have to imagine what his Mammoth people would say if they knew. He had only to look at their faces to know. They loathed him.

"The mammoth hunt," said Lern firmly, "begins today!" With one last mocking glance at Mamut, he spun on his heel and walked away.

Mamut's humiliation was complete.

Chapter 34

Mamut headed down the short path to the river. He had not failed to notice how the others now shunned him. When he passed Benaleese coming back from the river with a bison bladder full of water, she yanked her tunic hem out of his way, careful not to let the garment touch him. "My child will not be a coward such as you," she hissed.

Mamut clenched his fists and ignored her as he strode by. *I must accustom and harden myself to this,* he counseled himself. *They are not going to change. The Mammoth People respect bravery. They have no need of cowards.*

He sat down on a rock beside the water and stared into the swirling depths. The hunters were leaving, and he turned to watch them make their way upstream. His obsidian eyes followed them as they blended like shadows into the yellow willows that grew beside the river.

Farther upriver, at a wide spot, the mammoth herd sunned itself by one of the pools. The herd numbered the same as the fingers on a man's two hands. They were all females, and four of them had calves. The biggest one was the gray-tipped grandmother who led the herd. Mamut could hear her snuffle once in a while as she browsed in the willows for food.

The Mammoth hunters were reconnoitering their prey. They would study the great beasts to learn how best to kill them.

Mamut sighed, castigating himself because he had been reluctant to accompany the hunters. He did not think he could face their contempt. But sitting by the river sighing was hardly a satisfactory alternative. He stiffened when he heard light footsteps behind him.

"Mamut?"

He recognized Terah's voice but did not turn around. He braced himself against her forthcoming taunts.

Terah stared at his stiff back. She could see that he did not want to talk to her. Should she bide her time? She was still angry at being recaptured. Perhaps she should wait and speak with him later, when his humiliation was not so fresh. She should just let him suffer, she thought, and then wondered why she did not. After all, he had not helped her. He had stolen her from her own people. Now she wondered why. Was her cooking so tasty, her hide tanning abilities so wonderful—

or was it that he stole her just because he did not want to pay the bride price, as other Mammoth men had to do? She sighed. She would never understand this man.

"Mamut?" She tried again. He would have to chase her away, she decided, if he did not want to speak with her.

Mamut stared across the river, his back to her. What did the Bison woman want? Could she not see that he was cast out and reviled by his own people? Had she come to taunt him too? He wished she would get it over with. No doubt Bison men were ten times braver than *he* was. "What is it?" he growled at last.

"What did Lern mean back there, when he said you were a coward?"

Mamut knew the Bison woman was no fool. She wanted him to condemn himself in his own words. Perhaps then she would go away. "It is true," he answered at last. "My people consider me a coward."

Terah came over and sat down cross-legged a little distance from him when she saw that he was willing to talk. She did not say anything, afraid to jeopardize his newly found openness.

"Everything that Lern says is true," Mamut continued brutally. "My father, Kran, was killed when a mammoth attacked him. My father died with my name on his lips, pleading for my help. I—I ran away."

Terah's eyes widened in horror, and she could not stifle a gasp.

Why is she still sitting here? wondered Mamut.

371

Does she wish to hear more of my cowardly ways?
Aloud he condemned himself further. "I never
told anyone what happened. As you have learned,
the Mammoth People do not tolerate cowards.
They thought that I had done everything I could
to help my father." He snorted in self-disgust.
"But instead, I ran."

He turned to look at her, and his gaze locked
on hers. "So you see what kind of a man wants
you, Terah. A coward." His voice was even. "You
had better go now."

"Go where?" she responded. "Back to my people?"

He grinned then, the first sign of humor from
him that she had seen in many a day. His lips
curved, and she could not help staring at them.
When she was able to lift her eyes to meet his
black gaze, her heart started pounding. She put
a hand over her chest to slow the beat.

"Do you think that I would let you go after all
I went through to recapture you?" He shook his
head. "No. Even Mammoth cowards have their
needs, their desires." His eyes were hot as he
gazed at her, and Terah felt a shiver go up and
down her spine. "Since I am being honest with
you," he added wryly, "I will tell you now that
I will not let you go. I am keeping you with me,
make no mistake about that."

"Why?" she cried in frustration. "You do not
want to marry me! You do not love me! You
can easily trade bison furs for a willing woman
at the Meet-meet. You are wealthy enough now.
All the Mammoth People are wealthy now." Her

frustration showed in her green eyes.

He reached over and dragged her to him. He held her and looked down at her trembling lips. A wanting so strong that it was uncontrollable filled him. He crushed her to him and plundered her mouth. When the kiss was over, he held her away from him. "Does that answer your question?"

She put a shaking hand to her lips as though to brush away his touch. His lambent gaze followed her hand, and she saw the anger flare in those obsidian depths.

"Accept it," he snarled. "You are mine! I will not let you go. No matter what my people say to you against me, it counts for naught. I will never let you go!"

She scrambled back away from him, heedless of the rough stone ground. He read her fear, her revulsion.

"And if you so hate it that you are the mate of a coward, so be it," he growled. "I care not what you think!"

She rose to her feet, her limbs trembling so much they could barely support her.

He watched her with thinly veiled, sardonic amusement. "And if you seek so hard for explanations, Bison woman," he said softly, "then here is one—I keep you because no other woman will come to a man such as I am now, a known coward. My people will tell the story far and wide, and no woman of any mettle would seek to be my mate now. You are the only hope I have for a woman, for children." He laughed cruelly as though at a jest. "So you see now why I will not let you go."

She thought she saw a flash of deep sorrow in his eyes, but it was swiftly gone. Perhaps she had imagined it.

She took a breath and stood as straight and as tall as she could. In a shaky voice, she announced, "I—I am going for a walk. I have much to ponder."

It surprised him that she showed so much restraint. He shrugged. Well, what of it? Screaming and denouncing him now, or screaming and denouncing him later, it was all the same to him. He nodded as though he had the power to release her to go for her walk. "Begone, then."

He watched her slim-hipped, lithe figure as she walked away, and the sorrow he had been holding back flooded into his heart. "If only it could have been otherwise, sweet Terah," he whispered. "If only I could have had your love, your respect. I would have given anything on this earth to keep this knowledge from you." He felt moisture gather in his eyes and closed them. "Now I have lost you."

The only answer that came to him was the cool touch of the autumn breeze. It caressed his cheek and forehead and foretold a cold, lonely winter ahead.

Chapter 35

The shaman stopped. He heard a low, keening sound coming from the Frog Tent. It was late afternoon, and few people were in the camp. He frowned and muttered to himself. Then he hobbled over to the Frog Tent. "Rana," he called out. "Are you in there?"

Some sniffs answered him. Then, to his surprise, Terah crawled out of the tent doorway. The shaman took a step back. "I did not know you were visiting Rana," he said. Then he leaned forward to peer into the tent. "Is she hurt? I heard crying."

Terah sighed. "I fear she is hurt," she said sadly. "Very badly. Her arm will not work correctly."

The shaman looked puzzled.

"Rana," Terah called softly. "Come out here."

There were several audible sniffs then silence.

"Rana?" Terah guessed that the Great Frog woman would rather hide in her tent than show the shaman what Lern had done to her this time. She shrugged and said, "I think that Rana does not want to show you—"

"I am coming out, Terah," came Rana's muffled voice. "Just give me a little time."

The shaman's dark eyes met Terah's in silent understanding. "She must make the decision to defend herself," he murmured. "You and I cannot make it for her."

Terah felt drawn to the compassion she saw in those dark, wise eyes.

"No matter how much we may wish to do so," the shaman added. He smiled kindly as they waited.

Rana poked her head out of the tent. "Greetings, Shaman," she said as she emerged from the tent. She held her arm at a strange angle. The shaman frowned and touched it lightly. Rana winced and drew her body stiffly away. "Hurts," she whimpered.

The shaman looked at Rana. "I must touch it to set the bone," he said. "But I can do that later. First tell me, how did you injure your arm thusly?"

Rana poked at the dirt with her big toe. She would not meet Terah's eyes or the shaman's. "I—I fell."

"No, that is not what you told me, Rana." Terah's lips were tight in anger. "You told me that Lern beat you. Again."

Rana looked at her. "You have betrayed me."

"I!" snorted Terah. "You have betrayed yourself! It is you who refuses to acknowledge what that man has done to you! You keep getting hurt!" She pointed her chin at Rana's arm.

Rana swung away, placing her body between Terah's angry gaze and her broken arm. "It—it is difficult for me to leave him. Where will I go? What will I eat?"

"You can stay in your own tent. Get him to leave," suggested the shaman. "As for food, I and some of the other hunters supply food for Lame Leg. We can do as much for you."

Rana was silent, and Terah hoped she was considering the shaman's words. He had just neatly removed two of the biggest obstacles to Rana's safety. But the biggest obstacle of all, thought Terah irritably, was the woman's own stubbornness.

"I—I must think about it."

"How long will you think about it, Rana?" asked the shaman gently. "A day? A handful of days? A season? Until the next beating? How long?" He watched Rana and shook his head. "In this camp I have heard your cries many times. Yet never have you come to me, or to others. Until you ask for help, we cannot give it."

"I did not think you would help me," Rana said sullenly. "Many times have you defended Lern."

Terah thought the shaman looked guilty. Then Rana was quiet for a long time. Terah began to think she had not heard what the shaman said.

Finally, Rana turned to face them, and she was calm. "I ask for your help then." Her words were quiet, her demeanor dignified. "I can no longer let him hit me. One day he will kill me." Terah was surprised to hear those words. Had she not said the very same to Rana on another occasion? She shrugged. It mattered little. What mattered was that Rana saw how hurtful Lern was to her. "And I want him out of *my* Frog tent."

"You want him to be the one to move."

"Yes."

Terah understood. If Lern moved, this would give a measure of power, of strength to Rana.

"It is good," grunted the shaman. "Now, let me look at your arm." He frowned at what he saw. Then he began chanting. After the chant, he shifted the bone back into place. Sweat popped out on the older woman's forehead, but she did not cry out. Next the shaman bound dried leather strips on either side of her broken arm. Rana's face was drawn and pale with the pain.

Terah made a poultice of leaves and moss to take away the hurt. Rana seemed so fragile, thought Terah as she placed the poultice on the arm. It was surprising that Lern had not broken any of her bones before this. Terah consoled herself with the hope that he would not break any more.

After the evening meal, the shaman called the Mammoth People over to his fire. The people grouped themselves around the flames, talking in small groups of two and three. When every member was accounted for, the shaman walked over to stand near Rana. Rana clutched a small leather shape stuffed with straw tightly to her. Terah had seen it before and knew it was a frog-shaped icon.

"We must talk," the shaman said. "We have something important to discuss."

Spearpoint, Lern, Spark and the others waited respectfully. Benaleese plopped herself down on a rock and yawned. Lame Leg played with stones on the ground.

Mamut hung back behind the others, and Terah's heart constricted when she saw how his people ignored him. Wolf Boy, unaware of Mamut's public shame, came up to him and sniffed and wagged his tail. Mamut patted the dog, and Terah could read his profound gratitude in the small action. She had to turn away and focus on the shaman to quell the tears.

"Lern has said that Mamut is a coward."

Mamut flinched and straightened, now fully alert to the proceedings. He felt Wolf Boy tense beside him. The dog understood a threat, too.

"Lern says that he saw Mamut run away when his father called him for help."

Terah was bewildered. Why was the shaman talking about Mamut? He was supposed to talk about Rana! She edged closer to Rana and touched the woman reassuringly. She wanted to convey that even if the shaman had forgotten about her, Terah had not. Rana smiled back with trembling lips.

Lern was nodding at what the shaman had said. So were several others.

"We must talk about this," said the shaman. "Where were you, Lern, when you saw Mamut run?"

Lern flushed and looked round at the listening men. He shifted his feet and his forehead began to glisten. "I—I was watching from behind a boulder."

"Why did you not call for help?" The shaman's face was stern.

"I was too far away. It happened so fast. . . ."

"Why did you not go to Mamut's aid?"

"I was too far away." Something in his voice told Mamut he was lying.

The other men's faces were somber.

"You watched my father die!" cried Mamut. "And you did nothing to help him. To help me!"

"I had no spear."

"That is a lie. You received the spear of manliness before I did."

Lern said nothing. His face reddened, and his eyes flashed.

"That is why you have hated me all these years," goaded Mamut. "You, too, acted the coward!" Suddenly the revelation made sense of all the years of sly innuendos and insults.

Lern glowered. "I did not want to help you," he hissed. "You had a father. I did not! Why should I be the only boy without a father?"

Mamut stared at Lern. "Your father died when

you were eight summers old," he muttered. "As did your mother. They left you and your younger sister orphans."

Benaleese looked pale. Terah remembered then that Benaleese and Lern were brother and sister. That meant that Benaleese, too, had been orphaned when very young. Sadness for her welled inside Terah.

"Yes!" growled Lern. "We had no mother or father to care about us. What I needed was a man to teach me to hunt. To care about me! I watched you go hunting with your father day after day, season after season. Bison hunting. Antelope hunting. Mammoth hunting! And not once did you invite me along! I had no one!" Lern's eyes squeezed shut, and his body shook. His rage and hatred reached out and wrapped around Mamut, and for a moment Mamut too felt the strength of Lern's rage.

It left Mamut shaken. Years of insults, insidious cruelties—it had all been because of jealousy. If only Mamut had known how Lern had felt. He would have invited him to hunt, shared his father. No, he thought, he could not be certain he would have shared his father. . . .

"My father died, killed by a vicious pack of dire wolves, when I was eight," Lern's voice was shaking. "And no one helped me. Oh, they took me along on hunting trips as an afterthought. But no one looked at me. Helped me. Noticed me!"

His words fell into the stunned silence of the listening men and women.

At last the shaman said sadly, "You were told,

Theresa Scott

Lern, that your father died in an attack by dire wolves."

Lern nodded. "You told me so."

"But there is more," continued the shaman. "Did you ever ask yourself why he was out in the tundra that day—alone?"

Lern, watching Mamut with a hostile gaze, did not at first understand the medicine man's words.

"What do you mean?" demanded Lern. "That is how he died! That is what I have been told ever since he died! *You* told me that!"

The shaman was sadly nodding his head. "Yes," he acknowledged quietly. "But I left out a part of the truth when I told you only about the wolves." He sighed heavily, then took a breath as though he summoned his strength. "I left out part of what happened to your father so that you could be proud of your father." He faced Lern. "I lied to you."

Lern's eyes widened. He took a step backward. "What are you telling me, Shaman?"

The shaman stood quietly leaning on the stout stick he always carried with him. "Your father died because he was banished from our people. He was forced out into the tundra. That is how the wolves got him."

"Why?" rasped Lern, his eyes riveted on the shaman. *"Why was he banished?"*

"Because he beat your mother—to death. When we found her, there was nothing we could do to help her. She was able to tell us what happened before—before she died."

"You lie!" screamed Lern. "You lied to me once!

382

You are lying again! I can believe nothing you tell me!"

"He speaks the truth." It was Spark's deep voice. He looked sadly at his young wife, Benaleese, who was staring in frozen disbelief at him. "I was there."

"No!" raged Lern. "My father would not do such a thing! Not to my mother! You lie!" He howled his outrage. *"You lie!"*

He lunged for the shaman. Mamut and Spark and Spearpoint pulled him away from the old man before he could strike him.

"You were very little and did not know what had happened." The shaman's voice was sad. Terah thought that he now deeply regretted his decision to lie to Lern about his father. "Our people would not allow your father to stay with us anymore. He was forced to leave. Banished."

Lern howled. "No! No! You lie! All of you! Liars!"

All that greeted him was a sad, profound silence. He read the terrible truth in the shaman's face, in that of Spark. And lastly in Benaleese's eyes. "No!" he yelled at his sister.

"Yes," she said hoarsely. She passed a hand over her eyes. "I remember."

Lern glared at her, his rage and anger very much upon him.

Terah reached for her white chert knife. If he attacked Benaleese, Terah would stop him. But he did not attack. Before her eyes, Lern sagged and shrank. "No," he muttered. "It cannot be."

Benaleese got up from the rock where she had

been sitting. She walked over to him and touched his arm. "It is true, my brother." She reached up and hugged him.

And then Lern cried. Great, hoarse, rasping sobs. Terah wanted to run out into the night to get away from his pain. But she stood her ground.

Mamut wanted to run away from Lern's terrible cries. But, he warned himself, he had run enough in his life. He would not run from this. Lern needed him to stay. And accept.

Rana walked over to Lern. There was a hushed silence as everyone waited for her to speak.

"I will no longer live with you, Lern."

Terah let out her breath in a relieved sigh.

The older woman looked dignified and proud and calm. "I will no longer let you beat me."

Lern lifted his head and pulled away from Benaleese's clasp. His face was haggard. Tears streaked his countenance, but he was calm after the storm of his weeping. "I will not be like my father. I will no longer beat you."

She shook her head. "No, I will not stay with you."

He seemed to crumple into himself. Dully, he looked at her. At last he nodded. "Very well. Go."

He walked her over to her Frog tent. In a short while, he returned to the shaman's fire. Alone. He carried with him a bison bedrobe and his spears and hunkered down by the fire.

Benaleese looked at Spark. Her husband nodded.

"You may stay with us," offered Benaleese.

Lern shook his head. "No," he said. "I have much thinking to do. I do not want to disturb you."

"Thinking will not disturb us," said Spark.

"No," responded Lern. "I—need some time to think. Alone." He looked lonely and despondent in the firelight.

The others slowly drifted away, leaving him at the shaman's fire. Terah felt relieved that Rana was safe at last. She said good-night and went back to her tent.

As she crawled into the bedrobes, she thought, *tomorrow is the mammoth hunt. How am I going to save Mamut?*

Chapter 36

"What are you doing, Terah?" asked Rana.

Terah jumped guiltily. The mist was so thick and she had been so intent upon laying the broad green leaves carefully in the water that she had not noticed anyone. It was just before dawn, and she had deliberately made her visit to the mammoth drinking hole at a time when the Mammoth People were asleep. No one must see her.

She stared at Rana through the fog. Could she trust her? She thought she could, but with this important mission, she would not take the risk. "I am picking water plants," she lied.

Rana frowned. "It does not look like you are picking them *from* the water," she answered. "It looks like you are putting them *in* the water."

Terah sighed. Lying was not something she

did well, she decided. She wiped her weary forehead with a muddy hand. She had risked her life
in coming to the mammoth pool, too. She had
hoped that the dire wolves and lions and saber-
toothed tigers would be feeding on the game they
had caught earlier in the night and would be too
busy to notice one frail human walking in the
water. She had not reckoned with Rana, however.

"Why do you do this?" Rana asked curiously.

Terah tightened her lips. Her friend could ask;
that did not mean Terah must answer.

When no answer was forthcoming, Rana took
the hint. "Very well," she said, and Terah could
hear the hurt in her voice, "do not tell me." Rana
began to wade over to where Terah had carefully
laid out several broad leaves that floated just
under the water. Rana bent to take a drink.

"Do not!" cried Terah. At her cry, several water
fowl cackled and flew into the air. She ignored
the disturbed birds. "Do not," she said again,
a little calmer this time. "You may drink from
where the water flows swiftly." She pointed with
her chin to where the river flowed past. Rana
could not see very well in the dim light, however,
and was not to be put off.

"I must drink," she complained. "I am thirsty."

Terah waded over to her friend and bent down
until their eyes met. "Rana," Terah said as evenly
as she could. "If you drink from this water, you
will get very sick, perhaps even die."

Rana's shrewd eyes met hers. She took a step
back. "Very well, then, I will drink farther
upriver."

"Good," answered Terah. Rana moved away, and Terah watched her go until she was certain the older woman was safely out of the way. Then she began carefully laying more broad leaves.

She was just laying the last leaf when she heard a lion roar. "Time to go back," she cautioned herself. "I do not want to become food for lions while doing this deed." She waded to shore and gave a little jump when she saw that Rana had come up silently behind her.

Dawn's light was starting to filter through the hills, and Terah could see that the old woman smiled. Her eyes looked less puffy, the bruises were fading. "You are helping that man of yours, are you not?" guessed Rana.

Terah frowned discouragingly. She would not tell Rana a word of her purpose. She did not want to jeopardize her delicate plan, so she shrugged carelessly. "I felt like fishing," she said.

"Fishing?"

"Yes. Those leaves will stun the fish, and later I can come back here and scoop them up in a basket." Which was true. Her Bison People used the leaves to stun fish. But the number of leaves that Terah had placed in the water could stun more than fish. Their poison could stun much bigger game. She hoped Rana would accept the explanation.

"Oh." Rana sounded disappointed. As they walked back through the low-lying mist to the sleeping camp, she asked, "Could you make me another poultice for my arm? That last poultice you made took away my pain very swiftly."

Theresa Scott

Terah nodded with relief, her mind turning back to the forthcoming mammoth hunt. This was the day the mammoth hunters had chosen to spear the great beasts. The shaman had told them the day was not auspicious—none of the upcoming days were, he warned. He could not promise that the hunt would go well. But the Mammoth men, goaded by an impatient Lern, wanted the hunt over with so they could move south. Winter was coming.

Terah was afraid. She did not want to leave the mammoth hunt to chance. There was one person and one person only whose welfare she cared about. The hunt *must* be a success. And she would do everything in her power to make it that way.

She was so busy with her plans that she did not have time to stop and ask herself why it mattered so much that he succeed.

Chapter 37

Mamut groped drowsily for Terah. She was not there. He rolled out of bed. *If she has escaped again, I will make her pay. . . .*

On that ill thought, Terah entered the tent. Her legs were wet and her feet were muddy.

"You cannot get into my bed like that," he joked, pretending that he had not rushed out of bed to look for her.

She smiled wanly at him, understanding how difficult it must be for him to jest. She brushed the mud off her legs with dried grass. She watched as he sat down on the dirt floor of the dwelling.

"Breakfast?" she asked.

He stared at her. She was going to make him breakfast? What ailed the woman? Did she not know he was an outcast among his own people? Bison women were strange, he decided. He would not encourage the Mammoth people to marry into them. Who knew what rude surprises awaited a man married to one such as this? He nodded, not trusting himself to speak.

She brought him a freshly roasted fish.

"You have been fishing early this morning," he observed as he ate.

She answered with a noncommittal nod, concentrating on her own breakfast.

When Mamut was done with his meal, he retrieved something very valuable from its hiding place. It was the white chert blade he had found on the Mountain of the Badger. Holding it reverently in his hand, he closed his eyes and squeezed his fingers gently around the blade. It was solid. Thick.

He could feel the strength of the blade. It would aid him in his hunt. It would help him kill a mammoth. Mamut reached for the leather sack full of white blades he had earlier flaked off the white core he had also found on the mountaintop. Carefully, he had laboriously notched and fluted every single one of them.

They looked very fine, but not one of them approached the superb workmanship of the blade the Great Spirit had given him. He smiled to himself. He strode to the tent entry. Terah's voice halted him. "Do you go hunting this day?"

Did she not know that this was the day of the mammoth hunt? "Yes," he answered. "I go mammoth hunting."

He thought he heard a swift intake of breath, but when he narrowed his eyes at her, she was wearing a bland expression on her lovely face. "May your prey die swiftly and your spear run with blood," she answered politely.

"I will share," he responded just as politely and ducked out of the tent. He found himself walking jauntily through the mist now that she had wished him the traditional farewell of his people. He hoped that the hunt truly did go well, that the mammoths died swiftly and that his spear ran rivers of their rich, strong mammoth blood.

The other hunters had already gathered at the shaman's fire. Stacked around them was every single spear the Mammoth hunters owned. Each spear had been meticulously cleaned and checked. New bindings had been tied on to hold the spear point to the wooden shaft of the spear. The speartips themselves had been carefully retouched, and small pieces of stone had been flaked off along the cutting edges so that the sharp fluted blades would slice neatly through thick mammoth hide and into a heart or lung.

When Mamut approached, several of the hunters, Spearpoint among them, turned their faces aside—but not before Mamut spied the disgust in their expressions. Lern, however, met his gaze boldly. "We would do better to take Wolf Boy than you. Wolf Boy is brave."

Mamut restrained himself with a massive effort. He wondered if the loss of Lern's wife had made the tattooed man meaner than before. "No doubt Wolf Boy is brave," Mamut answered evenly when he could speak. "But Wolf Boy will warn the mammoths we seek them." He paused, relieved that no one had yet walked away. "I will not warn them."

Lern laughed. "You seek to kill a mammoth, *boy?*"

The others snickered.

Mamut had never known the pain that mere words could inflict. He felt as though he were tied to a tree and his people were spearing him. He met their contemptuous faces with a stony gaze. "I would join you."

"You will run," predicted a mocking Lern.

Mamut speared his foe with a glance. "I will not run."

"I do not believe you."

Mamut shrugged as though he faced such insults daily. *Perhaps,* he thought, *I do. Perhaps I face a lifetime of such insults.* "Believe what you want," he said hoarsely.

"Coward," said Lern.

Never in his life had Mamut known such pain as that of his people turning upon him. If he survived the hunt, perhaps he would take Terah and go into a wandering exile, he thought. Finally Mamut answered, "You are in no position to call me coward. You fled, too."

Lern glared at Mamut and turned away, effectively silenced.

None of the hunters said anything more. They moved out into the mist. They had studied the mammoth herd well enough to know that the calves liked to play in the pool at dawn. The older cows were sluggish then and still sleepy. Early morning was the preferred time for slaughter.

No one noticed the shadowy figure of a young woman slip from a tent and follow the hunters. In her hand was a dully gleaming white chert knife.

"The hunt goes well!" cried a jubilant Lern. Already four mammoth cows lay dying with many spears bristling out of their sides. Mamut counted as many spears sticking those animals as a man had fingers and toes. The bellowing calves made a cacophonous din. He watched as several hunters swiftly dispatched the calves. The noise ceased.

"Our children will eat!" cried Spark. His impending fatherhood added to his hunting success.

Hope glowed on the other hunters' faces. This kill would bring much meat to the Mammoth People. Now none of their people would go hungry this winter.

The last remaining animal, the huge matriarch of the herd, shook her head and swung her trunk. She flapped her tiny ears back and forth, and her eyes rolled wildly. She trumpeted her fear and anger and confusion.

Lern grabbed two spears and raced toward the angry, stomping beast. He ran in under her trunk and laughed wildly as he plunged his spear in and under, aiming for one of her lungs. He missed. In his haste to back away, he tripped and fell.

The maddened beast whirled on him, her huge forefeet plunging up and down in a frenzied attempt to stomp him to death. One huge forefoot came hurtling through the air— down, down, to smash Lern. Suddenly Mamut grabbed Lern by one arm and dragged him across the stony ground. He pulled Lern as fast as he could, but the mammoth was almost on top of them.

Spearpoint saw the danger and yelled to Spark and the shaman. Together, the three ran in with their spears and with powerful thrusts stabbed several times at the beast. The combined shock of their ferocious attack sent the animal reeling back, and she screamed as she sank to her knees. Lern, holding one arm, watched in safety from behind a rock where Mamut had dragged him. As the mammoth's great head swung back and forth, she gave a last trumpeting scream and died.

There was a throbbing stillness, a vibrating silence after the beast died. Then the shaman dropped his spear and lifted his voice in song. As he sang, he danced and weaved his way around the dead bodies of the beasts, stopping at each one and bowing and raising his arms to the Great Spirit. In the song he thanked the Great Spirit for delivering the mammoths up to the hunters. He sang about how bravely the mammoths had fought, how vigorously they had defended their young, how nobly the grandmother had fought for her family. He expressed much admiration for the animals and thanked each one of them for delivering herself up to the Mammoth hunters. Now the hunters and their families would eat and live happily because of the gift of meat and bones and ivory to the hunters.

The other Mammoth hunters stood listening, each with his own private thoughts and prayers, until the shaman was finished. Then they danced and yelled and cried out their happiness at the success of the hunt. When they had finished cavorting amongst the animals, they set about cutting into the hides to get at the meat.

The joyous women came running to help, crying and laughing in their elation.

Terah, smiling, waved to Mamut and walked over to where he was slicing at the stomach of a carcass. "It was a good hunt," she said, her eyes sparkling. Part of her wanted to blurt out her secret, but another part cautioned her. She did not want to crush the pride she'd seen on his face.

"It went very well," he agreed. "The mammoths fought bravely, but we were the stronger. The old one, the leader"—he pointed with his chin at the biggest carcass—"gave us the most difficulty."

Perhaps the mammoth matriarch did not drink much of the water, thought Terah. Never would Terah tell Mamut about the poisonous leaves she had placed in the water. She would die before she would let him know that that was why the hunt had gone so successfully. She contented herself with a gracious smile whenever Mamut looked at her. "Did Lern thank you for saving his life?" she asked.

Mamut stared at her. When had she seen that? He shrugged. "No."

Terah frowned. She was just bending down to examine the entrails of the beast that they were butchering when a motion out of the corner of one eye caught her attention. She stared into the mist. "Mamut!" she gasped.

He whirled when he heard the fear in her voice. Looming out of the mist, striding toward them, came a huge, hoary, white mammoth.

Mamut grabbed his spear. It was the mammoth of his vision!

Chapter 38

Mamut watched in dumbstruck horror as the giant behemoth loomed out of the fog. Suddenly he seemed to come to his senses and yelled at the others, "Get back! Bull mammoth!"

The men and women of the Mammoth People glanced up from where they were happily slicing meat and breaking the great bones. Their jaws dropped in terror. Benaleese's husband, Spark, stared in horrified disbelief. Lern and Spearpoint gaped.

Mamut knew why. The beast looked to be not of this earth, so white and ghostly was it coming out of the fog. "Move!" he yelled at the frozen people. "Flee!"

Finally, as though they each had great rocks

tied to their legs, the Mammoth men and women began to back ever so slowly away from the carcasses.

Wolf Boy started barking, and Lame Leg tottered after Rana in an attempt to escape. The dog's barks seemed to awaken the others out of their horror and disbelief. Several of the men snatched up their spears. Mamut glanced at the spears he had grabbed in his haste. One was the red spear with the white chert spearpoint, his gift from the Great Spirit.

A calmness settled over Mamut. Ahead of him was the greatest fight of his life. If he succeeded in battling the great white mammoth, he would be a man—in his own eyes and in those of his people. If he failed, he would die.

He started to run toward the beast. The elephantine animal had stopped and was casting its long trunk in swaying circles, trying to find the scent of the enemy.

"It is the son of the mammoth grandmother," pronounced the shaman in his deep voice. "He has come to avenge his dead!"

Shivers rippled through Mamut at this disclosure. The mammoth would be very angry and fierce in his revenge for his family.

Out of the corner of his eye, Mamut saw Spark pause, and Lern too, as they considered the shaman's somber words. "Let us fight him!" cried Spearpoint.

Eight of the Mammoth hunters ran closer to the great beast. The remaining two hunters fell back to protect the fleeing women and Lame

Leg, keeping between them and the beast for a desperate defense if the others could not kill the animal.

The eight—among them Spearpoint, Spark, Lern, the shaman, and Mamut—positioned themselves in a circle around the hoary beast. Mamut stood just to the side of the animal and out of reach of the mighty trunk. He remembered his vision. He did not want to feel that trunk snaking around his body as it had in his vision.

Terah watched in frozen horror, unable to flee. The bull mammoth before her was the tallest, heaviest animal she had ever seen in her life. A full-grown man would barely reach his stomach. And the animal was furious.

Suddenly a sickening thought jolted her. This bull had not drunk from the poisoned pool. He had come from the other direction! Mamut was about to fight a fully alert, enraged bull mammoth!

She pulled out her little white chert knife and ran to Mamut.

"Get back," he yelled, momentarily distracted. His gaze darted from Terah to the bull and back again. "Get back!"

"But I want to help!" she cried, waving her knife.

The snaking trunk swung in her direction and stopped, the sniffing tip aloft. Transfixed, she watched the hairy white trunk weave in front of her, delicately fixing her position. Then the great beast lumbered toward her. Too late,

Terah realized that she was the animal's target now!

She gazed unblinking and hopelessly up at the behemoth as it charged toward her. Her feet would not move.

"Run!" cried Mamut, waving his arms to distract the animal from Terah. "Run!"

Still she stood there. It was Mamut's worst nightmare. The charging mammoth, the person he loved—it was his father's death all over again! Only this time it was Terah, the woman he loved, who would die.

He willed himself to move forward. He took a step, then another. Two more steps and he could touch the heaving flank of the great beast.

He raised the red spear. He had one chance. A single chance to kill. The spear must enter the great beast's heart. To do so it must pierce first through thick, shaggy hair the length of a man's fingers. Then the speartip must pierce through thick, leathery hide. It must be thrust with such force that it drove between the ribs and penetrated the heart. This knowledge came to Mamut in the flash of a moment. He knew where the skin was thinnest and access to the heart greatest—the belly.

He ran in under the animal. He took a breath and concentrated the force of his life, his whole being, upon the tiny spot where the ribs met. Behind that moving point pounded the huge heart.

Be with me, Great Spirit. When Mamut expelled

his breath, out came a fierce, guttural cry. Power surged through him. With every fiber of his body, every muscle, every sinew, Mamut drove the red spear up—up and in!

The sharp white point buried itself in the animal's chest. The red wooden shaft followed to the very hilt. The spearpoint had penetrated. Deeply. Mamut dashed out from under the beast before it toppled on him.

The mammoth took one more step, its rolling eyes glazed. It sank back, crushing the spear shaft like a twig.

Terah could smell the animal. It smelled of warmth and earth and its own peculiar mammoth smell. The yellow-white hairy trunk grazed her skin as the animal sank to its knees. The touch, a mere whispery thin feel of it, galvanized her. She came alive and darted out of the way.

The Mammoth People watched transfixed as the great white beast sank to its knees. It raised its trunk once more and gave a wild, screaming trumpet.

"He sings his death chant," cried the shaman.

All the people listened as the keening sound died away to an eerie silence. Then the white mammoth closed its eyes. Its huge head lowered. It never moved again.

Mamut stared at the dead animal. He had killed it. He had killed it! The realization slowly sank into his benumbed brain. The charging mammoth was dead. By his hand. Relief scoured through him. He was tired unto his very soul. He was elated too. He staggered over to a rock and sat down.

All was changed for him now. He had killed the mammoth. He had restored his life. He was a man.

Chapter 39

The Mammoth People went wild in their jubilation. They jumped up and down and yelled and shrieked and danced. Benaleese held her bulging stomach and dipped and swayed carefully. Spark threw back his head and yelled his delight. Rana pounded a spear shaft against the earth as she had once pounded it to call forth toads. Terah stood dazed, sweating, empty. Alive.

Lame Leg danced in little awkward skips and hops. Wolf Boy pranced and barked. The shaman sang a song of thanks. Lern danced and cavorted. Spearpoint stared at Mamut.

Mamut stared back. He felt too elated, too tired to let his friend's past betrayal intrude upon the moment. He had killed the mammoth! No longer did he need to feel the coward.

Spearpoint sauntered over. "That was a big mammoth that you killed. Huge."

Mamut grunted.

Spearpoint glanced around at the celebrating people, unable to meet Mamut's eyes. "I—I—" At last his gaze swung to Mamut's. "It was a brave thing to do." Then he walked away.

Mamut shrugged. He recognized that Spearpoint had come as close to saying "I was wrong" as he would ever get.

Mamut was musing upon this when he felt a gentle touch upon his arm. He held up his arm to look at his trembling hand. He was, he marveled, still shaking from killing the beast.

He looked up to see Terah studying him.

"Thank you," she said softly. "You saved my life."

Mamut inclined his head in acknowledgment. It was good that he had saved her. He said a prayer of thanks to the Great Spirit for His help.

Then he stared thoughtfully at Terah. He was free now. Free to tell her about himself. Free to love her. Free to marry her. "Terah—" he began.

She shook her head and placed a hand over his lips. "Mamut," she said gently. "Please listen to me."

He watched her, his obsidian gaze unnerving. She swallowed, wondering how she was going to say what she knew must be said. "Your people will accept you now. That is good. You no longer need to hold on to me because no other woman will be your mate. Therefore I tell you, Mamut—" she hesitated.

He felt lost in her somber green eyes. He leaned forward, anxious to hear every word. Dread started a slow coil in his gut.

"I must leave you, Mamut. I must return to my people. I thought—I thought I could leave my people and go with you. I thought that I could live with you and be your woman—" She felt proud of the strength in her voice. Proud that she had not said "wife." "But I find I cannot. I cannot be separated so cruelly from my Bison People. I cannot live with a man who does not want to receive the spears my father wishes to offer for me."

Green eyes burned into brown. "You no longer need me," she continued. "You can go to the Meet-meet. You can exchange mammoth ivory or bison robes for a wife. Your people accept you, respect you."

This is difficult beyond words, she thought. Her heart was breaking as she spoke. He had saved her. He had been kind to her. And she loved him. But she could not, would not, stay with him as a captive. And though he could physically stop her from walking away, some wise part of her knew that he would not. He was different now— restored, complete—and he no longer needed to hold on to her.

Mamut's face closed, and he looked to be carved of stone. Inside him bitterness churned. He remembered the contempt in her eyes when Lern had told everyone of his cowardice. *She still believes me to be a coward*, he thought.

And then he sagged where he sat. If Terah did not want to stay with him, he would no longer force her. If she thought him a coward, so be it. She could leave. He inclined his head once again, as though it cost him nothing. Never would he tell her of the anger, the betrayal, the bitterness, the despair, he was feeling. Better that she knew nothing.

"Benaleese has yet to have her baby," he said pointing with his chin to the dancing woman.

Startled, Terah looked at him.

"My people will wait here for a time, until Benaleese has birthed her child," he explained. "While they wait, I will travel back to the Bison People with you. You will need protection," he added when he saw that she was about to protest. "The saber-tooths . . ."

She flushed. "It is good," she murmured. She felt perversely hurt that he was able to let her go with not even a protest. Did he not care for her— even a tiny bit?

"My brother, Bron," she began awkwardly, feeling the need to explain that she did not think Mamut was ever a coward, "was killed by a saber-tooth."

"Yes, you told me," Mamut observed curtly.

She met his cold gaze and shrank inwardly. This man looked as if he cared little what she had to say. *No doubt he is anxious to find a new woman at the Meet-meet*, she thought in irritation, *and he no longer wants to be bothered with me.*

"He—he tested his bravery against the animal and lost."

Mamut stared at her, his obsidian gaze impenetrable. Was it not enough that he had saved her life? Did she feel compelled to insult him by comparing him to her brave brother? He heaved himself off the rock and stood gazing down at her. "Your brother was very brave," he acknowledged coldly.

"My brother," she said, and her face flushed a becoming pink, "was very foolish." With that, she turned on her heel and walked away.

Mamut frowned as his unwilling gaze followed her. What was she trying to tell him? He ground his teeth in frustration. What did women want, anyway?

It was a bleak day when they found the Bison People. The huge bowl of sky was gray and overcast. Geese flew overhead. Autumn was full upon the land.

The Bison People were huddled in a small encampment. Mamut spied Tika and Kell from the hilltop where he and Terah stood. "There they are," he said at last. He had hoped with a fanciful part of his mind never to find the Bison People. Alas, his excellent tracking skills had for once proved a disadvantage. He had found Terah's relatives rapidly.

"Yes," she agreed, wondering why she still stood rooted to the hilltop as though she were a scrub pine tree. "Yes," she murmured once more. She took a step forward. Should she tell him she still cared for him? Loved him? Wanted still for him to ask her father for him?

No, she warned herself silently. If he wanted her, he would ask her father for her. And from the cold, implacable look upon Mamut's face, she decided that he was relieved to let her go.

With her heart twisting in her breast, she faced into the wind, looking away from him. *How it hurts to say good-bye*, she thought. Never had she felt such pain, such agony, as this.

She brushed her hand across her face, as though to brush her hair out of her face. Her hand came away wet. She blinked. "Farewell." She should feel proud that she could utter the word without sobbing.

Mamut waited. Was this what it all came to? he wondered. The love they had shared? His hopes for a life together? Yes, he thought savagely. It all came down to a cool good-bye on a windy hilltop overlooking the Gift of Life River.

He had won back his dignity as a man. It was a cruel blow that he had lost the woman he loved.

Chapter 40

45 days later

The shores of the Giver of Life River were crowded with people. It was the time of the Meet-meet. A festive air prevailed. Each band had set up their tents in their own area.

The people all mingled near the trading mats placed around a huge, central firepit. Each night men and women danced in the light of the glowing fire. Each day children darted between tents, men talked in small groups or sauntered about with their families, and women visited with friends they had not seen since the last Meet-meet three autumns before. Some women sat beside carefully worked wares laid out enticingly on well-tanned hides. Prospective buyers walked past, half-listening to their friends and half-eyeing the wares.

A sick child or adult could be cured here. Medicine men from the different bands were solicited for their healing skills. And of course a thoughtful gift to the shaman was not considered amiss after a successful cure.

A variety of implements and jewelry were displayed. The Duck Netting People showed off beautiful ivory bone needles and awls to make a woman's sewing easier.

The Great Frog People were known for their neatly sewn moccasins and vests and tunics.

White shell bead necklaces and bracelets made by the Groundsloth Eating People were delicately wrought to grace a lithe brown arm.

The finely flaked obsidian blades of the unsociable Grassy Plains People were always sought after. So were their beautifully crafted obsidian knives that sliced smoothly through an antelope hindquarter.

The Always Crying People were known for their fluted brown chert spearpoints, ideal to aid a man in killing the winter's meat. Red ochre for decorating spears and hides was also available.

Birch sticks, fire-tempered by the Salmon Spawning People, made stout spear shafts and were especially in demand.

The Mammoth People displayed bison skins for making warm robes for the coming snows. Many of the visitors marveled over the vast width of the bison horns that were displayed, but it was the costly chunks of mammoth ivory that drew the most admiring gasps from visitors.

The Mammoth People had set their tents near the river. Mamut leaned against a rock, arms crossed over his bronzed chest. From where he was he could see the different bands' encampments. He had already wandered among the displays, gazed at this chert knife or that intricately carved spear shaft. He had even seen a beautifully worked white shell necklace that would have looked lovely on Terah. Sadly, he had turned his back on the necklace, a painful reminder. Terah—the reason he was not enjoying himself.

The people around Mamut were happy, but he felt detached from their gaiety. He had observed the various women, of course. All the Mammoth men did. Spearpoint was in the middle of negotiations for a lovely Duck Netting woman whose big brown eyes he rhapsodized about each evening to Mamut. The five other Mammoth hunters had each offered for a woman of their choosing.

Benaleese had seen her husband, Spark, speaking with one curvaceous young Groundsloth beauty, a prospective co-wife. With narrowed eyes, Benaleese had wordlessly thrust Spark's tiny new daughter into his arms as he stood smiling at the woman. Benaleese sauntered around the camp and returned just in time to find her husband standing by himself and looking bewildered as he tried to calm a howling baby. The curvaceous beauty was nowhere to be seen. Benaleese smiled sweetly and took the child from her husband. Spark remained close at her side after that, all thoughts of a second wife ostensibly forgotten.

Rana was enjoying a loud reunion with her Great Frog relatives and proudly introducing her new daughter, once called Lame Leg, now called Blossom. Were it not for her limp, Mamut would not have recognized the clean and tidy Blossom with her carefully combed and braided hair. Her shy, smiling face was actually pretty, he saw in astonishment. Rana had done much for the child. And the child had done much for Rana, too, giving her someone to care for now that she no longer lived with Lern. Rana looked happy as she hugged relatives and laughed with them.

Lern and the shaman had decided not to choose wives at the Meet-meet.

Mamut wondered if Lern would ever take another wife. Certainly the man had been quiet and somber since he had accepted Rana's decision to leave him. Lern had somehow matured, too. Ever since Mamut had rescued him from the mammoth, Lern no longer made offensive remarks.

Mamut sighed. He supposed he should consider taking a wife; the Meet-meet was his best chance to find an acceptable woman. But the women he had seen here, while many were comely and skilled in tanning and preparing food and building tents, did nothing to his heart. There was no little frisson of excitement when he looked into a woman's eyes. There was no leap of joy in his heart when he heard her lilt of laughter. He sighed. He could not fault the woman.

She was not Terah. Perhaps by the next Meet-meet, he would be over grieving for her, he told himself. Yes, perhaps in three or four years, at the next Meet-meet, he would be ready to find a wife.

A small straggling group of strangers approached the camp at the far end from where the Mammoth People were. They set up their tents at the edge of the Meet-meet and lit their fires and began cooking and fetching water from the river.

Mamut glanced over desultorily and then his heart stopped. It was the Bison People. He got to his feet and strained to see them. Terah was with them!

His heart started pounding again. He knew what he must do.

Chapter 41

Terah walked along looking at the displayed wares, her best, newly tanned tunic feeling stiff against her flesh. Her hair hung down her back. Chee had combed it until it reflected the sun's beauty. Terah's mother and father walked beside her.

With a tiny smile, she remembered her daydream. She would come to the Meet-meet, looking her loveliest; Mamut would see her and be overcome with love for her. He would want to marry her. He would beg and plead and get down on his knees in the dirt. Perhaps he would cry a tear or two. She, of course, would regally turn aside and choose some other handsome suitor from a group of admirers. And Mamut would be left standing alone. And rejected. And lonely. And regretful that he had ever treated her so poorly. And sadly he would turn away, crushed and broken, knowing that she would never be his bride.

It was a satisfying daydream, she mused. Then she sighed. Unfortunately, the person who felt alone and rejected and lonely and regretful and sad was not Mamut. It was Terah.

She glanced behind her. Ah, the group of suitors. There they were, following her. There must be five or six. She smiled to herself. How handsome the one was with the brown hair, the half-smile, the slanted obsidian eyes. . . . She frowned at the reminder of another pair of obsidian eyes and swung back to watch where she was walking.

And came up against a broad, naked chest. She lifted her eyes. "Mamut!" she gasped.

He stared down at her. "Terah."

She glanced nervously behind her. Her day-dream—which suitor was she supposed to choose? She could not remember. Not with Mamut so close to her. She met his obsidian eyes. "How—how pleasant to see you," she murmured, shifting from foot to foot.

His eyes burned into hers. He could feel his desire for her. Time had not dulled it, only strengthened it. He turned to her father, "Greetings, Bison Man."

Terah's father grunted. "Come, Terah," he said warily as he and Terah's mother attempted to step around Mamut.

Mamut shifted to block their path. "I would

offer for your daughter," he said arrogantly.

Terah could not stem her swift intake of breath.

"Terah?" her father glanced at her.

Her eyes wide, Terah met her father's questioning stare with her own question. *Oh, what am I going to do?*

She glanced at her small crowd of suitors. In her daydream, at this moment, she was supposed to choose one of them and cast Mamut away. But this was not a daydream. This was real.

Mamut followed the shift of her eyes. His sculpted lips tightened, but he said nothing. His gaze narrowed as he stared at someone behind her.

One Shoe came running up. Bear too. Both had avoided Terah since she had returned to her people. Now, sensing a fight, they each rested a hand eagerly on a knife.

"Terah?" asked her father again.

She looked at him then, the gray hair, the beloved stooped figure.

"Is this the man, Terah?"

She knew what he was asking. Was this the man who had captured her and stolen her heart? "Yes, Father," she affirmed. "It is he."

Her father grunted. He took several shuffling steps forward, and Terah wanted to cry. He looked so small and thin facing up to Mamut.

Mamut stared down at the smaller man. If his father had lived, Kran would be younger than this man. Still, the Bison man before him was a father. Mamut could see that in the worried

419

glances he gave his daughter, in his protective stance even now, when he could not hope to win a physical fight with Mamut. The wife, Terah's mother, walked forward and joined him, her hand resting on his arm, whether to steady him or show support, Mamut could not tell. They both peered up at him.

Mamut smiled. He could see now where Terah got her bravery.

"I wish to marry your daughter," he said. "Amongst my people, when a man wants to marry a woman, he gives gifts to her family for her. I wish to give gifts for Terah."

Her father frowned and cleared his throat. "Amongst our people, young man, *we* are the ones to give the gifts. Spears, of course, are the best gifts. I have eight of them saved up to give for Terah. It is a huge dowry. One that many young men would be happy to marry for." He turned to his wife. "Is that not correct, beloved?"

Terah's mother nodded. "Yes," she said. The wrinkles around her eyes from many years of squinting against the sun almost hid her eyes. Wooden bracelets clacked on her arms whenever she moved. "You must tell this young man that it is also customary amongst our people to obtain the bride's consent." She turned to Terah.

Terah smiled and opened her mouth. "Ye—" she began.

"But of course," interrupted her mother, "we know what Terah's answer is. It is 'no.' She would not want to marry a man who stole her away from her people."

Mamut wanted to gnash his teeth. "Why do you not ask her?" he ground out.

"No need, no need," said her father. "We have several other offers to consider."

Terah stared. There were no other offers that she knew about. Whatever was her father talking about?

Her father coughed nervously. "Furthermore, I do not understand how this marriage could take place. Our customs are too different. You want to give gifts to us, we want to give spears to you. Who will the children belong to?" He shook his head. "No, this is too confusing. Not the orderly Bison way of doing things. Not at all. We will have to reject your offer, young man."

Mamut did gnash his teeth.

"Father!" Terah stepped forward. Now that Mamut had asked to marry her, she was not about to have her father drive him away because of insignificant differences in marriage gift customs! "Surely we can work out a way," she began.

Her father shook his head. "No. I do not believe we can. His people are too different. And they live too far away. We would never see you again."

He saw his daughter tighten her lips, an ominous sign to family members. "And of course I have all those spears to give away. . . . And all those other suitors. No, I do not see how it can be done." He took a shuffling step forward. "Come, beloved. We must see the rest of the wares on display. Beautiful jewelry over there." He pointed with his chin. "Shall we look at it?"

"Yes," said Terah's mother as she tottered after him.

"Father! Mother! Come back here," wailed Terah. "We must come to an agreement. . . ."

They ignored her and tottered on. One by one, Terah's admirers drifted away. One Shoe and Bear, seeing that a fight was no longer imminent, sauntered off in search of more excitement.

Mamut was left staring at Terah. "Your father has eight spears to give away, an unheard-of number among the Bison People. That is what you told me. Then why is it that he does not want to give them away to *me*?"

Terah shrugged, misery in her lovely green eyes. "I do not know. I would think they would be happy to marry me off to a fine hunter. I have been so unhappy of late, moping about the tent and crying. I would think they would be happy to be rid of me. . . ." She stopped. Perhaps she had said too much.

Mamut touched her cheek. "Moping, Terah?" he asked softly. "Crying?"

She nodded.

He swallowed. Dared he hope that she had longed for him?

"Terah," he asked gently. "Do you want to marry me?"

"Oh, yes," she said. Her eyes were full of love as she looked at him.

He hugged her to him. "I thought," he began, "that you did not want me. I thought that you despised me when you heard what Lern had to say about my running from the mammoth that

422

killed my father. That was why I let you go. I could not bear the pain of loving a woman who held me in utter contempt."

His eyes burned into hers. She saw the naked love there. "Oh, Mamut," she groaned. "I love you too! I left because I knew that after you killed the white mammoth, you were free from whatever had tormented you. That meant you could choose a woman of your own, not have to keep someone you had captured. And," she added softly, gazing into his eyes, "I could no longer live my life as your captive."

He saw her soul in those green eyes.

"Freedom is important to me, Mamut. As important as love. I loved you, but I could not be your slave. Something precious inside me was dying. I had to be free."

"I understand," he agreed. "Freedom is important to me, too, though in a different way. Now I have freedom from my past. And freedom from the fear of Father-Killer. Those are tough bindings that I worked for years to sever." He drew her closer. "I did not want to tell you what had happened to me as a young man. That was the reason I chose not to marry you."

She frowned in puzzlement.

"I knew that if I married you," he continued, "I would tell you my thoughts and feelings. And then one day I would want to tell you what happened that day with Father-killer. I did not want to watch your love for me turn to disgust and hate. I reasoned that if I kept you as my captive, I need not tell you the truth about myself." He smiled

423

sadly. "When Lern told the truth about me, I was ready to believe that you had turned against me in disgust."

"No, Mamut," she murmured, leaning into him. "I was remembering my brother, Bron's, needless bravery when he fought the saber-tooth. I was thinking of his death, and I was glad that you had run that day. I was glad that you saved yourself," she said fiercely. "A fourteen-year-old boy is no match for a charging mammoth! You would have been killed along with your father." Her eyes held his. "I know that your Mammoth People expect bravery at all times, but I think it is a foolish expectation. There is a time to be brave and there is a time to run."

He smiled into her eyes, pleased at her spirited defense of him. Of course she was wrong, but it pleased him nonetheless to hear her defend him.

"And Mamut," she said sweetly, diverting his attention from her lips back to her eyes. "If you had been killed, then who would I marry?"

He smiled. "Bear, perhaps," he teased.

She shook her head. "I would as soon live alone."

"Perhaps we had better renegotiate this," interjected her father as he shuffled up to Mamut and Terah. "I see that this young man is just not going to go away." He sighed. "I suppose I must give him my eight valuable white chert spearpoints set on stout birchwood spear shafts and painted with red ochre."

"Yes," agreed her mother. "And I suppose we

must accept his gifts." She sighed.

Mamut frowned. "My gifts are very fine," he reproved. "I am giving you beautiful mammoth ivory, a set of huge bison horns, and two warm bison robes."

"Pah," said her father. "What will two old people like us do with two warm bison robes, beloved?"

"I am sure I do not know," answered his wife.

"Winter is coming," sighed her father. "I suppose we will find a use for the robes." He smiled at his wife. "Come, beloved." They tottered away.

Terah and Mamut were left alone once more. Terah smiled at Mamut and reached for his hand. She took it in hers, lifted it to her lips and kissed it.

"And I have a gift for the groom," Terah said, her eyes twinkling.

"I have a gift for the bride," said Mamut. After he had caught sight of Terah, he had traded for the beautiful white necklace. It was hidden in his tent.

"You do?" Terah looked most interested. "What is my gift?"

Mamut smiled. "I will show you. But you have to come with me. To my tent."

Terah grinned knowingly.

Mamut's heated glance ran up and down her figure and returned to meet her eyes.

She loved that hot look in those obsidian eyes.

"And what is *my* gift?" Mamut's voice was a

low growl. He could not take his eyes off her loved face.

Terah patted her slightly rounded stomach. "A child."

"Terah!" He picked her up and danced around with her. Dogs barked, people stared, and everyone smiled at the love that shone from the two beaming faces of the dancing man and the laughing woman.

Epilogue

One year later

"What are you doing, husband?" asked Terah.

Though it was early evening, Mamut shaded his eyes and looked up at her from where he kneeled in the sand near the banks of a small blue lake. Great scoops of dirt lay around the edges of a hole he had been digging. Slowly he rose to his feet.

"Why are my dowry spears here? What are you doing with them? And the white chert spearpoint that the Great Spirit gave you in your vision. What is it doing here?"

He smiled at her and at the babies nestled in the crook of each of her arms. "Is it not too hot for the twins?" he asked instead of answering her question.

"They love the sun," she answered. "They want to feel every last ray of warmth before the long, cold winter ahead. And they are happy to be walking in the land of the mammoth and bison." She touched her lips to first one little forehead, then the other. "Our daughters Spear and Truth are so beautiful. I love them so," she murmured.

"As do I," he concurred. He stood gazing at his wife and children and knew supreme happiness.

Terah lifted her head once more, and a breeze blew her shining brown hair away from her face. "You still have not explained to me what you are doing, Mamut."

He swung his gaze past her, across the land that they had returned to. The Mammoth People had wintered and summered in the south, along the banks of Giver of Life River. But once again it was fall, in the Moon of the Geese Flying, and the Mammoth People had come north to hunt. They had come to the land where Mamut had first captured his wife.

The breeze brought the smoky smell of drying, smoking bison meat. There had been another successful bison hunt, and the Mammoth People would be returning south in the next few days, laden with meat and warm robes.

"Mamut?"

"Let me have your knife," he said.

She shrugged, both arms filled with babies. She did not protest when he plucked the little white chert knife from her waist. Terah watched in surprise as he sliced through the leather thong he wore at his neck. The yellowed ivory bead that he had always worn slid off the thong and into the palm of his hand. He held the bead up and eyed it carefully. "I will be glad to say farewell to *this*."

Terah watched, perplexed.

Then Mamut threw the bead into the pit he had dug.

"Husband? What *are* you doing?"

He bent over and picked up the spears that were her dowry. Their tips caught the sun's rays and glowed as if filled with a living spirit. The red ochre paint on the spear shafts contrasted beautifully with the white tips. Carefully he laid the spears in the pit. Lastly, he placed in the pit his most precious white spearpoint, the one the Great Spirit had given him.

"You are burying them? All of them?"

"Yes," he answered at last. "I am burying them."

"But why? They are valuable! You have used them to kill bison, to kill mammoths, to hunt for our children! Why, Mamut? I do not understand."

He gazed at his beautiful wife, his healthy, strong children. "I am giving these weapons and tools to the Great Spirit," he said at last. "I have everything I need. A healthy family, a woman who loves me."

"But the weapons—you need them!"

"The Great Spirit will provide," he said at last. "That much have I learned. When the time comes, and I need a spear, the Great Spirit will provide.

I realize now that the Great Spirit has provided everything for me all my life. I do not need these spearpoints to hang on to. I can give them back to the Great Spirit and know that He will provide more."

Terah watched in silence, turning over his words in her mind. "I think I understand," she said at last. "You are thanking the Great Spirit."

Mamut nodded.

"By giving Him your valued possessions."

He nodded once more.

"You are thanking him for your children, for me, for your very life."

He smiled. The Great Spirit had provided well. He had given Mamut a wife who understood him.

"Please wait, Mamut," said Terah. "I will return soon."

He sat down to wait. She returned a little while later, carrying a small bundle. Behind her walked Rana carrying Spear and Blossom carrying Truth. Blossom, her black, shining hair neatly braided, walked carefully so that her limp did not jostle the sleeping baby. Beside her trotted Wolf Boy, tail wagging.

Terah walked up to the side of the pit. Carefully she laid a bone awl, a carved piece of ivory, and several other implements in the pit. Then she placed a chunk of white chert in the hole. "I was saving it to make knives," she explained to Mamut. Lastly, she laid her little white chert knife beside the other implements.

He smiled. "There will be more."

"Yes," she answered, looking at him with all the love in her heart.

Mamut covered up the pit with dirt and there, at the edge of the small blue lake, he, Terah and their two friends chanted a song of thanks to the Great Spirit.

As the sun set, a fiery red light exploded to the west, and the sky lit up red and orange and yellow. Far away a volcano was erupting.

"The Great Spirit likes our gift," murmured Terah as she snuggled up to Mamut. He smiled and wrapped his arm around her. Behind them they could hear the soft snores of the sleeping babies and the gentle murmurs of Rana and her daughter.

"It is good," answered Mamut.

Author's Note

The cache of fine-quality tools that Mamut
and Terah buried so long ago was finally
found by two orchard workers in Wenatchee,
Washington, in 1987.

The tools range in color from white translucent chalcedony (a chert-like stone) to a
caramel-colored, banded brown. They were
determined to be of the Clovis archeological
culture, a descriptive term given to similarly
fashioned tools found across the United States
and Canada and falling within the dates of
11,000 to 11,500 years before the present.

The spearheads are beautifully flaked in a
fluted shape and are about 12″ high. Arche-
ologists tested the white translucent spearheads and discovered trace elements of rabbit,
deer, bison, and human blood. At the base of

the spearheads were tiny amounts of red ochre, a red clay mixed with grease.

Not all of the site has been excavated, and archaeologists have yet to recover the yellowed ivory bead that Mamut once wore.

Theresa Scott loves to hear from readers. Send an SASE to:

P.O. Box 832
Olympia, WA 98507

References

Avey, Michael   1991. *Fluted Point Occur-
                       rences in Washington
                       State.* Self-published.

Barsness, Larry   1985. *Heads, Hides and
                       Horns.* Texas Christian
                       University Press, Fort
                       Worth, TX.

Canby, Thomas Y.   1979. "The Search for The
                       First Americans" in *Na-
                       tional Geographic,* Vol.
                       156, No. 3, September.
                       pp.330–363.

Cruikshank, Julie   1982. *Early Yukon Cul-
                       tures.* Dept. of Education,

Gov't of Yukon Territory, Whitehorse, Yukon, Canada.

Frison, George C. 1978. *Prehistoric Hunters of the High Plains*. Academic Press. NY.

Frison, George C. and Lawrence C. Todd 1986. *The Colby Mammoth Site: Taphonomy and Archaeology of a Clovis Kill in Northern Wyoming*. University of New Mexico Press. Albuquerque, NM.

Frison, George C., Editor 1974. *The Casper Site: A Hell Gap Bison Kill on the High Plains*. Academic Press, Inc., NY.

Gramly, R.M. *The Adkins Site: A Palaeo-Indian Habitation and Associated Stone Structure.*

Gramly, G. M. *Guide to the Palaeo-Indian Artifacts of North America*. pp. 1–63.

Gramly, G.M. 1991. "Blood Residues Upon Tools from the East Wenatchee Clovis Site, Douglas County, Washington" in *Ohio Ar-*

chaeologist, Vol. 41, No. 4, Fall. pp. 4–9.

Haynes, C. Vance — 1980. "The Clovis Culture" in *Canadian Journal of Anthropology* 1(1)pp. 115–122.

McKenny, Margaret, rev. by Daniel E. Sturtz — 1971. *The Savory Wild Mushroom*. University of Washington Press. Seattle, WA.

Mehringer, Peter J., Jr. — 1988. "Clovis Cache Found: Weapons of Ancient Americans" in *National Geographic*. Vol. 174, No. 4, October, pp. 500–503.

Meltzer, David Jeffrey — 1984. *Late Pleistocene Human Adaptations in Eastern North America*. PhD. University of Washington, Seattle, WA.

Orenstein, Ronald, editor — 1991. *Elephants: The Deciding Decade*. Sierra Club Books. San Francisco, CA.

Orr, Phil C. — 1968. *Prehistory of Santa Rosa Island*. Santa Barbara Museum of Natural History. Schauer Printing Studio, Santa Barbara, CA.

Pielou, E.C.   1991. *After the Ice Age: The Return of Life to Glaciated North America.* University of Chicago Press. Chicago, IL.

Putman, John J.   1988. "The Search for Modern Humans" in *National Geographic,* Vol 174, No. 4. October, pp. 439–477.

Romain, William F.   *Calendric Information Evident in the Adena Tablets.* Brookly, OH

Sutcliffe, Antony J.   1985. *On the Track of Ice Age Mammals.* Harvard University Press. Cambridge, MA.

Waitt, Richard B.,   1985. *Case for Periodic, Jr.   Colossal Jokulhlaups from Pleistocene Glacial Lake Missoula.* Geological Society of America Bulletin. Vol. 96, pp. 1271–1286, Oct. 1985.

Waitt, Richard B.   1987. *Evidence for Dozens of Stupendous Floods from Glacial Lake Missoula in Eastern Washington, Idaho, and Montana.* Geological Society of America Centennial Field Guide. Cordilleran Section. Pp. 345–346. U.S. Geological Survey, Vancouver, WA

Wormington, H.M.   1957. *Ancient Man in North America.* Denver Museum of Natural History. Popular Series No. 4. Denver, CO.

LOVE SPELL

THE MAGIC OF ROMANCE PAST, PRESENT, AND FUTURE....

Dorchester Publishing Co., Inc., the leader in romantic fiction, is pleased to unveil its newest line—Love Spell. Every month, beginning in August 1993, Love Spell will publish one book in each of four categories:

1) *Timeswept Romance*—Modern-day heroines travel to the past to find the men who fulfill their hearts' desires.

2) *Futuristic Romance*—Love on distant worlds where passion is the lifeblood of every man and woman.

3) *Historical Romance*—Full of desire, adventure and intrigue, these stories will thrill readers everywhere.

4) *Contemporary Romance*—With novels by Lori Copeland, Heather Graham, and Jayne Ann Krentz, Love Spell's line of contemporary romance is first-rate.

Exploding with soaring passion and fiery sensuality, Love Spell romances are destined to take you to dazzling new heights of ecstasy.

COMING IN JANUARY!
TIMESWEPT ROMANCE

TIME OF THE ROSE
By Bonita Clifton

When the silver-haired cowboy brings Madison Calloway to his run-down ranch, she thinks for sure he is senile. Certain he'll bring harm to himself, Madison follows the man into a thunderstorm and back to the wild days of his youth in the Old West.

The dread of all his enemies and the desire of all the ladies, Colton Chase does not stand a chance against the spunky beauty who has tracked him through time. And after one passion-drenched night, Colt is ready to surrender his heart to the most tempting spitfire anywhere in time.

_51922-4 $4.99 US/$5.99 CAN

A FUTURISTIC ROMANCE

AWAKENINGS
By Saranne Dawson

Fearless and bold, Justan rules his domain with an iron hand, but nothing short of the Dammai's magic will bring his warring people peace. He claims he needs Rozlynd—a bewitching beauty and the last of the Dammai—for her sorcery alone, yet inside him stirs an unexpected yearning to savor the temptress's charms, to sample her sweet innocence. And as her silken spell ensnares him, Justan battles to vanquish a power whose like he has never encountered—the power of Rozlynd's love.

_51921-6 $4.99 US/$5.99 CAN

LOVE SPELL
ATTN: Order Department
Dorchester Publishing Co., Inc.
276 5th Avenue, New York, NY 10001

Please add $1.50 for shipping and handling for the first book and $.35 for each book thereafter. PA., N.Y.S. and N.Y.C. residents, please add appropriate sales tax. No cash, stamps, or C.O.D.s. All orders shipped within 6 weeks via postal service book rate. Canadian orders require $2.00 extra postage and must be paid in U.S. dollars through a U.S. banking facility.

Name _____

Address _____

City _____ State _____ Zip _____

I have enclosed $_____ in payment for the checked book(s). Payment <u>must</u> accompany all orders.☐ Please send a free catalog.

FROM LOVE SPELL
FUTURISTIC ROMANCE
NO OTHER LOVE
Flora Speer
Bestselling Author of *A Time To Love Again*

Only Herne sees the woman. To the other explorers of the ruined city she remains unseen, unknown. But after an illicit joining she is gone, and Herne finds he cannot forget his beautiful seductress, or ignore her uncanny resemblance to another member of the exploration party. Determined to unravel the puzzle, Herne begins a seduction of his own—one that will unleash a whirlwind of danger and desire.

_51916-X $4.99 US/$5.99 CAN

TIMESWEPT ROMANCE
LOVE'S TIMELESS DANCE
Vivian Knight-Jenkins

Although the pressure from her company's upcoming show is driving Leeanne Sullivan crazy, she refuses to believe she can be dancing in her studio one minute—and with a seventeenth-century Highlander the next. A liberated woman like Leeanne will have no problem teaching virile Iain MacBride a new step or two, and soon she'll have him begging for lessons in love.

_51917-8 $4.99 US/$5.99 CAN

LOVE SPELL
ATTN: Order Department
Dorchester Publishing Company, Inc.
276 5th Avenue, New York, NY 10001

Please add $1.50 for shipping and handling for the first book and $.35 for each book thereafter. PA., N.Y.S. and N.Y.C. residents, please add appropriate sales tax. No cash, stamps, or C.O.D.s. All orders shipped within 6 weeks via postal service book rate. Canadian orders require $2.00 extra postage and must be paid in U.S. dollars through a U.S. banking facility.

Name_____

Address_____

City _____ State_____ Zip_____

I have enclosed $_____in payment for the checked book(s).
Payment **must** accompany all orders.□ Please send a free catalog.

FROM LOVE SPELL
HISTORICAL ROMANCE
THE PASSIONATE REBEL
Helene Lehr

A beautiful American patriot, Gillian Winthrop is horrified to learn that her grandmother means her to wed a traitor to the American Revolution. Her body yearns for Philip Meredith's masterful touch, but she is determined not to give her hand—or any other part of herself—to the handsome Tory, until he convinces her that he too is a passionate rebel.

__51918-6 $4.99 US/$5.99 CAN

CONTEMPORARY ROMANCE
THE TAWNY GOLD MAN
Amii Lorin

Bestselling Author Of More Than 5 Million Books In Print!

Long ago, in a moment of wild, rioting ecstasy, Jud Cammeron vowed to love her always. Now, as Anne Moore looks at her stepbrother, she sees a total stranger, a man who plans to take control of his father's estate and everyone on it. Anne knows things are different—she is a grown woman with a fiance—but something tells her she still belongs to the tawny gold man.

__51919-4 $4.99 US/$5.99 CAN

LOVE SPELL
ATTN: Order Department
Dorchester Publishing Company, Inc.
276 5th Avenue, New York, NY 10001

Please add $1.50 for shipping and handling for the first book and $.35 for each book thereafter. PA., N.Y.S. and N.Y.C. residents, please add appropriate sales tax. No cash, stamps, or C.O.D.s. All orders shipped within 6 weeks via postal service book rate. Canadian orders require $2.00 extra postage and must be paid in U.S. dollars through a U.S. banking facility.

Name_____
Address_____
City _____ State_____Zip_____
I have enclosed $_____in payment for the checked book(s).
Payment <u>must</u> accompany all orders.☐ Please send a free catalog.

AN HISTORICAL ROMANCE
GILDED SPLENDOR
By Elizabeth Parker

Bound for the London stage, sheltered Amanda Prescott has no idea that fate has already cast her first role as a rakehell's true love. But while visiting Patrick Winter's country estate, she succumbs to the dashing peer's burning desire. Amid the glittering milieu of wealth and glamour, Amanda and Patrick banish forever their harsh past and make all their fantasies a passionate reality.

_51914-3 $4.99 US/$5.99 CAN

A CONTEMPORARY ROMANCE
MADE FOR EACH OTHER/RAVISHED
By Parris Afton Bonds
Bestselling Author of *The Captive*

In *Made for Each Other*, reporter Julie Dever thinks she knows everything about Senator Nicholas Raffer—until he rescues her from a car wreck and shares with her a passion she never dared hope for. And in *Ravished*, a Mexican vacation changes nurse Nelli Walzchak's life when she is kidnapped by a handsome stranger who needs more than her professional help.

_51915-1 $4.99 US/$5.99 CAN

LEISURE BOOKS
ATTN: Order Department
276 5th Avenue, New York, NY 10001

Please add $1.50 for shipping and handling for the first book and $.35 for each book thereafter. PA., N.Y.S. and N.Y.C. residents, please add appropriate sales tax. No cash, stamps, or C.O.D.s. All orders shipped within 6 weeks via postal service book rate. Canadian orders require $2.00 extra postage and must be paid in U.S. dollars through a U.S. banking facility.

Name _____
Address _____
City _____ State _____ Zip _____
I have enclosed $_____ in payment for the checked book(s).
Payment <u>must</u> accompany all orders. ☐ Please send a free catalog.

TIMESWEPT ROMANCE
A TIME-TRAVEL CHRISTMAS
By Megan Daniel, Vivian Knight-Jenkins, Eugenia Riley, and Flora Speer

In these four passionate time-travel historical romance stories, modern-day heroines journey everywhere from Dickens's London to a medieval castle as they fulfill their deepest desires on Christmases past.

_51912-7 $4.99 US/$5.99 CAN

A FUTURISTIC ROMANCE
MOON OF DESIRE
By Pam Rock

Future leader of his order, Logan has vanquished enemies, so he expects no trouble when a sinister plot brings a mere woman to him. But as the three moons of the planet Thurlow move into alignment, Logan and Calla head for a collision of heavenly bodies that will bring them ecstasy—or utter devastation.

_51913-5 $4.99 US/$5.99 CAN

LEISURE BOOKS
ATTN: Order Department
276 5th Avenue, New York, NY 10001

Please add $1.50 for shipping and handling for the first book and $.35 for each book thereafter. PA., N.Y.S. and N.Y.C. residents, please add appropriate sales tax. No cash, stamps, or C.O.D.s. All orders shipped within 6 weeks via postal service book rate. Canadian orders require $2.00 extra postage and must be paid in U.S. dollars through a U.S. banking facility.

Name _____
Address _____
City _____ State _____ Zip _____
I have enclosed $_____ in payment for the checked book(s).
Payment <u>must</u> accompany all orders.☐ Please send a free catalog.

HISTORICAL ROMANCE
DANGEROUS DESIRES
Louise Clark

Miserable and homesick, Stephanie de la Riviere will sell her family jewels or pose as a highwayman—whatever it takes to see her beloved father again. And her harebrained schemes might succeed if not for her watchful custodian—the only man who can match her fiery spirit with his own burning desire.

__0-505-51910-0 $4.99 US/$5.99 CAN

CONTEMPORARY ROMANCE
ONLY THE BEST
Lori Copeland
Author of More Than 6 Million Books in Print!

Stranded in a tiny Wyoming town after her car fails, Rana Alcott doesn't think her life can get much worse. And though she'd rather die than accept help from arrogant Gunner Montay, she soon realizes she is fighting a losing battle against temptation.

__0-505-51911-9 $3.99 US/$4.99 CAN

LEISURE BOOKS
ATTN: Order Department
276 5th Avenue, New York, NY 10001

Please add $1.50 for shipping and handling for the first book and $.35 for each book thereafter. PA., N.Y.S. and N.Y.C. residents, please add appropriate sales tax. No cash, stamps, or C.O.D.s All orders shipped within 6 weeks via postal service book rate. Canadian orders require $2.00 extra postage and must be paid in U.S. dollars through a U.S. banking facility.

Name_____
Address_____
City _____ State_____ Zip_____
I have enclosed $_____in payment for the checked book(s).
Payment <u>must</u> accompany all orders.☐ Please send a free catalog.

FUTURISTIC ROMANCE
FIRESTAR
Kathleen Morgan
Bestselling Author of *The Knowing Crystal*

From the moment Meriel lays eyes on the virile slave chosen to breed with her, the heir to the Tenuan throne is loath to perform her imperial duty and produce a child. Yet despite her resolve, Meriel soon succumbs to Gage Bardwin—the one man who can save her planet.

_0-505-51908-9 $4.99 US/$5.99 CAN

TIMESWEPT ROMANCE
ALL THE TIME WE NEED
Megan Daniel

Nearly drowned after trying to save a client, musical agent Charli Stewart wakes up in New Orleans's finest brothel—run by the mother of the city's most virile man—on the eve of the Civil War. Unsure if she'll ever return to her own era, Charli gambles her heart on a love that might end as quickly as it began.

_0-505-51909-7 $4.99 US/$5.99 CAN

LEISURE BOOKS
ATTN: Order Department
276 5th Avenue, New York, NY 10001

Please add $1.50 for shipping and handling for the first book and $.35 for each book thereafter. PA., N.Y.S. and N.Y.C. residents, please add appropriate sales tax. No cash, stamps, or C.O.D.s. All orders shipped within 6 weeks via postal service book rate. Canadian orders require $2.00 extra postage and must be paid in U.S. dollars through a U.S. banking facility.

Name _____
Address _____
City _____ State _____ Zip _____
I have enclosed $_____ in payment for the checked book(s). Payment <u>must</u> accompany all orders.☐ Please send a free catalog.

HISTORICAL ROMANCE
TEMPTATION
Jane Harrison

He broke her heart once before, but Shadoe Sinclair is a temptation that Lilly McFall cannot deny. And when he saunters back into the frontier town he left years earlier, Lilly will do whatever it takes to make the handsome rogue her own.

__0-505-51906-2   .$4.99 US/$5.99 CAN

CONTEMPORARY ROMANCE
WHIRLWIND COURTSHIP
Jayne Ann Krentz writing as Jayne Taylor
Bestselling Author of *Family Man*

When Phoebe Hampton arrives by accident on Harlan Garand's doorstep, he's convinced she's another marriage-minded female sent by his matchmaking aunt. But a sudden snowstorm traps them together for a few days and shows Harlan there's a lot more to Phoebe than meets the eye.

__0-505-51907-0 $3.99 US/$4.99 CAN

LEISURE BOOKS
ATTN: Order Department
276 5th Avenue, New York, NY 10001

Please add $1.50 for shipping and handling for the first book and $.35 for each book thereafter. PA., N.Y.S. and N.Y.C. residents, please add appropriate sales tax. No cash, stamps, or C.O.D.s. All orders shipped within 6 weeks via postal service book rate. Canadian orders require $2.00 extra postage and must be paid in U.S. dollars through a U.S. banking facility.

Name_____
Address_____
City _____ State _____ Zip _____
I have enclosed $_____in payment for the checked book(s).
Payment must accompany all orders.☐ Please send a free catalog.